Under the Mistletoe with You

T0349283

Lizzie Huxley-Jones is an autistic author based in London. They are the author of the queer holiday rom-coms *Make You Mine This Christmas* and *Under the Mistletoe With You*; *Hits Different*, co-written with Tasha Ghouri; and the Vivi Conway series for children including the Waterstones Children's Book Prize shortlisted *Vivi Conway and the Sword of Legend* followed by *Vivi Conway and the Haunted Quest*. They are the editor of *Stim*: an autistic anthology. They write joyful stories that centre queerness and disability, and can be found as @littlehux on social media.

They tweet too much and enjoy taking breaks to walk their dog, Nerys.

Also by Lizzie Huxley-Jones:
Make You Mine This Christmas

LIZZIE HUXLEY-JONES

UNDER THE MISTLETOE WITH YOU

HODDER &
STOUGHTON

First published in Great Britain in 2024 by Hodder & Stoughton Limited
An Hachette UK company

1

Copyright © Lizzie Huxley-Jones 2024

The right of Lizzie Huxley-Jones to be identified as the Author of the
Work has been asserted by them in accordance with the Copyright,
Designs and Patents Act 1988.

All rights reserved. No part of this publication may be reproduced, stored
in a retrieval system, or transmitted, in any form or by any means without
the prior written permission of the publisher, nor be otherwise circulated in
any form of binding or cover other than that in which it is published and
without a similar condition being imposed on the subsequent purchaser.

All characters in this publication are fictitious and any resemblance
to real persons, living or dead, is purely coincidental.

A CIP catalogue record for this title is available from the British Library

Paperback ISBN 978 1 399 70083 2
Hardback (special edition) 978 1 399 74329 7

Typeset in Plantin Light by Manipal Technologies Limited

Printed and bound in Great Britain by Clays Ltd, Elcograf S.p.A.

Hodder & Stoughton policy is to use papers that are natural, renewable
and recyclable products and made from wood grown in sustainable forests.
The logging and manufacturing processes are expected to conform to the
environmental regulations of the country of origin.

Hodder & Stoughton Limited
Carmelite House
50 Victoria Embankment
London EC4Y 0DZ

The authorised representative in the EEA is Hachette Ireland, 8 Castlecourt
Centre, Castleknock Road, Castleknock, Dublin 15, D15 YF6A, Ireland

www.hodder.co.uk

For my brave and brilliant boys:
Cameron, Charlie, Dylan & Krish

Chapter One

Christopher

To Christopher Calloway, the best things about Christmas are usually building the gingerbread house, making a wish at midnight, diving back into one of his favourite children's fantasy novels, and eating as much as is physically possible.

This year, though, the thing he is most looking forward to is a break.

An actual break.

Well, and the gingerbread house. No matter what happens, he will *always* want to build the gingerbread house.

Tomorrow, he'll be in York with his sister, Kit, and her girlfriend, Haf, who happens to also be his best friend, for a very restful, do-nothing-eat-lots Christmas break.

He needs it. He's exhausted. When he worked in his less-effort-than-it-looked finance job, everyone clocked off early at Christmas, the last few days spent physically there, but mentally checked out. Usually thinking of new things to bake, if he's honest, while moving his mouse *just* often enough that his computer didn't go to sleep. Now that he actually *owns* his dream bakery, he doesn't miss those soulless days, but he does miss how tired he *wasn't*.

And although part of him feels a little bad for closing up on 20th December, he needs the rest.

'Need me to do anything else?' asks Tegan, his teenage shop assistant, who has already hung up her apron and is reaching for her bag in a way that suggests she doesn't want him to say yes.

There really isn't anything else for her to do. They've not had a customer in over an hour. It may only be 20th December, but it feels as if the world is shutting down for the holidays already. Maybe things just stop earlier in this little town. He's still running on London time.

The bakery has been busy all morning with customers collecting orders of Christmas puddings and a few marzipan-topped boozy Christmas cakes, and buying fresh bread and pastries. Christmas makes people want fancy bread, it seems. It might be the most loaves he's sold in a day ever. But now . . . nothing.

Tegan had cleaned basically every inch of the café side of the bakery. If anything, she'd gone above and beyond. There really isn't anything else for either of them to do. He may as well let her go home early.

'No, go ahead. Thank you, Tegan. Merry Christmas,' he calls after her as she darts out the door with a 'Nadolig llawen!'

He regrets letting her go after a minute. Time goes much slower when you're desperate to close up but have hours to go *and* are now on your own. Not that he and Tegan have particularly in-depth conversations, seeing as she's a teen-age Goth who barely tolerates him, even though he's her employer. The company is nice though.

There are a few Christmas puddings awaiting collection, plus a few more loaves and biscuits to sell if he can. Plus, the bakery is normally open until five.

At least the one thing he won't have to worry about is the bakery over Christmas. Kit had suggested he offer it up as a holiday let in case anyone local had family coming in from out of town. After all those window displays and buying an entirely new business, his bank balance was looking a bit . . . slim. Luckily, it was quickly snapped up by someone coming over from America. He's written up a very thorough hand-over document about staying in the flat, so all he needs to do tomorrow morning is give them the keys, show them round, and head to the train station.

In want of a task that isn't clock-watching, Christopher wipes down the counter for possibly the twentieth time that day. At least something is happening, even if it's potentially damaging the already battered wood.

He probably should have saved making treats for his family for this lull, but he finished them yesterday – a Christmas pudding, of course, but also shortbread stars to hang on the tree, some gingerbread (not in house form, for ease of transport), and little bags of peppermint candies, sea-salt fudge and chocolate truffles. The last three hadn't even been part of the plan – they were what he'd whipped up in the very early hours of this morning when he was too wide awake *not* to make a sweet shop's worth of treats. Hopefully, he can pack them all into his suitcase for the train journey, but if he ends up with spillover tote bags at least he can bribe anyone he ends up squishing with some sweets.

Three hours. Three hours and then he can lock the door, be done for Christmas and the whole of this intense year. He's never been so excited to check out mentally.

But there are still three hours to go, so wiping the counters it is.

* * *

It doesn't help his sense of time that the last year has gone by at two very different speeds – horrifyingly fast, and drudgingly slow.

It had all started last Christmas. For reasons he is admittedly a little embarrassed about now, he'd spent the holidays in his family home with a fake girlfriend, Haf, in a hare-brained scheme to deflect any questions about him potentially taking over his father's business, and to avoid being set up with anyone else. Naturally, the course of terrible schemes and fake romance never did run smooth. For a start, Haf fell in love with his sister, Kit, in a matter of days, which is totally preposterous. And then Christopher rejected a job from his dad at the Christmas dinner table. On the drive home, he had instead started to form his own plan for a very different future.

Barely a month later, he had jacked in his fiscally sensible but soul-destroying job and was studying 'Pâtisserie and Boulangerie' at the most prestigious cooking school in the country. Six months of full-time kitchen life, covering everything from the foundations of breadmaking all the way up to fiddly and complex molecular gastronomy, surrounded by other hungry people determined to work in kitchens around the world. There was really nothing like it. It was the happiest – and busiest – time of his life.

And then, it was over, so suddenly – frankly, it's no wonder his sense of time is entirely warped now – but he wasn't ready to slow down; he *couldn't*. While he was looking for jobs, he had offhandedly mentioned to Haf and Kit that really, what he wanted was his own kitchen. This somehow made its way to Haf's mum, Mari, who mentioned the bakery a few towns down from her on the North Welsh coast, which stood empty. He should come and look at Pantri Bach, they had said. Someone needed to reopen it.

It was silly to even consider it. And yet, the thought kept *nagging* at him.

It made sense to just look it up, he decided.

Looking it up quickly turned to driving up to view it in person with Kit and Haf. The town, Pen-y-Môr, was so close to the sea that he couldn't believe it. He'd grown up in the landlocked Cotswolds and lived in London for so long that he couldn't imagine a town could be literally on the seafront. It was small, perhaps smaller than he originally imagined, with one long high street running from the sea up to the coastal mountains that crowded in at the back of the town. It was probably only a little larger than Oxlea, where he grew up, a few thousand people clustered together. But he liked that idea: the intentional intimacy as opposed to the anonymity of London. After all, the biggest towns nearby were either Llandudno or Bangor, still significantly smaller than London. Living here carried the prospect of a whole new way of life.

When he got to the bakery, it was clear the insides needed more than a lick of paint, but the estate agent insisted the recently serviced kitchen with all the equipment was included in the price. Upstairs was a tiny little run-down flat he could live in, with views of the sea and the mountains. Even his architect sister agreed it looked as if it had good bones, despite the peeling wallpaper and holey walls where pictures had been taken down. With some cosmetic fixes, some new furniture in, café side, and a decent coffee machine, it could be something totally new. Something that belonged to him.

He couldn't stop looking at the light, by God, the *light*. You only get light like that with big skies.

Could it be a home to him? It felt as if it could be.

His friends seemed to think so, too.

Before he could overthink it, he'd put in an offer for as much as he could afford, and he'd put his flat in London on the market too. Somehow, his offer was accepted, his flat sold, and before he could really blink or breathe or think about what the hell he'd done, his friends were loading up a moving van to drive him to Wales.

It had been a trial, not necessarily one by fire, but certainly something painful and tricky to navigate. Perhaps trial-by-swamp, if that was a thing. For the first few weeks, he worried every night that he'd made a terrible decision, but all his friends seemed so on board with it that he hoped they were right. They usually were. His brain often got the better of him, after all.

And now, he is happy.

He *is*.

It's just been . . . harder than he thought it would be. Thinking about what he could sell had been great, but now he has to think about things like overheads, profit, turnover

. . . keeping the lights on. And that buzz, that spark he felt at cookery school, seems to have just dulled, or perhaps burned down.

And he's barely made any friends here. It's hard to be so far from everyone he loves.

Needless to say, he hasn't hung up any mistletoe in here this Christmas. Call him superstitious, but he doesn't want to tempt fate. There's been enough chaos in his life for one year.

★ ★ ★

When Christopher glances up at the clock, somehow only a few more minutes have passed. What torture is this? When he was procrastinating in his old job, he would dream up new things to bake, but, well, that creative spark hasn't really been burning quite the way it used to. The little creative energy he has left has gone on the aesthetics of the café and the few reliable if basic things he can regularly make and sell.

At least the Christmas puddings look nice, wrapped in coloured paper and tied up in ribbons – a touch his mother had insisted on, because if he was going to sell things for a special occasion, they should look *special*. She was right, of course. Turns out a bit of ribbon goes a long way. Perhaps it was Esther who had all the business sense. His father, Otto, might have been the businessman, but she ran the house, and half the town, based on all the committees she was on.

It wasn't just the puddings he'd made look special, either. Ever since he opened the bakery, Christopher had made sure there was an intricate window display. Yes, they took time and a lot of effort, but people did stop and stare and even very occasionally come in to buy something. In truth, he did it more for himself than his customers. When he couldn't sleep, he would sketch out plans for seasonal themes. Currently, he was working on a romantic set piece to be in the window from St Dwynwen's Day to Valentine's Day – a riot of reds and pinks and flowers, both real and sugar.

The Christmas window was probably his favourite one so far. Jewel-colour-wrapped presents – empty boxes of course – nestled in leftover white packing peanuts that looked like snow if you didn't get too close, sailed over by gingerbread reindeer and angels and stars, suspended from the ceiling on wire. Around them he'd placed empty Christmas pudding bowls wrapped in bright paper, and an upturned cake tin that he'd decorated with icing and marzipan to look like a real Christmas cake.

Thanks to the fact that the bakery sat on the main road that ran through Pen-y-Môr, the displays always drew looks from people heading down to the beach or train station, and the other way, up into the town, towards the other shops. It wasn't a roaring trade, but he was getting by . . . just about, despite his extravagant taste for window displays (which admittedly he'd partly paid for out of his own pocket a few times). But he had a few loyal customers, and he'd started to recognise the faces peering into the window, even if they didn't come in very often.

A little sprucing goes a long way, Esther had said.

Before he can ruminate on the inevitability of becoming his parents, the bell over the door jingles. Shaz stalks in, dressed in an enormous knee-length puffy coat, complete with woolly hat and mittens, all in various lurid shades of yellow.

'It's pure witches' tits out there,' she says, flinging herself into a chair right in front of the counter. As she pulls her woolly hat off her head, her thick, almost-silver-blond hair sticks up with static.

'Afternoon to you too, Shaz,' Christopher says, resisting the urge to wipe the counter down once more.

She groans. 'Don't remind me. If it's afternoon, then I'm officially behind on my to-do list, and I'd rather live in ignorance if that's all right with you.'

'Good . . . day?' Christopher offers.

'Better. I've come to get the pud, but if it's peachy with you, can I just sit here with my eyes closed for a few minutes?'

'That bad?'

Eyes firmly closed, Shaz makes a noise that Christopher takes to mean *absolutely*.

Not only was she the first friend he made here, Shaz is also his first friend with kids. It turns out that having multiple children of indeterminate age – somehow he's never managed to work that out and now it's absolutely too late for him to ask – means you live with a permanent look of confused fear etched onto your face.

When Christopher had opened the bakery in September after a furious month of redecorating, Shaz was the first customer who walked in. Loud, brash, Scouse, and determined to get him talking, Shaz was like a hurricane in Christopher's absolutely dead bakery. At first, he was worried she was a competitor or just trying to get the gossip on why he, an arguably plummy Englishman, was in this little Welsh town. But he quickly realised that, for some reason, she liked him, and she showed up every single day the bakery was open. Since then, she occasionally will literally drag other people in with her and heavily insist they buy something, especially towards the end of the month when the frown lines get deeper.

From what Christopher can gather, Shaz used to work at the primary school doing slightly too many jobs for one person. A bit of admin and finance, some teaching assistance. But then the school budget shrank, and she was out of a job (or five). Perhaps that's why she's in here basically every day – he's her water cooler.

No matter the reason, Shaz brought life to the café – and to Christopher – when he most needed it.

Plus, the gingerbread reindeer biscuits he'd started making in November had become the talk of the town thanks to her. And luckily for her, he'd decided to make one last-minute batch that morning.

'Would a gingerbread reindeer help?'

One eye opens and fixes on him. 'A biscuit I don't have to share with piranhas masquerading as children? You're offering me a Christmas miracle.'

Christopher slips two reindeer into a paper bag. 'And one to hide in the car, for later.'

'You're a good man.' She violently bites the head off. Her eyes close again, this time with the joy of eating. Christopher will never get tired of that look.

Without another word, he makes her usual frothy latte with many packets of sugar on the side and deposits it in front of her.

'Oh, you absolute beaut.' Shaz dunks a bit of leg into the hot froth. 'Must you close for Christmas? How will I get by without this every day? I'm too used to it. And you. You've ruined me. Plus, I heard the pub had a burst pipe and the whole place is wrecked so that'll be shut too. Where am I going to hide from my children if you leave?'

'You'd have to buy a lot more coffees for me to stay open over the holidays.'

She snorts. 'I'm already metaphorically shitting myself over Gar's mum coming for the holidays. I don't need to be *literally* shitting myself too.'

'A truly delightful image. Is it that bad? Now I feel bad for leaving.'

The tiredness must show on his face because she adds, 'I'll put my big pants on. Just this once, mind, don't you get cosy with all this leaving business. But I suppose you'll need to recharge your energy so you can come up with a new seasonal biccie for me.'

'I could keep doing gingerbread out of season.'

'Just for me?'

'Just for you. And hopefully some other customers.'

'Yeah, but they matter less than me. Are you all ready for your trip?'

'I think so. Just the last of these to get out the door,' he says, indicating the Christmas puddings. He passes hers over and sets it just far enough away from her that it won't get splattered with coffee or gingerbread.

'Diolch bab. Have you downloaded any films for the train?'

'If you mean, am I still working through your several-pages-long list of essential Christmas romcoms, then yes.'

The other thing that Shaz brought into his life was an appreciation for Christmas romcoms. Back in September when he started making the Christmas puddings, she insisted he needed festive inspiration, and sent a list of seasonal romcoms to watch.

Determined to nurture their new friendship, he decided to watch one, just to say that he had. Over that week, he'd watched five. One each evening, with two repeats. And he had *opinions* about them. He was absolutely completely and utterly hooked. He wasn't sure if it was the guaranteed happy endings or the high ratio of bakers to literally any other profession, but he couldn't stop watching. The only thing Christopher had ever felt that invested in before was baking.

He hadn't even heard of most of them, but then festive romcoms hadn't been something he'd sought out. At Christmas, he normally just passively watched whatever was put on. Maybe he should have been paying better attention. Apart from the few queer film titles he vaguely recognised, Shaz's list skewed to heterosexual romances, and of those, most featured one particular actor, Nash Nadeau – a blond-haired, perfectly stubbled, slightly hench American man on the cusp of thirty who, well, Christopher found rather handsome. There was just something so charismatic and warm about him. Or perhaps his characters. But still.

At first, he kept this new obsession all to himself, but eventually, once he had completed Nash Nadeau's infamous *Christmas at the Clinic* series (casually known by fans as the

'Christmas Vet' films), it all came tumbling out. The last movie in the series, unless there were more unannounced to come, ended on a cliffhanger – a cliffhanger, for Christ's sake! Would the veterinarian played by Nash Nadeau ever get back together with the witty and brilliant schoolteacher played by Barbie Glynn? The films had been teasing it all the way through the series. And now, they'd left the final movie on a *cliffhanger*.

When Shaz walked into the bakery the next day, Christopher had yelled, 'They can't just end a film on a cliffhanger!' With one throaty chuckle from Shaz, their friendship was officially cemented.

'I've rinsed all the new ones for this year already,' she sighs now, sadly, swirling the coffee in its cup. 'I'm going to have to *rewatch* some.'

'Heaven forbid.'

'Don't be cheeky now. You'll be in my position any moment at your rate.'

She wasn't wrong. He had watched *a lot* of Christmas movies in the last four months. It had become a kind of routine: he'd close up the bakery and wind down while watching some glittering, joyful Christmas romance, regardless of the time of year. After all, romance isn't just for Christmas. There was nothing more comforting than knowing things would be all right in the end, no matter what you were put through. Christopher wished real life had that level of certainty.

'Yes but I'll just watch all of Nash Nadeau's back catalogue again, and be glad of it,' he says.

'I would love to see that man's back catalogue,' says Shaz.

Me too, Christopher thinks to himself. Nash Nadeau's various characters had started turning up in his dreams, always to whisk him off to some snow-dipped destination where they would kiss by the fireside and eat delicious food.

It was getting a little ridiculous. The last time he had a crush this intense was after he saw *The Mummy Returns* playing on ITV as a child, and had suddenly developed a fascination for both Rachel Weisz and Brendan Fraser.

'Now, are you definitely sure you don't want to stay here for your first Welsh Christmas? I'm sure we could squeeze you in on the kids' table. I mean, you'd be wedged firmly into someone else's armpit, but you'd be welcome.'

'Thank you, but I'm sure. I wouldn't want to impose anyway.'

'It's not imposing if I've offered. Plus, you're on your way to being a local here – hardly anyone calls you "that one from London" or "English" any more. Sure, they don't know your name yet, but at least they know you're the baker guy.'

'I'm practically born and bred.'

'Don't get any notions,' she laughs. 'Unless you were making a bread pun. Born and bread, get it?'

'I wasn't, but I wish I had.'

'You're staying with your sister and your ex-girlfriend-now-friend-slash-her-real-girlfriend, right?'

Christopher sighs, regretting that he had ever explained the intricacies of his family drama from last year to Shaz. 'Haf and I weren't ever *technically* dating.'

'Oh yeah, fake-dating or whatever you kids call it,' she says, as though this is something people regularly do, or as though she's much older than him – Christopher is fairly sure there's only a decade between them.

'My parents are stopping by on the way to my grandparents' up in Scotland. And I think our friends, Ambrose and Laurel, will come up the day after Boxing Day.'

'Ah yes, Laurel. Your real ex-girlfriend.'

'Correct.'

'That sounds like a nice big reunion. Send me some photos so I can remember what grown-up Christmases look like while I'm being screamed at about Lego and *Frozen* and whether someone can have another snack.' She already looks tired. 'Before I forget, you're leaving the bakery keys with the house guest, yeah?'

'Oh. I was going to take them with me?'

Shaz fixes him with a look that says, *You're an absolute dingbat*, though she'd probably say something much ruder than that.

'Pop them through mine on your way, or if you run out of time, I'll pick them up from your guest. I'd tell you to bring them over tonight, but the piranhas will be in the middle of their feeding frenzy, and trust me, you don't need to see that. Plus, I figure you'll want to check you've turned everything off a good few times before you go.'

It's a little scary how well she knows him already.

'Thanks, Shaz. That's really kind of you.'

'I know, I'm a saint.'

'But if anything goes wrong—'

'It *won't*. And if I'm not sure of anything, I'll get Tegan to come have a look. And if I'm *really* not sure, I'll call you, all right?'

That seemed like a pretty decent plan, he had to admit.

'What's their name anyway?'

Christopher pulls up the booking confirmation on his phone. 'Tessa Nichols?'

'Hmm. Never heard of her. Must be a hermit.'

'She's not a hermit . . . I presume. She's probably just visiting family.'

'Nah, I'd recognise the name. Not like there're many Nicholses around. Anyway, I'll know her what with her being inside your house and all. I'll make sure she doesn't nick anything.' She's joking, what with her wink and raised bicep, but Shaz is truly quite terrifying in that *mums know what is happening at all times* kind of way.

She downs the last of her coffee and hops to her feet, keys jingling in her hand. She rushes round the counter, where she *knows* she's not allowed to be, and pulls him into a big hug. 'All right, I've got to go find out where I left my kids. Text me when you go tomorrow, yeah? And wrap up warm. The weather says it's going to get somehow even worse.'

'Will do.'

She peers over the counter. 'Who is left to pick up their puds?'

He checks the labels. 'Oh, these are all for the Yangs.'

'Give them here. Tammy lives on my street. Then you can close up.'

'It's too early. What if someone else comes?'

She looks around. 'My sweet friend, it is deader than a graveyard in here. Plus, did I mention it's witches' tits out there. Everyone will be heading home if they have sense. Come on, lock the door behind me and finish for the day. What's the worst that could happen?'

'That's not a thing to ask me.' He laughs awkwardly.

'I'm telling you, it'll be fine. You need a bath and an early night.'

The voice in his head that sounds worryingly like his mother tuts, but Shaz is right. If anyone does come, he'd hear them knocking on the bakery door anyway.

'Are you sure?'

'Christopher, give me the puds.'

He hands them over, and she runs off to the front door with all her bags before he can change his mind. 'See you next year!' she shouts as she rushes out, only pausing outside the big window to mime opening champagne, filling glasses and doing shots. Christopher takes this to be some kind of promise or perhaps a threat of a future celebration.

And once again, it's just Christopher and his bakery. But this time, he can lock the door.

Thanks to Shaz, his break has officially begun.

Chapter Two

Christopher

The next morning starts in the same way pretty much any holiday does for Christopher. He gets up nice and early to shower, and once he uses something, he packs it in his travel bag, so everything is present and accounted for.

The only difference is, today he goes into host mode, setting out fresh sheets and towels, and fresh, fancy miniatures to replace his hidden-away half-used bottles. It looks nice in the end. Rustic.

Seeing as his mother would be proud, he takes a picture of his handiwork for her. For some reason, it won't send, though that's not unusual. The phone and Wi-Fi signal is always all over the place here, fluctuating even when you're standing still; hopefully it'll send when he's downstairs.

The very last thing he does is open the curtains.

Outside, there is snow.

A *lot* of snow.

So much snow in fact that the broken-down bakery van, which he also got from the bakery's previous owners, is completely submerged.

When he first moved here, he had somewhat falsely presumed winters would be snowy. But something about being so close to the sea meant it was too warm for snow, and instead the coast got whipping icy winds and sleet. And yet . . .

This is fine, he tells himself. *Absolutely fine. No need to panic yet.*

Admittedly, it is a bit startling to discover a lot of snow when you're not expecting it, but still. He carries his cases downstairs and decides to make a coffee. It is a little expensive to run the huge bakery coffee machine just for him, but it is delicious and will give him something to do to settle his nerves. Not that drinking coffee has ever made him feel particularly chilled out. But going through the motions of grinding the beans, tamping down the softly powdered coffee, and running the steaming hot water through it slows his brain down. He breathes deeply, purposefully, as he watches the *crema* layer over the top.

Coffee in hand, he leans against the counter, connects his phone to the café's Wi-Fi, and navigates to the Met Office website.

He's greeted by an alarming amount of red.

There are, somehow, *multiple* severe weather warnings – for snow, clearly, but also for ice, for wind, for general inclement weather. In the north and south of the UK, there are flood warnings. It's somewhat apocalyptic.

And worst of all, warning banners across the page announce that no one should travel unless there is a medical emergency. Christopher is fairly sure being a little burned out does not count.

From the big bakery windows, he looks out across the village. Everything is less snow-dusted and more snow-buried. Piles of snow seem to climb up against the buildings where it's been blown around.

And somehow, it's still coming down. Sideways.

Normally, he is happy to see snow. A sprinkling feels magical, like the icing sugar dusted over gingerbread houses. This is . . . possibly cursed.

He unlocks the front door and steps out, almost losing a slipper in the process. It's really, really cold outside. Once back inside, he has to shake a flurry off his clothes.

His phone pings with a notification from his group chat with Kit and Haf.

Kit: Bud are you ok? I just saw there's snow on your end.
Christopher: Yeah, there's a lot.
Haf: We never got snow growing up!! I'm so jel.
Haf: This is probably not helpful is it
Kit: No babe. xxx
Kit: It's bad here too. The snow volunteers are already out shovelling and salting.
Haf: I'm still mad you wouldn't let me join them
Kit: We are not spending Christmas in A&E.
Christopher: Are you two just sitting next to each other texting me?
Kit: No
Haf: Obvs

He sends them a few pictures of the view outside.

Kit: Shit.
Haf: There's no way the trains are running. They barely run at the best of times so
Haf: I'm doing it again aren't I
K: Yes

His train ticket app shows a similarly red vibe. When he checks his route, all the trains have a totally-not-alarming question mark next to them. They *must* be running later on. *This can't be that bad*, he thinks. It's just a bit of snow!

As the websites are a sea of unhelpful panic, he decides to walk down to the train station just down the road by the sea. His train isn't for ages, but because Pen-y-Môr is a request stop, you have to either tell the guard you want to get off or furiously wave one down like you're in *The Railway Children*, so usually there's someone around.

Walking boots laced and warmest coat on, Christopher steps outside. Or rather, he pushes himself outside. Since he last went out, the door is now wedged firmly with snow, and it takes a good few shoves to get it open enough for him to squeeze out.

The snow is thigh-deep on him, which for a six-foot-tall man is a bad sign. He winces as the cold seeps through his jeans.

The weather is so bad, it takes him the best part of twenty minutes to wade down the high street to the train station. The red-brick station building is open but inside he finds the ticket booth closed.

'Hello?' Christopher calls.

'Over here,' calls a thick, sing-song Southern Welsh voice, which he follows out onto the sea-facing platform. It looks angry out there. Grey, and white-tipped.

The railway tracks are covered in just as much snow as the roads. A station guard stands, hands on hips, surveying the mess.

'Bore da,' Christopher says in nervous Welsh. He's been learning on his own. He'd ask Shaz to practise, but she is somehow worse than he is.

'Morning fella.'

'Is the 11:23 to Manchester still running?'

'There'll be no trains going today, boyo,' sniffs the guard.

'None?'

'Not a sausage.'

'From just here or . . . ?'

'Anywhere. The whole network is down. Too much snow for the trains to drive safely. Not enough drivers who can get to the trains. And nowhere near enough engineering teams to deal with all the situations we've got. We've not even managed to get the rail replacement buses going because all the coach companies are having variations on the same problem.'

'Christ.'

'Not his fault.'

'Feels pretty biblical.'

'Not sure there was a snowstorm in Egypt, but I get your point.'

Christopher resists pointing out that Jesus wasn't around for that, but arguing his Sunday School knowledge in the middle of an ongoing snowstorm seems futile.

'Is it *just* the snow? Do you think it might clear up later today and things will get on the move again?'

The station guard chuckles. '*Just*, he says. I doubt it'll melt in this cold. Plus, I'd say that's a pretty big problem,' he adds, pointing at something a little way up the tracks.

Christopher follows his pointed finger until he sees a huge tree has crashed over the whole line.

Christopher sighs. 'Well. That's quite definitive, isn't it?'

The station guard's eyes soften. 'Sorry to be the bearer of bad news on a day like this. I think we're in for a worse-before-it-gets-better-type situation. I'm sorry, but it might be no trains until after Christmas from what I'm hearing.'

Deep down, Christopher knew the guard was going to say this. He takes a photo for the group chat, sends it and pockets his phone.

'Going somewhere were you?' the guard asks, when Christopher says nothing.

'Not anymore.'

'Sorry, lad.'

'Thank you for your help. I appreciate it.'

'Stay safe now.' The guard pats him on the shoulder as he heads back inside.

★ ★ ★

The miserable hike home takes even longer as it's uphill and against the wind. Christopher is convinced the wind changed direction just to spite him. There are a few scary moments when he almost falls over, but luckily he manages to get home with no injuries. Just a heartache. It's another battle to get inside, and he flings his snowy walking boots against the door with frustration.

After that walk, he's grateful that he indulged in turning the coffee machine on after all. As his hand settles on a tub of hot chocolate – because boy does he need a hot chocolate right now – his phone buzzes with a video call from Kit.

She and Haf appear on screen, both wearing Santa hats. Kit's new bob sharply pokes out underneath the trimming. Despite the hat, Haf's hair is, as usual, somehow everywhere.

God, he needed this Christmas with them.

And now he's here. Alone.

'Hey. Are your parents okay?' he asks Haf. After all, they only live down the coast from him. They will have been hit with this too.

'Yeah, they're fine,' Haf says. 'Mum has enough packets of quinoa in the pantry to last an apocalypse. I think they're mostly bothered about whether they're going to make their New Year's cruise.'

'I'm so sad,' says Kit flatly.

'Me too,' Christopher says.

'This was supposed to be our grown-up, calm Christmas!' Haf wails.

'I don't think it was ever going to be exactly that,' murmurs Kit, which earns a weak chuckle from Christopher. 'Fuck this weather.'

'What are you going to do?' asks Haf sadly. 'Do you even have any food in?'

'I'm not sure,' he admits. 'There's fish fingers in the freezer, and there's some bakery stock.'

'I mean, a Christmas where you live off cake isn't too far off what we'd normally be doing,' says Kit.

'I don't want you to be alone,' whispers Haf.

'It's okay. My friend Shaz invited me over to hers yesterday.' Even if it was just an offhand comment, he knows she'll strong-arm him into coming when she finds out he's home alone. Hopefully, anyway.

'And the weather could all change by Christmas Day,' he says, even though this is counter to what the station guard told him. 'There're still four days until Christmas. Anything could happen!'

Kit and Haf nod with forced smiles.

'Have you heard from the person coming to house-sit?' asks Kit.

'Oh Christ,' Christopher says, wiping a hand down his face. 'I hadn't even thought about her. Hang on.'

Christopher clicks out of the app and scrolls through his email to see if Tessa has reached out, but there's nothing. Just brand emails promising last-minute gifts and teasing Boxing Day sales. And she has his number, but there are no missed calls. Maybe she got held up? Or her flight from America got cancelled? He sends her a quick text asking if she is on her way.

'Nothing from her yet. I bet her flight was cancelled,' Christopher sighs, slumping down over the extremely clean counter. 'I can't believe I'm stuck here.'

'You can come as soon as the snow clears. They'll honour your tickets, right?' says Kit.

'They have to; it's Christmas!' insists Haf. 'Maybe you'll still make it?'

None of them wants to say the true thing.

'We can just have a Christmas as soon as you get here,' she continues, keeping her tone light. 'It can't stay like this *all* week.'

He can't help but laugh at her determined face. 'I admire your optimism, Haf, but I don't think Mother Nature is going to change her plans just because you said.'

'Well, she *should*,' she huffs. 'Maybe this is some kind of climate—'

'And that's enough of that,' growls Kit, covering Haf's mouth with her hands. 'No existential dread today, please.'

She squeaks as Haf bites her hand and they start fighting, wobbling the phone around. It would be adorable if Christopher wasn't feeling quite so lonely.

'Look, I should go,' Christopher says, as they continue to wrestle. 'I'm going to call Tessa and work out what's going on.'

'OKAY WE LOVE YOU,' yells Haf from underneath Kit's armpit as he hangs up.

★ ★ ★

His call to Tessa goes to voicemail, hopefully a sign that she's still at home.

There's no point wallowing. If he's learned anything this year, it's that you have to keep going. He can wallow later.

He puts on Cher's Christmas album, which is just the right tone to convince himself that nothing bad is happening, and takes his case back upstairs. At least he's got a fresh bed to sink into. He lies back and makes a to-do list on his phone. After all, he needs a plan. Inventory food, then pick some new recipes to bake. He can do this. It feels like just enough of a plan to keep him going.

He'll start enacting it later. For now, he needs some comfort. Something to ground himself. He auto-pilots to the couch and puts on one of his favourite films from the past few months. In *Christmas at the Rink*, Nash Nadeau and Barbie Glynn (an iconic duo, honestly) play rival high-school ice hockey coaches and fall in love. It's a classic, clearly. His favourites don't *all* have Nash Nadeau in them. Just . . . a lot of them. There's something about that man's smile that puts him at ease, makes him feel . . . almost safe.

Christ, he needs to get back on the dating scene. It's been so long since he kissed someone that he's falling in love with fictional characters.

But there had been no time for falling in love this year. And things aren't looking hopeful for the coming year, either.

Not that long ago, Haf had shared into the group chat that she, Christopher and Kit have with Laurel and Ambrose (a group chat still named St Pancs Squad since *last* Christmas, though which Haf insists is actually named Spanks Squad) a map of where all the queer people lived in the UK, created by census data. He's pretty sure the minuscule figure for Pen-y-Môr meant there were perhaps three people, including himself. It's not exactly London here. Maybe all the queer people moved away from home, like he did.

He's not ruling out dating women, though he's not met any of them either. Well, he's met Shaz, obviously, but they are deeply friends vibes.

It's just . . . ever since he told Haf last year that he was bisexual too, he's been thinking more and more about what that means to him. He'd lived in London for years before the big *fake date quit job upheave life*, and while not directly exploring his queerness, he'd done a tiny tour of the museum Queer Britain, the bookshop Gay's the Word and some art exhibitions.

But that wasn't enough, really. He wanted more. He *needed* more. And so, he had approached the project of his own queerness with much the same resolve as any other big change in his life: throw himself in head first with little thought beforehand, and then worry incessantly while living through it.

Sensing he needed a kind of emotional guide, Ambrose, Haf's best friend, had taken him out to a drag night featuring some of the best British Queens. It's strange that Ambrose has only been in Christopher's life for the last year, because they are such an enormous presence. After last Christmas's shenanigans, Ambrose and Laurel had set up a fashion label together. They wove their way into the fabric of Christopher's life as though they had always been there.

Maybe that's why Ambrose was so easily able to convince Christopher to go dancing at G-A-Y, because they insisted he *had* to do it once (even though the pair of them left after an hour to get pizza). Christopher has always been a nurse-a-drink-at-the-bar rather than dance-in-a-club kind of guy, but everything felt a little different through this new lens of bisexual freedom. He wanted to try more things.

And it had yielded some . . . experiences, to say the least. He'd kissed some boys, and more than that too. Several firsts for him. There were a couple of people in London when he was studying – you don't spend that long in close proximity with people without a few sparks flying – though it was all sexual chemistry and the stress of deflating souf-fles, rather than any emotional connection. He'd spent a glorious weekend with a non-binary person with the most glorious laugh, who looked like JVN dressed head to toe in sequins.

Hell, the Spanks Squad even went to the tiny gay bar in York when he was there visiting, and while there was no kiss-ing (for him at least), it was a nice time to just be somewhere he was allowed to be himself, or even somewhere he allowed himself to be.

Nothing lasted though. He didn't have time. All his major focus had to be the baking. And then he'd suddenly moved and bought a business and all that exploration went on the back burner.

No wonder he had become so parasocially attached to Nash Nadeau.

It was just nice to have a little crush.

★ ★ ★

Two movies down, Christopher remembers that he never actually made himself a hot chocolate, after all that faffing.

It's dark when he gets downstairs, the sun already low in the sky. It's weird not to have the bakery open, though he supposes he'd be closing around now anyway. There's a guilty pang in his stomach over this impromptu day off, but a quick glance out of the window suggests that the storm is by no means better, and almost certainly worse than it was before he started his mini movie marathon.

He can feel the urge to wallow, so focuses instead on hunting down toppings to make a luxurious hot chocolate. Tegan must have thrown out the whipped cream yesterday, but he finds some slightly dried-out marshmallows left over from the melting snowman cookies he made last week. He reaches in for a handful and then, on second thought, decides he'll take the whole bag with him.

He gets so lost in the slow blending of pink and white marshmallows as they melt that, at first, he thinks he imagines the banging on the front door.

There's only one person he knows who carries that much fury in her general person. But when he looks up, it's not Shaz. He'd recognise her outline with her mounds of knitwear anywhere. How odd.

He fishes in his pocket for the front door key as he wanders over, and it's only when he opens the door and the light spills out from the bakery into the evening gloom that he recognises the man. For a second, he wonders if he fell asleep upstairs, because the very same person has invaded his dreams for months on end.

The man who dominates Shaz's Christmas film list.

The star of the film he was watching mere minutes ago.

His *little crush*.

In the doorway to Christopher's tiny village bakery, inexplicably, stands Nash Nadeau.

Chapter Three

Christopher

Nash Nadeau.

Is here.

In Christopher's bakery.

What the hell is happening!?

It's as if he stepped out of one of his own Christmas movies.

Or, well, not exactly like that. He tends to be dressed in elaborately knitted Nordic jumpers or, if he's playing a veterinarian, as he often does, scrubs.

Today, for some reason, he's wearing a leather jacket, a truly terrible outerwear choice for Wales in the middle of winter.

Plus, this Nash looks as if he's been through one hell of a snowstorm. Which of course he has.

But it *is* undeniably him. Christopher would recognise him anywhere. He could probably draw that face from memory. The aquiline nose and strong jaw. The peppering of just the right length stubble. The man is all broad shoulders and strong arms, but not in the usual stocky British rugby player way. There's still something lithe to him, a nimbleness. Despite the dark purple under his eyes, there's still a playfulness about him. Nash's golden blond hair is mussed, presumably from the hat he was just wearing. It makes Christopher want to push it back from his face.

Several questions run through Christopher's mind at once.

First of all, how did he even get here in the middle of the worst snowstorm in history? And *why* is he here? He's pretty sure that Nash lives in California. London or Edinburgh would make sense, especially if he was filming. But if he was coming to Wales, you'd expect he'd be in the capital, Cardiff, or maybe somewhere fancy and picturesque in Pembroke-shire, or perhaps even at a Wrexham game with Ryan Reynolds and the other one. But Pen-y-Môr is just a normal small town. And if they were filming something here, even he would have heard about it from Shaz. News travels fast in Pen-y-Môr.

He falls back on the *probably dreaming* explanation. Per-haps in the stress, his brain has decided to conjure a relaxing scenario for him. This is plausible if he ignores how much he can hear, smell, taste and how much he's in control of his body. Well, sort of – he's frozen, clutching the half-empty bag of marshmallows.

Anything seems more realistic than Nash Nadeau actually being here.

The whirring in Christopher's head is promptly interrupted when Nash Nadeau steps through the door and drops his bags to the floor with a clatter. With the air of someone who has just absolutely had enough, he proclaims, 'Fuck me, I didn't think I was going to Narnia.'

In all possible scenarios, this wasn't what he was expecting him to say. Not even a 'Hello' or a 'Where am I?'

Christopher realises that he is wide awake and, in his stupor, he hasn't actually said anything yet. And for some bizarre reason, the thing he responds with is, 'I believe you have to step through a wardrobe to get to Narnia. That's just a regular front door.'

Not 'Hello, why are you storming into my bakery?' Just correcting Nash Nadeau on the lore of C. S. Lewis's chil-dren's fantasy series. Okay.

Could this day get any weirder? The bag of marshmal-lows crinkles, and he drops it on the counter before he rips it apart with nerves.

Nash drops a flapped hat on the table next to him and rubs at his shockingly pink cheeks and ears. 'Honestly, buddy, given the day I've had, having to walk through a wardrobe into another world wouldn't feel that out of place. In fact, I think it would have been a major step up from some of the transportation I've been on today. It definitely beats the truck full of sheep.'

This might possibly be the most bizarre conversation Christopher has ever had in the history of his life. 'Hopefully you didn't have to sit with the sheep?' he offers incredulously.

'Luckily not. Though I think it would have been slightly better company than the driver. That man was no Mr Tumnus.'

'No goat legs?'

'I didn't think to check. Look, sorry to barge in here yelling about satyrs, but I'm lost, half frozen, and dying for a coffee.'

'Oh! Um, we're not actually open I'm afraid,' Christopher says, dazed from this whiplash of a conversation.

'You opened the door?' says Nash, with a confused twitch of his eyebrows and a flash of teeth as his mouth pulls up at the corner.

Hang on a moment. 'Yes, because you were banging on it?'

'Right. But we're both in here right now, and that coffee machine is on. You were making yourself a drink when I showed up.'

Well. Nash does have him there.

'And you must own this place, right? Why else would you be here when it's closed?' For emphasis, he adds air quotations around 'closed'.

'I do,' says Christopher a little tartly, and points at the door. 'But the sign was turned to closed.'

To be fair, Nash does at least glance over his shoulder to look at it. 'Okay, but no one's going to get in trouble if you make me a coffee, seeing as you own the place? I've had one hell of a journey, it's basically Christmas, and I will literally pay you.'

All this rankles Christopher in a way he can't put his finger on. If he'd been given a moment to process any of what was happening, he would have offered to do that anyway. He doesn't need to be *told*.

But this guy stormed in as if he owned the place. In fact, it reminds him of some of the people he went to school with. A bit of money in the family pocket meant people felt they owned the world, and that everyone else's job was to bow to their whims. It's the attitude that he's fought against all his life because it's just so blinkered and cruel. Someone's fortune of birth shouldn't be meted out in unkindness to other people.

Maybe he's thinking too deeply about this – it wouldn't be the first time. It is snowing and miserable. The last thing he wants to be is unkind. If he's honest with himself, he's probably experiencing some kind of parasocial whiplash that's feeling like salt in the wound. They say *never meet your heroes*, and maybe the same could be said for your celebrity crushes.

But even if he doesn't like Nash's attitude, he doesn't need to be a prick back. It's not as if he likes every customer he ever meets. Plus, didn't Nash say he was lost? It would only be right for Christopher to help him out. So, he begrudgingly agrees.

'Sure. One coffee coming up.' He walks behind the counter to add beans to the grinder, enough for both of them.

'I'll take an espresso if you guys have that here,' Nash calls to him.

Christopher is thankful his back is turned because he rolls his eyes at what feels very much like an insult to his bakery and the town. Sure, they're not in LA, but it's not as if they don't drink proper coffee here. He takes a deep breath, trying to ignore the irritation prickling under his skin. He tries to keep his tone jolly as he replies, 'We are in Europe. Of course we have espresso.'

'Oh great. I was just thinking, you know, proper Europe feels so far away from here. And didn't you guys leave or something?'

He's saved from snapping back by the very loud rumbling of the grinder. Instead, he watches as Nash peels off his sodden jacket and hangs it on the back of a different chair, where it proceeds to drip meltwater all over the floor. He must be soaked.

The grinding stops, and Christopher calmly explains, despite Nash's apparent ignorance. 'We left the European *Union*. The UK is still part of Europe. I don't think you can choose to leave a continent.' He tries to channel his most sunny, helpful self. 'By the way, you can change in there if you need to.' He thumbs in the direction of the café bathroom.

'Oh thanks.' Nash immediately wheels his suitcase over there as Christopher continues making them both espressos.

It'll be fine. They can sit down, drink their coffees, and he can send Nash on his merry way. Deep breaths.

What a weird day. What a terribly weird day.

Chapter Four

Nash

God, what a fucking day.

What a *fucking day*.

This all serves him right really. Maybe it's some kind of karma? Run away from your responsibilities and bam, you're stuck in a freak snowstorm in Europe begging a barista who might hate you to make you a hot drink.

All Nash had wanted was a Christmas alone where no one could bother him. That was why he picked somewhere no one would expect him to go, after all. He's never even been to the UK before, and so, rather than go for the usual touristy experience of London, or even Edinburgh at the very least, he's now in the middle of nowhere in Wales.

The thing is, he had to get out of LA. Even just for a little while.

In fact, Tessa, his assistant, is the only person who knows where he is. She's a great assistant so didn't pry into why he was fleeing the country. Didn't even enquire. Discreet is part of the job description, and her general demeanour of being slightly uninterested helps too – if he remembers right, she's some director's kid writing a screenplay and wanted some experience 'doing a normal job'.

Although, thinking about her, he should probably let her know he is alive at some point. Maybe when he's not completely soaked. His parents would never let him live it down when he was a teenager if he dressed weather-inappropriate, and he gets a pang of that old *well I told you so* in his head as he peels away his sodden jeans. Critical error, there.

Not helped by the fact that what he's going to put on . . . are also jeans.

Maybe he can find a Walmart or whatever the equivalent is here when the weather is a little less apocalyptic.

Either way, he's definitely stuck here for now. Serves him right for leaving.

People were always fleeing the city – it was easy to get tired of LA. The cars, the smog, the people. Well, not *all* the people, but a lot of them. Plus, he'd been getting tired of the whole one-season thing. You don't grow up in Canada without occasionally missing snow, though he's pretty sure after this snow-cursed trip he'll never think that again.

Anyway, now it seems he's stuck here. And it had all seemed like a great idea at the time, or if not *great* it was certainly *an* idea. And when he left LA yesterday there was no sign of a storm. As far as he knew, anyway. There were probably meteorologists talking about it somewhere . . .

And so, it was a shock to land in Manchester to snow *everywhere*. It turns out that snow grinds *everything* to a halt in the UK. For some reason, everyone seems to be surprised that it snows here. And yes, this might be snow beyond the usual levels (from what he can tell) but still, it's not as if the UK is a tropical country? Why was no one prepared? Maybe he'll email Hugh Grant about it when he's back home. Hugh loves a cause.

So far, it was not the relaxing escape into obscurity he was hoping for, let's just say that. They were the last plane to land on UK soil, as all the rest seemed to be diverted to mainland Europe (just his luck that he didn't end up stranded somewhere *not* snowed under), and then it turned out all the trains had been called off too – definitely a problem when he was planning to get one the whole way from Manchester to the apartment he'd rented.

Uber was so in demand, the app wouldn't even load.

He considered walking to the nearest airport hotel and begging for help, but something in his jet-lagged lizard brain told him he had to get to Wales. That address was the only guaranteed bed he had. Plus, how far could it be? A few hours' drive? How bad could that be?

Apparently, *pretty bad* according to the fourteen taxi drivers in a row who insisted they weren't leaving Manchester for love nor money.

Taxi driver number fifteen agreed to drive him as far as he thought safe for a significant bank transfer and an autograph, once he'd wheedled out of Nash that he was an actor. Unfortunately, *as far as he could go* turned out to be a service station outside Chester, which wasn't even *in* Wales. The man simply refused to cross the border, as though things were going to get that much worse if he tried.

Granted, he might have been onto something.

It was pure luck (or perhaps, on reflection, terribly bad luck) that, just as the taxi zoomed off, a huge truck full of sheep had pulled up alongside him, ready to fuel up at the gas station. Nash is recognisable, he knows that. He has 'The Look' of an actor, so to speak, and globally, enough people have the streaming services that host his various films that they've at least scrolled past his face, if not watched something he was in. Unless he meets a real connoisseur of the romance genre, he doesn't get outright recognised as much as *hey you look familiar*-ed.

This together with his generally helpless situation made it even more improbable that the driver of said sheep truck, Gethin, the very Welsh farmer, was not only a huge Nash Nadeau fan, but was heading back home to Wales *and* would be passing the town where Nash was staying. Despite years of festive-themed films, Nash has never stopped to consider whether a Christmas miracle was a real thing, until now.

And sure, Gethin's truck reeked of sheep – a smell he's convinced he's never experienced so intensely before now – and Gethin was a little strange and over-enthusiastic, but he was also Nash's best chance of escaping that service station.

Nash paid for the gas, because that only seemed polite, but wow is it expensive in the UK.

The drive took a couple of hours, and from Gethin's enthusiastic questioning, Nash isn't entirely convinced the man didn't go well out of his way for an exclusive interview. But what was the cost of a few incredibly invasive questions in exchange for a possibly lifesaving lift? A few sanity points that he would have definitely lost if he'd been stranded in Chester.

Anyway. At least he's here. Well, he's definitely . . . *some-where*, and Gethin was insistent this was the right place. If only Nash's phone would work, he could dig all the information out. This is why people print things still; just in case they're stuck in a catastrophic snowstorm in the middle of nowhere.

Now, he rubs at his soaked, wind-blown hair with the damp top he just took off, which typically just makes his reflection in the mirror look even more like he's been on the journey from hell. Which, well, he might have been.

The dry, clean, and crucially not-smelling-of-sheep clothes do brighten his mood enough that he can face leaving the bathroom and talking again with the ornery café owner.

God knows why that guy is acting as if Nash's entire existence is his own personal cross to bear. Like, come on, it's a *snowstorm*, dude. Help a guy out? Nash only asked him for a coffee. It's not as if he asked the man to polish his boots, or give him a piggyback through the snow. Though, given he's going to have to go out into the snow in jeans again, maybe he should ask to be carried.

All he needs to do is get this weird, gangly British man to direct him to the place Tessa booked, and then he can get out of here. Be alone, *finally*.

Thank fuck he packed too many clothes and a full bottle of testosterone gel.

Get it together, Nadeau. The show must go on and all that crap.

All he needs to do is slap on some good old North American charm, like every miserable press circuit has taught him to do.

This is nothing. This is just one weird dude.

He can do this.

Be polite, ask for help, get the fuck out of there. Easy.

And with that, he opens the bathroom door.

Chapter Five

Christopher

While Nash is changing, Christopher somehow finds himself further down an anxiety spiral. He's not the best in novel social situations, and this is *really fucking novel*.

It's a very weird thing to meet someone you feel you know. But really, it's Nash's *characters* he knows – perhaps that's why the man himself feels so alien.

Nadeau himself is famously rather private. There never seem to be interviews or profiles of him. The last thing Christopher remembers was one of those Google autocomplete video interviews by *Wired*, where Nash said he liked tacos and found it weird that so many of the questions were about who he was dating and where he lived. The number of interviews he'd done really dropped off after *Parental Units*, his first role in a family drama where he played a trans teenager. After going through puberty on screen, perhaps it was understandable that he wouldn't want to subsequently share much else with a world so obsessively curious about trans bodies.

The thing Christopher had noticed about Nash was that he always seemed to be alone. Some kind of island, apart from the others. He was never papped, and never posted pictures of himself with his famous friends. At one time, Christopher had thought it was just privacy, but on the Christmas-movie Reddit that Christopher followed way too intently, someone who had assisted on one of Nash's film sets said that Nash was just like that. Kept to himself.

Is it weird that he knows all this?

It is, isn't it?

As Nash will be on his way back into the main café any moment, all being well, Christopher decides that he will just have to pretend he doesn't know who Nash is. Yes, that'll be much more casual and won't prolong the situation. Hopefully, Christopher can keep his cool and Nash can just chalk up any prior awkwardness to him being British.

Nash returns from the bathroom in a clean pair of dark blue jeans and a brown checked shirt that appears to be lined with faux fur. In his hands are his damp clothes. 'Is it okay if I hang these up for a second?'

Christopher points to a radiator. 'Hang them on there.'

Nash does as he's told, thankfully, before taking a seat. In front of him, Christopher deposits a steaming hot cup of espresso in a tiny cup on a saucer, with a wrapped-up Biscoff biscuit on the side – he keeps a box of them under the counter just in case. Normally, they're unofficial Tegan snacks.

'Thanks for all this. You're a lifesaver.'

Nash gives him a lopsided smile that makes Christopher feel strangely exposed. Christopher nods awkwardly and returns to the safety of his counter, where he can pretend he's doing anything other than noticing how handsome Nash is. Because he really is. He might scowl down at his phone, but it's kind of *hot*. And when he takes a sip of his espresso, Christopher finds himself licking his own lips.

What exactly are you supposed to do when the man of your dreams walks into your life? Especially when he arrives underdressed and exhausted. Ask for his number, probably. Make him a hot drink at the very least, and he's done that. What now? Kit would absolutely tell him to get a grip and help him.

Nash drags him from his horny reverie with a 'What do I owe you?' In his hand, he holds a black credit card, one of the ones that Christopher is pretty sure only exist for the seriously famous or seriously rich. The tills are all booted down – because *they are closed*.

'It's on the house. Call it a Christmas miracle.'

'Thanks. This coffee is the best thing that's happened to me today.'

Christopher clears his throat and stares intently at the counter he was permanently wiping before Nash Nadeau walked into his life. And for some reason, he says, 'Just so you know, sheep truck is not a standard form of public transport here.'

'Oh yeah? I figured it kind of made sense given how old everything is here in Merry Old England.'

'Wales.'

'Sorry?'

'You're not in England. You're in Wales,' Christopher says a little haughtily.

'Isn't Wales like part of England, though? Isn't that why there's a Prince of Wales or whatever?'

Christopher has been in Wales long enough to know exactly how some people feel about *that* particular royal title. And that's apart from the way Wales gets lumped in with England all the time. Haf had told him that people never properly recognise Wales as a country seemingly as if to purposely annoy her – she likes to bring this up during the rugby, when she gets particularly patriotic.

'No. It's not. There are four countries, and the United Kingdom or Britain is them put together.' He's pretty sure there's a lot more nuance to it than that, but this will have to do.

Nash nods, taking this in. 'Noted. Sorry, I just need to check something.' He goes back to his phone without another word, and so Christopher takes the hint to busy himself until he's needed.

On the back of a paper bag, he decides to take inventory of the bakery contents he could eat over the next few days. It feels wrong, but needs must – after all, who knows what state the supermarkets are in and there's no way he's going out in that weather again today. Though, he's going to need a supply run if he wants to avoid rickets.

From across the café, he hears Nash swear. He looks up through the service window to see Nash waving his phone over his head.

Christopher takes one of the little cards with the Wi-Fi code on from the counter and lays it on Nash's table. 'The signal can be wonky, but luckily we have Wi-Fi in this country.'

He meant it as a joke, but if he's honest with himself, he's quietly pleased with the look of embarrassment that washes over Nash's face.

'Thanks,' Nash says, somewhat chastened.

From his safe place behind the counter, Christopher says, 'Do you need any help by the way? You said you might be lost?'

'Yeah, I'm trying to work that out.'

'I think *trying to work out if you're lost* probably counts as being lost.'

'I think you're right,' sighs Nash. 'I'm supposed to be staying . . . well, I hope it's nearby. I had some stuff open on my phone but at some point it refreshed and now it won't load. But I had shown the sheep-truck guy and he said he'd dropped me off in the right place, but who knows.'

'Are you here on holiday?'

The page on Nash's phone loads incredibly slowly.

'You could say that. It's more like a solo escape. Though looking at this weather I feel as if it's more like *a trap*.'

'You're here on your own?'

'Just me and my mountain of soaked laundry.'

'So, are you visiting friends or family?' Christopher asks, though if that was the case, surely Nash would be calling someone.

'God no,' Nash answers. After a second, he looks up. 'Not that I hate them or anything. I just mean, I don't have family here.'

This is all very strange, though. This confirms no one is filming anything, and if he was here for work, there'd be some kind of entourage, surely.

The page finishes loading. Unfortunately, Nash looks as baffled as he is relieved. He cranes his neck to look out the front window from his seat.

'Well, do you need some directions?' Christopher offers, equally baffled.

'I think I need some pronunciation help. I should have Duolingo'd before I came, but man, I really hate that owl.'

'Show me?'

Nash walks over to the counter, and when Christopher takes the phone from him, their fingers touch ever so briefly. A glorious shock runs up Christopher's arm that he tries really very hard to ignore. Thank goodness for the counter, though it would be easier if Nash wasn't leaning over it towards him.

He's shorter than Christopher expected, but that's because he half presumes all famous people will be taller than he is, even though *he's* taller than most people. As though there's some kind of special height-enhancement available just for celebrities, along with all the other slightly horrifying surgical options.

It would be so easy to just look up and see how long Nash's eyelashes are in person.

How soft his gently curved lips look.

His eyes are green, his traitor brain says.

Christopher gulps down the frog in his throat. It takes him a few seconds to realise that Nash spoke.

'All this just serves me right for making my assistant book for me.'

Wait. His assistant?

A nagging prickle runs up the back of his neck.

It can't be.

When Christopher glances down at the phone, he sees a booking confirmation. And right there is *his* address. Pantri Bach, Station Road, Pen-y-Môr.

Oh no.

This can't be.

'Do you know where this is? Penny Mire?' Nash nudges him, clearly confused by his total lack of response. 'Is it far from here?'

'Pen-y-Môr,' Christopher croaks.

'So you know it?'

'You're here, actually. Or there. Pen-y-Môr is this town.'

What the hell is he going to do? Nash Nadeau, *the* Nash Nadeau, can't possibly stay here.

'Man, what a relief,' Nash says, his voice sounding hollow in Christopher's ears. 'I was right to have trusted Gethin the sheep guy with my life after all.'

Christopher feels as if he might be about to pass out. He still can't bring himself to say anything helpful.

This Christmas was already turning out weird, even before he discovered his celebrity crush was supposed to be house-sitting for him.

Except now, Christopher can't leave. He has to stay here *himself.*

And now he has to tell Nash that . . . what? That he can't stay here after all? There is no script for this and Christopher feels so desperately lost.

'I . . . you're here.'

'Yeah, you said.'

'No, I mean. It's the flat upstairs. Sorry, I was expecting a Tessa.'

'That could be my name,' Nash says airily, which makes it Christopher's turn to look embarrassed. 'I'm just razzing you – I'm Nash.' He holds out his hand to shake, which Christopher takes in his. 'Nash Nadeau.'

Christopher does his absolute best not to react. That was the plan, right? Pretend you don't know who he is. This is the moment where his path could diverge; he could say *oh yeah, are you that guy from the Christmas films* or he could keep up this ruse that he definitely does not owe his mental health to Nash's IMDb credits.

In the end, he chooses the original plan.

'Christopher Calloway.'

'Nice to meet you. So... can you show me up to the place?'

Christopher shuts his eyes, bites his lip and takes a deep breath. 'I'm afraid there's a problem.'

'A problem?'

'Yes.'

'With the flat?'

'Well, not just the flat.'

'Okay . . . are you going to tell me what it is or are we going to continue this cryptic back and forth?'

'The flat is no longer empty, as it was going to be when advertised, due to a change of circumstances.'

'But I booked it? So, I should be able to stay here?'

'Yes, but as you're well aware, there's been an enormous snowstorm.'

'My guy,' Nash says, wiping his face with his hands, 'I am so exhausted. Can you drop the very British politeness, and just straight up tell me what's going on? Please.'

Christopher takes a deep breath. 'I own the flat, yes, and I also usually *live* in the flat. And I was supposed to go to stay with family in Yorkshire while you were staying here.'

Realisation dawns on Nash's face. 'But you couldn't get there because of the weather.'

'Precisely.'

'Right.' Nash runs his fingers through his hair. 'Crap, I really should have thought this through.'

All of a sudden, Nash looks much smaller than he did a few moments ago. The brash swagger has all melted away. He looks desperate.

'Is there anywhere else to stay in this town? I mean, could you help me find somewhere? I really, truly do not know where I am and I can't get hold of Tessa and you're literally the only person I know in possibly the whole country so . . .'

In his heart of hearts, Christopher knows the answer is no. Didn't Shaz say yesterday that the pub is totally out of action? None of the other holiday flats will be empty at this time of year, and even if they are, how will they even get Nash there? He doesn't know anyone well enough to ask them to put Nash up apart from Shaz, who has her mother-in-law staying in the spare room.

At least for tonight, there really is nowhere else.

As if in confirmation, the wind howls outside, battering the windows in their frames. Since Nash arrived, the snow has resumed falling with such vigour that Christopher suspects he might have to dig them out when they do try to leave. They're going nowhere today. Not unless either of them has survival skills and a death wish.

And Christopher can't leave Nash without somewhere to stay. Turning him away would be pretty counter to the whole Nativity story aspect of Christmas. If he hadn't rented his flat out, Nash wouldn't be here. As weird as it is, he's Christopher's responsibility now.

And it's going to be *extremely* weird.

Christopher hopes that, at the very least, his television upstairs has gone to sleep so that Nash doesn't walk into the flat to see a huge picture of himself on the screen. The universe owes him that one, surely.

'Look, you're just going to have to stay with me for tonight, at least while we work this out. The flat is small, but there's just enough space for both of us. Tomorrow, if the weather is better, we can look at finding you somewhere else, but we're not going anywhere in that unless you can call back Gethin the sheep farmer.'

'The one time I regret not getting someone's number,' Nash mutters to himself.

This rattles Christopher from his speech for just a second, but he keeps going. 'I really think it's safest if you just stay here, even if that means you're shacking up with a stranger. I'm sorry, this probably isn't what you were expecting.'

Nash doesn't say anything for a minute, presumably thinking his way to the same inevitability Christopher has already reached. 'Are you sure?'

'Yes.'

'Okay then,' he says, and for the first time, that earnest look that Christopher recognises from his films appears on Nash's face. 'Thank you for this, man.'

As Christopher locks the front door he murmurs, 'Don't thank me just yet.'

Chapter Six

Christopher

It doesn't take very long for Christopher to start wondering whether the innkeeper was onto something when he told Mary and Joseph to go and stay in the barn.

Nash takes up a lot of space. Even just drinking his coffee and gathering his wet things, his movements feel much bigger than his person. He does wash his cup up in the small sink behind the counter without being asked, which gets him a couple of points, but they are quickly cancelled out by him saying, 'You know, I'm pretty sure several horror movies start this way. Tiny rural town, trapped in a snowstorm . . .'

Christopher ignores him and instead leads him through the bakery's kitchen so they can take the internal stairs up to his flat.

'See? Plenty of weapons to hand . . .' Nash nods at the kitchen knives hanging on the wall. 'Hang on, are these your initials?' he asks, looking at them more closely.

'Yes, we had to label them at cookery school so no one would get their sets mixed up,' Christopher defends himself, stiffly.

'Sure.'

He wants to add, 'Of course we have knives, they're slightly integral to a kitchen,' but he's not sure how an exhausted North American would take a dose of British sarcasm, and even if Nash is annoying him, he doesn't really want to upset this actual stranger before they share his tiny flat for the night.

Be polite. Be normal. This is a weird situation and yes you're feeling a bit emotionally tested but you can get through one night.

He loves this kitchen. It isn't large, but the sense of calm he always feels in here washes over him, even now. The gleaming stainless steel. The permanent smell of butter and sugar that hangs in the air. The flour-dusted floor tiles that never get completely clean, as though the flour is baked into them from all the people walking through. His Christmas might have taken a turn for the . . . *bizarre*, but at least he is at the bakery. At least he has his safe haven.

And now Nash is trying to joke it could be the site of some kind of murder?

Someone is going to get murdered at this rate, Christopher thinks darkly.

A tiny little corridor leads round the back of the building to the stairs up to the flat. 'This is it.'

Christopher takes off his shoes at the bottom of the stairs. To his relief, Nash has the manners to do the same.

It's a weird thing seeing your own home through someone else's eyes. This was precisely what he was hoping to avoid; originally, he was hoping he could just meet Tessa outside the bakery before scarpering off for his train.

He hovers uselessly while Nash appraises his slightly ramshackle flat. Christopher has always liked it, even though it's pokey and a bit cold and the walls look slightly wonky. Cosy, that's what the estate agent called it. But now, he can't help but see the cookbooks stuffed everywhere, even if he did clean up all the piles and consolidate them into one tall pile against the very full bookshelf. The hallway console table is decorated with a vase Laurel gave him, which is empty – perhaps that was a little thoughtless? The kitchen is a standard, slightly battered IKEA set-up that basically every student house has, and the fridge is so little that he has to bend down to put stuff in it. The TV is thankfully on standby. He can't imagine what Nash thinks of this place.

But Nash just asks, 'So, where should I put my case?'

'In here,' Christopher says, ushering him to the bedroom. This room looks the most normal. He tried to keep it as clean and empty as possible when he moved in so that his brain would have fewer things to latch onto, and so he painted it a deep, calming forest green. The fresh towels are still folded on the end of the bed, which is made up with clean jersey sheets from Uniqlo for the extra warmth. He had picked up the dark wood bed and the matching furniture from another house clearance sale when he moved here – Facebook truly does have one good use still. It all creaks but he revarnished it with Kit one afternoon in the sun, so it looks pretty good at least. It's his favourite room. And now, he has to give it up.

Which, yes, he was always going to do, but he wasn't going to have to sleep on the couch next door while it was occupied. Obviously, he's going to have to sleep on the couch, because there's no way he's letting a guest sleep there. That's, like, Hospitality 101. He'd never hear the end of it from his mother.

'You can unpack your things into the chest of drawers there, and there's space in the wardrobe too.'

Nash sets his case at the end of the bed, and sits down on it, bouncing slightly. 'Man, this is so much better than sleeping on the plane. Or the sheep truck.'

Christopher looks longingly at his bed, and quietly bids it goodbye for now.

'Let me know if you need anything. I'll leave you to unpack.'

He retrieves his own suitcase and sets it in the corner of the living room. That'll have to do.

Now what?

What exactly do you do with yourself when an actor you're pretending to know nothing about is making themselves at home in your bedroom? Especially when you've already cleaned everything in anticipation of guests.

He primps cushions, rearranges the already neatly folded blankets, and straightens the huge baking bibles that live permanently on his coffee table. Christopher very quickly runs out of tasks, and so resorts to British basic programming: he makes tea.

Nash has left the bedroom door open, but he still knocks to be polite.

'Tea?'

Nash grins. 'I wondered how long it would take for you to offer me tea. I've heard it's a compulsion for you guys. That was a whole five minutes. You must have been dying inside.'

'Well . . . yes. It is one of those stereotypes that's mostly true,' Christopher says with a smile. 'How do you take it?'

Nash raises his eyebrows and gives him a smirk. 'Depends who's asking.'

Christopher can feel his face go completely beetroot. At this moment, he would quite like to escape his own skin, never mind the flat.

Hopefully oblivious, Nash just laughs at his own joke. 'I dunno, man, milk and sugar, I guess? Our tea tastes like piss so I drink freshly ground drip coffee at home. I'll take it however you have it.'

It's a strange experience being simultaneously attracted to someone and irritated by everything they say. Imagine having such a blasé attitude to how you take tea; and of course he'd be a *has-opinions* coffee drinker.

Be nice, Christopher. Just be nice!

Christopher makes tea in two of the nice stoneware ceramic mugs that Laurel got him for the new flat. He puts an extra sugar in Nash's because Americans love sugar, but then remembers LA people probably think it's the devil. Either way, it's too late.

As he squeezes out the teabags, he hears Nash in the bedroom say, in the worst cockney accent ever, 'One cuppa, governor.' Against his best intentions, he can't help but chuckle. But only a very little one.

His phone buzzes, and he's relieved to see a text from Shaz.

Shaz: Oi, you all right? Did you leave? Any word from Tessa? Let me know if you need me to pop over. Sorry for not messaging earlier. Gar was clearing the snow off the drive and pavement this morning, fell over on some ice, and has a probably broken ankle according to Priti (have you met her? Nurse, nice) who came over to help. The Piranhas have been up since four. Merry Christmas???? I need more gingerbread!!!!

Christopher: Oh no! Is Gar okay? Do you need anything? Good job I gave you two reindeer.

Shaz: Gar is Gar. Stoic but also sleeping it off in front of Frozen 2 with the kids. And my mother-in-law has helpfully told me the bath needs cleaning. Reindeer are long gone.

Shaz: Wait are you still here then?

Christopher: Yes. No trains running.

Shaz: Ah shite, I'm sorry! Wanna come over? What happened to Tessa the hermit?

Christopher: Tomorrow? Need to sort some things out. Will bring gingerbread.

'Sort some things out' seems like the world's biggest euphemism. And sure, telling her that Nash Nadeau is here might give her the distraction that *she* needs, but Christopher himself is still wrapping his head around it all. At least promising her gingerbread means he has A Task to focus on.

After all, how do you even condense the enormity of *yes that film star we're mutually obsessed with is currently putting his things away in my chest of drawers and also I feel conflicted because turns out he is terribly annoying* into a single text message?

Perhaps he is thinking about it all too much.

Nash has closed the bedroom door, so Christopher calls 'Tea!' to no answer, and sets Nash's tea down on the coffee table. This reminds Christopher he should process a refund for Nash – yes he's technically staying in Christopher's bed tonight, but it's really not right to keep the money.

The wind roars outside again. It's pitch black out there now. It makes him want to light candles and curl up in a blanket fort.

What a weird fucking day. So many thoughts have been racing – and continue to race – around his head that this brief pause means he finally notices he's got a cracking headache. He presses the warm cup against it, hoping the heat will ease the tension, but it is quickly too hot. He almost spills the cup all over himself as he thrusts it away and back to the table.

Everything is officially Too Much.

'This is a cute little place you've got here.' Nash has re-entered the living area, presumably on the hunt for his freshly made mug of tea.

He sits down next to Christopher and the three-seater couch suddenly feels a lot smaller, not least because Nash is spread out all over it, legs apart and head back.

Make yourself at home, Christopher thinks sourly, and then feels immediately guilty for not being charitable about it all.

No wonder he has a headache.

Christopher blinks a few times, and realises Nash is staring at him with intense concentration. 'Yes?' he asks nervously.

'What did you do to your head?'

'Sorry?'

'You've got a big pink mark on it.'

'Oh Christ.' Christopher feels the skin with the back of his hand. Hot but not burned, at least. 'Occupational hazard.'

'Extreme-sports version of making tea, was it?'

'Something like that.'

Christopher normally likes silence, but unearned silence with a stranger is far from companionable. He feels as if he should be entertaining Nash, but Christ, he's tired. He doesn't trust his slightly burned brain to not come out with absolute nonsense. The wind rattles the windows again, as if to highlight how much 'not speaking' is going on inside.

It could be worse. He could have fallen and maybe broken a leg and be being forced to watch *Frozen 2* with multiple children.

But even if it could be worse, it doesn't make it *not* annoying. To Christopher's growing irritation, whenever Nash takes a sip of tea, he follows it by breathing out with an *ahh*.

Every single time.

Be charitable. Be nice. Calm down, Christopher repeats to himself over and over again. And then . . .

'Are all British places so little?' Nash asks. He does this so airily, which somehow makes it seem all the more annoying.

Unstoppable irritation bubbles under Christopher's skin. 'It might not be the biggest, but it's the right size for me,' he replies, coldly.

At this, Nash does that raised-eyebrow-smirking thing again.

Realising what he's just said, Christopher splutters. 'That's not what I mean. It's small but perfectly formed.'

This sends Nash's eyebrows right up into his stupidly perfect hair, a laugh rumbling in his chest.

How? *How* did he make it worse?

All Christopher can do is grab his too-hot cup of tea and take a huge sip. He winces with the heat, but it's a relief from the constant hum of stress under his skin.

'I'm just razzing you,' says Nash with a lazy smile.

Christopher can't decide what is more mortifying – how obviously embarrassed he is, or how clearly aware of that Nash is.

'What I was trying to say,' Christopher says, a little too conscious of his words, 'is that that there's enough space for me for now *in this flat*, and yes, I suppose our buildings are much smaller over here.'

'Do you have a spare room too? Like an office?'

'Yes, but it's rather full. I didn't have time to unpack everything when I moved here. I really had to just focus on getting the bakery up and running.'

The spare room really is a dumping ground. If he's honest with himself, he has no idea what half the stuff is. There are boxes that haven't been opened or thought about, plus all his home baking equipment because the flat's kitchen is way too small for it. It's not as if he needs it with a professional bakery downstairs, but he can't bear to get rid of it all.

The only thing he really did unpack was all the cookbooks. There's a lifetime's worth of them in here. Once they were boxed up, he did have some regrets about not culling them, but it was too late at that point.

The thing is, he hadn't thought of his move as downsizing, because it's not as if his London flat was big. It's just, somehow, this flat is even smaller.

He's been waiting for a free weekend to sort it, but there's not been a spare moment where he's had the energy to sit upright, never mind unpack a room of boxes, or even a single one.

And so, the spare room remains full of stuff.

'Wait, if that's full of stuff, and I'm sleeping in the bed . . . where are *you* going to sleep?'

Christopher looks down at the couch. 'Here,' he says, trying to sound casual.

'Oh.'

'It's fine. Honestly. It's just for one night and then we'll get everything sorted out.'

'Are you sure? It's a pretty small couch. And you're . . . you know.'

'What?'

'Extremely tall.'

'I'm not *extremely* tall. I'm just tall.'

Nash 'hmms' in disagreement.

'I'll be fine,' Christopher says, hoping to close the matter.

The flat might be small, but surely they can keep out of each other's hair, at least for just one night.

How hard can it be?

As if in answer, Nash knocks back the last of his tea so that his cup is nearly vertical over his head, followed by one very long *ahhhhhh*.

Despite all the fantasies and dreams, Christopher realises that Nash Nadeau might just be the most annoying man he has ever met.

Chapter Seven

Nash

Nash is pretty certain that this Christopher Calloway guy is the most annoying man he has *ever* met.

Perhaps being stuck in a tiny apartment with the world's prissiest Englishman drinking tea awkwardly on a couch that's definitely too small for the guy to sleep on is some kind of divine retribution for lying and running away from his problems.

And sure, Christopher is probably not going to murder Nash in his sleep, but unless Christopher gives him some space, Nash might take that option himself.

The only upside to being squished on the tiny couch is that Christopher also seems annoyed, which is quite funny. And at least the tea is good.

But what happens now? Do they both sit here until it's time to go to sleep? Nash could pretend to work in the bedroom, but he knows he'll just lie there and stare at the ceiling listening to the quiet sounds of Christopher being tall and awkward on the other side of the door, which somehow feels worse.

He really is very tall and awkward. Far too tall for a place this small. It's like seeing an elk in a stable. Nash swears he saw Christopher stoop to pass through the door. Why the hell would you buy an apartment with doors too short for you? Is everything in Britain built for hobbits?

This tense silence is excruciating, and so he decides to do the thing he's been avoiding: he checks his messages. And there are a lot of messages.

Christopher looks over, but not like a normal person. He doesn't turn his head and say *hey you've got a lot of messages*. He just side-eyes as he's sipping his tea, looking like that meme of Kermit the frog.

Oh man, that's who he reminds him of.

Kermit.

But English.

Most of the messages are from Kurt, his agent. A man who, if you met him, you'd be sure surfed professionally or ran a marijuana-dispensary-cum-wellness café, rather than being a hard-nosed talent agent. He's been by Nash's side since his career took off properly, and has never steered him wrong.

Obviously, Nash knows why Kurt is trying to get hold of him. That's half of why he ran away in the first place. All he wanted was a bit of peace and quiet so he could think everything through and escape the industry for a few days – especially when it's an industry that doesn't care about the holidays, not when a deal is on the table. A deal that might be the most important one of his life.

And he's not sure he even wants it.

Sure, maybe if he'd acted like an adult and had a proper conversation with Kurt about what he actually wants instead of running away, he wouldn't be here worrying about being locked into another multi-film contract playing characters he can't relate to.

But he's too chicken. So, he ran away to Wales.

He's not ready to reply to Kurt. A pang of guilt shoots through his chest when he reads Tessa's increasingly frantic messages. She deserves a raise when he gets home. That's if he ever escapes the snowpocalypse.

Nash: Hey Tessa. Sorry for not getting back to you earlier. I made it to Wales safely, and just got internet. Happy holidays!

Next to him, Christopher shuffles awkwardly in his seat. He's probably just shifting to get comfortable, though given the height-to-space ratio, Nash is convinced this man has never felt comfortable in his entire life. It's almost as though Christopher is purposefully trying to remind Nash that he's still there.

As if he could forget!

Before he can make a pointed remark about Christopher's constant presence, another notification from Kurt comes through. This time it's a phone call. Now Nash knows he's *really* in trouble. But if he sends him to voicemail, Nash is just postponing the inevitable. It'll be so much worse to have to go through all those voicemails and *then* ring him back.

With a sigh, he gets up and walks to the bedroom, connecting the call as he does.

'Hey man,' he answers, in the most casual tone he can muster.

'Dude! There you are!' Kurt doesn't speak so much as yell in the same cadence of a happily barking golden retriever. 'I've been trying to get hold of you. I was three steps away from calling round the hospitals, or even your parents.'

Yikes, he must have been really worried.

'You owe Tessa a raise, by the way. She was insisting you were fine but unavailable – are you on a hook-up or something? No, don't tell me. Just let me know you're okay?'

Nash feels immediately guilty about Kurt's concern. He probably thinks it's something really serious rather than *I ran away to Europe*.

'Sorry, I didn't mean to scare you,' Nash says, pulling the door closed. 'I'm fine. Just got some stuff going on.'

'Oh yeah?'

Rather than implicate himself or come up with an elaborate lie on the spot, he just says, 'Yep.'

After a pause, Kurt asks, 'Are you safe?'

'Yes.'

'All right then.' Satisfied, Kurt gets down to business. 'Did you see the email from Chuck?'

'A new one, or the one from two days ago?'

There's a small pause. The magical thing about Kurt is that he never lets Nash know exactly how annoyed he is with him, or at least he doesn't think he does. Over the years they've worked together, Nash has learned to read it in his silences and the various intonations of '*dude*'.

'The ones sent yesterday.'

'No then, I haven't seen those yet.'

'Well look, it's my job to know how to best represent you. I can't do that unless I know what's going on for you. So, can you read them, dude?'

'Will do. But, you know, I really would like to think about this after Christmas, if that's possible?' He hears a car honk and Kurt swear under his breath. 'Are you calling me from the car?'

'Business never sleeps, my good dude. Especially in this town.' Kurt laughs heartily, which makes Nash miss him and feel almost bad for not being honest. Kurt adopts his Serious Agent Voice, and adds, 'I'll try and stall them for as long as I can. We can let them know that you've got some . . . personal situation going on, which might buy us some time. Just know that they're getting twitchy over there, Nash.'

Nash sighs, sitting down on the bed.

'I don't think they're going to cancel the offer, but you know, it might be harder to get all the terms *you* want if we're down to the wire, deadline wise. You can talk to me, you know?'

The swirling guilt in Nash's stomach grows into a whirl-pool.

'They all think you're holding out for more money. It's not just money, is it?'

'No, but—'

'Well?'

This is it. Kurt is giving him an opener to just talk about it. But the words just don't come.

This happens to him sometimes. There comes a point where he just can't *think* about something any more. It's not that he doesn't want to – hell, it'd be easier if he could just explain all his thoughts to Kurt – and he knows that Kurt will have his best interests at heart no matter what. But he's just *so* tired. A whole situation that's not been helped by this failure of a vacation. He was supposed to have some time to think, to collect his thoughts.

A car door slams and he hears footsteps. He imagines Kurt walking to one of the really good taco trucks.

Right up until the point he hears a very familiar doorbell. No one else has a poor recreation of the *Parks and Recreation* theme song as their doorbell, he's pretty sure. He set it that way once when he was a bit high and he's never worked out how to change it. But Kurt can't possibly be at his house?

'Kurt, where are you?'

The theme song plays again from the other end of the phone call.

Nash winces. This is about to get really awkward.

'Kurt. Are you at my house?'

'Obviously I'm at your house. I have come to stage an intervention. I brought the catfish tacos you like from Tacos Baja and everything.'

There's a third ring of the doorbell.

'And . . . you're not here, are you?'

'No.'

There's silence on the line for a little too long.

'Fancy telling me where you are while I sit on your door-step eating these delicious tacos you're missing out on?' Nash can hear the strain as Kurt tries to remain chipper.

He could pretend their call is breaking up, but that would be the ultimate dick move. But also, he can't *tell* Kurt. That would be . . . really embarrassing.

Plus, he'll be back home in a few days. The weather will wear off soon, and he'll just get a flight out early. Then he'll take Kurt out for make-up tacos while they talk this all over. Kurt will never need to know he left the country. And continent.

'Look, I know it's weird but I can't tell you right now. But I promise I'm safe, and I just need some help stalling them. Please. I promise I'm thinking about it.'

The word *promise* curdles in his stomach.

The thing is, signing that new contract isn't *just* about him. His deals are how Kurt gets paid, and there are all the other people who want to keep going. Barbie, for one. He knows she's already in. That's before he even considers basically everyone involved – the film crews, the directors, hell, the marketers at the streaming company. If he doesn't work out what he's doing, all those people's jobs are on the line. That's one hell of a lot to carry. His shoulders may be broad, but it's a lot.

'Okay, look, I know that you've got . . . something mysterious going on that I respect your boundary about, that's fine. You don't have to tell me if you don't want to. The only issue is that today the studio set a deadline for a decision on that contract for Christmas Eve.'

Three days, with a little extra thanks to the time difference. 'Oh . . . shit.'

'Yeah, I thought you might say that.'

'Do you think you can stall them until after Christmas? Say my grandma is sick or something.'

'*Is* your grandma sick?'

'. . . No,' he admits, immediately regretting that he did not take that wide open goal when he had the chance.

'Nash, that's not something to lie about,' huffs Kurt.

'Well, she died in 2005 and was a total dick, so I don't mind us using her as an excuse.'

'I feel morally conflicted,' Kurt sighs. 'You know I hate it when I feel morally conflicted.'

'Fine, forget the grandma.'

'Nash, I'm going to be real with you a second. You might be their leading man and yes they might want you for this film series. But they can and will recast you if you fuck them around. I've seen them do it for properties just as big as *Christmas at the Clinic*. Look at *The Witcher*! They recast Henry Cavill even though everyone and their mom fancied him. Being the fan favourite isn't enough.'

Kurt clears his throat and softens his tone. 'I don't know how much longer I can make them wait. If you piss them off, they might gamble that Barbie has enough star power alone, and that the fanbase might accept someone a bit more studio friendly.'

Kurt's right. He's running out of time. He taps his chest with his knuckles. 'Okay. Let me reread the contracts.'

Kurt sighs, or possibly slurps sauce from somewhere; it's not so clear over this long-distance connection. 'Good. Meanwhile, I'll try to stall them.'

'Thank you.'

'Just put that beautiful face of yours onto thinking about this.'

'I don't think you think with your face.'

'Eh, whatever. I'm not the writer.'

Something uncurls in Nash's chest, but before he can speak, it squishes back up, a hard little stone deep inside him.

'I will think about it. I promise.'

'All right. It's the 21st now. I'll call you in two days, okay? We need a decision for Christmas Eve if I can't stall them. Speak to you in a few days, bud.'

And with that, he hangs up. Probably off to surf on a big wave or some kind of activity that you have to get extra insurance for if you go on vacation. Nash can't really think of anything worse.

Though being stuck in a tiny apartment with a Kermitty stranger is definitely up there.

★ ★ ★

Nash lies in guilty silence for some time, until his stomach rumbles so loudly he realises he's starving. When did he last eat? He doesn't even know.

He finds Christopher in the kitchen frowning as he crouches in front of a shockingly small fridge with pen and paper in his hand. His round-frame glasses slide ever so slightly down his nose.

He's quite handsome when he concentrates. Not in the LA way where everyone is all daily gym sessions and green smoothies and golden and slightly unreal. But he is undeniably attractive. Those big baby blues, and softly pink lips. Nash can't help but notice the freckles peppering Christopher's forearms, where his sleeves are rolled up.

Yes, he might be inordinately tall, but he'd probably look good in a suit. As long as he didn't talk or move. It's easier to appreciate him when he's not flapping around.

Christopher's 90s-leading-man foppishness is probably a hit with women. And he'd probably kill with the Americans – that accent can take you a long way. Not that there's any sign of long-term girlfriends here. Nash is almost certain a man like Christopher didn't buy the vase in the hallway, but even so, if he had a girlfriend around, it wouldn't be empty – there'd be flowers or dried ornamental twigs or something in it.

He's been staring, Nash realises. Not that Christopher has noticed him. Nash tells himself it's just because he was waiting for Christopher's glasses to slide right off the end of his nose and crash to the floor. But he feels uncomfortable now that he's lurking, so he announces himself. 'Anything good in there?'

Christopher startles and looks from Nash to the paper in his hand. 'Well, unfortunately I spent the week eating everything so that the fridge would be empty for you.'

'Hospitable of you, even if we now don't have anything to eat.'

'Did you or Tessa book in a shop or anything?'

Nash shrugs. 'No, in the before-times I just figured I'd go to the grocery store when I got here.'

'We don't have a greengrocer's in the village,' Christopher says, standing up. His knees click as he stands. 'Oh, sorry, you mean a supermarket, don't you? Here, a green-grocer's just sells fruits and vegetables. I think there's one a few towns over.'

'Thank you for that thrilling translation,' Nash snarks. 'I'm excited to get a cultural exchange thrown in with the accommodation.'

To his surprise, this prompts a very tiny smile in the corner of Christopher's mouth. Apparently he *does* have a sense of humour. It must be buried deep inside him along with everything else the British repress.

'If it helps, I don't mind missing out on the leftovers and sad bags of salad you must have thrown out,' he adds.

A huge gale rattles the windows and the lights above them flicker just for a second. 'I think the storm is trying to tell you not to look a gift horse in the mouth,' says Christopher.

'I'm sorry, can you repeat that completely ridiculous sentence you just said to me?'

'Don't look a gift horse in the mouth? Is it that weird a saying?'

'English really is another language over here.'

'I suppose it has the same meaning as "beggars can't be choosers".'

'Oh yes, an equally complicated phrase. I can absolutely see why you chose an idiom like "gift horse" over that.'

He is almost certain that Christopher shuts his eyes for a few seconds as if he's counting for patience. 'We've got a few bits in here, and the tin cupboard is full, so we won't go hungry tonight at least,' Christopher announces a little too cheerily.

Nash feels a little thrill that he's annoyed him. 'Tinned stuff is British cuisine at its finest, isn't it? Sardines and cold baked beans by candlelight?'

'It's not that dire. We still have power after all.'

And with that, as if in answer from the gods, the lights all go out. The fridge makes an ominous groan.

'You *had* to say it, didn't you?' mutters Nash, turning on the torch on his phone.

'Christ.' Christopher tentatively walks to the window and looks out across the town. 'Everyone's power is out.'

With a deep sigh, Christopher sets down his list onto the counter and impressively digs out a fresh box of taper candles and matches from a drawer.

'That was alarmingly well prepared. This is very Boy Scouts of America,' Nash comments.

'We just call them Scouts here.'

'Fine, very *golden boy* of you,' Nash says, lighting the way through the cramped apartment to the living room with his phone torch. Christopher follows with a candle holder, which he sets down on the coffee table and wedges the tapered candles into. It takes a couple of matches to light all the candles as a rogue breeze from somewhere seems to be snuffing them out.

There's nothing else to do but sit back down on the couch together. This time, they are bathed in the low golden light of the candles, and the sounds of the snowstorm.

Still, it's eerily quiet – where are the cars and neighbours and planes and signs of goddamn life? *Maybe I'm dead*, Nash thinks. That could explain it. Though if he had died and gone to hell, they could have found a better torture than being cooped up with an awkward giraffe man.

'What now?' Nash says, wanting to fill the void with anything.

Christopher doesn't reply straight away. But eventually, quietly, he says, 'We just wait.'

He says it so simply, like this is just a normal occurrence.

'Great.'

'There's nothing to be done. Sometimes it goes out when the weather is bad. Hopefully it'll be fixed by the morning. Maybe later because of the weather.'

'Wow, I really am in the sticks.'

'Is . . . everything all right?' Christopher asks, tentatively. 'I promise I wasn't trying to listen to your phone call, but the flat is so small.' Tentativeness quickly turns to babbling. 'I suppose your family and friends must be worried about you being here in bad weather? Sorry, is that too much to ask? I shouldn't have listened.'

He splutters on, over-explaining himself for a little longer and Nash lets him because, frankly, it is funny. 'I don't know what privacy laws are like in the States—'

'Christopher.'

'Yes?'

'It's fine. I'm not going to sue you for overhearing me on the phone. Yet.'

Christopher stiffens.

'I'm joking.'

'Ah.'

'For a start, I don't want your *tiny flat*.' The last bit he says in a bad English accent, and the whole thing garners an extremely British sound from Christopher that can only be described as a *harrumph*. 'Just don't make a habit of listening to my conversations. I'm pretty sure that's against some kind of short-term let customer–proprietor rules.'

'I think, given the situation, those are probably out the window.'

'Only if we're agreeing to get rid of basic courtesy,' Nash says a little too sharply. He adds, more softly, 'Just a tricky call with my agent.'

'Oh,' Christopher says slowly.

And then he doesn't say anything else.

This immediately arouses Nash's suspicions. Whenever he mentions that he has an agent, the next question is usually about what he does for a living that requires an agent, because that's kind of weird and rare. Pretty much everyone knows in theory what an agent is, thanks to Estelle from *Friends*. And while he doesn't necessarily *want* to have the whole *yes I'm an actor yes you can watch my films on*

Netflix chat, it is always inevitable. From there it is either *wow that sounds so cool* or *do you make any money* or, his least favourite, *can I get a picture with you*, which, when you think about it, is deeply weird, because presumably that person didn't want a photo with him before he declared he was a potentially famous person, upon which he immediately becomes an object of consumption . . . or whatever.

He gets too stressed out if he thinks about the parasocial relationship aspect of fame.

But this conversation is different. Silence is unusual. And while there have been plenty of awkward pauses today, it is suspicious that the man, who initially seemed keen on prying, is now faking casualness. No follow-up question comes.

There is no doubt in Nash's mind that this man knows *exactly* who he is and yet, for some reason, is pretending to have never seen him before in his life.

This trip is deeply cursed.

Chapter Eight

Christopher

He *almost* walked right into it. For a moment, Christopher did think he should probably come clean about knowing who Nash is, especially now they are temporarily cohabiting.

But then Nash just kept being snippy and weird after the phone call, and the admittedly rather petty part of Christopher thought, no, Nash doesn't deserve the satisfaction of discovering he knows his extensive list of IMDb credits.

Plus, if he's honest with himself, it's probably too late to casually reveal it now. How would he even start that conversation? *Oh hi, so remember how I have pretended to not know who you are and now you're trapped in my house with me in the dark? Well actually I'm a huge fan.*

That would go down faster than an undercooked souffle.

But Christ, he doesn't like this pretence. Sure, he operates on a steady thrum of anxiety at the best of times, but this isn't exactly a situation he could prepare for. His heart beats so loud that he swears Nash must be able to hear it from across the couch.

No, stop worrying, he didn't notice. You're making it more weird.

Clearly, Nash was expecting Christopher to fawn over him or something, because when he doesn't respond, Nash eventually turns to look at him.

Just act normal. Just be a normal person who doesn't know anything about movies. That seems fine.

After a while, Nash offers, 'My agent, because I'm an actor.'

If you think about it, that's a very weird fragment of a sentence to say after a solid beat of complete silence.

'That must be . . . interesting work,' Christopher replies.

Nailed it.

'It can be.'

The awkward pauses return, like a chasm that Christopher would like to throw himself into. God, he's going to have to keep talking about it but be purposefully vague. If he stays calm and uninterested, it'll be fine.

'What sort of acting do you do?'

'I started out in TV originally when I was a teenager doing the odd supporting role, but now I'm predominantly in movies for streaming.'

'Oh. Nice.' His voice is perhaps a little too flat that time.

There's a tiny movement where he sees Nash's eyebrows do this kind of frustrated waggle. It's truly amazing they can both fit in the room along with this man's gigantic ego. It's quite funny really. He has to bite down on his lip to stop himself from laughing.

If he was feeling *really* petty, he'd ask Nash to suggest some things he might have seen him in, but there's no way he could control himself. Perhaps if he gets desperate he can try that one tomorrow. This is right out of the Esther Calloway playbook – *never let them know how much you know.* It should horrify him that he's potentially turning into his mother, but he'll worry about that later when he's finished torturing Nash Nadeau.

Plus, teasing him is a good distraction from the fact that they are sitting in the dark together.

Luckily, before he can think any more about that, the lights come back on.

'Phew,' says Nash beside him. 'I was worried we were going to have to sit there awkwardly watching the candle all night.'

Nash can be quite funny, he'll give him that.

Christopher gets up and goes to the kitchen to check all the appliances are back on properly. The fridge hums healthily, which is a relief – not that there's any food in there.

The smell of blown-out candle wafts through and Nash appears, leaning against the door frame.

'Shall we eat something? Just in case—'

'Don't even say it,' Nash says, raising his eyebrows.

Logically, he has known his kitchen is small, hence why half his stuff is in the spare room in boxes. But with Nash standing in the doorway, he realises how little space there is in his kitchen. Is this what the next twenty-four hours are going to be like? Dodging around each other, pretending he doesn't know who Nash Nadeau the actor is, and acting relatively normal? At least cooking will be a distraction.

'Does some kind of pasta sound all right to you?'

Nash gives him a nod, and when he turns to look in the cupboards for ingredients, he lets out a tense breath. Food. Focus on the food. That's what you're good at. He finds enough bits and bobs to whip up puttanesca, Nigella-style. Not the most Christmassy of meals, but the chilli flakes will warm their bones and it does okay as leftovers. He sets all the ingredients on the counter, including the pans, and gets to work finely chopping some admittedly sad-looking garlic.

Without a word, Nash squeezes past him and takes the big pan that permanently lives on the hob and fills it with water. Christopher tries not to, but he holds his breath as Nash passes, his whole body freezing from the almost-contact. He's just so *everywhere*. It's annoying.

When Nash goes back to the hob, he makes a conscious effort to breathe like a normal person. At least Nash salts the water liberally – just as he should – though this possibly contradicts all Christopher's presumptions about joyless Hollywood diets.

'Is this all right? Sorry, I should have asked if you had any dietary restrictions or anything.'

'No, this is great. Thanks,' Nash says, peering down at the cloudy water. 'And I'm not filming right now, so I don't have to think about it so much. An upside of not doing well-paid action movies is that no one expects me to look like a slab of sirloin.'

He's still pretty buff though, Christopher thinks. The muscles in his arms are visible through his long-sleeved shirt, and somehow look more pronounced in person than on camera. Probably because he's not wearing a ton of knitwear.

The room steams up as the water boils, and Christopher feels as if he can't get enough air, so he opens the window.

'Is there anything else I can do?' Nash asks.

'No, please. Go sit down. I'll call you in.'

It's a relief when he's gone because Christopher can just lose himself in the act of cooking. Soon, the air is heavy with the smell of anchovies cooked down in good olive oil, with sharp bursts from the little chilli flakes and garlic. He loses himself in the rhythm of it. The stir and the chop and the add and the taste.

This is why he started baking, really. Yes, the end result is great and he loves to feed people. But the act of it all settles something inside him. It's a calm kind of focus where only flavour matters. He once tried to explain this to Kit, but she accused him of sounding like the rat from *Ratatouille*.

The sauce thickens as he adds a good glug of salted starchy pasta water, and soon it's all plated up together. He picks a few leaves off the parsley plant on his windowsill to finish it, and even though it doesn't really need Parmesan, he grates some just to be polite. The deep pasta bowls shine with delish hearty dinner. Nothing can be bad when you have pasta.

* * *

Christopher finds Nash in the living room, curled up in the corner of the couch on the edge of sleep. His breathing is soft and slow, and Christopher almost feels bad waking him. He must be really tired and probably jet-lagged – isn't LA eight hours behind Wales? Something like that.

'Nash?' he calls quietly. But there's no response. Maybe he really is asleep? 'Hey, Nash. Wake up.'

'Mmhmm?' Nash replies sleepily. It's a funny thing seeing a man you're so used to seeing on TV all sparkly and perfectly chiselled look like a toddler who's had too much fun and is desperately fighting off bedtime.

'Dinner's ready.'

Nash yawns widely, the kind of full body yawn that leaves you blinking. He seems to suddenly remember where he is, and leaps up to standing.

'Hi,' Christopher says.

Christopher is pretty sure that Nash tries to subtly wipe a slick of drool from his chin.

At the table, they both dig in hungrily, twirling spaghetti and sauce into neat little curls.

Once his bowl is nearly wiped clean, Nash sighs contentedly.

'There's more in the pan.'

'Oh, thanks,' he says, getting up. 'More for you?'

'No, I'm fine.'

'Are you sure? This might be the last hot meal we have with this temperamental electricity.'

'I thought you said we shouldn't say it in case we jinx it?'

'I said *you* shouldn't say it because last time *you* jinxed it. I am, so far, apparently not angering the gods.'

'It was just a coincidence,' Christopher huffs, wiping a little spot of sauce from his bowl with his pinkie finger.

Nash returns with another full portion, and Christopher wonders if he even ate today, other than the biscuit with his espresso.

'I can't remember the last time someone cooked for me,' Nash finally says, breaking Christopher's train of thought.

'Not a dinner party kind of person?'

'It's not so much that,' he says, yawning before taking another bite. 'LA is just so big that you always find somewhere to meet in the middle, and then when I'm working I'm usually not in town anyway, so then it's all Kraft services and ordering in to the hotel room.'

He pauses, his cutlery frozen in motion as he thinks.

'What I'm saying is, thank you. It was kind of you to cook for me.'

That's another thing to give him credit for, along with salting the pasta water. At least the man always says thank you, even if it's just some kind of American reflex. Perhaps earlier he was just desperate and tired.

Either way, Christopher can't find the words to reply, because his eyes are locked on the tiny smudge of sauce in the corner of Nash's lips. If this was one of his dreams about one of Nash's characters, he could reach forward and wipe it away gently.

But this is real life, and he needs to get a hold of himself.

'Oh, erm, you've—' he mumbles, tapping the same place on his lips.

'I'm always a messy eater,' Nash says. With one finger, he delicately wipes the smudge away in a move that makes Christopher's stomach ache.

Nash takes the empty plates to the sink and yawns widely. 'I'm really sorry but I need to sleep, like, now. I guess it's probably too early, but that pasta has knocked me out.'

'Go, go. I'll wash up—' Christopher says.

He was expecting Nash to protest and offer to help, and then they could have a back-and-forth but . . . he just leaves. Like he said he would, and like Christopher told him to. So why does he feel so unsettled? Irritated, even. Is it the lack of the overly polite back-and-forth that forms the social contract? He doesn't really care about that stuff usually, so why now? Maybe he's just looking for petty things to be annoyed by for the distraction.

Instead, he thinks back to the Christmas he was going to have. No, *will* have. This weather can't hold out much longer. The trains will be running, or at least some miserable rail replacement bus, but he'll take it. Then Nash can just stay here alone.

It'll all be fine in the morning, he tells himself firmly. It *has* to be. He doesn't want to think about what happens tomorrow if both he and Nash are stuck here.

As usual, Christopher puts his feelings into scrubbing furiously at a pan, and soon the cookware and crockery are clean, dry and put away. The counter gleams.

All that remains is for him to get some sleep.

* * *

But before he can turn his mind to it, his phone begins to buzz. It's his mother. Typical really that one of the rare times he actually gets signal up here, it's a call from Esther. He wants to let it ring out and call her back in the morning, but there's a snowstorm across the country – what if something's happened to her?

'Hello, Mother,' he says, keeping his voice low. 'Are you and Dad doing all right?'

The first thing she says in her clipped tones is, 'Why are you whispering, Christopher?'

'I'm not whispering.'

'Well, you're speaking very quietly. I'm not losing my hearing yet, but it feels like you're testing me.'

'Sorry, Mother, is that better?'

'Your father and I are fine, to answer your first question.'

'Are you still at home?'

'Yes we are. Our initial plan was to drive north tomorrow to meet you at Katharine's, but of course that's on hold now.'

'Have you decided not to risk it?' He doesn't want to outright ask them if it's safe for them to drive in tricky weather – Esther's right, they aren't old, but they are older every year.

'Darling, have you not looked outside all day? I can't imagine it's much better for you, but I'd have to dig the cars out. The motorways are practically ski slopes.'

'It can't go on for that long though, can it?'

Esther fills him in about various news reports and statements from politicians, and he tries to make sure he's doing a good job of sounding as if he's listening, rather than slowly sinking into a pit of despair. That's that, then. Unless there's a Christmas miracle involving a sudden heatwave, which given the state of the climate he's not sure he particularly wants, he's stuck here.

Nash appears in the doorway again, dressed in a scoop-neck white T-shirt and sweatpants. 'Sorry, can I just grab a glass of water?' he whispers, before slipping around Christopher to take a glass from the cupboard. 'Night,' he mouths as he leaves.

It's only when Esther is practically yelling his name in his ear that he realises he completely zoned out from their conversation.

'Sorry, Mother, what was that?'

'I asked you why there's a man in your house?'

Shit. How did she hear that? He barely heard him.

'Oh . . . well. He's just staying. You know, because of the storm.'

There's a pause, which with Esther could go either way. 'A last-minute visit from a *friend* of yours? Does that mean we will get to meet him?'

Uh-oh. The emphasis on *friend* is very clear. That glimmer of excitement.

The one downside to having parents who are very accepting of the idea – and reality – that both of their children are queer, whether or not it's been verbally confirmed to them or not, is that they always want to talk about it. Kit's been out for years, but the act of moving in with Haf seems to have turned Esther and Otto into parents competing for World's Greatest Allies. He fully expects Esther is trying to organise a Pride in Oxlea on the download.

He knows he shouldn't feel this way, but for right now it would be nice if his parents were a bit more repressed about this, *specifically* to save him from this conversation. They are about practically everything else.

'No, Mother. Remember I said someone was going to stay in the flat while I was away at Kit's? Well, he arrived this afternoon.'

'And you're just letting him stay?'

'Mother, I can hardly throw the man out into the cold.'

'He's a stranger, Christopher. I know he was renting the place but it's different when you are still there. And I imagine you haven't sorted out your spare room yet, so what, you're sleeping on the couch?'

It pains him that she knows him so well.

'It's just for one night.'

'We must be looking at very different weather forecasts.'

'We are in different countries, Mother.'

'I'm well aware of that. Otto, come here will you?'

In the background, he hears the familiar folding up of a newspaper that always signalled his father was about to do something. 'My boy!' he bellows down the phone. 'I hope you're all right in this snowstorm!'

'I'm fine, Dad—'

'He is not fine,' snaps Esther. 'Otto, he has a strange man staying with him.'

'What's so strange about him, dear?' Otto teases.

Christopher bites down on his lip to stop himself from laughing.

'Don't twist my words. You know I meant a stranger.'

'Has he never spoken to the man?'

'We've spoken and even shared a meal together.'

'Well now, he doesn't sound like a stranger to me if they've broken bread.'

'It was spaghetti, but close enough.'

'Give me that newspaper. I want to whack you with it. You're supposed to be on my side,' Esther hisses.

'I am always on your side,' Otto says softly. 'But if Christopher is happy to offer hospitality to this gentleman in his time of need, then we should just be pleased that our son is so thoughtful. No?'

There are a few beats where she mulls this over. 'It wouldn't be very Christian of you to throw him out,' she relents.

'True, though I'm not very Christian at the best of times. Nor are you really.'

'That's true,' agrees Otto. 'We haven't been to a service that wasn't a wedding or a funeral in years.'

'It's an *expression*,' she says, exasperated. Eventually, she concedes. 'It's very kind of you to let him stay for tonight.' There's a very slight emphasis on *for tonight*, as though she's reminding him that it would be unconscionable to let Nash stay any longer.

'I'm glad you're both safe,' he says. 'But I really need to get to sleep. It's been a long day.'

'Right-oh,' cries Otto. 'Sleep well.'

'Goodnight, darling,' says Esther softly before hanging up. What a day. What a totally weird day.

Christopher makes the executive decision to ignore all the notifications on WhatsApp until tomorrow. No more talking to anyone tonight.

His bedroom door is firmly closed, and boy does he miss his bed already. The couch is small and old and in certain places there are springs that are a little *too* springy and dig right in. The chill in the air tells him it's going to be a cold night, so he gathers every single blanket including the ones that are just to cover up how worn some of the inherited chairs look, and layers them up over him like a lasagne. Although it's been a long day, it's still too early to sleep. Maybe he can find something familiar to bake, he thinks to himself, as he's probably stuck here for at least another day. So he gathers a couple of Christmas cookery books from the spare room and takes them to read in his nest. *The Little Library Christmas* and a frankly enormous Nigella one balance in his lap, and slowly he flicks through the recipes.

He doesn't have any of the key ingredients for Christmas – not a single chestnut or sprout in sight. Naturally, he has an obscene amount of nutmeg and cinnamon downstairs but that's not going to go very far without the rest. Before he owned the bakery, he'd be able to come up with alternatives, or even just dream up things irrespective of what was on his hurriedly scribbled inventory list. In the end, his brain whirrs too much for him to lose himself in the recipes. He sets them down on the floor and lies back, willing sleep to find him.

But here lies the problem.

The only way he's managed to fall asleep for the last few months is by putting on a film. Practically speaking, he can still watch something. He has a bunch downloaded on his tablet, so he doesn't have to turn on the TV, and he can use his headphones to listen so as not to wake Nash. Although, from the snoring currently rumbling from the bedroom, he's pretty sure that Nash is completely flat out.

But he doesn't watch just any film to fall asleep. He watches *Nash's* films. And he's not sure he could take the mortification of Nash walking in on Christopher watching one.

No, he'll just have to fall asleep the old-fashioned way.

Except, his mind keeps turning to the snoring from the other room. No one else has been up here in months.

You get used to being lonely, he's realised. It becomes a constant dullness. But now, amongst all this change and chaos, it feels magnified. Suddenly, Christopher can't help but think that not being alone at night would be quite nice.

Time, his old enemy, returns to pass by excruciatingly slowly. Christopher is in for a long, lonely night.

Chapter Nine

Christopher

Christopher wakes with a start as an enormous crash resounds through the bakery below him.

What on earth was that?

He leaps to his feet, or at least, he tries to and spectacularly fails. Clearly, the part of him automatically reacting was operating on the presumption that he was in his bed. He's so tangled in blankets that he sprawls over the coffee table and bangs his knees hard.

'Christ!' he yells, kicking his feet free.

It's still dark outside, and he has no idea if it's the middle of the night or morning. Who would be breaking in on 22nd December? Did he even lock the front door after Nash arrived?

His mind races as fast as his pounding feet, as he whirls down the stairs and into the bakery kitchen.

Nothing could have prepared him for the sight before him.

First of all, everything is white.

Like, *everything*.

For a brief, horrifying moment, he imagines the café windows have smashed, letting in all the snow. But the white doesn't seep through his socks. It's not cold. And neither is the air . . . well, no more than usual.

He scoops some up in his hand, and with a very different, rather confused kind of horror, he discovers it's flour.

Why is there flour *everywhere*?

'Christ,' he mutters.

A rustle sounds across the kitchen, as if in response.

'Who is there?' he barks, arming himself with a very big pair of tongs. He advances towards the noise, which seems to be coming from the other side of the huge work table that runs down the middle of the kitchen, makeshift weapon thrust forward. 'Show yourself.'

In reply, he hears a groan. 'A little help?' calls a familiar voice.

He rounds the corner of the table and finds Nash on the floor, flour-drenched.

'What in the bloody hell are you doing in here in the middle of the night?'

'It's morning.'

'All right, what are you doing in my bakery – which, if you remember the terms of your stay, is off-limits – in the morning?'

Nash groans again. 'Can you just help me up?'

'Not until you tell me what you're doing in here, and why you've covered the place in flour. And why can't you get up yourself?'

The man on the floor has the grace to at least look ashamed. 'I'm stuck.'

'You're stuck?'

'That's what I said. Also, there's flour in my eye and I can't see, and my arm is pinned under something. Just help me.' His tone softens pathetically. 'Please.'

Adrenalin dissipating and fury calming (just a little), Christopher finally takes a moment to step back and assess the bizarre scene in front of him. Nash lies under one of the massive wholesale sacks of flour that are so heavy Christopher has to wheel them in on a trolley. And, for some reason, there's what looks like the stick of his broom snapped over Nash in an arch, half of which appears to be wedged under one of the ovens. And over his legs is a second massive sack of flour, though it's lost all structural integrity and has burst open – probably the source of the avalanche all over the room.

What the hell was he doing?

It takes him a few goes but Christopher manages to drag the two sacks away, and as he does, the broom handle simply falls apart.

Freed from the prison of his own creation, Nash wipes the flour out of his eyes and sits up. With an offered hand, Christopher yanks Nash to his feet. Flour plumes into the air around them.

'Now talk,' Christopher says, dusting flour from his pyjama top.

Except . . .

A memory sparks of sometime around 3am when he'd got too hot under his lasagne of blankets, and so had thrown off his pyjamas rather than disturb the integrity of the layers. Pyjamas that he hadn't put back on when he ran downstairs, too desperate to find out what the hell was going on.

And so, instead, he simply wipes flour off his right nipple.

At least he still has his underwear on. If only they weren't the novelty Love Hearts-sweets-patterned ones that Haf bought him for fake Valentine's last year.

Oh God, and he's wearing socks too. Novelty pants and socks.

And he just wiped his nipple.

This is absolutely mortifying.

'I was . . .' Nash trails off and looks up at the ceiling, evidently also realising that Christopher is mostly naked. Except, because Christopher is taller than him, it looks as if Nash is staring intently at his hairline, which he's not sure is much better. Nash's gaze hops about, settling on a chart about handwashing hygiene above the sink. 'I woke up really early and you were asleep, and I really needed to get some exercise done as I was going mad, and I didn't want to disturb you so I came down here and figured I'd just construct a barbell out of some sacks of flour and this broom, except the broom didn't hold—'

It all rushes out in one enormous hurried and embarrassed sentence.

At least they are as embarrassed as each other.

'Hang on. Let's walk that back a moment. You tried to weight-lift flour?'

'Yes.'

'Why?'

'It seemed like a good idea at the time and was the only thing that wasn't sharp,' he says, eyeing the tongs in Christopher's hand. 'Hang on. Why didn't you grab a knife? What if I had been an intruder? You're going to *select* me to death?'

'Why are you obsessed with the knives in here?'

'I'm just thinking practically!'

'Clearly.' Christopher rolls his eyes in annoyance and surveys the mess all around them. 'Christ, man, you could have impaled yourself. And, if you had, that would have probably affected my insurance. You're not even supposed to be down here. It was all in the welcome documents I sent Tessa.'

'Oh. Yes, which I *definitely* read,' Nash says flatly.

'Why would you go somewhere without reading the pertinent information first?'

'I don't know, Christopher. Maybe because I'm a normal person who just wants to go somewhere and relax.'

'Knowing what I'm doing and the rules of the place *is* relaxing.'

'Maybe if you're Type A.'

'I am not *Type A*. Not least because that's some kind of stereotyping nonsense.' Christopher folds his arms. There's nothing wrong with being organised. Yes, perhaps it would be good if he could be more of an impulsive person, but he used up all his impulsivity last year faking a relationship, quitting his career and buying a business on a whim. Excuse him if he's a bit tetchy about sticking to the details.

With one glance at the floured kitchen, he remembers what he's actually supposed to be annoyed about. 'Hang on, how did you spin this around to me?'

Nash laughs, his mouth a wolfish grin. 'It's just too easy.'

With a furious huff, Christopher hands him the other, non-broken, broom, and says, 'Clean it up. All of it has to go in the bin.'

'Even the stuff still in the bag?'

'Yes, Nash, even that. It's all contaminated. I can't sell it.'

'Well, now I feel bad,' mutters Nash as he starts to brush flour into small piles.

'Good.'

Working together, it doesn't take too long to get most of the floor-flour into a neat pile. The only problem is, it's still everywhere else. They dust it off the shelves and work surfaces onto the floor as there's no saving any of it. With a sigh, he realises he's going to have to Ajax all the stainless steel later as it all looks dusty and ancient, rather than clean and well maintained like it had done yesterday. He hates doing that stuff. But a job in the bakery kitchen gets him out of the tiny flat, so you win some, you lose some.

Kneeling on the now slightly cleaner floor, he brushes the mound of floor-and-flour-stuff into the dustpan with the little brush.

'Wait, let me do that,' says Nash, squatting down and reaching over to grab the dustpan.

'No, I can do it.'

'Yeah, but I made the mess. Let me fix it.'

'It's *fine*.'

'I think, when said with that tone, things are specifically not fine,' Nash says, tugging at the dustpan insistently.

'You're making it worse,' growls Christopher, pulling back.

'No, I'm not!'

And that's when, in this final struggle, the dustpan flies up into the air, covering them both with floor-flour. It's such a shock that, for a long moment, Christopher says nothing. He sits still as a statue, eyes shut and lips sealed so the flour doesn't get in. He then wipes at his eyes with the back of his hand, which he can only hope is slightly less disgusting than the flour rapidly turning to a sticky paste from the sweat on his face.

Eyes clear, he fixes Nash with a glare.

'Oh crap,' groans Nash, picking clumps of flour out of his once-blond now-grey hair.

'If you brush it off you and down into the dustpan—' Christopher says, just as Nash enthusiastically shakes himself like a wet dog.

The flour that they had brushed off the entire kitchen is now back everywhere, just in different places.

Nash surveys the damage. 'That didn't work as well as I thought it would.'

'This must be a nightmare,' Christopher says, still carefully brushing the flour off himself. 'That's the only explanation for this. I'm being tortured. My brain has concocted the worst scenario it could possibly think of and now it's playing out. Thank you very much, sleep paralysis demon.'

'Round two?' Nash says, and without another word, they clean up the kitchen. Again. This time, Nash doesn't argue. They're so caked in flour so there's only so much cleaning they can do without shedding little squalls of white.

Once it's as good as it's going to get, Christopher decides it's time to temporarily give up. 'I am going for a shower. Go upstairs and wait for your turn. When we're clean, we'll work out what we're going to do with you.'

As they ascend the stairs, Nash murmurs, 'At your command. You know, when you're bossing me about, it almost sounds exciting.'

A furious flush creeps all over Christopher's body, and before he can give a second's thought about his body turning the colour of a very ripe strawberry, he storms into the bathroom and slams the door.

It takes a moment for the shower to heat up, so he lets it run, and almost jumps out of his skin when he catches his eerily pale reflection in the bathroom mirror. He looks like a ghost thanks to Nash's little home gym situation.

Obviously, today was going to be complicated, but he hadn't expected it to involve a veritable bomb of flour. And he doesn't even want to think about how much that cost, on top of the refund for Nash's stay. That minus number in his bank account is growing by the second. Maybe he can get a refund for his train tickets as he couldn't go yesterday? Perhaps Nash will offer to cover the flour? He hates talking about money, but he might have to.

The shower doesn't help, really. Being a baker, he probably should have remembered that flour and water makes a sticky proto-dough paste, and so he's halfway to making a decent flatbread by the time he realises. Naturally, it doesn't go down the drain. It gathers in sad-looking clumps around his feet. The shower needs a clean now, but that can wait until Nash has de-floured too. Two shampoos gets much of it out, and once he's wrapped in clean towels and moisturised, Christopher feels a little bit more himself.

His clothes wait outside in the suitcase, and while he doesn't really want to go wandering around in just his towel, given Nash just saw him in pants and socks, it can't get much worse.

When he leaves the bathroom, he sees that Nash is still standing at the top of the stairs, arms held out from his side as if he's malfunctioned.

'What are you doing?' Christopher asks.

'I'm not moving, as you instructed.'

Is Nash taking the piss or behaving? It's unclear, so he splits the difference and ignores this comment. 'Your turn. There are towels in there.'

'Thanks.' With a stiff and very careful walk, presumably so as not to dislodge any more flour, Nash waddles into the bathroom. At the top of the stairs where he was standing is a small mound of flour.

It's freezing cold in the living room, so Christopher turns up the heating and hopes this doesn't mean the weather is worse today. He hasn't even been able to check, with the rude awakening and all the chaos. There's no gale battering the windows though.

Worried Nash is going to appear again, he dresses hurriedly under his towel into a pair of nice blue jeans and a warm oatmeal Henley top under a thickly knitted jumper with a high collar. His hairdryer is in the bedroom, but as he doesn't want to risk another semi-naked Nash interaction, he does his best with the towel.

He is damp and cold and annoyed, and he hates to be any of those individually, never mind all three at once.

To add salt into the wound, the doorbell rings.

Christ. Who on earth could that be?

He slings his damp towel on the hallway radiator – optimistic, as it very rarely manages to churn out any heat, no matter how often he bleeds it – and stomps down the stairs. When he flings open the door, he does so with a little too much gusto, causing it to bang against the internal wall.

'All right, drama,' croaks Shaz.

'Shaz!' he cries with relief, pulling her into a hug. She's wrapped up in her enormous puffer and so much knitwear that only the pink tip of her nose peeps out. He's pretty sure she's wearing two scarves today.

'I knew you couldn't last without me,' she laughs.

'Come in. There's no reindeer as I didn't get a chance to bake yet, but I can do a coffee.'

'Oh, you treasure, if you insist.' She knocks her knee-high snow boots against the door frame as she comes in, dislodging snow onto the mat. It reminds Christopher of this morning.

'Come through the kitchen.'

'Ooh, the behind-the-scenes tour. I feel special. You've never let me in here before.'

'Christmas treat. But don't get too excited. And, err, don't touch anything.' He flicks the lights back on, and Shaz gasps. Even though they swept up and dusted off a lot of the flour, there's still a fine layer of it everywhere.

'Bloody hell, what happened in here? Looks like Miss Havisham's place.'

'Well, that's part of the whole . . . situation. Come on.'

As they walk through, he realises how cold and quiet it is in here. It's weird, not having the machines on at this time of day, nothing baking or proving or cooling. It's like a dusty old mausoleum.

In the café side, Shaz de-robes, creating a little Shaz-shaped pile of outdoor wear on one of the counter stools. Free of her many layers, she joins him behind the counter, which she knows she's not allowed to do. But he lets her off; it's not as if there are customers here. She's leaning against the cupboard with the Biscoff biscuits. He gestures for her to open it up and when she finds them, she makes a low noise of glee.

'How is Gar doing?' Christopher asks as he fires up the coffee machine.

In answer, she shakes her head and shrugs at once. 'Still mostly sleeping, which I think is the best thing for healing really. Made me come out to see you while the kids were watching *The Muppet Christmas Carol*. The power those Muppets have over my kids is truly impressive. I might have to get a Gonzo to speak through.'

'Is your mother-in-law helping?'

'Yeah, she's not that bad is our Kathy. I just need a bitch and a moan. It's just tricky. I want her to like me, you know?'

'It must be hard.'

'What's up with Tessa then? And why did she nuke your kitchen?' Shaz asks, barrelling past any opportunity to talk about her feelings. 'Is she a wee freak?'

'You're not going to believe me if I tell you.'

'Oh, go on, let me guess. Did she bring a weird pet, like a massive snake? You know, like Britney in that music video.'

'I'm pretty sure snakes need temperatures a little warmer than this.'

'Not if they have a massive tank and a big light too, but I see your point. The snake's out. No pets at all?'

'Not that I've seen yet.'

'There's still time.'

'Why does that feel like a threat?'

'Okay, give me a moment, I'm still guessing. But what are you going to do now you're staying here?'

'I'm still working that out.'

'You know what you could do while you're working it out . . .' She eyes the kitchen.

'I *suppose* I could make a small batch of gingerbread reindeer, seeing as you're here. Once I've cleaned enough that I won't give you some kind of communicable disease.'

'It's giving you something to do. I'm just that generous. And I'll even pay for some of them.'

'Don't get ahead of yourself.'

'It's the Christmas spirit running through me. Go on then, I'm out of guesses. Just tell me what's up with her.'

This is, of course, the very moment that Nash saunters in. And typically, he looks *particularly* good in a plaid shirt over a white T-shirt and black jeans. A kind of famous-person shine emanates off him, Christopher swears. Turns out, Nash cleans up really well when he hasn't been travelling halfway across the world.

The *bastard*.

For the first time since he's known her, and quite possibly the first time in her entire life, Shaz is silent.

'Hey there,' Nash greets her with a nod.

She wears a confused grimace that Christopher's pretty sure is supposed to be a smile.

'I heard you talking down here. Just wanted to make sure you weren't talking to yourself,' he says to Christopher.

Behind him, Shaz's eyes are wide with *what the actual fuck*. Her mouth falls open, but nothing comes out except a small croak, like she's a fish on land.

'I left the hairdryer out in case you need it.'

'Thanks,' Christopher says, trying to simultaneously ignore how chilly his damp ears are and signal to Shaz with his eyes that she's being incredibly weird.

He's trying to make up for it. Be calm. Don't let him get to you. He'll be gone soon. Probably.

'I was just thinking I'd go for a walk round the block,' Nash says, his eyes darting from Christopher to Shaz, and back.

'Sure, just don't go too far,' Christopher says.

The ice in his chest thaws a little. They both need to cool down. He can't begrudge Nash being courteous; that's all he wants, after all. Either way, they're both on their best behaviour in front of their unnervingly silent witness.

'I won't get lost. Sea's that way; the mountain's up there, right?' he asks with a smile, pointing for good measure.

'That's right. Do you have my number in case you do?'

Nash nods. 'Got it off the booking details. And if there's no signal, I'll send up a flare. Worst case, I swim home to LA.'

'A little extreme. And cold.'

'The novelty will do me good, won't it?' Nash says this to Shaz, as if to include her in the joke, but she doesn't say anything. 'Well . . . bye then!'

Nash disappears back through the bakery kitchen and when the back door slams, Shaz comes to life. 'I'm sorry, am I hallucinating or was that *Nash fucking Nadeau*?'

'It really was,' Christopher says, still hardly believing it himself. Shaz bearing witness has made this all much more real than it already was.

'What the fuck?!'

'I know,' he sighs, the weight of it all hitting him now.

'What in the—'

'I *know*.'

'Wait . . . who the hell is Tessa?'

'His assistant.'

'Ohhh. I wondered if it was his hotel code name or something. Wow. So *he* was going to housesit for you?'

'Apparently.'

She frowns, her eyebrows meeting in the middle. 'Hang on. Is the man too tight to pay for a proper hotel?'

At this, both Shaz and Christopher burst into body-shaking, keeled-over, eyes-streaming laughter.

'Just gets by . . . couch-surfing,' gasps Christopher.

'Knocks on random doors asking for a bed for the night.'

He can barely catch his breath, and when the giggles settle, they start all over again.

It all spills out of him, all the feelings he's been holding in, in racking laughs.

'They keep putting the subscription price up every other month, so he can't be that short,' Shaz says, wiping at her eyes. 'Maybe I'll give it direct to him in coins in a little envelope.'

This sets them both off again.

Once they finally get a hold of themselves, Shaz clearly remembers something. 'WAIT,' she yells, grabbing the collar of his top to pull him closer and lowering her voice to a whisper. 'That's only a one-bed flat up there. Christopher Calloway, you have to tell me. Be honest with me. Are you sharing the bed with him?'

Christopher can feel himself go beetroot. 'I slept on the couch.'

'Ah, what a shame.' She lets him go, clearly a bit disappointed. 'So that's why you've got the countenance of a cold cowpat this morning.'

'I do not,' he insists. Behind him the coffee machine rumbles. 'Do you want this coffee or not?'

'Yes, obviously.'

'Then stop trying to distract me.'

'I bet he's distracting you far more than me just asking you about it. God, he's so fit in real life. I thought maybe it was just that thick make-up they slather on for the HD cameras, but he is really good-looking isn't he?'

'I wouldn't know.'

'You absolute liar.' She cackles and Christopher places all his attention on making this coffee for her. 'Maybe you *should* share the bed with him. It's so cold out, and just think of the savings on your bills. You know, get a little cosy?'

'I think that would be highly inappropriate.'

'Let a girl dream, will you? I think it would be *highly hot*.'

'Speaking of,' he says, setting down an espresso in front of her.

'So, what are you going to do with him?'

'Well, it doesn't look like the snow has cleared so I was going to see if there was anywhere nearby that could put him up.'

'Chance would be a fine thing. I've already called them all.'

Christopher raises his eyebrows. 'I didn't realise you had attained psychic administrative powers during the last thirty seconds of this conversation.'

Shaz rolls her eyes at him. 'Ha ha, but no, I may have got desperate yesterday after Gar's accident and rang round everywhere just in case someone could take Kathy. I even got desperate and rang a few places almost as far as Chester – though God knows how we'd even get there in this weather – and they near laughed at me before hanging up.'

'Is she really that bad?'

She sighs loudly. 'I'm just being dramatic. I just got annoyed when she had recleaned the house because I hadn't done a good enough job the first time. It's not as exciting as your situation, I'll tell you that.'

Christopher pulls a sad face. 'You mean she's not a looker?'

Shaz snorts and gives him a playful whack on the arm. 'I wish. I didn't bleach half my skin off cleaning for her to think it wasn't a good enough job.'

She isn't being hyperbolic. Her poor hands are cracked and red. The cold must be making it so sore. He slips into the kitchen and collects a hand lotion from beside the sink, which Laurel sent him as an advance Christmas present, all while trying not to notice what a complete bombsite his beloved kitchen is.

'Here, use this,' he says, handing it over to her. 'It's soothing.'

'You're a sweetheart.' She takes the tube and dabs a glob on the back of her hand, then sniffs. 'Ooh. It smells posh. A Laurel gift or an Esther gift?'

'Laurel.'

'Truly, what would you do without your ex?'

'Probably be still working in finance.'

He knows his relationship with Laurel is strange to some people, but they were childhood friends, then dated for ten years through the tricky teenage years and their mid-twenties. After they broke up, things were a little strained, but ironically the chaotic situation of last Christmas brought them closer together again, but just as friends. She's a fashion designer now, sharing a size-inclusive brand with Ambrose, having built her audience up from being an influencer. She really helped him make the leap from boring finance drudgery to cookery school.

And she is very good at choosing thoughtful gifts – pretty much everything nice in Christopher's house is from her.

'Well, I am much better off for her interferences, either way.' She rubs the cream over her sore skin and sighs with relief.

'Good?'

'Good. With Kathy, it is what it is, isn't it? Mother and daughter-in-law dynamics are not known for being uncomplicated. We just have to learn to live with each other, and instead of pissing myself when she oversteps, I need to tell her to piss off or just let it go.'

'A lot of piss,' he says sagely, before realising what he's just said. 'Christ.'

'Tis his season, yes. Anyway, yes, hate to be the bearer of bad news, but it's horrendous out there. You're still not going anywhere, in case you were hoping.'

'I was hoping.' There it is, then. He confirms it with a glance at his phone – all the trains are cancelled still, the weather forecast says not to travel, and there are hundreds of notifications on his WhatsApp.

'It looks like you'll be stuck with the gorgeous film star for a little longer. What a disaster for you,' she drawls.

'A really annoying gorgeous film star.'

'What did he do to annoy you?'

He nods his head back to the kitchen. 'He's Miss Havisham.'

'Oh yeah, I could see that would grind your gears. You agree he's gorgeous though?'

Christopher groans and walks back into the bakery kitchen to start cleaning up so he can make some gingerbread. He gives her a death glare, spray cleaner in hand. 'Do you want me to make these reindeer or not?'

'Pretty please.'

He gives in, because of course he does. It's Shaz. He'd do anything for her.

* * *

In the end, it doesn't take too long to get the central table clean and sanitised. It's nice, the companionable silence. Shaz must need it too, as she sips at her coffee quietly.

When he finally starts laying out the ingredients for the gingerbread, she asks, 'So, did you downplay how much of a fan of his you are?'

'Oh. Um.'

'Um?' She raises her eyebrows.

'Well, you can't just tell someone that kind of thing. That's weird. I think they call it being *parasocial* or something, right?' He's still not one hundred per cent sure that's quite right given he's trying to pretend he doesn't know who Nash is, but Laurel and Ambrose complain a lot about the way people mistake them as being people they know personally, even though they only see them on their phones. It makes both of them feel uncomfortable, and he just doesn't want to make anyone feel that way, even Nash.

'So . . . ?'

'So, I just . . . pretended not to know who he was. Just played ignorant when he mentioned his job. Plus, he keeps being so annoying that I don't want to give him the satisfaction. I'm sure his ego doesn't need another boost.'

Shaz bursts out laughing, a raucous, echoing sound in the empty building. 'Oh *brilliant*. Oh my God, Christopher. This is going to end in disaster, I can see it already.'

'It'll be fine.'

'It will be *something*, all right! And now it's been too long to admit that you're a fan and you two are stuck up there together. What are you going to do? Just never turn on the TV so he can't see your Netflix watch history?'

'Something like that.'

Shaz literally slaps her thigh, which Christopher didn't think people did outside movies. 'Oh, this is good. This is really good.'

'Please revel slightly less in my pain.'

'I will not.'

'And you can't let on that you know who he is either.'

'Why's that now?'

'Well . . . I don't know! It'll just be easier that way, won't it?'

'So, what, he just thinks I'm some weird rude staring person?'

Christopher shrugs. 'I'm sure you can flesh out the back story there.'

She thinks this over as he mixes up the gingerbread dough. 'All right, I'll go along with your little scheme, even if only for my own amusement.'

A simple melodica tune plays out, and Shaz pulls her phone out of her pocket. 'I'm being summoned. I'll be back later for the reindeer and a minor revel.'

It takes her quite a while to shuck back on her coat and many scarves.

Nash appears at the front door to the café, tapping on the glass to be let in, just as she turns to leave.

'Hello again,' Nash says, as Shaz opens the door. But she just slips past him with only a cackle as she disappears off into the snow.

Nash shuts the door behind him after a pause. 'Goodbye then? Is everyone so talkative here?' He hovers in the kitchen doorway. 'Um. Am I allowed in?'

'Depends; are you going to attempt to make another home gym?'

'No.'

'Then yes. Provided you don't touch anything.'

For some reason, Nash looks rather dishevelled and a little dirty.

'Where on earth have you been? You look like you crawled out of a coal scuttle.'

'I'm sorry, a what now? A *coal scuttle*?'

'Yes, where you keep coal.'

'All right, Mr Victorian England. What are you making?' Strange that he moves the conversation swiftly along, Christopher thinks. Perhaps he fell in the snow and doesn't want to admit it. That would be rather funny, at least.

'Gingerbread reindeer. Shaz's favourite.'

'And that was Shaz, I presume?'

'The one and only. She'll be back later.'

'I look forward to another thrilling in-depth conversation.'

'Speaking of, she did mention that we might have a small issue.'

'Shoot.'

'There's no room at the inns. Metaphorically or literally.'

'Ah. Shall I just check Airbnb, in case there've been cancellations?'

'Go ahead, but I think you'll find the same,' Christopher says, rolling out the gingerbread dough on the counter.

'That smells pretty good by the way,' Nash says without looking up from his phone.

'It's even better when it's baked.'

They don't speak any more, even as Christopher cuts out the dough into reindeer shapes and lays them on a tray. For the first time, Christopher doesn't feel completely unsettled in Nash's silent presence. It must be the baking. The room is soon flooded with the sweet scent of gingerbread cooking as Christopher washes up the pans and sets everything away. It's a reset, or perhaps a bubble of normality.

Eventually, Nash looks up and puts his phone inside his shirt pocket. 'You're right. There's nothing.'

'And I can't get to Yorkshire to see my family either.'

The understanding that they are stuck together hangs in the air. But before they can discuss it, Shaz comes back through the bakery front door.

'They've not even finished baking,' Christopher calls, before realising she's on the phone.

'All right, love, I'll see if we can get anyone up to you,' Shaz says, one finger in her ear. 'I'll call you back in ten, okay?'

She pockets her phone.

'Everything okay?' Christopher asks.

'We've got our first snow-based emergency.'

Chapter Ten

Christopher

Christopher is not convinced that anything happening now could constitute the *first* snow-based emergency, given all that has happened to him in the last twenty-four hours, but he ushers Shaz over all the same.

'By any chance do you know Myffy Evans? Nice lady, little older than me. Face like an angel. Rollickingly dirty jokes. Uses a wheelchair when she's down in town.'

'No, I've never met her I don't think.'

'Well, she lives up at the top of the village, and her carer just called in sick for the day. Normally that wouldn't be a massive issue as her husband Mohan can work from home and help her out, but *he's* stuck in London. Myffy needs someone to pick up her prescription quite urgently, plus probably a little help at home. I can sort the prescription now as it's just down the road, but . . .'

There's no way Shaz has time to trudge up the village with Gar and the kids.

'I can take it to her. What's her address?'

'Are you sure? It's a long walk uphill. I wouldn't ask if it wasn't—'

'I want to help. And I have hiking boots.'

'And longer legs than me. Sorry, I'd offer you the car—'

'You need that just in case for Gar. It's fine, Shaz.'

Somewhat foolishly, he had left his little car with his parents when he moved to Wales, as he'd had to drive a rental van laden with all of his stuff during the move itself and he'd figured that he wouldn't be massively in need of a car when he got here. That was very silly as it quickly turned out he couldn't really get anywhere without relying on the under-funded, barely there public transport system.

'If you weren't being so helpful I'd tell you off for inter-rupting me. All right, I'm sending her your number, and her address to you.'

The maps app on his phone tells him it's a twenty-five-minute walk. Given how long it took him to get to the train station and back yesterday, he's mentally doubling that. At least. He should probably take a thermos.

'We don't need to walk,' says Nash.

The 'we' of that sentence throws him, but also, obviously they need to walk. Christopher gestures outside. 'Erm, yes we do?'

'Well, that's the thing,' says Nash, mirroring Christopher's movement, but in a way that doesn't feel mocking. 'This morning, I dug out your truck before I did all the, err, ill-advised home gym.'

This gets two raised eyebrows from Shaz, who still hasn't heard the full story. 'No, don't tell me,' she says, stopping him with a hand. 'What I'm imagining is way better.'

'Thank you for clearing the snow, but that van hasn't worked for years.' The former owners had called it 'non-operational', which he assumed was code for 'ready for the scrapheap'. He'd never even attempted to look at it, and was just waiting to find someone to come and scrap it for him.

'Oh. It does now.'

'What?'

'That's what I was doing outside. It just needed a tune-up, some oil and some air in the tyres. And all that stuff was in the little shed by the side of the house – the lock on that is bust, by the way. So yeah, long story short, I fixed it.'

'And broke into the shed by the sounds of things,' Shaz adds.

Christopher can't quite compute what Nash is saying. 'You *fixed* the van?'

'Yeah. It was really easy. Didn't need much to get it going. I think it could do with a few new parts but you're not going to get them today. It'll last if I keep an eye on it. Will get us to Myffy's house, at least. It should be able to drive through the snow easier than anyone's car.'

'Bloody hell. Thank you.'

'It's no big deal. I just needed something to take my mind off . . . things.'

Shaz gives Nash an approving look, but Christopher is still barely processing.

He fixed the van?

'I've got my licence upstairs, and I think I insured it when I got it just in case,' Christopher says, mostly to himself. 'I haven't driven around here in the snow before. There're a lot more hills than in Oxlea.'

'Just go slow and hope for the best,' Shaz offers.

'Wow, thanks.'

'Sorry, mildly supportive aphorisms are all I can offer. I'll go get her meds. You two can get loaded up. See you in a tick.'

* * *

Twenty minutes later, outside the bakery, Christopher exchanges a paper bag of fresh-out-of-the-oven gingerbread reindeer with a prescription from the pharmacy down the road with Shaz.

'This feels like an illicit deal,' she says, waggling her eyebrows.

'They might be a bit wonky. I didn't have enough time to cool them properly, so who knows what shapes they've set in. And they're not decorated.'

'Err, stop apologising, will you? Wonky or no, it's a win for me. Drive safely. Call me if you need anything?'

'Will do,' he says, locking up the bakery behind him. It's incredibly cold outside, but thankfully it has stopped actively snowing. The sky is murky grey, clouds still heavy with snow.

He rounds the corner and finds Nash doing last check-ups on the van, which is gently humming. Even if it doesn't sound as if it's going to be capable of driving him to York-shire, finally having his own means of transport feels like a huge relief. Perhaps he can actually explore this new country he's moved to.

The short driveway that runs down the side of the bakery has been cleared of snow, and a small bank of it sits neatly at the edge. 'Thanks for clearing the snow,' Christopher says.

Nash pops his head up from under the bonnet of the van. 'No worries. I only did your drive. I wasn't sure if you guys have rules about who can clear the sidewalk, you know, in case someone sues.'

Christopher hops onto the worn leather of the front seat, to get himself familiar with the van. Despite its general neglect, it's clean inside, though he's not entirely unconvinced that wasn't another Nash Nadeau morning task. What a strange man he is.

'You do a lot of pavement-clearing in LA, then?' Christo-pher asks.

'Not in LA, but I'm Canadian.'

'*Are you?*' asks Christopher, before instantly regretting what a giveaway the surprised squeak in his voice is.

Nash closes the bonnet of the van and fixes him with a puzzled grin. 'Yes?'

Christopher pretends to be distracted by cleaning the mirror. 'Is clearing snow a genetic predisposition?' he asks casually.

'No, I just had to do it a lot as a kid. Why are you so inter-ested that I'm Canadian?'

'Just don't meet a lot of Canadians,' Christopher replies quickly.

Behind him, the back door to the van opens and Nash piles a bunch of tools inside.

Christopher raises his eyebrows. 'One, where did you get those? And two, why do you think we'll need a saw exactly? We're hardly going on an expedition. It's just to the top of the village.'

'From the shed I broke into; and you never know what is going to be helpful in a snowstorm,' Nash replies, slamming the doors shut. 'When I was a kid in Canada, I was taught to always make sure you have the things you need on the road.'

Christopher tries to resist rolling his eyes. 'Come on, I've got the prescription. Do you want to drive?'

To his surprise, Nash slinks around the car and sits in the passenger side. 'You're already there. Go ahead.'

Damn. If he's being honest, he hoped Nash would test-drive it, especially as he is apparently Canadian and presumably very familiar with the snow. He must have driven in the snow more than Christopher has.

'You can drive it if you want? Especially seeing as you fixed it.'

'I'm good. Wrong side of the road and I don't have insurance for here.'

'Honestly, you get used to the little roads quite quickly, and it's not that big a van—'

'No. Thanks.'

'No?'

'Really, no.'

'All right then.' Christopher adjusts the mirrors and his seat height until he's satisfied, and then does another round of checks, just to be safe. He can do this. It's just driving a formerly defunct vehicle uphill in a snowstorm to deliver important medication to an alone and possibly vulnerable woman. Easy.

'You're going to run out of gas if you take much longer,' Nash drawls, a map open on his lap.

Christopher ignores him. 'I'm just being safe. Can you direct me?'

'According to this massive X that Shaz has marked, you need to go straight up after the crossroads.'

After stalling the van . . . twice . . . Christopher eventually manages to reverse it onto the main road. He drives cautiously through the freshly snow-covered roads, wishing they had some snow chains on the tyres. If this wasn't an emergency of sorts, he would not be behind the wheel. At least there's a lull in the snowfall right now so his windscreen is clear. But it's been so cold he's worried there could be ice under the snow, so he drives very slowly. He's always been afraid of driving on ice. Are you supposed to turn into a skid, or away? This is the sort of thing from his driving test that he has completely forgotten after living in London for years, and only using his car in Oxlea when he was visiting his parents.

It's still bitterly cold so hardly anyone is out. The few people they pass are wrapped up to the nines in knitwear and mountain boots, clearing snow from their paths with big shovels, or trudging through the thick snow on some small adventure. It really does feel like day two of Snowmageddon.

The road to Myffy's curls up the mountain. This high up they can see the whole valley mouth unfurl beneath them to one side, and the angry grey of the sea on the other. The clashing white and dark grey is somewhat ominous.

'Wow,' murmurs Nash, his face pressed to the window.

'It's quite beautiful, isn't it?'

'Yeah, in like a dramatic, possibly depressing kind of way. Feels like the background to a shoot where someone is about to get murdered in a coal mine.'

Christopher rolls his eyes. 'You're *obsessed* with murder.'

'Can you keep your eyes on the road. I swear you almost nicked that mailbox.' Nash stares straight ahead, holding onto the map for dear life.

'Postbox,' mutters Christopher.

'What did you say?'

'It's called a *post*box.'

'I know. We use both names in Canada, where I grew up. Anyway, stop.'

The van lurches to a halt as Christopher slams on the brakes. 'What?!' His heart is thudding in his chest.

Nash looks from the map up to the house. 'I think we're here.'

'Some warning might have been nice,' Christopher grumbles.

'You were too busy complaining about North American English being a whole other language.'

They're parked up in front of a pebble-dashed bungalow with a cherry-red front door. The path and drive up to the house are covered in knee-deep snow.

'Good job I brought all those unnecessary tools,' says Nash, as he hops out of the van. Christopher is briefly worried this means he's found a reason to use the saw.

Christopher locks the van and catches Nash giving him a look.

'What?'

'Why did you lock it?'

'I always lock the car.'

'Okay, but who is going to break into a truck that's on its knees, especially when we're the only people out here?'

Nash has a point, but still. Some habits can't be broken. He's only been out of London for six months, after all.

The doorbell chimes out a sweet little song, and after it ends they hear a distant 'I'm coming, just a minute!'

Christopher flips open the letterbox in the door. 'Take your time, Myffy.' He doesn't want her falling over *in* the house when they're this close to helping.

When the door eventually opens, they're greeted by a rosy-cheeked woman with wild curls of brown hair and the biggest smile in the world, standing with the assistance of a bright pink rollator. 'Did you bring the goods?'

she asks, dropping her smile and raising her eyebrows conspiratorially.

'We've got your drugs, ma'am,' says Nash cheerily.

'Shh, they'll hear you,' she giggles and steps back to let them in. 'What handsome rescuers. At least I hope that's who you are, or this day is about to take a really interesting turn.'

'We're the rescuers, I promise,' Christopher says with a smile, hoping it reads as non-threatening rather than strange. He's not particularly good at this bit with new people.

'Come through and warm up, duckies.' They follow her through her blessedly warm house to the kitchen at the back, where Nash places the paper prescription bag on the centre of the dining table.

'Diolch, darling. Paned?' Myffy asks.

'Allow me,' says Christopher, filling the kettle, and taking three clean mugs from the drainer on the side.

'I'll get us the biscuits then,' she insists, but Nash reaches over and grabs the obvious biscuit tin from a counter just out of her reach, setting them on the table too.

'Please, allow us,' he says, holding out a chair for her.

'Crikey. What a delightful day this is to have two strapping young men waiting on me. A girl could get used to this.'

She sits down at the kitchen table and opens the bag to check her medicines. 'All present and correct. And what a relief, to be honest with you. Thank you ever so much for bringing this up to me. This cold is a nightmare for my joints, and I wasn't fancying going cold turkey.'

Nash sits down next to her, while Christopher finishes making the teas. 'We're happy to help. Is there anything else we can do while we're here?'

'Ah, let's get a hot drink in you first before I start ordering you around.'

It appears that Myffy's mug collection is somewhat eccentric. It's only as Christopher pours water into the mugs that he notices the decorations. All the mugs must be part of a set, as they all feature people in rather rude poses that seem to be getting *ruder* as the mug heats up. Christopher can't help but blush a little as he sets the cups down on the table.

'Diolch, love,' Myffy says.

Nash inspects his mug, only to burst out laughing as he realises what he's looking at. 'My, my.'

Myffy grins. 'A good lark, aren't they?'

'I'm guessing "paned" means tea?'

'You got it in one, sugar. So, I suppose you are Christopher, and that means you must be Nash, am I right?'

'How did you guess?'

'Shaz told me to expect an English one and an American.'

'I'm Canadian,' mutters Nash into his tea.

'Really? You've never mentioned it,' says Christopher, blowing on his tea.

'I told you like half an hour ago.'

'And since then you've told me three more times.'

Nash huffs and folds his arms, much to the delight of Myffy. 'Look at you two. Such a funny pair.'

The blush on Christopher's cheeks refuses to go away. 'Is there anything else we can help you with? Shaz mentioned your PA can't make it today.'

'I'm guessing your version of a PA might be different from mine?' asks Nash.

'In some ways it's the same. I'm no Miranda Priestly tormenting young fashionistas, but a care personal assistant can do similar things,' Myffy says kindly. 'My care team help me out with tasks around the house and admin and things like going to get my medicine. But one of my girls, Selina, is up in Scotland for Christmas – she got out just in time but is probably stuck up there now – and my main PA, Polly, couldn't make it today as she's sick *and* snowed in, which seems doubly unfair to her. And my lovely husband Mohan is stuck in London! So I'm in a bit of a pickle, boys.'

'Can the council not get you anyone from a care bank or agency as it's an emergency?' asks Christopher.

'Well, normally I don't love having someone I don't know well for helping with some things, though I was willing to just go with it given the circumstances. But when Mohan called them they said that, given the weather, it's quite possible that I'm stuck with no one for now.' Myffy takes a sip of her tea and turns to Christopher. 'You know a lot about this stuff. Do you work in healthcare? A very *handsome* English doctor perhaps?'

Christopher tries not to choke on his tea. He's not used to older women aggressively flirting with him. Or anyone, for that matter. 'My sister is disabled so I know bits of how the system works, or doesn't work. And no, I bought Pantri Bach down on the high street last summer. I'm a baker, but I do have my first aid training at least.'

'Oh, gorgeous news! I didn't realise it was back open. I'll be down there like a shot once this snow is cleared out. Hell of a sweet tooth on me.'

'We're fully accessible too, not a step in sight, and the bathroom is accessible and has plenty of turning space. The same sister is an architect so she made sure everything was up to code and actually usable.'

'That's what I like to hear. But you know, you won't be rid of me at this rate,' she teases. 'What's the best thing you sell?'

'Well, I'm probably going to make some croissants with a pistachio filling when we reopen in January. I think they will be quite good.'

'Sold!' she laughs heartily. 'Consider that my pre-order.'

As Christopher sips tea from his X-rated mug, he catches Nash eyeing him. But as he looks up, Nash looks away. Strange.

Instead, Nash asks, 'Well, if Polly was here today, what would she be doing to help? Maybe we can help you with a few things.'

Of course, this is what Christopher *should* have been asking, not talking about his bakery. Typically, Nash Nadeau, Fixer of Vans and Clearer of Snow, would remember to help. It's a little annoying *how* helpful he's trying to be today.

Myffy chuckles. 'Well, she was going to help me bathe today, which I think might be an ask too far of you and too much fun for me.'

Christopher knows she's making light of it, but that must be awful, to not be able to do the things she needs to or wants to do.

'Don't stress,' Myffy continues. 'I can sort me out a flannel wash later. And hopefully Polly will be back tomorrow. Or Mohan if we're really lucky. I do have a few things on my shopping list that aren't desperate, but that would help. Maybe you could pick these bits up if you're safe to drive a bit longer? Other than that, clearing the snow off the path just in case I need to go out would be marvellous. And I've got some washing in the machine that needs hanging, and some to put away, if you wouldn't mind?'

Nash takes a sip of his tea, and stands, saluting Myffy. 'Your sidewalks will have never been so clear.' At that, he disappears off out of the front door.

'He's a bit bloody handsome, isn't he? Got that sort of made-for-television face. I feel all a-fluster with you both around.'

'Yes, well, he's an actor,' Christopher says a little reluctantly.

'What he's doing here then? Going method for a part as a farmer?'

'Wanted to come for a quiet holiday apparently – he was going to stay in the flat over the bakery while I was away. Unfortunately, he's stuck here *with* me, as I couldn't get out in time.'

'Tricky for you, that.'

'Not being able to go away for Christmas?'

'No, I mean being cooped up with that gorgeous face. I wouldn't be able to contain myself. You must have a stronger will than I do. That bottom!'

It turns out Myffy has the dirtiest laugh he's ever heard, and it's absolutely infectious. She's not wrong, though. Nash does have a very nice bum, although obviously Christopher already knew that from watching his movies.

And also in real life.

Not that he's been looking.

Well, he might have looked, but it was accidental. Probably.

It makes him feel rather strange to hear someone else being gooey over him, especially someone who doesn't recognise him from TV. He can't pin down the feeling. Perhaps he's just jealous that Nash seems to find being all attentive and helpful and charismatic natural and much easier than Christopher does.

The bastard.

Enough. Nash Nadeau is taking up far too much real estate in his mind right now. Time to get to work.

Myffy makes a shopping list while Christopher folds her laundry neatly – just like his mother taught him – and hangs the clean clothes in her wardrobe, led by Myffy's very specific directions. After all, what good is a wardrobe if things aren't organised by season, then mood and sub-sectioned by colour?

By the time they're done with the tasks inside the house, Nash returns to explain that he has piled the snow up in neat banks close to the drains on the road, so that when the snow starts to melt, the meltwater won't flood her house.

'By God, that's a bit clever,' Myffy says.

'Careful, his head will get too big for him to use the door,' Christopher murmurs, earning a look from Nash.

With a flirtatious smile for Myffy only, Nash says, 'Piling up snow is kind of my thing, ma'am.'

Christopher swears he hears Myffy say under her breath, 'Well then call me Frosty.'

She tries to hand Christopher an envelope of cash, which he refuses. 'Let's work it out later when we've got your shopping,' he says instead. 'I couldn't bear if we took your money and got stranded somewhere.'

'You're a kind boy, Christopher. Isn't he a lovely one?' she says to Nash, who nods stiffly.

They wave Myffy goodbye and hop once again into the icy-cold van. As the heating splutters to life, Christopher checks if the big supermarket in the next town over is open, and luckily, somehow it is. They just have to hope the van will get them there, and the supermarket has any food left to sell.

He shoots Shaz an update.

Christopher: Medicine all dropped off.

Shaz: Oh I know. She texted me the minute you left thanking me for her Christmas present of two hot helper elves. You both have a fan.

Christopher: We're off to the big Sainsbury's to shop for Myffy. Do you need anything?

Shaz: A babysitter, a holiday, and a good shag.

Christopher: I can't help with any of those.

Shaz: Pity. I bet Saino's is out of stock of them too. I'll send you a list in a minute once I've gotten out the cupboard.

Christopher: Why are you in the cupboard?

Shaz: Hiding from my kids, obviously.

Chapter Eleven

Nash

They drive back down the mountain, away from Myffy and towards the sea, just as the weather starts to turn again. After the last decade and a half in LA, Nash is admittedly unused to the stormy, grey fury before him. The Californian beaches are pristine and beautiful and filled with astonishingly fit people playing frisbee or surfing, like Kurt. Not that he gets out there very often. Travelling anywhere in LA is way too much effort, especially the beach.

Nash snaps a photo of the furious white-capped waves to send to Kurt. He almost sends it before remembering that he's not supposed to be in Wales. The problem with being friends with someone you do business with is when you're hiding from the business part, you have to forget the friendship part too.

And the thing is, he still hasn't worked out a way to say *sorry but actually I don't want to be an actor any more, I want to write or maybe produce or do anything behind the camera that isn't being the face.*

It's not the fact that he's only in romantic comedies – hell, he *loves* them, and that's what he wants to write. He's just . . . done with being an actor. And the thing is, if he says that, finally says it and pushes back on this multi-movie contract, it has ramifications for basically everyone else he works with, not least his co-star, Barbie. He knows the whole *Christmas Vet* fandom has been desperate for their movie together.

As if on cue, a text from Barbie herself comes through.

Barbie: hey doll, my agent said Kurt pushed your contract negoshh for personal reasons. hope youre safe and okii

He can practically hear the purr of her voice. He should text her back, so she doesn't worry he's really sick, but then if he does, he'll start thinking about this whole contract situation again. He pockets his phone and resolves to reply later.

Just put it away and forget about it, like everything else. Like, how he's barely dated for years because of how badly his last relationship ended, or how he's not even sure what he's doing with his life. Or how he feels as if some of the spark has gone.

But there's categorically no time for wallowing, not that he's even convinced that he deserves to wallow. He just needs to get a grip and focus on helping out someone with a genuine need, rather than thinking about his own deeply First World problems.

Plus, going to a supermarket when he's on vacation in another country is usually his favourite thing to do. There's nothing quite like finding an exciting new food he doesn't recognise or something he's always wanted to try. He'll never forget buying a durian when he was travelling in the Philippines – a delicious, stinky cheese-fruit. Or all the different flavours of soda he picked up in Japan, though he could do without ever having to drink the jellied one that tasted of grass again.

However, when they arrive at the supermarket, the slightly apocalyptic vibe really throws the joyful escapism off. The car park is fairly empty, but it turns out, so are the shelves inside, and they pass a handful of stressed staff who are basically rearranging the deckchairs at this point. There really isn't much at all.

Christopher looks at the list on his phone optimistically. 'I'm sure we can get *some* of the things we need, at least? We just have to be creative.'

Nash's eyes land on a single sad potato in a green plastic crate. 'I didn't realise your talent extended to creating food out of nothing.'

There's no other produce hidden in the crates underneath it either. This is really it. It feels wrong to leave the solitary potato behind, so he picks it up and puts it in the trolley. 'I'll push the cart.'

'Trolley,' Christopher corrects.

In the most overexaggerated American-doing-a-cockney accent he can muster, Nash repeats, 'Trolleyyyy'.

'I do not sound like that,' Christopher huffs.

They weave through the aisles, and Nash shivers as they pause by the fridges. The shelves are pretty empty here too. How depressing. Christopher sticks his head all the way into a fridge to grab something from the back, so Nash creeps up behind him and yells, ''Ello, sister!'

He hears a satisfying clunk as Christopher knocks his head on the shelf.

'I'm here to push the trolley. Fancy a cuppa?'

As Christopher stands upright, he spins round to face Nash, wielding a fridge-burned pack of bacon like a weapon. 'Stop that.'

Nash laughs. 'I will not. It's much too fun to annoy you.'

With a haughty little eye roll, Christopher drops the bacon into the trolley and stalks off ahead in search of the next thing from his list.

'To be fair, you sound more like a posh Bond villain or Stephen Fry than my terrible attempt, which is probably more *evil CW character that's going to turn me into a diamond*.'

'I'm sorry, did you say turn you into a diamond?'

'Yeah. You know, evil English stuff.'

'I worry about what they're teaching you over there.'

'Teaching us? It's just television.'

'*Precisely* my point. It's amazing that we supposedly speak the same language and yet sometimes I have not a clue what you're saying.'

'Not a single clue,' Nash replies in his terrible English accent, and when Christopher turns his back, he slyly gives him the finger.

He trails Christopher with the trolley. Slowly, it fills with items from the list, though it's by no means anywhere near *full*. A packet of skinny-looking sausages that go out of date that day, and some bags of rice and pasta. A box of tea. Nothing looks particularly Christmassy, though given Nash wasn't planning on doing a whole Christmas dinner situation just for himself, it hardly changes things for him. Plus, he knew he wasn't going to be able to find some of his favourites here, like the too-sweet almost-candied yams Americans cook, usually for Thanksgiving. It's been years since he went back to Canada for Christmas. The last time must have been when he was still on *Parental Units*.

The one thing the supermarket does have is cheese. Lots and lots of it, wrapped in brightly coloured wax and some even stacked up and wrapped in cellophane, like an easy cheesy gift. It's all the fancy cheeseboard stuff, but still, he adds a few things to their cart because there's no point ignoring the one food that's available.

'We could make a fondue? Or twelve,' Nash suggests, to the back of Christopher's head.

Christopher *harrumphs* again, the sort of overdramatic sound that a Muppet might make, while he glares at his phone.

'Are we missing lots?'

'Quite a few things.' Christopher hands him the phone with the list, where he has put a tick emoji next to the few things they do have. That surprises Nash a little; Christopher doesn't particularly seem like a man who is even aware of the emoji keyboard. He would have thought he'd do a smiley face like old people do, with a colon for eyes, line dash for a nose and a bracket for a smile.

'I'm worried. There are no ready meals or easy cooking stuff at all, which Myffy needs,' Christopher says, running his hands through his hair. 'And there's hardly any of the stuff that Shaz wanted for the kids.'

'Do you need to get those specific ones? Like, does anyone have allergies or anything?'

'I could call and check. Why?'

'We could make some food for them?' The thought comes from his mouth before he can really think it through. 'If ease is what they need, I mean. We can use the list as guidance to try and make something like the things they asked for, and then it's a whole meal they can heat up, right? We have your massive empty bakery, and it's not like we've got anything better to do in this weather. Plus, it might be better use of my energy than making homemade weights or us sniping at each other. And I've fixed the van already, so what else am I going to do? This place must sell Tupperware we can use, or maybe you have something like that in the bakery?' He trails off as he watches a soft, lazy smile blossom on Christopher's face. The kind that makes his stomach ache.

'That's really very thoughtful of you, Nash.'

'I can be thoughtful,' he sniffs, brushing off the compliment. 'It'll be like Meals on Wheels, right? You can cook, and I'll be sous chef. I'm good at taking direction.'

Christopher snorts at this for some reason, but makes the necessary phone calls to Shaz and Myffy, directing Nash to add a few notes on his own phone of likes and dislikes and an *absolutely do not bring that into my house* from Shaz about blue cheese.

The next hour goes quickly, and to Nash's surprise, it's because he's having fun. They raid the canned food and the frozen vegetables sections and Nash is surprised by the sheer joy he feels at finding some normal non-Christmas Cheddar for Shaz's kids.

With all their goods, they decide to make a vegetarian as-many-beans-as-possible chilli for the adults, a low-on-the-seasonings bolognese for Shaz's kids with lots of hidden canned vegetables, and a big thick soup with crispy bacon or fish finger croutons for the topping. Solid dishes they can batch-cook in massive quantities this afternoon without it taking hours and hours. There's no spaghetti for the bolognese, but they hope the kids will enjoy the novelty of the miscellaneous bags of pasta shapes they pick up. Strangely enough, the dietary section is another part of the store relatively untouched by the plague of locusts that must have come through, so they stock up on long-life oat-based cream for the soup.

Although he was a little unsure about the whole idea to start with, Christopher really comes alive when he realises he could bake things for people, too. He suggests sourdough loaves, some flatbreads for the chilli, and perhaps a run of biscuits. He picks up a few things for the baking, grumbling at the price compared to wholesale, but still smiling when he adds them in.

'You load, I'll bag,' says Nash when they get to the tills. He passes the cashier, saying hello, but Christopher gets into a full conversation with the young girl. Typical.

Nash can't help but watch as Christopher leans over to pick up things to place gently on the conveyer belt. They lock eyes, but Nash styles it out by making a very big show of shaking open the carrier bags. His eyes wander again even as he bags things together. And when Christopher gets out his wallet to pay, he rolls up the sleeves of his shirt and jumper, as though he's about to do manual labour rather than simply tap a card against a reader. In the soft white underside of one arm is one lone freckle, and Nash has to bite down on his lip to drag his attention away. His mind wanders, imagining clasping his hand right over that freckle, and pinning Christopher's arm above his head.

God, really? Is this what Stockholm Syndrome feels like? Being held hostage and developing feelings for your captor? But instead of romantic feelings, Nash is just thinking about the way the freckles dapple across Christopher's shoulders.

He's pretty sure he listened to a podcast about how Stock-holm Syndrome was all made up anyway. Either way, it seems a little unfortunate that this weird guy's vibe seems to be doing this much for him at this very moment.

'Ready to go?' Christopher startles him so much that he drops a bag of canned goods a little too heavily into the trolley. All the nearby cashiers look over at them, alerted by the noise.

'Yes,' he says, a little too quickly.

'All right,' says Christopher, with that soft lazy smile that makes Nash want to . . . well.

This is bad. This is really bad, he thinks. He needs a cold shower. Perhaps a walk in the snow. Maybe he should get into that angry sea too, just to be safe. Swim home.

★ ★ ★

They load up the van, and as they pull out of the car park, Nash flicks on the radio. Someone is speaking in Welsh, but it quickly gives way to Caroline Polachek's 'So Hot You're Hurting My Feelings', which Christopher hums along to.

Against his better judgement, he decides to find out more about Christopher. 'So do you speak Welsh?' he asks.

'Why do you ask?'

'The radio, and I heard you saying a few things to the cashier.'

'I'm learning, or trying to. I've always been quite good at languages; the Latin-based ones are what I was most exposed to. I very much felt that if I was going to come here and open a business, the least I could do is learn the language.'

'Do lots of people speak it?'

'Apparently a third of the country, but it might take a while for them to speak to me.'

'Why's that?'

'I've got to prove myself, haven't I?' Christopher says simply, shrugging his shoulders ever so slightly. 'Plus, it's just easier for us all to speak in English if I'm doing a really bad job of Welsh. But also, I came here, and bought up retail space because I was lucky to have London property money. I'm young, so I guess it could seem like I'm not serious. Like I don't care about this community. But I do. I want to prove that.'

'I guess moving into a small community is always tricky but even more so when it's a different country.'

'Essentially. And I suspect you don't get taught much Welsh history at all – I certainly was not – but there's a history of English colonisation here. I don't want to inadvertently be another part of that. There're so many people here with holiday homes that are just never here, never giving back to the community. It's just . . . it's all on my mind. That privilege.'

'That's admirable,' Nash reluctantly admits. He kind of wishes Christopher would go back to being prissy and annoying, instead of earnest.

'It shouldn't be. It really is the least I should be doing. And my Welsh is truly atrocious. You just can't tell because you don't speak it.'

Nash wonders if Welsh is on Duolingo because making fun of Christopher in Welsh could be extra fun. But before he can open the app, he realises his screen is full of messages from Kurt. Variations on *my dude, let's talk*. He hesitates, not quite ready to click on them and find out the full extent of Kurt's messages yet. After all, they've got two more days, right? That's plenty of time to deliberate privately.

When they pull up to the bakery, Nash leaps out of the van and picks up the heaviest bags from the back. If he's not going to get a chance to do any proper lifting, this will have to do. At least Christopher seems happy to let him, and takes the remaining bag under one arm. Once inside and de-booted, Christopher goes to walk upstairs when Nash stops him. 'Where are you going?'

'To . . . put the shopping away? In my house?'

'Shouldn't we cook down here? Might just be easier if we're cooking for ten to do it in a kitchen where we can swing a cat.'

'Good point.'

They dump the bags on the floor of the bakery kitchen, and Nash starts grouping ingredients together into 'soup', 'bolognese' or 'chilli' on the massive table in the centre. While he loves to cook, he doesn't get to do much of it at home. Plus, the strict diets he ends up on pre-shooting aren't exactly a joy to cook – no inspiration ever came from plain grilled chicken. When he was little, he would cook with his nonna, and she always insisted on setting everything out ready before you even thought about prepping, never mind cooking. That's stuck with him.

British through and through, Christopher takes a few bags up with him, and goes upstairs to make them tea. Nash drags a stool over from a corner and settles on it, his elbows on the prep table in the centre of the room, and opens up his message chain with Barbie.

Nash: don't worry. I have been kidnapped but adopted by locals and am being looked after, though they insist that someone sends a lot of money before I'm allowed to leave, and they keep taking photos of me with the newspaper. All very weird.

Barbie: lol

Barbie: good.

Barbie: or not good? Is this even Nash I'm speaking to?

Nash: send over £100k and we'll tell you for sure

Barbie: hmm I'm not sure he's worth that

Nash: rude

Nash: I mean…

Nash: You should send it

Barbie: you should tell Nash that if he signs his new contract, they can get the money that way

Barbie: (sorry)

Nash: not you too

Barbie: babe you know I do not love the reality of the biz, but like I gotta eat, you gotta eat, the crew have to eat, let's just do the thinggggg

It all sounds so *reasonable* when she says it. But it's another year of his life, at least. More than that really, because this is actually a multi-year deal, multiple films. If it was just the last *Christmas at the Clinic* film then that would be a different conversation, but the execs made it very clear to him, before he fled LA, that if he didn't agree to do more films, it wouldn't just be hurting his career, but perhaps hers too. Not that he'd told Kurt that, because he'd then have to tell Kurt about all the rest of it.

At one point, this kind of deal and the security that comes with it had been his dream. But now it feels like a trap. A gilded cage.

All this feels so much worse now that Barbie is rightfully on his case. There's no way he can tell her that he's being blackmailed with her own career security, and that's part of the hold-up. Another thing that Kurt probably could advise on.

But the thing is, he needs to protect her. After *Parental Units* got cancelled and everyone went their separate ways, he was kind of afloat in the industry. He was a young adult actor in a sea of them, and even though Kurt was great at getting him into the audition room, Nash just wasn't having any luck. It was months and months of showing up and sitting alongside the same four or five guys who looked exactly like him – blond, slightly preppy, all built like greyhounds – reading the same scripts. It wasn't always the same guys, because every now and again someone else would get their big break – they'd get a season-long role or a nice guest star appearance, and someone else would rotate into his slot in the audition room instead.

Eventually, they ran out of greyhounds and he'd got lucky with a pretty terrible made-for-TV film role, but he and Kurt agreed the only reason to do it was the strangely high pay (thank you to all the product placement), as they all agreed the script was a dud.

But strange things can come from terrible movies, because Barbie Glynn, rising star of social media and darling of the girls-next-door, had seen him in that stinker of a movie and wanted *him* to play alongside her in her first movie. He'd been a little sceptical to begin with; how could he not be? It was her first movie, basically written for her, and arguably the execs had her follower numbers translating into dollar signs in their mind. She was a bit younger and he wasn't sure if she'd done any acting at all. Plus, they'd never met. And yet, she wanted him to audition for *Christmas at the Rink*, in which they'd play rival ice-skating coaches training their youth teams for sectionals, or regionals – he forgets which.

It turned out they had amazing on-screen chemistry. Like, the type that made Nash wonder very briefly if it wasn't real, but no, he tends to like his real-life love interests with more stubble. Even so, just watching the tapes back for the chemistry reads they did together, it was clear for everyone to see that they were *it*.

They had a good time filming, too. Mostly, he just got to drive the Zamboni while Barbie wore the most incredible yet impractical, aggressively fluffy faux-fur coats in every scene.

And then, it really took off. He was officially a leading man, albeit in small-budget, made-for-television or straight-to-streaming romantic comedies, but the work kept coming. Screenwriters wrote scripts with them in mind. It was kind of magical, while he wanted it.

If it wasn't for Barbie, he'd probably have left the industry by now. And it feels very much like the weight of her career is also on his shoulders. He writes back that he's 'working on it', hoping this is vague enough that she won't see all the way through to the void of *I can't think about this not even a little bit* in his brain.

Barbie: no probs, good luck escaping that hostage sitchhhhh

Yeah, he probably needs all the luck he can get. Especially given that the weather warnings seem to just keep getting redder. He sends back a thumbs-up emoji, possibly the least convincing way of conveying he's totally fine.

Before Nash's brain can run off into an anxiety-induced imagination spiral of whether Christopher could actually feasibly kidnap him, the man himself walks into the kitchen, teas in hand. He sets them down on the counter and brushes his hands together, as though brushing away flour that's not there.

'Ready to—' he begins, but they're interrupted by a knock on the back door. Christopher lopes off to open it and is greeted once again by Shaz-en-knitwear.

'Hiya boys. Get your warms on,' she says, rubbing her mittened hands together.

'Our what?' asks Christopher.

'You know, your coats and stuff.'

'I did not think that's what you meant,' Nash says.

'Hurry up, will you? You've got to come with me. Have you not seen the new weather forecast? They've put out a bunch more alerts on top of the alerts there already are. It's going to get worse overnight.'

Nash's stomach drops. He really isn't getting out of here any time soon.

'They've called an emergency town meeting to work out how to help everyone. And seeing as you two have already been such good little elves today, I figured you should come along.'

'You don't have to come,' Christopher whispers to Nash, which makes his stomach twist in a different way.

He's here, isn't he? He fixed the van. He helped with the shopping and was about to start cooking. Why does Christopher keep trying to leave him behind when having something to do is the only thing keeping his sanity in check? Does he think Nash is that much of a jerk? The thought makes him feel strangely small. Unseen, perhaps. He's not sure why it bothers him this much, but then, who likes being misunderstood? It's probably just that.

Hot irritation rushes up his neck. It makes him want to itch or fight or go for a run. 'Let's go,' he says, grabbing his coat from the hook.

'That's more like it, American boy,' says Shaz.

Chapter Twelve

Christopher

They follow Shaz over the road to the town's community centre, a single-storey red-brick building bordered by a low grey stone wall. On the wall outside is a memorial to soldiers who fought in WW1 and WW2, a huge board for event announcements with a map of the town and the odd handyman business card. It's a place that Christopher has passed many times but has never been in. Not because he wasn't sure he was allowed or anything; more that he'd never had the time to seek out what happened there, or what he could potentially be a part of. It was hard to take part in a community when you were so exhausted from quite literally serving it every day. Or trying to.

Though, right now, he does worry that he might not belong here. Sure, they helped out Myffy, and he and Nash are set to cook for her and Shaz's family too, but will the rest of the town want his help? He's still basically a stranger, and Nash is an entirely unknown quantity.

Luckily, he doesn't have time to dwell on any of that, because Shaz has been literally dragging him over there, her mittened hand clutched around his wrist.

They tap the snow off their boots outside the front door and step inside. It's not much warmer inside, and Christopher swears he can hear the clunking of the heating reluctantly firing up after being so rudely awakened. Shaz leads them into the large open room of the community centre, with painted white walls, ancient faux-wood linoleum on the floor, and thick green velvet curtains. The paint is peeling off the ceiling where damp must have got in, and the whole room has an air of shabbiness about it. He wonders when it was last redecorated, or if the council even has money to do that. At least it's warm.

There are a few cursory nods to Christmas – some sad tinsel taped up around the announcement boards, and up near the ceiling he can see the browned edges of tape leftover from Christmas decorations of years gone by. There's also a plastic Christmas tree in the corner that he is fairly sure must be as old as he is.

Shaz waves to a few people in greeting, and Christopher realises he doesn't recognise the majority of people here. Perhaps he's not done as well at ingratiating himself into the town as he thought he had, and he had pretty low expectations to start with.

In a crisis, you can always count on the fact that someone will have made an urn of tea to power everyone through, both physically and emotionally. And even this rather hurriedly set up town meeting doesn't stray from that intensely British blueprint. Shaz beckons them over to a fold-up table where there are two hot drink dispensers – one full of seemingly eye-wateringly strong tea, and one full of what looks like the weakest coffee known to man – along with a truly eclectic assortment of mugs, sugar and packet biscuits. It's weirdly comforting.

Looked on by an older woman with a short crop of curly hair, Shaz makes herself a cup of tea in a somewhat ancient Cadbury's Caramel rabbit mug. The woman does not offer to help. Her job seems to be more to ensure proper use, rather than to actually assist anyone in making a beverage. She smiles at Shaz before disappearing through a door that leads to a tiny, ancient-looking kitchen.

'Come on, make yourselves one,' Shaz says.

Christopher does as he's told and soon is holding an extremely hot cup of tea in a mug dedicated to the opening of a local bypass in the nineties, hoping he doesn't scald his palms off.

Nash doesn't move, too busy looking around at his surroundings. Shaz elbows him.

'Oi, hurry up.'

'Oh, thanks but I'm not really thirsty.'

She fixes him with a look that she must reserve for the kids and sets her mug down on the table. With the most terrifying smile on her lips, she places her hands on his shoulders, and says, 'Don't refuse the hospitality. Make yourself a drink. Just hold it. I'm dead serious.'

'Will people care that much?'

'Oh *yes*. They will. People still talk about the time Mina Jenkins said the tea was too weak, and that was in the early noughties.'

'What happened to her?' Christopher asks.

'She moved to Sweden in disgrace. Now, put a nice smile on that handsome face, and make yourself a terrible drink.'

As if to confirm this, the woman formerly behind the table returns with two jugs of lurid-coloured squash, and waits expectantly for Nash to make his selection.

With a Hollywood smile, Nash says, 'Good afternoon' to her. She seems to come to life, blushing and giggling like a teenager, while he makes himself a coffee.

'I've never seen Enid so . . . *animated*,' Shaz murmurs. 'It's disturbing.'

They all sit on fold-out chairs that have been laid out facing a small stage area next to a stack of yoga and crash mats, Christopher in the middle with Nash and Shaz on either side of him.

'What happens now?' Christopher asks.

Shaz blows aggressively on her tea. 'Oh, I'm sure Tammy will start us off soon. She'll just be waiting for everyone to arrive.'

'Are you sure it's all right for me to be here?' Christopher asks again.

'Yes?' She gives him a look as if he's just said something totally bonkers. 'You *live* here, you own a business here, you employ Tegan. You are part of the community, and you're also here to help out. Stop fretting.'

'I just still don't know anyone.'

'Well, now's the perfect time, isn't it, you wally?'

On the other side of him Nash laughs softly.

'If anyone's not supposed to be here, it's this one.' Shaz's laugh is interrupted by a confused look, and she sniffs the air, before grimacing down at the enormous Cadbury's Mini Eggs mug in Nash's hands. 'Urgh, did you get the coffee?'

'Yeah?'

'Terrible choice, terrible choice. I thought you Americans *liked* coffee. That stuff is older than my kids.'

'Well, *they* do. But I'm Canadian,' he says, with the tone of someone who has had to correct people on this many times. It reminds Christopher of Haf, the way she gets frustrated when everyone assumes she's English. He wonders if everyone else here has similar stories.

'Are you?!' she says with surprise, and Christopher discreetly gives her foot a kick. This might be new information for her, but they are both still pretending to not know who he is. Flustered, she adds, 'Your accent. I'd never have guessed.'

'I've been based in LA since I was a teenager. It comes out when I go home.'

'Do you say "buoy" the Canadian way?'

'You mean, the *correct* way? The way that makes sense if you're on a boat and need to alert someone that there's a boy the water, not just a buoy.'

He says it *boo-ee* and Christopher can't help but snigger, as does Shaz. 'Whatever you need to tell yourself, babe, but that sounds silly.'

Before they can continue arguing, Enid from the refreshments table claps to get everyone's attention, only to inform them they'll be starting in five minutes.

'That was a bit anticlimactic,' murmurs Shaz, blowing again on her tea. Christopher is pretty sure he's not seen her drink any of it. He risks sipping at his own cup, but it's still nuclear.

'Shaz?' whispers Nash, leaning across Christopher. 'I don't mean to be rude, but is there no one else young here?'

Shaz snorts. 'Oh sorry, is it not LA enough for you?'

Nash rolls his eyes. 'I meant more, are there people who might be able to *help* who haven't recently had a hip replacement and/or grandchildren. A lot of people here look more in *need* of help than available to do the helping. And there's hardly anyone here.'

He's not wrong. The room is fairly empty, despite the optimistic rows of seats. Initially, Christopher had chalked it up to the bad weather, meaning people were taking a little longer to get here. After all, they only had to cross a road so it was pretty quick for them. But since they've been sitting here, only a few more people have arrived.

'No, Nash, there are not many people your age here,' she says truthfully. 'Or my age, for that matter.'

'Oh, I'm sure there's no difference in our ages. With skin like that? You can't possibly be even in your thirties.' He says it so smoothly that even Christopher gets goosebumps.

'Stop flirting with me now, I'm a married woman.'

'I'll behave.' He very nearly takes a sip of his giant coffee but thinks better of it. 'So, go on. Explain why it looks like we're nearing the end of that film about the beach that makes you old.'

'First of all, there are basically no new jobs, except for muggins here.' She thumbs at Christopher, who immediately feels guilty that so far he's only employed one often-sullen, albeit efficient teenager. 'And two, no one can afford to stay here long-term. Not since people remembered Wales is a nice place to visit.'

'What do you mean?'

'Holiday homes that are empty, like, eleven months of the year. Airbnb, things like that. People having a flat to let to holidaymakers.'

At this, both Christopher and Nash look down at their shoes.

'Get over it. Renting one normally occupied flat for a few days is not the same as that. Put your egos away a second and think about the wider problem,' she says, sharply but not unkindly. 'The fact is, people can't afford to buy here because other people are buying up places as second properties, quite often to rent to holidaymakers as another income stream. And there's nowhere for normal people living here to rent because, again, it's all short-term lets for people on holidays instead. And that has knock-on effects, like schools closing down or there not being a doctor's nearby any more. That's why the town feels so empty. It's because it *is*.'

Nash nods along, taking this all in. 'So really it's up to us, isn't it? You weren't kidding about needing our help.'

Shaz nods. 'Pretty much. I know Christopher said you came here looking for a break or whatever, but—'

'No, I'm happy to help where I can,' Nash says seriously.

Christopher can't help it, but he feels kind of sceptical. This all feels . . . a bit *too* like one of Nash's film characters in a way. Not the man who just destroyed his kitchen and stock making a home gym. But then, he did fix the van. And help Myffy. God, it's so confusing. Christopher can't get a read on Nash at all. It's a weird situation, being stuck together with someone you don't really know but are inadvertently responsible for, for an unknowable length of time.

'Plus, it's still a good distraction from my own brain,' Nash continues, 'and better than sulking around the flat. My original plan was to just hike and pout, so I'll just . . . help and pout instead.'

What does Nash need to distract himself from? Is his life in LA too glamorous? His diamond shoes too tight? Though, it's not as if Christopher can't relate. Maybe there's something bigger going on, something to do with that phone call yesterday.

'He's good at the pouting bit,' Christopher teases, which earns a stuck-out tongue from Nash.

By the time a few more people have taken their seats, a woman that Christopher vaguely recognises stands upfront. Her beautifully tailored sapphire peacoat reminds him of something from Kit's wardrobe, and her rich brown hair softly curls at her shoulders. She looks organised and put together, but not just aesthetically. There's a vibe. She's a woman who can rally the people.

'Croeso pawb,' she announces, drawing everyone's attention. This garners a few bore das, hellos and hiyas from the crowd. 'Welcome, and thank you for braving the weather to come out to this emergency meeting. I see a few unfamiliar faces, so I'll introduce myself – I'm Tamara Yang, and I'm the councillor for Pen-y-Môr.'

That explains the air of confidence about her. She's a politician.

'Tammy and I went to school together,' Shaz whispers. 'She's good people.'

'I will try to keep things brief today for the sake of us not freezing over, but I am proposing that, due to the weather and the time of year, an action committee is formed today in order to ensure that any people without power or food or safe housing can be identified and helped by us. We can use the community centre as a base of operations, and coordinate assistance from here with a pool of volunteers once we've ascertained how everyone can help.'

A hand from someone in the front row shoots up, and Christopher is almost certain that Tamara stifles a grimace.

'Yes, Ursula?' she says, with a tone of weariness that suggests this is not the first time Ursula has had an opinion during an important meeting.

Taking this as a cue to address the room, Ursula stands and turns slightly so everyone can see her. 'I just wanted to encourage the democratic process before we embark on this new committee, as it's very important that everyone in the room gets a say about membership and leadership and how things are organised.' Her voice is high, clipped and nasal, and overall, she reminds Christopher of the girls he went to school with.

'You're right,' replies Tamara slowly. 'But as this is quite a pressing matter, Ursula, I think it's okay for us to move ahead. We need to get going in order to help people out.'

'We can't help if we don't know how things are organised,' gasps Ursula with what seems to be genuine horror. 'For example, who is going to lead us in these endeavours?'

'Well, as I'm sure you've ascertained, I was thinking me,' says Tamara, completely deadpan. 'Seeing as I called the meeting and I am literally leading it, and also given that I am an elected figure of the community.'

'Are they about to fight?' whispers Nash.

'It seems like it, doesn't it?' Christopher agrees.

'Is this how all your town meetings go?'

'I don't know. This is my first.'

'Shhh,' admonishes Shaz. 'The fighting is my *favourite* bit.'

'I don't want to put words in anyone's mouths,' continues Ursula, sounding very much like she actually would like that, 'but I think that an emergency situation is no reason to bypass due process. After all, I *am* Head of the PTA and the Neighbourhood Watch for Pen-y-Môr, so I have as much local seniority as *you*, Tamara.'

The room is a collective held breath as everyone waits for Tamara, who looks increasingly wearied, to respond. She takes a few seconds, that classic politician's pause, before turning to the audience and asking, 'Does someone want to nominate a leader of this emergency committee? Anyone?'

'I nominate Ms Yang,' shouts back a wiry little woman who looks like a lively bird. She is wrapped up in a huge knitted roll-neck navy jumper that seems to swallow her whole.

'Thank you, Priti.'

'Also good people?' asks Nash.

'Good people,' Shaz confirms.

'Well, I nominate Ursula Caldecott,' calls another voice. Everyone's heads turn to look at the speaker, a ruddy-faced boor of a man inexplicably wearing a short-sleeved shirt despite how desperately cold it is in here. He, somehow, reclines in his chair, his palms facing the sky in a *try me* gesture.

'Of course he does,' cackles Shaz quietly. 'That's the pub landlord, Mervyn. He fancies himself Ursula's second husband.'

'Not good people?' Nash asks.

'Total arsehole.'

'Noted.'

Christopher had had an inkling that local politics – or whatever isn't strictly politics but acts as if it is – was sometimes very dramatic given the stories his mother would recount to his father. No wonder she enjoyed it. Esther Calloway is not one to suffer fools or back down from fights. She would thrive here, and everyone would already be assigned into their roles. He can't imagine she would have taken much notice of this request for democracy, which could be a good or bad thing, depending on how you look at it.

Tamara, on the other hand, looks suddenly as if she's about to sack the whole lot in and go to bed.

Still standing, Ursula looks like the cat who got the cream. 'Why, thank you Mervyn. At least someone cares about due process and standards.'

She sinks slowly to her seat, not taking her eyes off Mervyn, and Christopher feels a little sick, as if he's just watched a kind of foreplay in public.

'Oh, we're all aware of your standards, Urs,' mutters Shaz a little too loudly. 'We all got the emails about our lawns being centimetres too tall over summer.'

Exasperated and quickly losing control of the meeting, Tamara taps her forehead with her hand. 'Right, everyone, can we please just skip to the voting? Your choice is Ursula or me. Let's get this over with.'

'Excuse me,' says Ursula, rising to her feet again. 'But are we not going to blind it? Or maybe we need someone impartial to count?'

'I'll do it.' Shaz gleefully waves an arm in the air. This is met with a polite but firm 'No, thank you' from Tamara and an 'Absolutely not' from Ursula.

'It needs to be someone impartial and you are not impartial, Sharon,' sneers Ursula.

'And why aren't you impartial?' whispers Nash.

'Oh, because I fucking hate her,' laughs Shaz, not even trying to keep her voice down.

'To be fair, Ursula, I think everyone in this room lives in Pen-y-Môr and knows both of you, so really no one is truly impartial,' says Priti. Her attempt to soothe the situation is met by a death glare from Ursula that could rival Medusa for petrification powers. The already-minute Priti shrinks in her seat.

Before Christopher realises that it's happening, Nash stands up and addresses everyone. 'Hi! Hello everyone! Could I get your attention just for one second please?'

The room falls silent.

'Sit back down,' Christopher hisses.

'Don't you dare,' says Shaz. 'Keep going!'

'Christ.'

Everyone looks at Nash, their faces a mixture of confusion and awe thanks to his general movie-star glow. He catches a few rumblings of 'an American?' from the audience.

'Sorry, who are . . . you?' Ursula's words slow and soften as she turns and realises just how handsome Nash is, all the bite falling out of her tone.

'Hi. Nice to meet you all. My name's Nash Nadeau.'

The silence turns to a rumble of gasps and outbursts as people clearly begin to recognise him.

'I'm here for the holidays in town and thankfully got stuck here with you. But I'm not from here and I only really know these two people—' There's a brief swivel of looks towards Shaz and Christopher. 'So really I'm very impartial. I'll do the count. Just tell me what to do.'

Neither Tamara nor Ursula say anything, and the whole room is transfixed on Nash as if he's hypnotised them.

'Bloody hell, he's American,' calls Mervyn.

'Canadian, actually,' Nash corrects, making his way to the front of the room where Tamara stands looking less frustrated and more somewhat amused. 'Now, Ms Ursula, was it? Could you come join us at the stage here?'

It's absolutely incredible how the roomful of people fall completely under his spell. The spell of charisma and extremely straight teeth.

Without another word, Ursula slinks forwards to him. 'Have we met before?' She holds out her hand as though he might kiss it, but instead he just shakes it.

'Oh, definitely not. I just have one of those faces.'

'What a liar,' hisses Christopher to Shaz, who is pissing herself laughing into her scarf at the whole affair. She'll be eating this up for months.

'Thank you, Mr Nadeau,' says Tamara, trying to bring the meeting back to order. 'Come on, Ursula.'

She takes Ursula by the arm and drags her into the tiny kitchen, shutting the door behind them.

Nash addresses the crowd. 'Okay, we'll go for a very simple show of hands. No speaking, all right? Let's all play fair now.'

The crowd rumbles in agreement.

'All in favour of Ms Ursula?'

Out of respect for democracy, Christopher tries very hard not to look around to see who is voting for who. However, out of the corner of his eye, he does see Mervyn and Enid, the refreshments lady, raise hands to vote. There's a reluctance to Enid's hand, as though she's being watched over by Ursula. Perhaps she is worried Ursula can sense votes by proximity.

'And for Ms Tamara?'

All the remaining hands, including Shaz's and Christopher's, are raised. It's not unanimous, but it's the majority by far.

'And just to be sure, any abstentions?'

No one raises their hand, but Enid looks as if she might, even though she's technically already voted.

'You can come back in now,' Shaz yells.

'Yes, thank you for that, Shaz,' Nash says, as Ursula strides in with a smirk, followed by Tamara.

They join Nash up at the front. 'Tamara has it,' he announces. This is met by a barely concealed but extremely furious look from Ursula.

'Thank you for your assistance, Mr Nadeau,' Tamara says. Nash gives her a nod as he retreats to his seat. 'Anyway, let's continue, shall we?'

The meeting moves quite swiftly after that. Tamara clearly had prepared a list of topics to cover, and runs through them, making notes as she goes. The roads need clearing, but the weather forecast insists another load of snow is due that evening and there's no road grit in the area, so instead she organises a group to clear pavements in front of shops the next morning. Nash volunteers himself to do around the bakery and as far as he can, while the couple who run the Post Office and corner shop agree to do the lower half of the high street together.

'We'll rope our son in,' the shop's owner, Carl Watkins, says. 'I'll steal the power cable from his PlayStation, and he can have it back when he's done.'

'We also need to work out who is going to help man the community centre,' says Tamara. 'That will be me, of course, but are there any other volunteers?'

Shaz shoots her hand up. 'I'll have to go back and forth to my house, but I can definitely help with organising.'

Ursula raises a hand. 'Same.'

The hot drinks lady also gives a little wave.

'Good, between us we can take shifts so there's always some-one covering.' Tamara ticks something off the list in her hand. 'My next concern is the vulnerable members of the community and making sure that we aren't leaving anyone alone.'

Shaz raises her hand, and Tamara nods for her to speak. 'Myffy Evans has authorised for me to speak for her here. Her partner Mohan is stuck in London due to the weather, and one of her PAs was sick today and unable to visit, so she might need some extra help over the next few days. I'm sure there're a few people in a similar boat.'

Priti raises her hand. 'Yes, we should definitely try and find out if anyone's care needs are being dropped.'

Tamara nods and makes a note. 'Let's make that priority number one.'

'We're taking Myffy a care package this evening of easy meals,' says Christopher.

Priti turns in her seat to face Christopher. 'I'll come with you tonight if that's all right? I'm a nurse at Myffy's GP sur-gery. I can speak to her and see if I can get some emergency provision for her – it might be a quicker response from social services coming from me, but no promises. Either way, she might be happier to talk to me if there're any issues. I can always go and help, but I don't have a car.'

'Sounds great to me,' says Christopher.

Priti gives him a spindly thumbs up, and Shaz texts them both each other's phone numbers.

Tamara leads a discussion on plans to get groceries up to those who need it – luckily the corner shop is fully stocked with the usual canned necessities, but also bread and milk and butter, unlike the supermarket – as well as setting up a group of people to walk around and knock on doors. Using printed-out maps of the town that Tamara's office usually use for election canvassing, the group split up the town into zones for people to check on the residents.

'Everyone, wrap up warm. Please write down your phone numbers and emails here on the sign-up sheet before you go,' says Tamara. 'Right. Let's get going.'

The community centre very quickly feels like a real centre of operations. As the meeting ends, everyone helps to put away the chairs. In their place, people gather supplies on a couple of spare tables – first-aid kits, spare food from the little kitchen, and a fresh round of substandard tea and coffee. From one of the huge cupboards come a number of snow shovels, ancient-looking things that possibly haven't been used in years, and a selection of unmatched hi-vis vests and helmets.

Once things are set up, Christopher gets ready to leave and get cooking, but to his surprise, Nash dons a hi-vis waistcoat and helmet.

'I thought I'd clear around the community centre now before it gets colder and this stuff freezes under new snow. That's lethal.'

To his surprise, Christopher feels disappointed. He can see the logic in Nash helping out now, even if some small part of him feels aggrieved at the change of plans. They need to get cooking, don't they? Shouldn't *that* be the priority?

He shrugs the confusing feelings off, and nods. 'Okay. See you in a bit.'

Chapter Thirteen

Christopher

By the time he gets home, Christopher is almost grateful for a few minutes to himself, but the moment he gets inside the bakery, the notifications on his phone start buzzing again.

He scrolls through the main Spanks Squad group chat, mostly just nice messages from everyone hoping he's okay and asking him to check in. Clearly, his mother has told Kit that they've spoken, because there's a brief back-and-forth of irritation that he'd answered the phone to her but not his favourite people in the world. He's almost finished catching up on messages when a new set of notifications appears, from his separate group chat with Laurel and Ambrose.

> **Laurel:** Toph, who is that absolute dish in the photo with you?
> **Ambrose:** omg what
> **Laurel:** He got tagged in something on Facebook. Hang on.
> **Ambrose:** why are you on facebook??

What follows is a screenshot of a post in a group called *Pen-y-Môr Community Action* that includes a photo taken in the community centre while they were rearranging the main hall. In the background, Christopher can be seen carrying a stack of chairs. Next to him, with his back mostly to the camera, is Nash.

Christopher lets out a slow breath. It wouldn't be ideal if the entirety of Facebook, and perhaps the world, worked out that Nash Nadeau was here thanks to a well-meaning photo in a Facebook group. He must tell Nash, and perhaps have a word with Tamara, or whoever took the photo. He doesn't really know how to handle the privacy of a famous person but an accidental public photo leak seems avoidable.

> **Christopher:** How do you know he's dishy? He's not even facing the camera.
> **Laurel:** I don't need to darling. What a pair of peaches he's got.
> **Ambrose:** hahahahhhha
> **Ambrose:** wait i recognise those peaches
> **Ambrose:** christopher why the hell are you hanging out with nash nadeau??????
> **Laurel:** Who is that? I'm googling him.
> **Christopher:** Why do you think that's him?
> **Ambrose:** smart of you to try and deflect my incredible detective skills iphy
> **Christopher:** please don't start using that nickname again
> **Laurel:** Oh I hope it is him. He is very nice looking, isn't he?
> **Ambrose:** obviously i watched a bunch of the movies you told me to when i've been in the bath or bleaching my hair so i know the nash nadeau outline very well thank you
> **Ambrose:** SPILL
> **Ambrose:** is he gay

Well. Shit. Before Christopher can reply 'No' or at least 'I don't know', Ambrose has replied.

> **Ambrose:** i looked it up he is gay
> **Laurel:** It's quite concerning how quickly you did that darling.
> **Ambrose:** I have skills that can't be contained by the internet

Ambrose sends a full-length red-carpet photo of Nash wearing an elegant, sweeping jacket, which almost looks like a cloak, over a softly frilled white shirt and slim black trousers. He looks so different, so delicate almost. Something catches in Christopher's throat.

> **Ambrose:** he's not wearing a boring suit
>
> **Christopher:** Is that all you have to go on? He likes men because he's not in a boring suit?
>
> **Laurel:** It is still black darling.
>
> **Ambrose:** yeah because he works in the most heterosexual corner of the industry ever
>
> **Ambrose:** he can't exactly wear a David Wojnarowicz at the met gala yet
>
> **Christopher:** Who?
>
> **Ambrose:** we'll pick that back up later, because you will not distract me from this!!
>
> **Laurel:** Yes darling, irrespective of all this you haven't told us why you are hanging out with him in village halls.
>
> **Laurel:** In fact, is he around for long? Do you think he'd be willing to do a brand deal with us? Do you have his agent's contact details?
>
> **Christopher:** I don't have anything except an annoying man in my bed

This was obviously the wrong thing to say because his phone practically vibrates off the table with the number of messages Ambrose sends through. Christopher can just picture the devilish grin on their face.

> **Christopher:** ALONE HE IS ALONE! I am not in the bed with him.
>
> **Ambrose:** boo!!!!
>
> **Laurel:** Boo!
>
> **Christopher:** Nash rented out my flat for Christmas, and he got here just as everything went to hell, so now we're both stuck here. I let him have the bed seeing as he travelled from LA and needed the sleep.

The brief silence in the chat is broken by Ambrose sending strings of confused and excited punctuation. The pair of them are a demonic duo and know just how to wind him up. He just hopes they don't tell Kit and Haf before he can. Not that he needs to, really. There's nothing much to tell . . . right?

Ambrose: i think i'm dying

Ambrose: Iphy are you in an 'only one bed' situation with a film star and opting to sleep on the floor

Christopher: Couch actually

Laurel: Cheese and rice, Christopher. That sofa is far too small to sleep on! You'll ruin your back, and you're exceptionally grumpy when you don't get a good night's sleep.

Christopher: No I'm not.

Ambrose: you are

Laurel: You are.

Ambrose: I am going to walk to Wales and slap some sense into you. brb

Christopher: Why has iphy caught back on? I hate it.

Laurel: They're quite right, though. Isn't he the one you've been lusting over for weeks?

Christopher: I wouldn't say lusting.

Christopher: He is very attractive in person.

Laurel: I'm a bit concerned how quiet Ambrose has gone. Do you think they're really walking to you?

Christopher: Maybe we need to say something they can turn into innuendo to summon them back?

Ambrose: in your endo haha

Ambrose: don't worry, i've never voluntarily walked anywhere in my life

Ambrose: i was just looking up pictures of him

Laurel: I just realised you said he was very attractive, Toph.

Christopher: Sure, but he's an actor. It's like saying a painting is attractive.

Ambrose: i have never been attracted to a painting

Christopher: You know what I mean! Most people would find him attractive. It's stating the obvious.

Ambrose: beauty is but in the eye of the beholder

Laurel: That's very deep for you at this time of day.

Ambrose: i had a nap earlier

Christopher: I mean, he is very handsome. And he smells good, but I think that's just because he has rich people shower gel and perfume. It's probably easy to smell very good if you're rich.

Christopher: But he's very irritating. He threw flour over the bakery kitchen.

Ambrose: omg did you have a sexy food fight

Christopher: I was only wearing my underpants.

He's a little pleased with himself when Ambrose sends another string of capital letters and exclamation marks.

Christopher: But no. The man tried to make a set of weights out of bags of flour.

Laurel: That's very clever.

Christopher: Except that they exploded all over my kitchen

Laurel: All good ideas need a few drafts.

Christopher: He did fix my van which was slightly better.

Ambrose: a handyman who likes to work out and is also a buff actor??

Ambrose: christopher i need to know what is wrong with you, like clinically but also emotionally

Laurel: If you don't want him, we'll have him.

Ambrose: i'm not keen on sharing

Laurel: Fine, Ambrose will have him.

Christopher: I don't think we can just decide this on his behalf.

Laurel: Ask him then. You can gauge his interest. See if he fancies you as much as you do him.

Christopher: I do not fancy him.

Laurel: You did call him attractive and go through that whole tortured painting metaphor.

Ambrose: you don't have to be in love with him to take him to bone town

Ambrose: the bone zone

Ambrose: the city of bones, population you

Laurel: indeed

Ambrose: I'd like to indeed that

Laurel: What does that mean?

Christopher: It means that Ambrose is being very uncouth.

Ambrose: I'd like to couth him too

Laurel: I'm positive that's not a thing.

Ambrose: it is if you try hard enough

Christopher: I am not going to couth him and I'm blocking you both.

Ambrose: you know we're right

★ ★ ★

The one good thing about Ajaxing an entire kitchen is that it really does concentrate the mind. Christopher is on his second or third play of 'Washing Machine Heart' by Mitski when he admits the kitchen is cleaner than ever.

When he takes the bins out, he almost walks straight into Nash. He is leaning against the van, pink-cheeked from the cold and face sheened with sweat from the shovelling. It's probably just because of the conversation he just had with Ambrose and Laurel, but still, Christopher's stomach flips.

'You should probably watch where you're going. You were about to walk into a big patch of ice,' Nash says. Christopher's mind whirs too much for him to think of what to say, so Nash continues, 'No seriously, you were. Right there.'

In front of him is a bit of the drive that is often wet from drain overflow, which has frozen hard. 'Oh. Thanks.' Christopher sidesteps it and throws the trash into the bin.

'Are you going let me in now?'

'Christ, sorry! I forgot you don't have a key.'

A playful smile breaks across his face. 'Nah, I just got here, but it was funny seeing you panic.'

Christopher rolls his eyes, but still holds the door open for Nash to come through. *Be civil. Get the cooking done.*

Christopher watches Nash shiver as the warmth of the bakery hits his skin, and then as he leans against the tiny radiator he dried his clothes on only yesterday. How was that only *yesterday*?

'What were you up to while I was outside doing all the dirty work?' Nash asks, breaking Christopher out of his reverie.

'Cleaning up the rest of your mess in the kitchen so we can safely cook.'

'Oh come on, it can't have been that bad.'

Christopher resists rolling his eyes again, just about. 'It's a commercial kitchen, Nash. I have rules that—'

'I take back the warning I gave you about the ice. Can you go back over there and fall on it? Bonk that big head of yours?' Nash laughs, and Christopher is pretty confident he's going to sustain some kind of ocular strain from all the eye rolling that this man provokes in him.

In the kitchen, all the food is still laid out, though it has moved back and forth slightly with Christopher's cleaning.

'Come on, we need to get cooking. I've got some recipes drafted out so we should be good to get going. I just need to get some seasonings and bits from upstairs.'

'I'll get them,' says Nash, peering at the notes on the counter. 'I could do with putting on dry socks.' He disappears out of view.

But then Christopher hears Nash go halfway up the stairs and . . . stop?

Christopher wanders to the bottom of the stairs and looks up, where he sees Nash inexplicably crouching, as though about to pounce. Sensing his presence, Nash doesn't turn but waves down the stairs to Christopher, beckoning him closer.

'What are you doing?' Christopher whispers, because it seems like a situation that calls for whispering. 'I thought you wanted to work in a kitchen that had cat-swinging spatial capabilities.'

'Shh. It's funny you should say that,' Nash whispers.

Something is . . . crinkling?

Christopher slinks up behind Nash, and follows Nash's pointed finger to the kitchen where, on the table, where Christopher had left the bag of supplies, is, rather inexplicably, a cat. A sleek but very small black cat that he's pretty sure is a little too thin. He's always surprised by how small cats can be, expecting them to be as chunky as his parents' Border terriers, Stella and Luna, but this cat is *tiny*. It can't be much more than a kitten.

How did it even get into the kitchen?

Christopher is a little worried they might frighten it just by being there. The poor creature needs some lunch. There must be a can of tuna in one of the cupboards.

But before they can do anything, the cat spots them both, and, as it raises its little head, Christopher sees there's a half-eaten sausage protruding from its mouth. A sausage from the only pack they found at the supermarket and were saving for dinner.

'Christ!' says Christopher, clambering over Nash to rescue the sausages. The tiny thief slips as smoothly as an eel through a gap in a pushed-open window, sausage in tow.

The window had been closed when they left, but upon inspection, Christopher can see the latch must have loosened in the bad weather so the window doesn't actually shut properly. The cat would have only had to get a claw at the right angle to open it.

'I didn't even know cats liked sausages,' Nash murmurs, admiring the wreckage the cat had left behind. 'I guess that's not your cat then?'

'I don't own a cat, and no, I've never seen that one before either.' Christopher turns back to the table and sees that, in the time they'd been downstairs busying themselves, the cat had snuck in and snaffled three sausages.

'That makes tea a bit thinner, I'm afraid. Sorry. It's my fault for forgetting to put them in the fridge before we left with Shaz.'

'Well, it's cold enough in here that it would have been okay, if it wasn't for the cat. The others will be fine if we cook them thoroughly.'

'That doesn't seem very LA of you.'

Nash shrugs. 'I like to camp and do cookouts. What's a bit of dirt, what's a bit of cat saliva, etc., etc.'

'Many health and safety risks, I can tell you.'

'Worst case, I get food poisoning and get to sample your famous National Health Service.'

Christopher was too busy thinking to listen to what Nash was saying. Is the cat okay? Why was it sneaking into his house to eat table sausages? Raw, uncooked sausages, at that. It seems quite desperate. Though, there really aren't many birds or small mammals around at this time of year, especially with the weather being so bad. It must be hard to be a cat, if you're not getting fed enough.

What if it's not getting fed enough? What if it never comes back and it starves?

'Christopher? Hello?'

Snapping back to himself, Christopher breaks his gaze from the window. 'Sorry. Let's go.'

He picks up the seasonings from his cupboards, while Nash changes into dry clothes, and they finally meet back downstairs in the kitchen for the third time lucky.

On autopilot, Christopher gathers chopping boards and pans and gets to work on a bolognese first of all, so that it can slow-cook on the hob while they get onto the next bits. They work in companionable quiet, Christopher directing Nash, who takes instructions without a retort or comeback, while Christopher slowly melts down a soffritto in a large wide pan.

After a little while, Nash asks, 'Still thinking about that cat?'

Christopher feels his cheeks heat up. 'Yes. Just hope it's okay.'

He expects Nash to tease him, or to say something cutting back. To start up the usual back-and-forth. But instead, he gives him a lazy, lopsided smile and says, 'We'll keep an eye out for it. I'm sure it'll come back now it knows there's food here. It'll be okay.'

He feels a warm stirring in his chest. It's probably just the thought of seeing the cat again. *Probably*.

Nash gets started on the soup, a real broth of odds-and-ends vegetables that they can blend down later. As he's on such good behaviour, Christopher doesn't make a comment when Nash starts playing a Christmas playlist without asking. This is what Christmas was supposed to be like this year – cooking together and no fighting, except instead of a wayward film star, it was meant to be his sister and best friend.

At least the music is nice. He checks Nash's screen occasionally to see what's playing – pretty much a mixture of Wrabel, She & Him, a little from the Sufjan Stevens' Christmas albums. Calming, beautiful, perhaps a little bittersweet. It surprises him, honestly. Nash is always so bursting with energy that he was expecting pop punk or maybe even some genre of dance music that Christopher would have no idea what to call. Ultimately, something loud with a beat, something to burn all that fire with. But it's the opposite. It's music to curl up to.

Maybe it's okay that this might be all his Christmas is? After all, there's some food. There're some people he cares about, albeit not everyone . . . and there's Nash, for now.

Isn't that what Christmas is about? Though perhaps the visit-from-a-film-star aspect is not universal.

The air swims with the deliciously warming smell of the soup – bundles of thyme and sage and a few bay leaves harmonise with the freshness of lemon and ginger, and just the tiniest kick of heat from some dried red chilli flakes. It doesn't matter that the vegetables are a random mix of whatever they could raid from the frozen and canned aisles. With the right care, some good flavouring and patience, it all comes together.

Once he gets it going, the as-many-beans-as-possible chilli smells like comfort, too. He melts in some dark chocolate with a very high cocoa rate, cracking chunks straight in and watching it slowly succumb to the rest of the mixture.

It's not just the music that's relaxing him; it's the cooking. Sure, Best-Bet Vegetable Soup and Every-Bean-You-Can-Find Chilli aren't the same as the multi-hour-long process of proving dough and baking a loaf, or decorating a cake just right, but there's still that centre of peace he can find in himself.

'So,' he begins, 'other than escaping to Wales, which I presume isn't a tradition, what do you normally do for Christmas? Are you usually on holiday break on the 22nd?'

'Sometimes. Most of the time I'd be travelling home to my parents', in order to minimise the amount of actual time I spent there.'

'I'm sorry,' Christopher says, regretting that he asked this question because surely someone doesn't cross the Atlantic for a solo Christmas without there being something up.

'Oh, no they're fine, and we are fine. They love me a lot; we just don't have a lot in common. They've been supportive of everything my whole life, including the acting, and they were pretty good at making sure I was only on sets that were safe when I was young. But we just don't have that kind of close relationship.'

'Did they live in LA with you?'

'Yeah, for a while when I was still a minor. Sometimes it would just be one of them, while the other went back to Canada to work for a bit. They both moved back home permanently when I turned eighteen – I don't think LA was really for them. They're proud of me and what I've achieved, but I think they don't really know what to talk to me about, and when I try to make a wedge into their lives . . . Sorry, you don't want to hear this.'

'I asked,' Christopher says, meeting Nash's eyes.

'I'm sure you were asking politely, not fishing for awkward family stories,' he smiles, which of course is correct. 'Otherwise, I do a waifs-and-strays Christmas with my friends, many of whom are *actually* estranged from their family for, you know, queer acceptance reasons.'

Well then, perhaps Ambrose's suit theory was correct? Either that, or Nash just happens to have a lot of queer friends, as he's an actor. 'That's nice of you.'

Nash shrugs. 'No one wants to go home and be called the wrong name, or asked not remotely subtle questions about when they're going to conform to heterosexuality. So, we all just gravitated together instead. Though, we haven't managed to do that for a few years. I'm often on the PR circuit at Christmas, you know? What about you?'

'My ex-girlfriend Laurel's family throws a ball for charity at their house, and it's a huge affair with live music and food. And my mother, Esther, she runs the Christmas fête. Usually, I'd be there helping with set-up or trying to stop everyone from fighting each other.'

'Are you close with all your exes, or just her?'

Christopher laughs. 'There's no "all". It's literally just her.'

'Wow. Like, *just* her or . . . ?'

He can feel the blush heat up his cheeks. 'There've been dates, but no one else. Apart from my fake ex-girlfriend.'

'Sorry, your what?'

Oh. Had he not talked about this yet? 'Last year, Haf and I met at a party. Kissed under some mistletoe that looked sad.'

Nash sets down his ladle. 'Looked sad?'

'It made sense at the time. Anyway, Laurel was there, which I didn't realise, and she accidentally told everyone I was dating Haf. Well . . . we kind of told her we were dating. So then she joined us for Christmas, and that's how she and my sister Kit met.'

'Wait, so your sister fell in love with your fake girlfriend while you were still fake together?'

'Yeah . . . kind of.'

'How incestuous.'

'It is not.'

'All right then, how *weird*.'

Well, he can hardly argue with that. 'It worked out well. We're all close. I was going to stay with Kit and Haf for Christmas at their place in Yorkshire.'

'Wild. Where is this wife-swapping home town?'

'Oxlea. It's in the Cotswolds. Though, as far as I know, the latter isn't that common an occurrence.'

Nash snickers. 'That's not a real place.'

'It is.'

'Is it posh?' he says, adopting a British accent.

Christopher squirms. 'I mean. Yes? Haf described Laurel as "terrifyingly posh" when they first met—'

'A bizarre thing to say when you are pretty posh yourself,' he says, now in a bad impression of Hugh Grant, stuttering speech and all.

'I really hope you don't have British accents on your CV or whatever actors have, because really you are not very good at them,' Christopher says with a smile.

'To *your* ears. You wouldn't believe what we can get away with over there.'

'Oh, I can. I've seen enough attempts.'

'And yet none of my movies, apparently? How interesting,' Nash lightly muses. 'Hang on a moment. Your sister's name is Kit?'

'Yes?'

'But isn't that short for Christopher?'

'No, her name is Katharine.'

Nash rolls his eyes. 'I figured your parents didn't name you both Christopher, even if they did basically call you the same name but gender flipped.'

'It's not the same name,' Christopher says, feeling a little defensive. 'It's similar. We're just matching.'

'And who is the oldest one? Kit, right? So you're named after her? Maybe I should start calling *you* Kit.'

'Don't you dare.'

'Oh, I always dare a little, Calloway,' Nash says with a smirk. But still, he does drop it, which is a relief because talking about Kit made Christopher miss her desperately.

They go back to companionable cooking, and Christopher feels strangely light for sharing a little of himself with Nash. It's odd – they aren't friends, they aren't strangers. They just *are*.

Christopher's a little surprised that he can find that place with Nash in here. Usually, he's so nervous when people who aren't also professionally trained are around when he's cooking, even though he's not a chef himself. They always have questions or opinions, and that's totally fine, but it's just a different mode of cooking. It's not switching off.

If he's honest with himself, it's why he hasn't hired another baker yet to help him in the bakery. Tegan just helps on the tills and with the customers – and is great in this role – but he doesn't trust her to do the actual baking yet. He doesn't want to have to train anyone else on how to make his recipes, or how his kitchen operates. And she does take some of the pressure off him. Just none of the 'waking up in the early hours to get things started' reality of it all.

Plus, there's the precarious financial gamble of hiring someone else. As he cooks, he tries not to think about the energy costs of being here over Christmas that he hadn't factored in, the loss of all that flour, and all the many other things he wants to worry about.

For now, there's just cooking and acoustic Christmas music.

It takes most of the late afternoon to cook, cool and pack all the food up for everyone. All the containers are labelled with what food it is, cooking times and temperatures, and what date to use by if kept in the fridge.

All that's left is to get in the van to make the deliveries. Christopher texts Priti and Myffy to let them know that they're on their way as Nash loads up the truck with food. Shaz is just round the corner from the bakery, so they nip to hers first.

As they pull up at Shaz's door to drop off her shopping and some meals, Christopher realises that he's never actually been here before, though he knows where it is, obviously. After all, Shaz always comes to the bakery.

It's not Shaz who opens the door though, but Kathy.

'Hello there!' Christopher says cheerily. 'Merry Christmas.'

There's a pause before she returns the greeting.

'I'm just dropping off some shopping Shaz asked us to get. And there were a few meal things she wanted that were out of stock, so I just made them.'

'You made them?' she asks in a tone that suggests this is the worst possible option he could have taken.

'Yes? I made them.'

'You.'

'Yes?'

'Right. Are you waiting to be paid or something?'

Before the conversation can get even more awkward, the three piranhas thankfully appear, crowding around Kathy's feet.

'Did you bring us treats?' one of them yells, but Christopher isn't sure which because they circle and cross each other like a pile of puppies, constantly moving.

'Yes, did you?' cries another.

The pile of children starts chanting the word *treat* over and over in a way that is decidedly horror-movie adjacent, and Christopher decides that it's time to get out of there.

'No payment needed, it's fine,' he says, backing away slowly. 'Bye!' He jumps into the truck where Nash is waiting and slams the door behind him.

'You all right? You look like you've seen a ghost?' Nash says.

'No, not a ghost,' says Christopher, starting up the truck. 'Just a glimpse into Shaz's life. I'm going to bake her *so many* reindeer.'

They pick up Priti from her house on the next street over. Nash gets into the back of the van and straps himself into one of the fold-down seats, giving Priti the passenger seat. It doesn't take them too long to drive now that Christopher knows the way to Myffy's, where she greets them at the door as rosy-cheeked and sparkly-eyed as before. 'My helper elves! Come in, come in.'

While Priti and Myffy discuss her care needs in the living room, Christopher and Nash busy themselves with washing and drying the crockery that's piled up in the kitchen sink from earlier. There's a calm in this, too, Christopher realises. The domesticity. Helping people. Being part of a community. He's tired, sure, but he feels at peace, too. It's new for him, but he likes it.

'I'm going to stay over tonight,' says Priti, coming into the kitchen to relieve them of their duty. 'Myffy needs a little extra help, especially as she's been without her carers all day. She's got a spare bed so I'm set.'

'Just text us if you want us to come get you tomorrow,' Nash says.

Not wanting to overstay their welcome, they say goodbye to Myffy, who blows them both big air kisses in return, and head back to the van.

'That's all our deliveries done,' sighs Christopher contentedly as he gets back behind the wheel.

'All two of them,' laughs Nash.

'Thank you. For all your help today.'

'It was nice.' His voice is quiet, gone are the barbed edges. He must be tired, Christopher thinks.

They lock eyes briefly, and there's a moment where Nash rearranges his face and body, as though making himself look more like his normal self. It's strange.

'Let's get home. Onwards, driver,' Nash says, before Christopher can question it any longer.

Chapter Fourteen

Nash

The soft orange glow of the streetlights combined with the lull of the van's engine are enough to send Nash almost all the way to sleep. There's such a stillness here. It's just him, Christopher and the navy-blue sky peppered with stars. It feels like a dream.

He is tired. Really tired, and even though he's been clearing snow left, right and centre, he has been ruminating. He hates that. After all, that's what all the working out is for, apart from the Hollywood-prescribed hot-bod requirements: keeping his mind quiet.

All day, he's been so busy. The meeting, shovelling the sidewalks, the supermarket and helping Myffy. The cat. The flour incident. That was just today, somehow. It feels like the longest day of his life.

He feels overtired. Like a little kid who has done too much and it's so past their bedtime that they feel wired and half asleep all at once.

And the thing is, there is one specific thought he keeps mulling over – one that isn't the big, wider *what the hell do I do about my career* thought. And it probably has to be voiced. Especially given how tired he is. And there's a good chance that he's not going to be here just one more night.

Is he really going to talk about this? It's not something he brings up with strangers, or really anyone outside his need-to-know circle, but maybe Christopher technically falls into that category now, especially as he's somewhat responsible for him. His old therapist would tell him to just talk about it, but that doesn't make it any easier.

Often, in fact, talking about it has actually been the problem.

What if it becomes a problem? After all, they're in one small apartment together, or, well, one small van right now. Is now the right time? Maybe he should wait until Christopher isn't behind the wheel, but this way Nash doesn't have to look at him or read Christopher's reactions as he takes in his secrets.

But then again, after watching how Christopher is with people – awkward but well-intentioned and thoughtful – maybe it'll be different this time.

And if not, well, it can't be as bad as the last time. Worst case, he finds someone at the community centre to drive him somewhere. Anywhere.

The people he lives with always find out eventually, and he and Christopher are so constantly in each other's way that there's no way he's not going to see it unless Nash is really lucky. Plus, Christopher seems kind of oblivious to some things. But they should have a conversation. As much as he'd rather throw himself out the van before they do that.

He clears his throat and stares out of the window at the bright moon over the mountains.

'The answer is, I can't, by the way.'

'The answer to what?' Christopher asks, glancing over briefly.

'Whether I can drive. You asked me earlier.'

'Oh.' There's a little surprised tone in his voice. 'I thought LA was basically one massive road.'

'It is.'

'You didn't learn there?'

'Oh, I did.' It's hard to just say it and explain what he means, and he knows he's making it worse by going round the houses about it.

Beside him, Christopher frowns, clearly trying to work out if he's missed something in Nash's half-deliberate obtuseness. But credit to the guy, he doesn't ask any more, waiting for Nash to fill in the silence rather than adding more questions into the mix.

Nash breathes out slowly, feels the tension loosen under his diaphragm. 'I'm . . . legally not allowed to drive, and before you get all excited, there's no scandal or anything that resulted in me losing my licence.'

'I wouldn't even consider it. Not a single imagined road-rage incident or dramatically wrecked car from arguing with someone while they were driving.'

'Yeah, yeah,' he drawls, a little relieved Christopher is keeping this light. With his eyes set on the dark shadow of the peak ahead, he says, 'I have seizures. I didn't as a kid, that's how I learned how to drive, but when I hit my twenties, I kept getting these weird moments pretty regularly. And I fall into this helpful little sweet spot where they don't really know what's going on or why, and none of the medication we've tried works, so I just . . . have to manage them. Things like making sure I eat right and sleep enough and don't get too stressed out. It doesn't stop them from happening, but it stops me having so many.'

Nash braces himself for the usual barrage of questions, or slightly awkward statements. After all, most people's major touchpoint for seizures is in medical dramas when someone's going downhill fast. So few people seem to know anyone who just has seizures and lives with them. But, Christopher pauses. Takes a moment. Eventually, he says, 'That must be tricky, to manage with work and life, especially if the seizures take a lot out of you.'

This wasn't quite what he was expecting and, in fact, Nash is fairly sure no one has ever said this as the first response before. Usually, it's an apology, as though it was their fault or a major disaster, rather than a fact of his life that he has to live with. Or platitudes, yes, he's used to those. And there was that one time, a freakout about whether it was contagious – he's glad to not repeat that.

But this is . . . different.

Christopher is different.

'Why are you giving me that look?'

'Keep your eyes on the road, Calloway.'

'Then stop giving me weird looks!'

'I'm just . . .' Suspicious. Surprised. A little taken aback. Trying to work it all out. He doesn't want to say all that out loud. 'That was a very considerate response,' he says, finally.

It delights him a little to see Christopher huff. 'I'm very considerate. You shouldn't be surprised by that.' He looks like a fluffed-up chicken.

'Sure.'

'I *am*.'

'I don't think it counts if you insist on it. Plus, the brand of considerate you showed me the last thirty-six hours is more like . . . deeply irritating.'

'Excuse me?' Christopher says, but there's a tiny laugh and a smile caught in there.

He's relieved. These conversations usually go a different way. It's so tricky to be vulnerable about this that he usually resorts to humour and then people get weird about it. At least Christopher seems willing to meet him there. 'You know what I mean.'

'I do not.'

'The way you just like, lurk around asking me if I need things. That whole flapping thing you do.'

'I have just been trying to be hospitable in an unexpected situation!' Nash can still see the telltale sign of a grin in the corner of Christopher's lips. 'If I'm so *annoying*, then stop saying yes to things.'

'Why would I do that when you keep doing things for me?'

They both laugh, and when a quiet settles between them, it's not sharp or brittle. It's . . . comfortable.

'And you don't have be suspicious about my reaction, by the way,' says Christopher, using what Nash is starting to recognise as his serious voice. 'My sister is disabled, though she doesn't have seizures. She has this thing called a connective tissue disorder—'

'Oh, Ehlers-Danlos Syndrome, right?'

Christopher's eyebrows practically shoot up into his hairline. 'Yes. You're the first person I've met who knows what that is.'

'Eyes on the road please,' Nash reminds him. 'Yeah, a lot of people with EDS have some flavour of seizures too. Clearly, the support groups are a wealth of surprisingly useful info for conversations in cars with near-strangers.'

The jokes are a comforting place to return to, a nonchalant head space where he can pretend it's not a big deal. Being earnest is hard because it means being honest about his feelings and his life, and that's not something that Nash particularly likes to do. But he's taken the lid off now.

'Would it be helpful to tell me about them? Like, in case you have one while you're here, or feel unwell, and need some help?' Christopher asks.

Nash desperately tries to ignore the clutching feeling in his chest, and instead lets out a teenage-esque groan. 'I suppose so. But honestly, you probably won't notice.'

'I'm pretty sure I'd notice a seizure.'

'You apparently didn't notice your sister was in love with your fake girlfriend.'

'You weren't even there. And that's different.'

'Is it?' he teases.

Christopher parks the van in the drive, and they both stomp inside out of the bitter cold.

'Tea?' Christopher asks, and Nash nods as they wander upstairs to the flat.

★ ★ ★

It all feels so . . . terrifyingly normal. Domestic. And Nash hates to admit it, but he feels relaxed. Comfortable.

The flat is slightly warmer now the window isn't wide open, and outside the orangey sunset turns quickly to a dark purple. There's not enough light in this country, it turns out.

Beside him, Christopher pours hot water into the cups and stirs. He's quiet, perhaps still taking in everything Nash said to him in the car.

'No rogue cats this time,' Nash says.

'No,' Christopher adds a little sadly.

'We'll go looking tomorrow.' He's not sure why he promises this but Christopher looks so downtrodden and is being so nice that it slips out of him.

They walk into the living room and sit down at either end of the couch.

'So, you were saying they're not easy to notice?' Christopher ventures, blowing on the hot tea.

'Yeah, there's no shaking or anything really. I think that's what most people think of. Kurt, that's my agent, says I look like I've powered down, and before it happens, I get a bit slurry. He says I look like a rabbit in the headlights.'

Actually, what Kurt had said was that he looked like someone had brought up the concept of commitment to him, but that's a whole other side to Nash that he has no desire to get into right now.

'Do you know they're happening? Or are you totally out?'

'It's weird, like, no I don't know they're happening necessarily, but I guess my brain or subconscious does know something is going on. Sometimes I get auras – those are actually small seizures – so like I smell smoke that isn't there, or occasionally my vision will glitch, like someone knocked a few pixels out. It can be a little disorienting.'

'And what is helpful for you during, and afterwards?'

God dammit. Why does he keep saying all the right things? This conversation is already excruciating to have with a near-stranger, but the fact that Christopher is responding the *exact way* that Nash always hopes people will is killing him. Not Kermit. Not this giant posh flappy anxious weirdo *getting it*. Nash outright refuses to feel squishy and cared for by this gigantic locust man.

Except, he does. There's the tingle in his chest. Respect. Care. Being treated like a person who matters. A feeling that he hasn't felt in so long outside work because he's kept people away, not least because so many of them run screaming about it being too serious for them. Or they did what Stefan did. After all, that's why he has barely dated for years. One of a few reasons, at least. He shivers and pushes those memories back away. He might be willing to lay out the intricacies of his disability to Christopher but . . . that? No. No, he never wants to talk about that.

'Don't call an ambulance unless it's been like five minutes, and you should time it to make sure if you can. Just let me ride it out, and make sure there's nothing I can hurt myself on. Then when I'm back, get me, like, a Snickers, and a drink of water. The seizures might be quick and look like nothing but they can knock me out for a day, maybe two if I'm really unlucky. I just need to sleep it off after.'

'Okay. Just Snickers, or is any chocolate bar suitable?'

'Just something in that vibe,' he sighs, pretending to be exasperated but it's hollow. He feels the need to act out, to spark up that back-and-forth, but Christopher just won't bite now. He doesn't want to outright yell *come on, argue with me* because that's weird behaviour, but part of him really does. This vulnerability is like an uncomfortable costume, itching at his skin.

'It doesn't have to be exactly the same thing. Just some kind of sugary salty snack. I don't even know if our Snickers is the same as your Snickers anyway.'

'Noted.' No *I'm just trying to help*, or anything like that. The man just takes Nash's stinky little attitude, even when he's putting it on, and swallows it, and the worst part is, it's making that tingly feeling grow more. They need to have a fight so he can dispel it, remember how annoying he is.

How annoyingly *nice* he is.

All the talk of Snickers reminds them that they haven't actually eaten anything for dinner yet. Given the cat already opened the packet, they decide on the remaining sausages fried up to make mustard-laced sandwiches. With a hot tea, it is somehow exactly what Nash needed. It's the sort of thing he craves after a seizure, really – carbs, protein, and some sugar. Comfort food that replaces all the energy he's lost into the void.

Nash silently volunteers to wash up, while Christopher dries and puts things away. It's quickly become an alarmingly domestic kind of evening. It's nice but a little unnerving. A little too familiar, maybe.

'Perhaps we should get an early night,' Christopher says, glancing at his watch. 'I'm bushed and you must be too.'

'I'm bushed,' laughs Nash in his bad impression of Christopher. 'You're what? A bush? Are bushes known for being tired here? All your topiary is wilting from exhaustion?'

Thank God. That feels better. It feels as if some of the hot energy got let out of him.

'All right, fair. I guess that one doesn't make sense.' Christopher gets up to grab his pile of blankets from the other side of the room.

And before he realises what he's saying, Nash hears the following words come out of his mouth. 'We should just share your bed.'

Christopher's entire face immediately goes bright red. Oh good, he's being weird about it.

'Calm down. I just mean, I don't take up all the bed, and it's silly for you to try and sleep on that couch again. You look like an adult trying to sleep in a kid's bed. It can't be comfortable. And seeing as you're the designated driver in this partnership,' – he tries to ignore the hitch in his chest at that word – 'I'd rather you were well rested so that you don't, you know, murder us both on the tiny roads here.'

Still red, Christopher ponders this, gnawing at his bottom lip.

'We can do a line of pillows down the centre if you're that worried,' Nash sighs, walking to the bedroom.

'That's not necessary. I've shared a bed before.'

Nash swears he can hear the gulp in Christopher's voice.

'Good for you.'

He splutters. 'With Haf, I was trying to say. Platonic bed-sharing.'

It's kind of cute how embarrassed this man gets about sharing space. Maybe what Nash needs is to take back some of the power this evening. He's been vulnerable and talked about all the seizure stuff. And clearly this sharing a bed business bothers Christopher in a way that Nash doesn't want to explore *too* deeply.

So instead, he whips off his jumper.

And with it goes his shirt.

It's amazing to see someone's skin change colour so rapidly, but Christopher's cheeks morph from their already slightly embarrassed strawberry pink to scarlet red.

And he practically throws himself into the bathroom, yelling a series of words that Nash is pretty sure were about brushing his teeth.

Holding the jumper to his mouth, Nash cackles loudly. That was worth it. If he's honest with himself, Nash kind of likes how nervous he can make Christopher.

It's . . . kind of cute.

Chapter Fifteen

Christopher

Once he's safely ensconced in the bathroom, several thoughts run through Christopher's head at once.

The first is whether it's possible for a person to safely live in a bathroom for several days, just long enough for the snow to melt and for Nash to leave. Sure, there's no food and sleeping in the bathtub is going to be hell, but he could put up with that. Of course, it's a one-bathroom flat, so unless Nash is going to have flannel washes in the café bathroom, there's going to be some serious logistical issues with this plan. But he can't face him again. Not after the way he just sprinted away from him.

The second thought is, how can a person go quite so pink? Is it some kind of heinous medical condition he wasn't aware of, or is it, as he fears, just a side effect of being a total dork. His cheeks are aflame, and the heat runs down his whole body – twitchy and nervous and horrible. And that was just from a torso!

A normal, nice torso.

Well, not *nice*. And not *not* nice either.

Christ.

It's not as if it's the first time he's ever seen a guy topless, for heaven's sake. He's seen plenty of bare torsos in his time – during rugby at school and also any time he's been near a pool or a beach. Or whenever the temperature in the UK gets over 25 degrees, when all the *topless-but-still-wearing-jeans* men seem to appear from nowhere, ready to baffle everyone in their wake.

However, this is, admittedly, the first time there's been a topless person other than himself in this flat.

In his *bedroom*.

About to get into his bed.

And let's be real, Nash isn't just any old person for him. Christopher is pretty sure he's had several dreams that started out with Nash stripping off...

Oh God.

He's been in the bathroom so long that there's a distinct possibility that Nash is now de-trousered on the other side of the door. Just the thought of Nash in his boxers is doing something strange to Christopher. His body feels like a box of shaken frogs – confused, wriggling, slightly . . . no. Get a grip.

Or, he could be completely naked – though it would be slightly weird for him to just be standing in the middle of the room, totally starkers. But then again, what if he sleeps naked?!

Surely he wouldn't if they had to share . . . that wouldn't be proper. And Nash might be somewhat uncouth on occasion, but he's not *weird*. He wouldn't just spring nakedness on Christopher.

That is, unless he thought it would be a very good joke. Christ.

The cold water he splashes on his face practically evaporates the moment it hits his skin. What the hell is he going to do? He needs to calm down. Get a grip, or get a hold of himself. He needs help.

And for some – probably rather daft – reason, he goes to Ambrose and Laurel.

Christopher: Mayday. I think. Help.

Ambrose: what did you do

Christopher: Nash kindly suggested that we should share a bed because the couch is too small for me to sleep on, which I did last night and he's not wrong it was horrible.

Ambrose: yeah you should
Laurel: I agree!
Christopher: Well I'm freaking out!!
Laurel: I thought you weren't interested in him. How's this any different from sharing with Haf?

Well. She has him there. It was so different with Haf, because despite their two occasions of kissing – one terrible snog that started the whole confusing mess off, and one pretend but arguably quite good kiss to keep up the charade – they just weren't attracted to each other in that way. It was more that she was another half of him, and he of her.

And the reason he's not texting her about this right now is that she would be even more overexcited about this than Ambrose and Laurel. And telling her means sort of telling Kit, and he's not sure he wants to talk to his sister about the potential pitfalls of sharing a bed with a man he might be attracted to.

Ambrose: i bet he doesn't bear hug in his sleep like haf does
Ambrose: it's like sleeping in a vice
Christopher: I'm not interested, so to speak. He's an actor and I'm only human. It's his literal job to be handsome.
Laurel: So you agree that he's handsome?
Ambrose: hahahahah
Christopher: I came here for moral support :(
Ambrose: hahahaha
Laurel: Toph, just put your big pants on, and go get in bed with that man. If you don't want to do anything, you don't have to do anything! It's very simple darling.
Christopher: I've never slept over with a guy before without the sex part. It just feels like a big deal and I'm not sure why.
Laurel: I have a few ideas hehe
Ambrose: oh no you're having a gay panic
Ambrose: this is so cute

Christopher: I'm not.

Christopher: Maybe a small one?

Laurel: I assure you it's not that different from sharing a bed with anyone else. It'll be like when I stayed over all the time.

Christopher: We were dating! That's my point!!!

Laurel: Darling, you were able to restrain yourself from jumping my bones every night, so I'm sure you can do the same with Nash Nadeau for one night.

Ambrose: did you just say jumping my bones

Ambrose: im dying

Ambrose: please, my bones, they are very sick

Christopher: I know, but it's not just one night. It'll be every night until he leaves if we set the precedent now.

Ambrose: Christopher. I'm going to be really serious for a second. Look I'm using capitals and everything.

Ambrose: Are you listening?

Christopher: Yes.

Ambrose: do you have lube

Christopher: I hate you.

Laurel: It's an important question darling.

Christopher: An irrelevant one! I'm not planning on having sex with him!! That's the whole point! I'm just!!

Laurel: Unless the opportunity arises because darling I think you should take it. Bonk the man of your Hallmark dreams!

Ambrose: get some get some

Christopher: I don't think he's interested even if I was, which to be clear I'm not!

Ambrose: well he should be! have you seen yourself, you're a hot little slice

Laurel: Americans love a Brit. It's the accent.

Christopher: He's Canadian

Laurel: I'm sure they love it too

There's no way he's going to do anything with this man. It's more that, well, the spectre of it all hangs over him. The *idea* of what could happen. It's been so long since he was intimate with anyone, even longer since it was someone he wasn't just letting off steam with.

He needs to get himself together. After all, this is probably all in his head and they're right, he's quite possibly making a bigger deal out of this than he needs to. And Nash must not think anything of it, else he wouldn't have suggested it, right?

These are the sorts of sensible things Kit and Haf probably would have said to him. In hindsight, he probably should have swallowed the shame of hitting up his sister for advice.

With a few deep breaths in and out, he imagines himself rolling out croissant dough. A triangle rolled up becomes a delicious layered laminated curl. The smell of butter and warmed pastry. The milky coffee he'd have with it. All of these images and smells fill his brain, and while they don't quite push out all the wriggling thoughts and feelings, they shrink them. They're pushed aside just enough for him to breathe them out. Or bake them into the imaginary pastry.

Time to be normal, he tells himself. Time to get ready for bed. It's just a normal day, a normal getting-ready-for-bed. Nothing to worry about. There's nothing different about tonight.

And just as he's very almost convinced himself of this, there's a knock on the bathroom door.

'Are you okay in there?'

'Do you mind? It's the bathroom,' he replies haughtily.

'Right, and I need to use it too. Just wanted to make sure you hadn't fallen in.'

'I'll be out in a minute,' he grumbles, and all the wild, wriggly feelings worm back in as he brushes his teeth a little too vigorously.

Just to be polite, he decides to put on some deodorant. After all, no one wants to share a bed with someone who smells as if they've been stress-sweating for the last ten minutes (which he has). It's just courtesy.

He puts on some moisturiser too. Just for good measure.

There are only so many ablutions he can do before it swings towards actively *making yourself look nice*, so Christopher calls it a day and instead cleans up the mess he's made, takes a deep breath and steps out into the bedroom.

And almost crashes right into Nash who is standing just on the other side of the door, leaning on the door frame. He's still topless, but thankfully not trouserless.

'Christ, sorry,' Christopher says as they both stumble away from each other. 'I wasn't expecting you to be listening in.'

'I really need to pee, so was coming to ask you to get out.' Nash rubs his forehead where Christopher's chin had bashed him.

'Sorry about that.'

'Can you move? I still need to pee.'

'Sorry!' Christopher squeaks, as he squeezes out of the way so Nash can use the bathroom.

All this means that he's then standing uselessly in the middle of his bedroom.

Keep it together. Just put on some pyjamas.

God knows where last night's pair went after he overheated in the blanket mound, and instead of faffing about looking for them, he decides to just put on a nice pair of button-up flannel pyjamas that his mother bought him for Christmas last year. After all, he's not getting new Christmas pyjamas this year, so these will have to do. He undresses and redresses at lightning speed, lest Nash catch him in his pants again – it was bad enough the first time, but somehow now would feel even more mortifying. But once he's dressed, he doesn't really know what to do next.

Should he get into the bed? Or is that a bit too suggestive, like he's waiting for him? Plus, he hasn't asked if Nash has a side preference and seeing as Nash's stuff is on both bedside tables, he can't infer either. Perhaps he just sleeps right down the middle. Either way, if Christopher gets in first he might be forcing him to sleep in the wrong place and that seems rather rude seeing as Nash invited him to share.

He's dithering, but his mind keeps whirring. And before he can make a decision, Nash leaves the bathroom, and dives onto the left side of the bed, pulling the duvet up over his chest to right under his chin. And, as though this wasn't a big deal, he just starts flicking through something on his phone.

Maybe it *isn't* a big deal to him at all.

Everything he does seems at once so intentional and also without hesitation or thought or worry. What must that be like? Christopher's brain is still whirring, and yet he hasn't moved an inch.

'Are you getting in? Your hovering is weirding me out,' Nash murmurs.

'Oh, err, sorry,' Christopher mumbles, abandoning the plan he was conjuring up to busy himself in the kitchen to put off the next step.

'Stop apologising too.'

'Right. I'll take this side then.' He folds back the duvet on the right-hand side, and sits down on the sheet, his feet on the floor. It's an improvement from standing awkwardly by the bed, at least. All he has to do is swing his legs up and lie down, and that's it.

Simple.

He'll just lie down next to an extremely attractive man in his bed.

This is fine.

Except, what if their feet touch when he does that? What if he's too close to Nash when he lies down and they both feel weird? How close to the edge of the bed should he be?

'Would you prefer to be on this one?' Nash asks, which sends alarms in Christopher's head blaring before he realises Nash is asking if they need to swap sides of the bed.

'No, this is fine. It's my usual side anyway.' This is a lie, of course. He normally sleeps on the left, but he's not going to say that now.

With a big sigh, he lies down under the covers. This is fine. They're not touching at all – thankfully Christopher's bed is wide enough for them both. But he can definitely feel the warmth of Nash's body.

Christopher is so tall that his feet stick out the end of the bed, which is unfortunately normal and he's grown used to sleeping with cool toes. But he hadn't banked on the fact that Nash is a bit of a duvet hog. Not only is it pulled up against him, but he's tucked it around himself, forming a neat little cocoon that leaves little for Christopher to manoeuvre with. There's a cold strip running down the length of his body where the duvet doesn't reach the mattress.

He tugs a little on the duvet but it holds fast. Another tug, and a wriggle, and still, nothing.

'Could you possibly cede some of the covers,' he sniffs, tugging once again.

'You've got more than enough.'

'I do not. I'm barely covered.'

'Yes but that's because you're freakishly long and not because I'm using more than my fair share,' says Nash from the other side of the bed, where he is almost certainly hogging over fifty per cent of the duvet.

'You are. You're not even that big and you're hogging it.'

'Maybe you're just not used to sharing.'

'Or maybe you're just bad at it.'

Nash groans and sits up to assess the situation. 'Christopher. The reason the duvet is barely covering you is because you've left a gulf the size of the Mariana Trench between us. Stop being a weirdo, lie on the bed normally, and the blanket will fit.'

Annoyingly, Nash isn't wrong. This is worse than Christopher thinking that Nash was just a selfish bed mate, because it means *Christopher* is being weird, and it's becoming *a thing*.

'Fine. Sorry.'

'Stop saying sorry.'

He shuffles sideways under the covers; the radiated heat gets stronger and stronger.

Until they make physical contact. They both jerk back, as though electrocuted by the touch.

'I said get closer, not get on top of me,' groans Nash, and Christopher can feel himself going deep maroon again.

'Goodnight!' he practically shouts, rolling over onto his side with his back to Nash. He leans over to the table on his side and flicks off the light. Now, only the lamp on Nash's side lights the room in a dusky orange glow.

'Night,' Nash sighs with exasperation, but Christopher swears there's a smile in there. There's a curve to his words, a softness.

But he doesn't settle down to sleep and the light is still on. From the small movements behind him, it seems as if he's still up reading things on his phone.

'I thought you were going to go to sleep?' murmurs Christopher after about ten minutes.

'Weren't you?'

'Clearly I'm attempting to.'

'I'll attempt you in a moment.'

Christopher rolls onto his back. 'What does that even mean? What are you doing anyway?'

'None of your business.' But after a beat he adds, 'Emails.'

'It's quite late.'

'Not in LA.'

'Is everything all right? Don't they know you're on holiday? Or is this an American work culture thing?'

'Eh, kinda, yes and probably also that.'

He wants to pry. And he also wants to take the phone and fling it away from Nash, especially now that he knows that sleeping is important to keeping his seizures under control. Which, now that he thinks about it, is probably why he just disappeared off to bed last night and was quite blunt. Obviously it's not Christopher's fault for not knowing, but he feels a bit bad about judging him so harshly now that he knows he was just looking after his brain. It must be pretty tricky to manage, after all.

But before he can find a way to suggest Nash settles down in a non-irritating, non-overbearing way, Nash says, 'Sorry. Do you want me to turn the light off?'

'No, it's fine.' And with a gulp of breath he adds, 'But maybe you should go to sleep? We've probably got another busy day coming up tomorrow.'

'All right, Mother.' Nash might growl at this, but he does set his phone down on the table and flick the light off.

Christopher rolls back over onto his side, facing the wall. 'I'm not your mother.'

'Thank God. Else this would be really weird.'

'But . . . you did come here to escape or relax or whatever, and it's hardly been that. And as we've probably got another big day tomorrow, you probably need your beauty sleep.'

He hears Nash grumble something about beauty sleep, but soon his soft breaths give way to light snores.

As they both settle down to sleep, Christopher can't help but think about how nice it is not to be alone up here. To have someone else with him. He really had been lonely. And that's probably the only reason why he's thinking about it, and noticing how close Nash is to him.

Definitely.

Sometime later, Christopher stirs from a dreamful sleep filled with gingerbread and reindeer and so much snow. When he opens his eyes, he finds himself facing Nash. In the night, they must have both rolled over in their sleep, and now their faces are close, so close that he can taste Nash's sweet breath.

It's as if they've been drawn to each other. Perhaps, in a way, they were. Not just in this bed but in a broader, cosmic sense. Christopher isn't one for superstition necessarily, other than enjoying blaming things going wrong on Mercury being retrograde and his and Kit's annual tradition of a Christmas wish, but he can't deny this whole situation feels . . . not magical, but *created*.

What a coincidence it is for Nash to be here in his bed when, for the last few months, he's been watching Nash act out so many magical stories on his tablet. And as much as he protested to Laurel and Ambrose about whether he's interested in Nash, he's undeniably attracted to him. There's something chemical. A spark that sometimes shocks, but maybe it could thrill too.

Part of him wants to stay here, capture this moment where this beautiful gremlin of a man is quiet and at peace, rather than frustrating the hell out of him. But sleep drags him back under. And, without either of them knowing, as they are too deeply asleep to truly feel it, their hands intertwine.

Chapter Sixteen

Christopher

When Christopher awakes, he's alone. The sheet is still warm to the touch on Nash's side, so he must have got up recently. Hopefully, Nash managed a good long sleep. From the growing sunshine outside, Christopher seems to have, and he definitely feels better for it.

As if summoned by his thoughts, Nash wanders back into the room, steaming cup of tea in hand and a paperback from Christopher's shelf under his arm.

'Oh, you're awake,' he says.

'Yeah I just woke up. Did you sleep okay?'

'Yeah thanks. I needed it.'

Good, thinks Christopher. *Good*.

Nash sets the cup down on top of the bureau with the book, which turns out to be *The Moon of Gomrath*.

'I didn't take you as a fantasy reader.'

'Oh, yeah. Loved that stuff as a kid. I decided to challenge myself by picking the most ridiculously named book on your shelf.'

'You missed *The Weirdstone of Brisingamen*.'

'I swear you're making that up. That cannot be an actual book's title.'

'I'm not. It's a real book by the same man, Alan Garner.'

'Well, either way, I guess I'm about to learn some exciting new British words.' He sits down on his side of the bed and pulls the cover up over his lap.

It's strangely intimate, perhaps even more so than sharing the bed to just sleep, because now they're choosing to share the same space.

Before Christopher can ponder that further, Nash says, 'Thanks for nagging me last night. I'm finding it hard to switch off from some work stuff, so on this occasion, it was appreciated.'

'You're welcome.'

Nash gives him a heavy-lidded look that Christopher can't translate, but doesn't say anything else for a few beats. Eventually, he says, 'Where did you get those pyjamas? You look like Kevin McCallister.'

Christopher huffs. 'You're the blond one here.'

'All right then, you look like a child from some kind of period drama. Or Christopher Robin.'

'That's who I was named after.'

'Of course you were.'

'My mother bought me them last Christmas,' he admits. 'We always do Christmas pyjamas.'

A pleased grin spreads across Nash's face. 'Oh, that's far too easy. Want anything?'

Christopher ignores the churn in his stomach. 'Make me a tea?'

'Okay. I'll make breakfast too, so we're fuelled up for the day.'

'That's kind of you.'

One thing he's quickly learning about Nash is that he takes compliments and criticism similarly – always with a little dose of snark in return. If he were a cat, the fur on his back would bristle. He mumbles something that sounds like 'No problem' mixed with 'Whatever.'

Christopher reaches over to the bedside table for his phone and checks the time. It's late for him, though still very early in the day. Normally, he'd be putting loaves in the oven having proved them for hours, ready for them to be served hot and fresh when the bakery doors opened. It's a Saturday, too, so prime for people popping by doing their shop or heading down to the beach. It feels weird to be in bed this late. He misses the routine of a day running the bakery, as much as the lie-in is nice.

First thing they should do today is check in at the community centre so that Tamara can direct them.

He gets out of bed with a stretch, and when he opens the curtains he sees another fresh layer of snow has fallen over the town. It's no deeper than before, but it's no better either. Just to be sure, he runs through the various transportation and weather websites he's been repeatedly checking over the last few days. The roads are being cleared in some places, but there's still a very clear *do not drive unless there's a serious emergency* warning in place due to black ice across the whole country. The trains are still a mess, and only a few lines down south are running a very small timetable. Everywhere else is frozen over. And obviously no planes are going either.

It looks as if Nash is going to be stuck here through Christmas, and perhaps it's better if they accept that now, rather than carry on with the pretence that he's just staying one more night, just one more night.

He fetches his suitcase from the living room, where the majority of his clothes still are, and puts on a clean navy shirt paired with some nice, but admittedly not particularly warm, chinos. December 23rd feels ever so slightly too early to break out the Christmas jumper, but he opts for a Christmas-adjacent Fair Isle red-and-white knitted jumper.

On the side table, his phone buzzes.

Kit: Hey, can you message us back, maybe in the group? I know you've checked in with Laurel and Ambrose, but I'm just a bit worried about you, and you know how I hate it when I must feel something. X

Well, that sounds as if Ambrose and Laurel haven't spilled the beans on his accidental lodger. That's one big conversation he needs to have today, but there's a bigger one he needs to get over and done with first, with said lodger.

He finds Nash in the kitchen standing at the hob, where he is heating up one of the big cast-iron pans, a square of butter swirling in the middle like molten gold. He wears one of Christopher's aprons over a thick knitted cardigan, the sleeves rolled up almost to the elbow, revealing the soft golden hair and unseasonal tan on his forearms. Or, presumably, seasonal for LA, where they don't seem to actually have seasons. Though to be fair, he's quickly learning that Wales doesn't have many – there's the cold rainy season and then, apparently, the warm rainy season, which he is supposed to look forward to.

'Nice sweater,' Nash says.

'Jumper. But yes, thank you. An old Christmas present from Laurel.'

'I'm making pancakes. American style, I can't do the crepe thing. You want?'

'Yes, thanks.'

He slides a cup of tea across the counter towards Christopher.

'I thought I'd better get you full of breakfast and caffeine if we're going to be driving around and cooking all day.'

'Careful, Nash, or you'll have me thinking you're *considerate*,' Christopher says with a smile, hoping it reads as a callback to last night. He can't be sure though, because Nash just looks kind of blank this morning. 'Do you need any help?' Christopher adds, when Nash responds with nothing.

Nash picks up the jug of batter and waggles it. 'No thank you. I can make pancakes just as good as you, Mr Professional Baker.'

Christopher watches as the batter slips into the pan, forming perfectly fat little circles. 'Unless they're crepes, of course,' Christopher retorts.

'Hmm, I've changed my mind. No pancakes for you.'

Christopher laughs. 'I might have some bits for toppings in the freezer, so I'll make myself useful and get those out. But I promise not to interrupt the delicate art of gently frying batter.'

'I'll allow it.' Nash tips the first pancake onto a baking sheet and slides it into the warm oven.

That's about as effusive a yes as he can expect from Nash, so Christopher busies himself gathering ingredients. From the cupboard, he finds an old slightly sticky bottle of maple syrup that prompts Nash into a disgruntled 'You call that syrup?', and in the bakery downstairs, he finds some chocolate for shavings, and icing sugar, and manages to retrieve a bag of frozen blueberries from the chest freezer. He doesn't usually use frozen, but they were cheap and good for making a sauce or ensuring he occasionally eats some fruit. He also finds some wrinkled lemons in his fridge in the flat – they might not have much juice in them, but there'll be just enough to make a nice compote.

'Are you particularly hungry?' asks Christopher, as he sidles up next to Nash at the hob to mix up the sugar, blueberries and lemon juice in a pan. On the countertop are multiple vats of pancake mix.

'Yes, why?'

'Just a lot of batter.'

'Well, it's not all for us, is it?' Nash says, clearly a little exasperated. 'I thought we could make some spares for anyone who wants some. They're quite good if you cool them down and wrap them up quickly so they can't go stale. And easy to heat up in the toaster.'

'Well. That's me told,' Christopher says, feeling the tips of his ears heat up with embarrassment. Christopher hates it when their gentle teasing reveals that Nash is actually doing something nice for someone else. If he's honest with himself, he likes the sparking back and forth, just a little.

The blueberries give into the heat, the juice releasing from them into the sugar and lemon, sending up a heavenly, zingy smell into the air.

He searches for something normal and casual to say and lands on, 'Happy twenty-third of December.'

'Is that its own holiday here? Like Boxing Day?'

'Sadly not.'

'Maybe we can make it one. Pancake day.'

'Oh, we have one of those already. You know, the day before Lent. We all eat pancakes for dinner.'

'Oh yeah, I think we used to do that as a kid in Canada. It's been way too long. The US don't really have it. We'll have to come up with something special for the twenty-third in this fascinating country I appear to be stuck in.'

'Ah, yeah. So, we should talk about that.'

Nash groans as he adds another short stack into the oven to keep warm.

The hairs prick up at the back of Christopher's neck. 'God, it's not that bad is it?' He didn't mean to say it out loud, though he did think it, and it came out all sharp and sulky like . . . what? Like they're *friends* and Nash has upset him? Nash doesn't owe him anything.

To Christopher's surprise, Nash holds up his spatula in a gesture of peace. 'It's not about you. Sorry, I'm just . . . there's some work stuff going on I need to deal with, and being here with the time difference makes it much harder.'

Heat gathers around Christopher's collar, but all he can get out is a small nod.

'From what I can tell, there's no chance I'm going to get out of the UK until after Christmas,' Nash continues.

'You can stay here,' Christopher blurts out. 'Obviously.'

'Obviously,' Nash repeats, as though it actually was not obvious. Then he changes his tone, 'Thank you. That's very kind,' he says, stiffly. 'Any way I can repay you, I will. Please just say.'

Still trying to find the middle ground between snapping and blurting, Christopher reverts back to his usual tight little nod. He swears he wasn't always like this, sharp and a little spiky and uncomfortable, but maybe he was? Maybe he spent so long pretending that he was fine, that he was coasting along the middle ground of quiet acceptance, that he couldn't pretend anymore and things started to unravel. In his heart, he knows that's probably in part the truth of it all. It's something he hasn't wanted to look at directly – that part of him that knows he finds the people-ing much harder than some of his friends seem to, and the way he habitually closes himself off when he gets too afraid of what random reaction is going to spill out of him.

'I think,' he begins slowly, feeling his way through the words, 'I think helping me help other people would actually help me.'

'That was a lot of *helps*, but I think I follow.'

'Are you sure you slept enough?' Christopher says, swerving the conversation away from logistics for now. They can pick it up later when he feels less like a barely held together ball of anxiety. 'I always thought I was an early riser but you always seem to beat me.'

'I think that's the jet lag, but yeah. Once I'm awake, I'm up. I find it hard to just sit still,' he admits, pouring the last of the batter into the pan. 'It's why acting works for me because there's always something to learn or I have to be up early in make-up, or doing press or whatever. Someone's always telling me where to go.'

'That sounds exhausting.'

'It is, but I think I thrive off it a little.'

While the compote slowly cooks down, Christopher sets the table for two. Once everything is ready, Nash piles up two short stacks of pancakes, topped with icing sugar and deliciously sweet blueberry goodness. It's a weirdly domestic situation, sitting here with him, eating pancakes. Really good pancakes, at that.

'Have you heard anything from Christmas HQ?' Nash asks, and when Christopher gives him a confused look adds, 'The town hall? Shaz.'

'Oh. I haven't checked my texts yet. Sorry, I thought you were asking if I'd had a message from Santa.'

'And have you?'

'Not this year.'

'Pity. Feel like he might have some philosophical insight into this deeply weird situation. Anyway, we should probably go be good helper elves and head over to the town hall after we've eaten.'

'Community centre.'

'Right, this place is not big enough for the *town* part.'

'It's a good thing your pancakes are delicious. And yes, I just need to check in with my sister before we go. I think she's a bit worried I'm ignoring her.'

'And are you?'

That throws him. Well, he's not *not* ignoring her. But the missing them and the whole Nash of it all means that there's a big conversation to be had when he finally does get in touch. 'Maybe a little,' he admits.

'I should probably speak to my agent too. I am avoiding him.'

'Perhaps we can be brave and face them both.'

Nash laughs. 'Oh, it'll take more than a pact over pancakes to psych me up for that call.'

He says no more, and Christopher still feels a little strange about probing given the whole *I know your entire film catalogue* of it all. Though, he does wonder what has got Nash all tangled up.

Full of sugar and pancakes, they clean down the kitchen, once again in companionable silence, but moving in a gentle rhythm around each other. Nash packs away the remaining pancakes, and Christopher puts them in the fridge to keep them fresh.

It's strange how in sync they are here even though Nash has only been here two days. *How has it only been two days?* And, given it's almost Christmas, he's going to be here at least three more nights. Maybe even longer.

'I didn't see any signs the cat had been back when I got up,' Nash says, checking the window is closed. 'Do you want to go look for it while we're out?'

'We should prioritise helping everyone out. But yes. Please.' Normally, he might have felt a little awkward admitting that he really wanted to go out into the snow to find a cat, but then there have been so many embarrassing moments in the last twenty-four hours that this barely even registers. 'I'm just going to text my sister. Shall we aim to leave in about fifteen, twenty minutes?'

Nash nods, and disappears off into the bedroom, perhaps to make his own excruciating phone call.

Christopher takes the sofa and makes an executive decision to not read back up through the Spanks Squad group chat. It'll take him ages, given that WhatsApp has stopped actually tallying how many messages he has and instead has just added a helpful plus sign to the number. He's also not sure he wants to see what they've been discussing, even though he knows that's avoidant of him. And true, he could message Kit and Haf directly, but somehow, with Laurel and Ambrose there too, this feels easier.

> **Christopher:** Morning everyone. Sorry I've been a bit AWOL. There was a meeting called yesterday and I've been helping out the other villagers, cooking and driving the van up to people. Just wanted to reassure you all I'm all right.
> **Haf:** oh thank God. I was worried you'd gone all hermit on us.
> **Christopher:** All hermit?
> **Ambrose:** she thought you were wallowing. i said you were fine.
> **Haf:** Yeah but he hadn't told ME that had he? Or Kit.
> **Kit:** Why am I the second option in this list?
> **Ambrose:** he's been busy shacking up with his favourite film star

Trust them to just blurt it out, but Christopher's a little relieved that they've given him an opening, despite the many rows of question marks sent by Haf and Kit. In one messy essay, he explains the whole *Tessa-is-actually-Nash-Nadeau* situation, and that Nash was going to be staying here a while longer, while assuring them that he's mostly okay, apart from the whole mess of feelings towards Nash part, which he glosses over a bit.

Perhaps for the first time in the history of their group chat, no one says anything for ages.

Kit: Well. That's really not what I was expecting you to say.
Christopher: What were you expecting?
Christopher: Actually, you don't need to answer that.
Haf: That you'd gone hermit and had a Nash Nadeau marathon.
Ambrose: theres still time for that if you know what i mean
Kit: We all know what you mean.
Christopher: Also, sorry but I did tell Laurel and Ambrose yesterday about Nash. I thought they might pass the message on.
Laurel: I learned my lesson about passing on gossip last year thank you very much darling
Ambrose: he was having a gay panic
Christopher: I wasn't
Ambrose: you were
Laurel: He was.

He can't help but notice Haf and Kit have been *typing* on and off for the last minute, and his stomach squirms.

Christopher: I hope you're not upset I didn't message you all about this earlier? It's just been a lot of things happening at once.
Haf: Sorry we were screaming about how mad this is. THIS IS WILD. NASH NADEAU!? WHAT
Kit: also C, you're forgiven for not telling your sister about your possibly very confusing sexual-fantasy-cum-real-life situation
Ambrose: haha cum

Kit: For fucks sake Ambrose
Laurel: Cheese and rice!

Phew. A weight he didn't really know he'd been carrying lifts from his shoulders. At least that's out in the open . . . or, well, with his people.

Christopher: Just please don't share this anywhere. He's not asked outright for privacy or anything but still, I don't want it getting out if we can avoid it.
Haf: Who am I going to tell? You are all the people I know.
Kit: I think that was a message for Ambrose.
Ambrose: yeh fair enough really
Laurel: Don't forget to ask him if he's taking brand deals. We've got some cute workout pieces he'd look wonderful in.
Christopher: I think he's got some work stuff going on, so I'm not going to ask him that. Go through his agent or whatever.
Ambrose: boo what use are you
Ambrose: have you boned him yet
Christopher: OK have to go now! I'll check in later.

Just before he pockets the phone, Christopher gets a message from Shaz telling them she'll be at the community centre in half an hour, and to meet her there. With a little time to kill, he decides to make a quick grab bag of useful things – the candles and matches he used the other night, his Swiss Army knife, a box of unopened table salt, and one of the couch blankets just in case. Perhaps Nash is rubbing off on him.

Nash appears, and peers into the bag as Christopher fills it up. 'What is the table salt for?'

'The ice.'

'Is there no team out gritting the roads?'

'No, in Britain we prefer to be shocked by snow when it happens every single year.'

He's about to pick up the bag, when Nash swings it up over his shoulder with ease. 'You drive. I carry stuff.'

'A fair division of our talents.' He could almost swear that Nash flexes his muscles the smallest amount. 'Let's go.'

It's blisteringly cold outside, much colder than the day before. Christopher wraps his coat tightly around himself, as though that might make it keep the wind out better. Perhaps he needs to borrow some of Shaz's knitted accessories.

Under the fresh layer of snow that fell overnight, the older stuff has packed down and frozen, creating a hidden slippy layer. Despite their good grip, Christopher's walking boots slide on a steep bit of pavement. He waves his arms furiously just to keep himself upright. And yet, beside him, Nash walks with ease.

'How are you doing that? I feel like Bambi on the pond.'

'I'm sure that's from having massive gangly legs. You must always feel like a baby deer.'

'Oh, very droll.' Christopher windmills his arms as he feels himself sliding again. He can't control what his body is doing, and he's going to fall, he can just feel it. It'll be just his luck when he lands solidly on his bum, or worse, his face. The last thing he needs is a trip to A&E, especially as he's the only one who can drive.

But before he can hit the ground, Nash reaches out and steadies him on his feet.

'Steady, Bambi,' Nash drawls, and Christopher isn't sure if the fluttering in his stomach is the leftover sensation of being completely out of control, or the way Nash is holding onto him. 'Canadian, remember?'

'How could I possibly forget? You've never once mentioned it.'

'To answer your question, I used to play hockey so I'm pretty familiar with getting around on ice, and this is near enough that.'

Given that his physical safety is literally in Nash's hands, Christopher resists the urge to point out that they call it ice hockey here to differentiate from the incredibly vicious version teenage girls play on land.

'Here, lean a bit more forward. Your centre of gravity needs to be right over your feet, which should be easy because you're practically Bigfoot.'

'I'm six foot three. That's not even that tall,' Christopher mutters, leaning forward like Nash tells him to.

'When you walk, try to put your whole foot down at once. Watch me.' He lets go of Christopher for just a second and shows him how to step lightly and evenly on the ice. 'See?'

'Somewhat.'

'Somewhat,' Nash laughs in British, reaching out for Christopher's hands. 'Come on, put those big feet to good use. You're basically wearing snowshoes.'

They're both wearing gloves, but when Christopher takes Nash's hands, he feels fizzing heat in his fingers.

'Do you always speak like you're in a period drama?'

'Well, yes because they're just speaking British English, aren't they?' Christopher huffs.

'No, I think it's more than that. Like, your whole vibe. It's very—'

'Please don't say *Downton Abbey*.'

'Well, it is. And look, you've been walking this whole time.'

Christopher realises that Nash is right. He was *distracting* him, the absolute bastard.

'Bloody hell,' Christopher laughs.

'It's amazing what you can achieve when you're irritated with me.' Nash flashes a wolfish grin, and irritation rises in Christopher's chest. Well. He's pretty sure it's irritation.

Typically, Nash's smart advice taken from experience works. Slowly, they make their way across the road to the community centre, which is already open and bustling with activity.

The refreshments table is already set up and being manned by the same woman as yesterday, though to his embarrassment Christopher realises that he's forgotten her name and instead can only think of her as the Hot Drinks

Lady. Hopefully he'll overhear someone speak to her so he can update his memory.

Shaz waves them over, a steaming cup of something molten in one mittened hand, and a gingerbread reindeer in the other. 'Morning, sunshines.'

'Where did you get that?' asks Nash with hungry eyes.

'Your man here,' she says, laughing when both of them look annoyed at the implication that either of them belong to the other. 'You pair of prickly pears. By the way, putting some in with the dinner yesterday – which was delish by the way – was very kind but the piranhas got to them. This was the only one I could prise away from their hands.'

'You stole a cookie from your kid?'

'And I'd do it again, so this one had better make some more.'

'Noted,' Christopher says.

Nash peers closer to the biscuit, sniffing at it. 'It smells good.'

With a groan, Shaz breaks off a piece and hands it to him. 'You owe me at least two now.'

But the words fly over Christopher's head, as his focus is all on Nash, eyes closed as he chews the gingerbread. A moment of pure bliss. The look. Chasing that on people's faces was part of what Christopher wanted when he opened the bakery. Somehow, it feels even more special right now, probably because the man never normally shuts up.

He will definitely make some more gingerbread later.

For *Shaz*, obviously.

'Hang on, what's in that massive great bag?' she says, peering around Nash.

'Supplies, in case we get in trouble. It's a go-bag, I guess.'

She squints her eyes at him. 'Are you a prepper? One of those guys with a basement full of guns?'

'Obviously not. The basement is for the nuclear bunker.'

'Oh aye, of course. Silly of me.' They both laugh at that, and Christopher is slightly lost but it's nice to see them getting on.

'So, where are we needed?' Christopher asks, dragging his eyes away from Nash's contented face.

Mouth now full of gingerbread, Shaz points to the other side of the room. Tamara stands in front of a whiteboard, pen in hand, while staring with deep concentration at a laptop on the table.

'Morning, Ms Yang,' Nash says as they approach.

Tamara looks up from the computer with a prepared politician's smile, the kind that expresses that they are glad to see you even if they have no idea who you really are, and that they would also like to confirm you are voting for them.

'Please, just Tamara is more than fine. Thank you so much for your help yesterday. I'm just getting things organised but it looks as if you and the van will be needed this morning to pick up Priti from Myffy's.'

'Me and Christopher can go get her. Anything else?'

'Well, what would be most helpful right now is if you could assist with checking in on everyone. We didn't get particularly far yesterday because of the weather, and the power keeps going on and off in some bits of the village so we can't rely on phoning everyone.'

She directs them to the canvassing map she'd used yesterday, where a number of houses have been coloured in. It's clear that people have been starting at the community centre and working outwards, because the streets off the high street are all marked in bright-pink highlighter. It's the roads further up the mountain that haven't even been touched.

'We can do those after we've checked in on Myffy and Priti. We'll be heading in that direction anyway,' Nash suggests.

'Excellent idea. What I'll need from you is to take note of who is in, and if there are any immediate needs.'

Shaz plonks a big stack of printed flyers on the table in front of them. 'And if no one answers, pop one of these through the door.'

They're pretty basic, in black and white with large text so that they can be easily read, explaining who the task force members are and what number to call for help.

'Do you need us to cook any more too?' Christopher asks.

'Can we let you know later?' Tamara says, handing him their own copy of the map, roads marked for them to visit. 'Sorry, I know it's a lot—'

'We can handle it.'

'Thank you.'

Shaz looks around at the map, then at the computer, and back up to Tamara. 'Tammy, have you slept?'

'Not since 1996. Why?'

In a mock whisper to Christopher, Shaz continues, 'I think you guys should make her some treats, just in case. Our lives are in her hands.'

'A bit of snow won't break me.'

A laugh sounds across the room, and Christopher turns to see Ursula walking in.

'That might though,' Tamara mutters under her breath.

For just a moment, Nash puts on the film star smile. The glow appears. 'All right then. We'll get going. You all stay warm and safe now, ma'am.'

And Christopher could swear that Tamara giggles like a schoolgirl behind her hand, before clearing her throat. 'Yes, you too.'

As they walk out of the community centre, Christopher says, 'That was quite impressive.'

'What?'

'The *ma'am*-ing.'

'Oh that. Easiest way to diffuse a situation.'

'Flirting?'

'Something like that.'

'I think you might have too much power.'

They carefully pick back across the road to the bakery, and Christopher finds it far easier this time. It would be easier if

Nash hadn't walked ahead, and if he could hold onto him to steady himself, but he makes it all the same.

They reach the van, which is somehow even colder inside than outside, and Nash slings the bag of supplies into the back. It doesn't take too long for the van to splutter to life, and a very small amount of heat to filter through.

'Any ideas about fixing the heating in here?' Christopher asks.

Nash shakes his head. 'That's beyond me, sorry.'

'Were you always very handy? Or interested in machines?' Christopher trails off, trying to find words that aren't so obviously about a *before*.

'You mean, it's surprising someone who can't drive knows how to repair a van, right?'

'Well . . . yes.'

'You English people love to talk around the houses. It's exhausting. And yes, it was what me and my dad bonded over when I was a kid, before all the acting stuff kicked off. He used to do up classic cars and sell them on for profit, so there was always some half-built banger in our garage.'

'That sounds nice.'

'Yeah, it was. And I used to drive a bit as a teenager. Like, I got my licence and then the seizures came right after.'

'Do you miss driving?'

'Yeah. I miss the independence. I miss not having to wait for someone to pick me up. It's probably the most annoying part of it all, if I'm honest. Well, apart from the seizures.'

'Yes, I can imagine they're quite irritating.'

They share a smile, but then Nash closes off the conversation with a glance at his phone. 'Sorry, I just have to check my emails for a minute while I've got signal.'

He's not quite sure what he feels. Dropped? A little sad for Nash? But ultimately glad he let him in a little. But Nash was quick to close the door, too. There are things he wants to know about Nash, and not because he is a fan. It's normal to want to know the man you're sharing your bed with, right?

Chapter Seventeen

Nash

It's not that he didn't want to talk about it, though. Well, he *kind* of didn't want to talk about the way his disability disables him at ten o'clock in the morning when he's about to have a long day of talking to people.

But also, he really needs to decide what he's going to tell Kurt.

He does genuinely open his inbox. There are a few more back-and-forth emails between Kurt and the execs that Nash has been cc'd into. Requests for more time, and clarity on some clauses in the contract, like whether they'll be wanting to show-pony him as the face of the network.

Tomorrow – that's the deadline he gave Kurt, wasn't it?

The other thing playing on his mind is whether someone is going to leak that he's here. You never know who is submitting to *DeuxMoi* these days, though Nash has got quite good at spotting people trying to take a sneaky photo. He doesn't mind those so much – it's kind of funny how subtle they think they are being and yet are absolutely failing to be. But if word reaches Kurt that he's stuck in some village in North Wales before he can tell him, that would be *really* bad.

No, that would suck. And it would probably hurt Kurt's feelings.

He has two options it seems. Either he's honest with Kurt and tells him that he can't discuss anything until after Christmas because he's fled the country, or he just makes up some reason as to why he can't talk about it. He's an actor, and you'd think that lying would come naturally to him, but this is different.

At Myffy's, Priti lets them both in while she goes to get her things, and they find Myffy tucked up in the front room with a stack of romance novels next to her.

'I've ranked them in order of smuttiness,' she announces with a cheeky smile. 'Good to keep a bit of heat in my bones, isn't it?'

'Do you need anything else today?' Christopher asks after he's finished chuckling. 'We're just in the area knocking on doors for the next few hours so we can be back pretty quickly.'

'I'm good for food, thanks to you lovely boys. Polly, my PA, is doing much better now – but do you think you could whizz her over later? I'll get Shaz to coordinate if you two are out and about.'

'Sounds good to me.'

Independence. That's what Christopher had been asking Nash about earlier, and now that Nash is in Myffy's house, he can't stop thinking about it. Relying on other people to look after you is tricky. There was some time a few years ago, when he was luckily out of contract from *Parental Units*, when his seizures went wild – the neurologist had tried him on a new medication, and it had done the opposite of what was intended. He'd been so ill and felt as if his brain was on fire all the time. There'd been so many seizures that he'd been in and out of hospital and wasn't safe to be home alone. It had been his friends who'd taken up looking after him in the gaps. Cooking for him, washing his clothes, helping him get around the house, picking him up after he'd had seizures. In the last decade, he'd lost touch with some of those people, but you never forget that care and love. He'll never not be grateful for it.

Not everyone could be relied on to love someone in that way.

'Have you heard anything from Mohan? Has he managed to get out of London yet?' Nash asks.

Myffy shakes her head sadly. 'No trains. He keeps camping out at Euston; that's the big station where the trains to North Wales go from. He's hoping for the best, but nothing is running still.'

'Damn,' sighs Christopher.

'It's a pity he didn't drive down as he'd probably have chanced it by now,' she adds. 'Anyroad, I'd rather he's warm and safe in his hotel.'

'That's one thing, at least,' Nash says, wishing there was a way they could bring Mohan home for her. If he was the kind of extremely rich feature-film star with Marvel money then maybe he'd be able to get him on a private plane; not that anything is flying and he's pretty sure there's not a suitable airspace anywhere nearby anyway. The point is, maybe he could *do* something, rather than just wish he could help.

The feeling gnaws at him a little, and if he's honest, it's nice to have something else to think about that's not his own – arguably rather trivial in the grand scheme of things – problems.

Even though they're off to drop off Priti and pick up Polly, and so will be back shortly, Nash still makes Myffy a tea before they go. It just seems right. Together, they drive Priti over to the GP surgery, which has managed to open in spite of the weather. Luckily, a few of the staff have their own cars and have been coordinating their own emergency response plan, assisted by Tamara in the community centre. It's kind of amazing really, what such a small community can do with a few resources. Then, they very slowly drive over to the next unpronounceable town to pick up Polly, a small and very smiley woman with a shock of black hair, who they drop off at Myffy's cherry-red front door.

'Call us if you need anything,' Christopher says, with the kind of deep seriousness usually reserved for movies set in wartime. To be fair, he does have the kind of face that wouldn't look out of place in World War Two costume. He'd have to lose the round glasses, of course – those are far too modern *New Yorker* essayist adjacent – but his slim face with all the potential sharp edges softened and those huge baby blues would make him perfect for a role of *kindhearted man just doing his best during the Blitz.* The sort of character who just wants to get back to his pregnant wife. Perhaps it's wrong to typecast him so readily, but the energy cannot be denied.

If anything, it's one of the things Nash likes about him, even if it's a bit irritating at times. But that's how it can be sometimes, can't it? The things you most like about someone can be their annoying habits. Perhaps it's just about memorability – nothing sticks in your mind more than being pissed off by someone.

God, where is his mind going? They're driving back up the hill now to start on their adventure in knocking on doors to check on everyone, and Nash can't help but glance over at the Boy Wonder himself. There's so much about this man that he doesn't know, which is on one hand kind of strange when they've shared a bed, and on the other, not at all. After all, he has shared a bed plenty of times with *someones*, their names lost to time. Admittedly, that was a very different Nash; a younger, more carefree Nash. A Nash who hadn't been hurt yet.

Urgh. That uncomfortable squishiness creeps in again. God, he's fed up with it.

Looking for anything else to think about, he settles on the scarf around Christopher's neck. 'I need to ask you something.'

'Go on,' Christopher says with trepidation.

'Is that Paddington Bear on your scarf?'

'It is. I didn't realise he was an internationally recognisable bear.'

'I think pretty much everyone has seen the movie by now.' The goal is wide open, so he takes the shot. 'So, a big *bear* fan, are you?'

That one was too easy. Christopher does that awkward shuffle as if his body is turning to stone, and his cheeks go that familiar uncomfortable scarlet. More evidence to confirm his suspicions, along with the general air of panic Christopher displays every time they get physically close. None of this is the behaviour of a straight man. In his experience, straight men barely pick up on what he means when he references the subcultures. Unless they've been 'forced' into watching endless series of *Drag Race* with their girlfriends, though that just tends to mean they mistakenly use queer lexicon as if it's their own and need to be talked down. Either way, they end up scrambling to say something that isn't gently homophobic, and that produces a very different kind of panic: allyship panic. Or, you know, straight-up homophobia, but he didn't suspect Christopher of that, or else he'd have turned around and left the moment he arrived.

If Christopher was straight and uncurious (an important distinction from the 'straight' guys Nash has been with), the panic from sharing a bed would be a very different flavour. Interesting. *Very* interesting.

Not that Nash should be dipping there, nor does he want to. Well, he's a bit curious. Anyone would be curious.

'It was my Christmas gift from Haf last year. Paddington is kind of our thing. It's surprisingly warm, even though I'm fairly sure it's for kids as it's very short.'

'Is everything you own something you've been gifted by a woman in your life?'

'Worryingly, I think you might be right. Also hang on, did you say "the *movie*"? As in *singular*?'

'I haven't seen the second.'

'Nash, there's *three* now. So we'll have to see to that then.'

'Is that a threat? It sounds like a threat.'

'It's just a really good film.'

'Big film buff, are you?'

Another open goal. Nash has been working on a theory that Christopher does, in fact, know precisely who Nash is, but without logging into his Netflix – which has been curiously logged out of on basically all the devices in Christopher's house – he can't prove anything. Until then, he can just poke and prod and see if a reaction comes out.

'I've seen a few things. Mostly with bears, or *bears*.'

Nash cackles. At least he can find that sense of humour deep down under all that earnestness and bat back occasionally.

They park up at the place marked on Tamara's map, a curving street of bungalows with small gardens in front, just like Myffy's place. They must have all been built around the same time, with the same covered porches and wide driveways, all of them covered in a thick layer of snow. Nash senses he might have a lot of snow-clearing in his immediate future.

'Do we split up and take one side of the street each, or go together?' Christopher asks, peering at the map in Nash's hands.

'I think together, seeing as there's only one of these. Plus, the horny old ladies can't overpower us if there're two of us.'

'Having met Myffy, I don't think we should put anything past them.'

The first couple of houses are dark; clearly some people are away for the holidays. Nash feels a bit awkward about peering into people's windows. It makes him feel like a kid again, really. Sneaking around the neighbourhood just to see how other people live, inadvertently looking for signs that they feel the same way he does about his life and himself. Not that you can tell that kind of thing from someone's house, obviously. In truth, he probably didn't really know what he was looking for, in the same way there were quite a few seemingly unknowable yet known things about himself. He just wanted some kind of recognition that he wasn't alone, perhaps.

The third door down is where things start to get interesting. The man, who will not share his name, refuses to open the door and only speaks to them through the letterbox, insisting that he is both fine and uninterested in any help they might be offering. Nash is suddenly very thankful that they don't have guns in this country, as this man is giving off all kinds of doomsday prepper, *don't step on my lawn or I'll shoot* energy. Well. He's pretty sure they don't have guns. Either way, they walk away from that one swiftly.

The next few are, thankfully, a bit more normal. Families who need some help getting some food in, and one woman whose American-sized car's battery needs a jump-start off their van so she can go and pick up her mother from down the coast, not that he's convinced she'll get much further than the Sainsbury's. Either way, Nash takes over this delicate operation and is quietly relieved when both the car springs to life and the van doesn't die, as it was a little touch and go on that front.

At another house, they clear the snow off an older couple's drive so they can get around more easily. It had nearly been a few shades of disaster as Mengsan and Nancy had been poised ready to pour a kettle's worth of boiling water all over their steps, and Nash yelling at them to stop had almost resulted in them throwing it all over *him* instead. God, do none of these people know anything about clearing snow? Seemingly not. Hot water on snow is only good for creating a slick of black ice.

In a sweet little house further down the road, an elderly lady asks Christopher to use his ridiculous height to hang up some fresh fat balls in the trees in her back garden for her birds. That's all Joan was worried about. Not her safety, not the limited food she had in the pantry. Just her birds. They all stand in her kitchen watching as the tiny little birds flock to the hanging fat balls, while Nash insists she make a small shopping list so they can pick her up some bits.

It takes them nearly two hours to cover both sides of one street. But all they can do is keep going.

A lithe old man in a smoking jacket-type velvet dressing gown informs them that no, he doesn't need anything as he's sorted and sharing resources with his neighbours in their cul-de-sac, but insists on lending them his hiking thermoses. Nash has never been more thankful for instant coffee, the feeling starting to come back into his fingers as the coffee works its magic and his brain wakes up. Their new friend Cecil also kindly offers to top it up with a bit of whisky, which Nash is reluctant to turn down but does, just to be good.

The rest of the cul-de-sac seem just as sorted, with a striking man in exercise gear called Ted finishing up clearing all the drives and paths, and taking charge of everyone's care. Upon seeing how little of their map they've managed, Ted insists they take his number so he can pick up where they would be leaving off later on.

Two more cul-de-sacs down – one of which has taken a similar approach to Ted and Cecil's gang, by organising themselves, and another where it seems as if everyone absolutely hates each other. Every single house visit ends with some comment about one of their neighbours. Given they're already flagging, it doesn't exactly brighten the spirits to hear from Marjorie that May is shacking up with Gerald only because he's got a hot tub, or to hear from May to disregard anything Marjorie tells them because she's a word-that's-not-suitable-to-be-repeated-in-polite-company.

As they walk out of this cul-de-sac of hell, Nash feels all the energy start to leak out of him. Really, he should probably warn Christopher that he's flagging, but he hasn't got The Headache yet, and another sip of Cecil's nuclear coffee spurs him on a bit longer.

Clearly, Christopher is flagging too. 'One more?' he asks with the weary determination of Tom Hanks in *Castaway* trying to get over that wave bank.

'One more,' agrees Nash.

They come across a few more empty houses – some family homes, some clearly houses that are rented out for holidaymakers in the summer – on the next street, one that has clear views of the sea. At the last house on the row, they find a couple called Pearl and Don, who seem to be doing all right. They're the kind of old people who could give him a run for his money in the healthiness stakes, all wiry and bright-cheeked.

Nash feels his phone ping, and as everything seems pretty okay, he takes the opportunity to check it. It's a message from Kurt. His stomach turns, but he opens it because he's going to have to get this over and done with today.

Except, it appears the universe has done him a solid today.

Kurt: Update re: contract – there's been a leak about one of the production companies trying to write off a movie for tax breaks, so they're dealing with the public backlash. Have asked to pick up the conversation after Christmas. Call you tomorrow still?

'Thank FUCK!!' Nash shouts, which alarms Christopher, Pearl and Don, and causes birds to flee their trees. Somewhere in the distance, a dog starts barking. 'Sorry. I just had some big news.'

Nash sprints away to the pavement to reread this message. This has saved him. Some cash-grabbing executives, determined to throw away the hard work of a team of creatives for the sake of a tax write-off, have saved his ass, for now. At least now there's a chance of him getting back to LA to talk all this through with Kurt face to face, rather than having to admit he's trapped in the UK. There's time. He has time. And yes, he might still be snowed in across the Atlantic, but there's a chance he can fix this.

He hears Christopher say a friendly goodbye to Pearl and Don, before he strides over and takes Nash by the elbow. 'Could you, perhaps, not shout obscenities next time we're trying to help people?' Christopher mutters sternly.

'Sorry. I just got a good bit of news.'

At this, Christopher just screws up his face, as though Nash told him he'd just picked them up some roadkill.

'What, Calloway?'

'It's nothing.'

Obviously it *is* something from the speed that Christopher stalks back in the direction of the van, but Nash has no idea what it could be.

'So . . . are we done?' Nash asks.

'For now.'

No further explanation required, apparently. Fine, they're done. He really needed to stop for the day anyway but he's sure he'd have preferred it to be a conversation, not just a diktat from Christopher.

'Right, so why don't you spit out whatever is bothering you while we're out here freezing our balls off?'

Nash is not sure he's ever seen someone so angrily open a vehicle door. 'It's just hard enough doing this without you not taking this whole situation seriously.'

'I'm always serious about snow safety,' Nash grins, hoping to defuse whatever pissy little mood Christopher has conjured. He clambers into the van and Christopher just won't look at him. 'So that's not it. What am I not being serious about then?'

Staring straight ahead, the words start to pour out of Christopher. 'No, I mean . . . you're not being serious about helping everyone. This isn't like one of your . . . I mean . . . one of those Christmas films where everyone saves the town. We have to help everyone out or someone could get really hurt.'

Nash arches an eyebrow. 'I want to help, Christopher. People need help, and I have the ability to do that. Mostly. And I'm really confused as to why you think I'm not taking it seriously.'

Christopher starts the engine, and Nash is grateful for the very small amount of heat that starts to flood through.

'Well, you did just scream fuck very loudly.'

'Right. Not my best moment. But I've been doing just as much as you this whole time. So, I don't get it, Calloway? What's your actual problem?'

Christopher's brows furrow and he shuts his eyes briefly, shaking his head, as though the words he's saying aren't quite right. 'I just don't want you to feel you have to just because . . .'

'Just because you're not throwing me out into the snow, is that it?'

The blush that takes over Christopher's face is a pretty solid answer. This might be the most confusing conversation Nash has ever had. How did they get from happily helping all these strangers out for two days, to Christopher accusing Nash of not taking things seriously, or doing it just because he felt he had to? Why does Christopher seem to have this impression of him being a total dickhead? Is this his fault? He thought they were just playfully bantering half the time, but maybe he's misjudged all of it.

'Christopher. Yes, you care about these people and yes, you need help to help them, and also yes, you are giving me shelter. All those things can be true at once. But that's not why I'm doing this. I don't feel *beholden* to you specifically – we barely know each other.'

Christopher seems to shrink a little at least.

'This is just the right thing to do. Plus, if I didn't help, I'd be an enormous prick.'

'I don't think the prick part is affected by whether you help or not,' Christopher says, and Nash can't tell if it's a joke or not.

'I might be a prick sometimes, but at least I know when I'm being one. You're acting like, just because I want to help, I pissed in your closet?'

'Wardrobe.'

'Keep correcting me, and I really will.'

'Will what?'

'Piss in your wardrobe.'

'Please don't.'

'Then what is this? Are you just upset that I'm muscling in on your home? Taking the Boy Scout glory? None of this is making *you* seem particularly *not* a prick, by the way.'

Quietly, Christopher starts the van's engine, and they start driving in tense silence. 'Look, I don't mean to seem like I'm upset you're taking my glory. That's not . . . that's not what I mean at all.'

'Then why don't you tell me what you mean instead of being such a—' Nash searches around desperately for a word that's not *prick* and for some reason lands on, 'Huffy-pants. Real Heffalump energy.'

'I am not huffy,' laughs Christopher, seemingly in spite of himself. 'I didn't even know you guys use that word?'

'It's just the right word for this general vibe, isn't it? You are the huffiest man alive. And God knows where I heard it, apparently I'm becoming a local. Connecting with the community. That's what I thought *you* wanted. Or didn't want, because who knows what's going on in this conversation any more?' he says, on the edge of snapping. His head hurts already from how much they've done today, but this confusing conversation is making it so much worse.

With a deep sigh, Christopher says, sadly, 'I really care about this place, Nash. It's my home and I really want everyone to see me as someone who cares about the community. And I want to be someone who *shows* they care. I'm sorry if it sounded like I was angry at you, I'm not. I just want to know that you're as serious as I am.'

'I don't think there's ever been a person in the history of the world as unfailingly serious as you, Christopher. But why do you think I would say I wanted to help if I didn't?'

'I don't know,' Christopher sighs, pulling into the bakery drive. 'That's precisely why I'm asking. You have a very . . .'

'A very what?'

'Misanthropic vibe about you, sometimes.'

Well. Fuck this guy, honestly. Nash has had enough of this conversation. He jumps out of the van and slams the van door shut hard behind him. He needs to get out of here, away from this man for enough time for him to cool down.

From the back of the van, he gets out the shovel because if he doesn't have something to do, he's going to blow up.

Christopher gets out and tries to follow him. 'I'm sorry, I didn't—'

Nash wheels round, holding up a hand to make Christopher stop following him. 'Just because people have let me down doesn't mean I should let down people who are relying on me. I'm not a prick, Calloway. Stop treating me like I am.'

Chapter Eighteen

Christopher

God, how did he mess that conversation up so much? Every word he said was the wrong one, and he just couldn't get any of his meaning out. The shutters came down over Nash's face when he was just trying to make light of this situation like they've been doing the whole time he's been here, but clearly Christopher has ballsed this all up.

Nash looked so distant. Pale. Christopher watches as he storms off, somehow shovelling as he goes.

And all Christopher can do is uselessly watch him leave.

In truth, he lost the thread of what was happening in that conversation somewhere near the beginning, and it feels as if he's still untangling it all in his head. But he just wanted to be sure that Nash cared the way *he* does. This is his *home* and all he's wanted this whole time was to find a way of belonging here. Now he's finally found a way to be involved and help, but it's only possible while paired with a man who flips so often between being his fake Hollywood self and a disaster, Christopher can't tell who Nash really is. If helping his community is reliant on Nash, a man who is admittedly helpful, but also prone to shouting *fuck* at the sky and exploding flour everywhere and irritating the hell out of him, then that makes Christopher feel a bit weird. Conflicted.

If he's honest, he can barely believe everyone is letting him help, never mind Nash, who doesn't even live here. He had genuinely just wanted to check. But . . . maybe he can admit he went about all this the wrong way.

Nash is halfway up the street, clearing parts of the path they'd not managed to touch yet. Even when they're fighting, Nash is still helping out the community that Christopher lives in. And all Christopher is doing is sulking about it.

Behind Nash, the moody sun looms over the mountains. This is why he is here, in part. He loved a lot of things about London, but now he can't imagine living somewhere where the landscape is made up of buildings instead of huge rock formations and grumbling seas.

'Are you going to go inside, or are you planning to stand here forever freezing your arse off?' Christopher looks up to find Shaz standing under the bakery awning, waiting for him.

'Have you been there long?'

'Long enough to see the tail end of whatever that little tiff was.'

'Hmm.'

'Why are you overthinking it? I recognise those frown lines.'

'Overthinking what?'

'Nash. Being here. Helping. He was your favourite before he got here. Is that what it is? Just all mixed up in your head?'

'Maybe.'

'Not maybe. I know that whirly brain.'

'It's very annoying when you do that.'

'So? What are you going to do about it? You can't both be steaming like that all night, though that's probably a good way to melt some of this snow.'

Christopher sighs. 'I'll just give him some space.'

Shaz laughs. 'Sure. *Space.* I'm sure that's exactly what you both need,' she says, popping half a Digestive she pulls from her pocket into her mouth.

'Do you have a better idea?'

At this, Shaz points at her biscuit-filled mouth, shrugs with apology. Given this would be the first time Shaz has not had an opinion on something, he's rather glad she's not giving it.

Christopher unlocks the door and they both walk in. 'Did you want something?'

Mouth now biscuit-free, she says, 'Just was heading home and thought I should check on you given the two of you were yelling in the street. Very *EastEnders* of you.'

Christopher groans. That's not exactly going to help with people taking him seriously here. 'I'm fine,' he insists.

'You know what would cheer you up?'

'What?'

'Making some gingerbread.'

'Oh yeah?'

'Not the reindeer ones for me, though you know I'm always gagging for some more. Why don't you make the house? You always talk about how you love doing that, and if you don't make time to do it, you won't.'

'Maybe. I think I need to just have an early night and apologise when he comes back. How was your day?'

'Oh, you know, grand.' Shaz begins listing things off on her fingers, but as she's still wearing her mittens it looks as if she's giving herself a very slow clap. 'Kathy threatened to lock the kids in the cupboard, whereas Gar loves to gentle-parent, so they had a massive argument. Ursula kept interrupting Tamara when she was speaking to people, as though she had the authority. A man whose door I knocked on asked me for a sexy sponge bath. You know, a mixed bag.'

'Christ, I'm sorry.'

'Not his fault, or yours either I hope, unless you put Dick up to it.'

'Is that really his name?'

'Really. Right, I'm going to go, but just do me a favour?'

'What?'

'Chill out a bit, will you? Not everything is riding on you, and everyone can see how much you're doing. Stop putting so much pressure on the both of youse.'

She's gone before he can reply, but she's not wrong.

Still, after the last few days, he feels as if he is being tested by the universe, he's pretty sure of it. Clearly some deity or higher power has decided that his patience and goodness need to be examined, and so has sent all the most annoying people into this tiny town just for the holidays when he needed a rest more than anything.

Christopher: Has something planetary turned retrograde?
Ambrose: your ass x

Helpful as always. Though, this does add further weight to that 'the universe is testing him' theory.

Not sure what to do with himself, he crosses back over the street to the community centre to update Tamara on their progress. It's quiet when he gets inside, everyone who's been helping throughout the day getting ready to swap with anyone there for the evening.

Tamara is, as ever, at her control centre, and barely looks up as she accepts their very folded and crumpled version of the map. 'Any issues?'

'None. Well, Nash swore extremely loudly in front of an old couple who were not impressed.'

Tamara shrugs wearily. 'Eh, they'll get over it.'

Well, maybe he really should go easier on Nash then, if their elected representative doesn't care.

'Do you need anything?'

She shakes her head. 'No, can you just update the spreadsheet while I go get a disgusting cup of coffee?'

'It's getting pretty late?'

'I told you already. I haven't slept since 1996. Now you know why.'

'You know, I could bring you a proper one from the café?'

Her eyes flash with hope, and he nips back across the street with a list of orders from the community centre. Luckily, for once, the Hot Drinks Lady is not there to offer up her horrifying concoctions, so he doesn't have to worry about hurting her feelings.

It takes him a while to walk back over the slippy road with a tray of hot drinks, but he manages it, along with some of the Biscoff biscuits he'd been saving. It seems to boost morale so intensely that he's half tempted to suggest they camp out in his bakery instead, but the space is so much smaller.

While everyone sips at their actually nice drinks, he takes his time filling in a spreadsheet of who needs what, along with their addresses from the notes he'd saved on his phone.

When he crosses back over the street, he sees Nash at the bakery door. Maybe he should give him a spare key, not that he can remember if there even is one.

'Hi,' Christopher offers, figuring he should be the one to break the figurative ice.

'Hey.'

'Did you get much . . . shovelling done?'

'Yeah, I got quite far,' Nash replies coolly. 'What were you doing?'

'I went and filled in the community centre on our progress while you were cooling down.'

'While *I* was cooling down?'

'Sorry, I mean . . . we. While *we* were cooling down.'

'Mmhmm.'

'I really am sorry,' Christopher says, unlocking the front door and holding it open for Nash.

'What are you sorry for, exactly?'

'For being a miscellaneous dickhead.' This, at least, gets a laugh out of Nash. 'Are we okay?'

'That depends. Are you going to keep being weird?' Nash walks through the door, and folds his arms, his head cocked to the side.

'I'm *not* being weird.'

'You are. Though, given you have been, historically, quite weird, maybe I'm asking too much. Are you even going to shut that door?'

'Christ,' gasps Christopher, realising he's been holding the door open this whole time. His fingers are freezing cold. He didn't even notice because Nash is just being . . . all *Nash* like. 'You could have told me.'

Nash smirks, and saunters past him into the kitchen. 'Just thought you might have needed to *cool down* some more.'

But in the light pouring out of the bakery, Christopher catches the quickest flash of black crossing the path. 'Little cat?' he calls. He does the *pspspsps* noise that everyone does to call cats for reasons he's never understood.

But there's nothing. The cat has gone, again, and it's so dark that there's no point Christopher standing out here in the snow. He'll have to try again tomorrow.

'I'll see you tomorrow, cat?' he says into the empty darkness. Christopher goes inside, locks the door behind him, and follows Nash upstairs to the flat.

The aches of a long day set in as he climbs the stairs. He is bone-tired, and he can't imagine how much worse Nash feels, especially after the added fury-induced shovelling.

The mediocre heat of his flat feels almost tropical having come in from such deep cold. Nash is in the kitchen, leaning on the counter, peering down at his phone. That complicated man who keeps surprising him. He's handsome when he concentrates. There's a soft frowning tilt to his eyebrows, and his dark eyes sparkle a little as they dart back and forth, filled with thought. And then there are his arms.

His arms.

Nash isn't superhero-movie-star jacked, but he's muscular and lithe, and Christopher can't help but admire the strong slant of his back.

It's a very different thing looking at someone in real life, even if you've watched them on film for what feels like forever.

He's so *real*.

What would it be like to kiss those strong shoulders? To bite into the muscle of his thighs? It must just be because he's tired – gone is the willpower to hold these thoughts and fantasies back. He really should get a hold of himself. It's not right to think this stuff when Nash is right there.

'Who were you speaking to?' Nash asks, not looking up, and for a moment Christopher worries that Nash might have been able to hear his horny thoughts. He feels naked. In a bad way.

'W-what?'

'Outside. I could hear you through this very poorly maintained window.'

'Oh. The cat.'

'You saw it again?'

'I think so. I mean, it could have been a fox. Or a badger.'

'I hope it's not a badger.'

'Why?'

'I just don't trust anything that only comes out at night.'

It's such a bizarre sentence that Christopher can't help but burst out laughing, and to his relief Nash joins in. 'Noted. A new Nash Nadeau fear – nocturnal creatures.'

Nash raises an eyebrow at him. 'I think being a little afraid of the unfamiliar dark is normal.'

'Do you not like camping then?'

'Yeah. Inside my tent. Where there are no badgers. Anyway, we're getting off track. I did something nice.'

He can't help the laugh that escapes him. 'I don't think it counts as doing something nice if you tell the other person it's nice.'

'Stop being a pedant. While we were out *cooling down*, I went to the corner shop and picked up some truly disgusting-looking frozen pizzas for us.'

So many of the muscles in Christopher's body seem to relax at once. 'That might be the most beautiful sentence I've ever heard.'

'Don't get too excited. It's real bottom-of-the-barrel stuff. One of them has the word "sloppy" in the title.'

'If it's cheese and bread, that's good enough.'

'Oven's heating up. Why don't we pick something to watch from Net—'

'NO.'

Christopher is about to rush to the coffee table to pre-emptively lose the TV remote, when Nash bursts out laughing.

'Man, that was too easy.'

'I'm just . . . very protective! Of my algorithm!'

'Okay, I'm sure that might be true, but is it also possible . . .' Nash pauses, not taking his eyes from Christopher, 'that you've known who I am the whole time and just decided to be a bit of a prick about it for your own amusement? Don't go into acting by the way. You're horrendous at it.'

Well.

Nash has him there.

'All right, so I've seen a *few* of your films.'

'And knew who I was.'

'*And* knew who you were. But I was trying to not freak you out. And then if you hadn't been so impossibly annoying the first night and next morning, then I probably would have told you. And then it just had been too long for me to casually bring it up without sounding like I'd trapped you into staying with me.'

Nash cackles so hard that he almost falls over.

'All right, I'll admit I wasn't my shiniest self when I got here,' Nash manages to get out in between his cackles, 'but in my defence I had just been in a truck with a load of sheep being questioned on which celebrity women I'd slept with.'

'I thought he was just a fan of your films?'

'Yeah, but Gethin seemed to think it was his duty to interview me. Perhaps he's the leader of some rabid fan community. Instead of Club Chalamet, perhaps Club Nadeau.'

Christopher tries to hide his discomfort about all this fandom chat, but can't help but say, 'That's barely alliterative. They must have a better name. Have you not googled them?'

'Calloway, I'm publicly trans. Whatever is said about me on the internet is not for my eyes.'

'Ah yes. Fair point.'

Christopher slides the pizzas out of their cardboard boxes, and sees that Nash really wasn't being hyperbolic about the quality of them. Sometimes, what you really need is just a poorly constructed food that may or may not contain actual cheese.

'Go on, go sit down. I'll get these in.'

Nash does as he's told, and it doesn't take Christopher long to get the pizzas onto some roughly appropriately sized baking sheets and in the oven. He's somewhat pleased to see that Nash hasn't even turned the television on, though obviously he'd already logged out of his streaming apps anyway.

'So . . . *is* that a hobby of yours?' Christopher asks, as he settles back onto the couch next to Nash.

'Riding with sheep?'

'Dating around. You seem to be . . . well, what I mean is the media don't seem to report on you much. You're quite private.'

Nash grins with glee and cackles. 'Oh god, is this a *Swimfan* situation. The fan becomes the obsessive? Or maybe *Der Fan*? Maybe that's too much of a deep cut. Perhaps Hitchcock's *Vertigo*?'

Christopher gets the sense that if he doesn't interrupt Nash now, he'll just keep going listing obscure films. 'I really do think you should give up on this line of thought.'

'I really do think you should give up on this line of thought,' Nash repeats in what sounds like a vague impression of Queen Elizabeth the Second.

'Stop that.'

'I will not. And to answer your question, no, I don't date much. I mean, I'm not a hermit. I have a life, I see people,' he says, with a yawn as though the conversation is so nothing-y to him that he can barely stay awake for it.

What must that be like, Christopher wonders, to be so casual about whether you're seeing people. But then again, didn't he say something weird earlier about being hurt? He hasn't learned to read Nash yet, but he's starting to get the sense that there are two Nashes. The Nash he shows everyone, and the Nash who occasionally appears, like during the conversation about his neurological disorder in the car.

'The reason you don't see it in the press is that I'm not that interesting to them, and I make it my job to be that way. I don't want the intrusion into my life, or the lives of my friends, you know?'

'That makes sense,' Christopher says. 'Sorry for googling you, I guess.'

'Why does that sound so dirty when you say it?' Nash cackles again.

'It does *not*.'

'It does! Everything you say sounds kind of smutty in that accent. And I don't mean my version of it. I mean your proper, silver-spoon accent.'

His mouth goes dry. Nash must just be joking, surely? 'I thought my accent made things sound ridiculous?'

'Depends what you're saying, I suppose.'

'Then what would you want me to say?'

Christopher didn't even mean to say it but when the words leave his lips, everything changes. He could swear there's a crackle in the air.

It must just be how tired they are, but then again, this feels new. A different kind of energy from their usual spats. It's heavier, charged. As if they're circling something.

Nash's eyes roam over Christopher's face. Is he wondering what the hell he's talking about or is it something else? Is . . . is Nash appraising him? Christopher feels as if he's being examined, and that he might like it.

'You want me to give you lines? Or are you asking for something else?' Nash asks, his voice deepening.

It has been a while, but Christopher recognises the hungry look in Nash's eyes. He's pretty sure it's written all over his face too.

His eyes flit from Nash's eyes down to his mouth and Christopher feels his stomach drop.

He could live inside that look.

Time slows down, just for a second, and all Christopher can hear is the beat of their hearts, a drumbeat of tension.

It's almost automatic and somewhat unconscious, but suddenly they are reaching for each other.

Christopher pulls him close as Nash clambers forward, ending up with Nash straddling Christopher's body. They're face to face, and just for a second they watch each other, as if confirming that this isn't a daydream for either of them. That this really could be happening.

That it *is*.

Hungrily, they kiss. It's a hard, demanding kiss, that pushes Christopher's head back against the headrest of the couch.

Nash's back is strong and firm under Christopher's touch, and as the kiss deepens, he drags Nash closer to him, their hips locked together.

Is this really happening? Christopher can't be entirely sure that it isn't another of his dreams, but the sensation of Nash cradling his face can't be imagined. Nash's hands, rougher than Christopher had imagined, trace the stubbled edge of his jaw.

It's electricity, and a sigh escapes Christopher's lips. It seems to please Nash, who smiles mischievously into their kiss.

And then Nash grinds his hips against Christopher. It's a little embarrassing how loudly Christopher gasps at the friction, but it's clear that Nash is enjoying this.

The smug bastard.

Christopher clutches the front of Nash's shirt in his fist, daring him to move again. He can't get enough of the air or Nash or this kiss. It's a delicious drowning, and he's drunk on it.

'You like that,' Nash whispers. It's not a question. It's truth. And in answer, a second grind of his hips is met with another moan.

It's too much.

It's been too long.

Nash leans back and fixes him with a sharp, satisfied grin of power. It's the grin of a nasty little fae king – a smile he's never seen him wear on film. This is all for them right now, and Christopher wants to fall into it.

It floods him with something new. A fiery confidence that flushes his senses.

'Take your shirt off,' Christopher growls, and Nash does so. It's quite possibly the first time Nash has ever done what he's told. And, while it's not the first time Christopher's seen Nash topless, it's the first time he's let himself *look*.

And he's just as beautiful as Christopher imagined. That softly sculpted chest, leading down to a firm and even more sculpted belly. He kisses softly at the hard muscle between Nash's shoulder and neck, and relishes the returned gasp he hears in his ear.

He traces fingers down Nash's chest, down, down to his belt. But before he can unbuckle it, Nash takes Christopher's hands and pins them back above his head.

Nash's eyes are fire and heat, and even though it feels like a war for power between them, he submits. He lies back as Nash gets to his knees and hungrily kisses Christopher's soft belly, pushing up his jumper as he goes.

And in one delicious breath, Nash undoes the flies on his jeans. His face hovers right over the thin cotton of Christopher's boxers. He can feel Nash's breath against him, and it makes him pulse with desire.

'Yes,' he gasps with want. 'Yes.'

There's one more flash of that satisfied shark grin. Nash's lips are warm and full and *oh god*. He sinks into the glorious pleasure of Nash's mouth, and whimpers under the grip of his hand.

It's a golden blur of ecstasy that builds and builds, and he knows he is *so damn close already*.

'Nash,' he bleats, trying not to buck his hips against the delicious pleasure. Upon hearing his name, Nash hums in reply. The sensation tips Christopher over the edge, right into the deep bliss of orgasm.

'Christ,' he whispers, once he can speak again.

Between his knees, Nash grins up at him and he knows that the only thing he wants to do now is bring this man down to a shivering, crumbling mess too.

'Get up here,' he growls, but Nash darts away towards the bedroom, reaching for Christopher as he goes.

Somehow, all while kissing each other, they make their way to the bed. Christopher pushes Nash down onto the mattress. He's removed his trousers, and so reclines back in a perfect pair of black hipster boxers. A greedy ache rushes through Christopher.

What is it about this man that drives him into such a frenzy? The bickering, the flirting, the push and pull of their sex. There's something he can't escape about Nash Nadeau.

He lies down alongside Nash, sliding his hand below the line of Nash's boxers. To his delight, Nash gasps as his fingers stroke lower, through the soft hair to the warm hard centre of it all.

'Say please.'

'Fuck you,' snarls Nash.

'Did you mean "*me*"?'

The surprise on Nash's face pleases him so much that Christopher feels as if he's ready to go again. Jesus.

'Please,' he purrs.

'Show me what you want.'

Nash guides Christopher's hand down. The pleasure of Nash melting beneath him is all new. He strokes down on Nash's hard cock, and the beautiful, spiky man turns to clay in his hands, whispering directions that thrill Christopher even more.

'Your mouth,' Nash commands.

He does what he's told, and as he takes Nash into his mouth, the man arches his back in the most delicious way. The only thing that matters in the world right now is making Nash Nadeau orgasm. And when he does, he releases in a wide-eyed gasp, hands clutched in Christopher's hair and nails digging into his skin.

They pant together in the heat they've created, their bodies glistening with sweat and recent desire.

Christopher can't believe he did that.

He can't believe *they* did that.

Even just a week ago, this would have been beyond his wildest dreams.

He wants to reach out to hold Nash, but he's so tired he can barely move.

Instead, Nash wriggles back against him. They curl together, Nash's body fitting so neatly under his chin that Christopher can barely breathe.

Somehow, this moment feels so much more intimate than anything else they just did. He wants to stay awake, learn every contour of Nash's body, but the radiating warmth of their entwined bodies threatens to lull him to sleep.

He feels . . . safe. Does Nash feel the same way? Does Christopher *want* Nash to feel that way, after everything? He wills his brain to quieten down, and just enjoy this delicious moment.

His internal whirring is broken open when Nash murmurs, 'Do you smell something?'

'Just tell me. I'm too tired for guessing games,' grumbles Christopher.

'Like . . . smoke.'

They leap out of bed at the exact same time, almost colliding in the doorway as they race to the kitchen to save the pizza. Luckily, they aren't entirely cremated, and the pair of them burst into laughter that they're both butt-naked standing in the kitchen.

'Imagine if this had caught fire.'

'I'd rather not,' Christopher shudders as he cuts up the very dark pizzas into approximate slices and plates them up. He hands a plate to Nash and nods towards the still-open bedroom door. There's no point pretending they aren't going to just eat them in bed.

'The firefighters would show up while we were naked. Or we'd have to go out into the snow in just our pants. Like when you came to rescue me from my prison of my own creation in the bakery kitchen.'

They climb back into bed, plates balanced on their laps. Clearly, Nash is as hungry as Christopher after the long day because the pizzas are gone in minutes, and soon their plates are abandoned on the floor and side table.

Nash lies back, his eyes heavy. 'God I needed that.'

'The pizza?'

But there's no smarmy reply from Nash, because moments later, he's asleep.

And where he goes, Christopher follows.

Chapter Nineteen

Nash

When Nash wakes, he finds Christopher curled up against him, like the world's gangliest little spoon. In the weak morning light, he counts the freckles that start behind Christopher's ear and run down his shoulders to the soft curve of his stomach, a constellation of dusted cinnamon. Nash can't help but look at his long eyelashes and listen to the soft not-quite-snores he makes as he sleeps. Thankfully, Christopher is also radiating enough heat to keep both of them warm.

Sleeping with him was probably not the smartest idea Nash has ever had. After all, it's only just Christmas Eve, and they are guaranteed to have to get through another few days with each other until it's time for Nash to go home.

Hopefully they can stick to their usual bickering and not make too big a deal out of things. It's just sex after all. Surely they can just carry on the way they were, even having seen each other naked. That's all Nash wants. But the way Nash watched Christopher's soul repeatedly try to exit his body over just sharing a bed makes him suspect it's *not* going to be so casual. Probably because Christopher's baseline behaviour is always a little awkward. He's not just gangly; he's *emotionally* gangly and misplaced and too big for the room.

Perhaps it was an inevitability that Nash would get swept up by those big blue eyes the minute Christopher turned his normal bossiness to something much more fun. Nash has always been a sucker for big guys who like to be bossed around in the bedroom. Turns out Christopher seems into it too.

Plus, it was really hot.

Like *really* hot.

Who knows if it will happen again. Really, they probably shouldn't. First rule of being slightly famous is, don't sleep with your fans, though he's not sure if that counts when they're so begrudgingly a fan of your work once they've met you.

Either way, he kind of hopes they get to do it again, even if they shouldn't. He'd like to. It was fun.

Christopher's soft snores form a gentle rhythm that his own breath matches. Nash wonders if they were like that in their sleep, just naturally in tune with each other. In some ways, it does feel as if they are.

His mind wanders back to last night, to the way Christopher's long hands trailed his body. To the little gasps Christopher made when Nash went down on him.

He's not had a connection like that for . . . well, quite a long time. Yes, there's been good sex, but this felt like *really* good sex. The kind of sex you have with a good friend or an ex you still like, or if it's a one-night stand, the kind you stretch out over a weekend. Almost as if . . . no, he's not going to go there.

It was just blowing off steam.

Blowing off *something*, anyway.

What a great nearly-Christmas present to end up in bed with a hot Englishman. He did always have a thing for the Hugh Grant type.

Christopher's alarm goes off on his phone, and he grumbles, patting the bed around him in order to turn it off. For someone that everyone else reads as affable and polite, it's quite funny that he wakes like an angry little creature who has been personally affronted by the morning. It's as if they swap personalities in their sleep.

But then, he's seen all sorts of sides of Christopher in the last few days.

Christopher wriggles away and a rush of cool air punctuates the separation of their bodies as the alarm stops.

'Morning,' Nash whispers and Christopher flinches.

Just as expected, there is no way this man is going to be casual about the fact they slept together. But at least that means Nash can have a little fun with it.

'Um, yes, good morning,' Christopher replies, looking very invested in whatever is happening on his phone screen.

'I'll make some coffee, shall I?'

Still not looking over to Nash, Christopher nods, pressing his lips firmly together.

'What was that?'

'Yes. Please. Thank you.'

Oh God, he's reverted to basic programming. A post-coital C-3P0.

Nash decides to make the coffee and give him some space, but when he comes back into the bedroom with steaming mugs and plates of toast for two, Christopher is somehow showered, fully dressed and has made the bed. And when he takes the cup and plate, Christopher just returns with a little nod and quiet thanks and goes to eat them on the couch.

So, he's going with stiff and distant. All right then.

This is the worst kind of awkward Christopher could have opted for, and if Nash is honest with himself, he feels a bit peeved. Like, man, is it that bad that Christopher slept with him? Shouldn't Nash be the one feeling weird? God, he doesn't even know how to feel now that Christopher is basically ignoring him.

He shuts the bedroom door and takes a hot shower, though it's only hot for approximately two minutes. British plumbing is not something he could ever get used to. Or British central heating. Or the weather in general.

He sits on top of the covers still in his towel. The bed is still kind of warm with their heat, and he has to resist the urge to clamber back in soggily. He quickly dries himself off and puts on some fresh underwear before deciding he needs to slow down.

There is, blissfully, nothing on his phone, probably because everyone is asleep. He opens his finsta and likes a few photos of his friends' dogs. His main account has been updated by Tessa for the last few weeks, mostly just photos from his last shoot, or shots from various holiday movies, reminding people that *nothing says Noel like Nadeau*. He has to hand it to her, that is pretty catchy.

He can't stay in here forever, as much as he'd like to. Because the sooner he leaves this room, the sooner he has to interact with robo-Christopher.

He takes a deep breath, and with one confidence-boosting smile at the mirror, he walks back to the living room. Awkwardness hangs in the air, like when you're trying to pass a stranger in a tight hallway and both of you are trying to let the other person go first. Is this how Christopher feels all the time? No wonder the man can't settle.

In another world, they could just be having breakfast together and talking about the day and not be shrouded in a cloud of weirdness just because they slept together. Apparently, this is beyond Christopher. They should get out of the house, give Christopher a task to do, rather than watch him try to absorb himself into the couch.

'Shall we go?' he asks, and Christopher near enough spills coffee everywhere.

He leans forward, his cup and it seems his face dripping coffee. 'Where?'

'Where else? Community centre. See what adventures await us.'

'Yes. I'll just . . . go clean myself up.'

Nash decides, just for once, to let that one go.

Once they're dressed (or re-dressed in Christopher's case), they're outside and over the road in a flash. Christo-bot storms ahead with his gigantic legs – which Nash can't stop thinking about wrapping himself around – without so much as a glance backwards to see how Nash is even doing.

It's so early that there's hardly anyone inside the community centre once they arrive. Even the lady who makes the horrible hot drinks isn't here.

'Hiya!' It's Shaz, here already, her voice echoing across the empty room from where she stands with Tamara.

'Good morning.' Christopher is still in polite robot mode, but to be fair, it's so close to his general awkward demeanour with strangers that Tamara seems not to notice. Shaz, however, does glance at Christopher before looking over at Nash with a searching glance.

'Don't look at me. He's always like that,' Nash mutters. 'Do we need to go up to Myffy's this morning?'

Tamara shakes her head. 'The bonus of living on a small-holding is that we have a 4 x 4 that can drive through most obstacles, so we whizzed Polly home and dropped Priti off there again first thing, so she's with her all day.'

'We'll pop in later, if you'd like?'

'That would be good, if you're up for it, but I have a possibly bizarre request for you both first.'

Finally, a task that can distract them.

'What's bizarre about it?' Nash asks.

'Well, I've had a rather interesting email.'

'Has someone told you you're cursed unless you forward it on to ten other people?' interrupts Shaz. 'Though I've always wondered how that would even de-curse you, because surely you're just sneezing the curse around?'

Tamara gives her the kind of withering look that only comes from knowing someone for far too long. 'Very witty. Here to escape the kids?'

'You bet. I told my mother-in-law she is on grandparent duties and the look she gave me was worth it all.'

Tamara continues, ignoring Shaz. 'I think you should all read it yourselves. See what you make of it.'

She spins the laptop round, and they all peer over. Naturally, Christopher has to crouch down to read the screen, the absolute giant.

Dear Ms Yang,
    I write to you today as a concerned constituent who hopes that you can knock some sense into one of your other constituents. My terribly stubborn neighbour, Dai Edwards, appears to have lost all his power (this is what happens when you don't install two backup generators like I suggested). The silly man will not leave his farm and while I have no intention of talking to him, I'd also rather he does not freeze to death. Please go sort him out.

Regards,
Anonymous

Underneath is a second email from the same account, replying to the chain, that just says *P.S. You never saw this email.*

'How very odd. I wonder why whoever this person is doesn't want Dai to know they're trying to help him?' murmurs Christopher.

'And why have they signed it "Anonymous" when their email address is right there?' asks Nash, expanding the email address out. 'thelmaagogo@gmail . . . is that someone's name?'

At this, Shaz barks with laughter and grabs at Tamara's extremely well-pressed coat. 'Oh my god, is it really?'

'*Really* really,' confirms Tamara, wearing a very unpolitician-like gleeful smile.

'I didn't think they were still fighting! How mad that she's trying to help him out?'

'That's the really strange bit to me, though. Don't you think it's strange?'

'I'd have thought she'd be glad he'd freeze his willy off.'

'Please don't make me think about his willy.'

'Too late.'

'Sorry to interrupt this charming discussion about willies,' Nash says, feeling Christopher physically panic as he says that word, 'but can you guys explain what on earth is going on?'

'Let me tell it, please?' Shaz presses her hands in prayer at Tamara, who gives her a gesture of 'Go ahead'. 'Okay, so the key players in this story are Dai and Thelma. They both come from farming families, and so they were always in each other's orbit growing up. Inseparable as kids apparently – obviously neither of us were alive then. But when they were teenagers . . .'

She pauses for effect for just a little too long.

'Sorry—' begins Christopher, who is immediately interrupted by Shaz yelling, 'THEY FELL IN LOVE.'

'Oooohh,' Nash replies, evoking his very best Dr Phil audience member, like he's in a studio audience and someone held up a sign that says, 'React excitedly.'

'And they were courting for like years, right?' Shaz continues. 'But then, something happened between them, that we've never really got to the bottom of. Like a really, *really* terrible break-up. The kind where people pick sides, and everyone becomes sworn enemies.'

'My mam said it was like they unanimously agreed to never speak again,' Tamara confirms.

'And they never did. It's been like fifty years or something?' Shaz adds.

'Holding a grudge for fifty years?' cries Christopher, which seems a little ironic to Nash, because if *anyone* has the emotional capacity to hold a pointless grudge for too long, he thinks it would be Christopher. 'Crikey.'

'Crikey indeed. They're both . . . you know, rather elderly now. Still running their farms and that. But whenever they're in the same room together, they completely blank each other. Not even a "Tell that man over there" type message thing. As far as they're concerned, the other person is dead to them.'

'Intense,' whispers Nash. 'Did they ever date anyone else?'

Shaz nods. 'Oh yeah, of course they did. Both of them married other people. Thelma's husband Eric died about ten years ago now. Their son, Liam moved up to London.'

'Hang on, isn't London south of here?' Nash asks.

'London is definitely south. It's just how she says it,' Christopher explains.

'For a moment there I was worried I was more lost than I thought.'

And he can't help but feel a little relieved that Christopher said something kind of normal to him. Nothing like reuniting some ornery old people to bring them together. Well, as long as Nash doesn't accidentally scream a swear word again.

'And Dai married my mother's sister Miriam, but they divorced a long time ago. I must have been barely ten,' adds Tamara. 'Honestly I don't think he got over Thelma underneath it all. As much as they love to act like they hate each other.'

'And so, it's *dead* weird that she is, like, breaking that unbreakable pact to tell you to go sort him out,' muses Shaz.

'Precisely what's worrying me.' Tamara spins the ring on her fourth finger. 'As far as I know, nothing before has driven them to speak to each other. Neither death nor divorce, so I'm worried. She might act like he's dead in her own reality, but she must care enough to not want him to, you know . . .'

'Freeze his willy off.'

'Quite. But I'm also worried *she* might not be okay either. After all, giving up on your lifelong grudges feels quite . . . you know . . .'

'Big stuff.'

Tamara leans down to look at something on the computer. 'I just thought, if she is having some difficulties, she might be trying to deal with it on her own, which means we should check in on her. She's always been fiercely independent. She still drives that bloody enormous tractor around herself, but she really is getting on a bit now. And it's not like we can propose putting either of them up in any of the local care homes because they would never leave the animals anyway.'

'So, I guess we'll just have to find another way to help them.'

Tamara nods, her mind elsewhere. She must be worried. 'I know it's a tricky situation but it's odd for her to reach out.'

'We'll go help,' says Christopher. 'Don't worry.'

'Thank you. I'd go up with you but—'

'You need to stay here and make sure Ursula doesn't take over,' mutters Shaz, which sparks the smallest of grins from Tamara.

'I need to just help make sure things are running and it helps that I'm the councillor, as most people know me or at least my name. People like to know who they can ask for help, so it makes sense for me to be here. They're both a little like family.' She takes a deep breath. 'And credit to her, the reason I know there's any capacity in the care homes in general is because Ursula, who runs the big one down on the seafront, went through their books to see if they could take anyone particularly vulnerable who needs some extra help.'

Shaz hmms, clearly not yet willing to give Ursula any credit.

'I can go, if you want to stay here,' Christopher murmurs to Nash, hoping the others won't hear it. He's giving him an out, an opportunity for a break from each other. Perhaps they need this.

'Why?' Tamara says, making Christopher wince. 'You've been doing everything together. You're the dream duo, I've heard.'

Well. So much for that.

★ ★ ★

Tamara hands them some directions and they head back to the van straight away. As it snowed a little bit overnight,

Nash takes the opportunity to do some checks before they head off, but everything seems to be running well.

'Where first?' he asks, clipping his seatbelt in.

'Dai, I presume? Find out what's wrong, and then when we've fixed it, we can go check in on Thelma? You'll have to navigate on the map, if that's all right?' He faces forward as though watching the road, even though they're still stationary.

'It's what we've been doing the whole time, Calloway.' He had hoped this familiarity might break some of the tension, but Christopher seems stiff in the bad way again. 'Did we need anything else for the prepper bag before we go?'

'You're the one who put a saw in the back of the van. I think we'll be okay.'

Nash manages to find the farms on the map thanks to the directions Tamara wrote down for them. Always good to have both to hand in a snowstorm.

He laughs to himself. 'It's all the Boy Scout skills at play this Christmas. If I'd known, I'd have done a refresher course or something.'

'I'm not sure you can do a refresher course on Scouting as an adult.'

'Pity. But luckily I've got the boy-scoutiest Boy Scout ever to scout his way in the driver's seat.'

This, at least, rouses a small smile from Christopher.

Nash has never been a nervous driver or passenger, but the tiny winding roads up around the mountain and into the farmlands are really testing his resolve. Even the roads in the countryside in Canada were bigger than this. These are definitely not the freeways of LA, though they're terrifying in a whole different way. He technically has the *ability* to drive (if not the legal okay) but he's pretty sure that nothing in his Drivers' Ed classes would have covered piloting a recently fixed bakery truck down curiously serpentine, snowed-in Welsh roads with an uptight Englishman.

'Hang on, can you slow down?' he asks, peering at the road, and to the map again.

Christopher complies. 'Do I need to turn back?'

'No, I'm . . . just not sure this is a road. It looks like a hiker's trail. Not that I can tell from all the snow.'

'I think, unfortunately, it is a proper road.'

Nash retraces their steps on the map, and it does appear to be an actual road for people to drive down, in theory. 'Drive on, I guess,' he says, a little nervously.

There's barely room for their truck, and as they drive, they take bits of snow-topped hedge from both sides with them. Beside him, Christopher winces at the occasional scraping sound on metal.

'It'll buff out,' Nash says, unsure if it will.

How do people even use these roads in normal weather? If another vehicle comes along, one of them will have to reverse because there's no room to pass each other.

And that's to say nothing of the visibility. *Everything* is white, and it's taking all their concentration to determine what bits of white are road, hedge or the huge dip that runs along the edge of the road. It's like driving in a meringue. As if to really get the point across, a few ominous snowflakes land on the windscreen.

Quickly followed by a lot more.

'Uh-oh,' whispers Christopher, turning on the windscreen wiper, which squeaks as it tries to furiously wipe away the snow.

'Uh-oh indeed,' murmurs Nash, clutching at the map for dear life. 'Maybe we should speed up a little? We're going to get snowed in here at this rate.'

'I don't think it's safe to drive any faster,' Christopher says quietly, concentrating hard on driving.

'The snow is falling faster than we're moving.' Nash bites his lip.

Without taking his eyes off the road and with a clenched jaw, Christopher mutters, 'Please stop backseat-driving me, Nash. I need to concentrate.'

'I'm not in the backseat. I'm shotgun.'

It's not productive to annoy the person driving him through a snowstorm, but perhaps it'll keep him moving. Alert with annoyance. His barbs are the spark that lights the wick. After all, he knows that flirting with Christopher makes him freeze up and go all robotic, but annoying him, like when Nash arguably destroyed his kitchen, made him move as if he was on 2x playback.

But then, he'd just really like Christopher to keep concentrating on not driving them into a hedge or a ditch or off a cliff. Who knows if there are even cliffs here!? Well, there is a map on his lap that suggests no, there aren't any, but what if there's been some kind of mass erosion incident?

God he's spent too much time around Christopher. And only two people from his world even know he's here!

For some reason, he starts thinking about how soft Christopher's deeply dreaming breaths were this morning. How they woke breathing in sync. How closely curled up together they were, like a pair of commas. As though searching for a moment of greater safety to ground him.

'I can't see any turnings off at all,' mutters Christopher, which startles Nash from his thoughts. He's frowning so hard that a crease appears between his eyebrows. 'Am I supposed to be straight still?'

What he wants to say is *probably not after last night,* but then Christopher would go out of his way to find a cliff to drive them off. 'Yeah, just keep going,' he says instead.

The road slowly climbs, then dips and winds as they get deeper into the valley. It's bordered by more mountains, which seems like a terrible place to farm, but then again Nash is more familiar with the Dorothy-from-Kansas-esque golden fields of corn than the idea of sheep clinging to mountainsides, which seems to be more the vibe here.

In the distance, Nash thinks he sees a building. He glances back down at the map. 'I think we're almost there.'

'Are you sure?' Christopher says, squinting at the building up ahead as he slows the truck down. 'It looks abandoned.'

'Didn't the email say his power was out? That might be why.'

'Good point. Can you see the turn-off for it on the map?'

Christopher slows to a plodding crawl, the kind that reminds Nash of the near-stationary traffic jams of LA and how they make him want to chew his arm off, because he could walk faster than that. Well, maybe not in this weather.

They come across what looks like it could be the entrance – a gate half propped open with a giant stone.

'I'm going to have to get out and move that, aren't I?' sighs Nash.

'If you wouldn't mind?'

'Oh, I really do mind.'

Still, he leaps out of the car, pulling his coat tightly around him as the cold mountain breezes try to tear it away. The expensive hiking jacket he'd bought for this trip was supposed to be for leisurely wanders up along the beach, not for wading through snowstorms, and its capability to keep him warm in the middle of one is really being tested.

Wading through the white, Nash desperately peers around for signs confirming this is actually the turn-off for Pentre Farm, and not a potentially dangerous mountain road that will lead to their untimely deaths. Luckily, he spies something attached to the top of the gate. With the sleeve of his coat, he wipes the snow away to read a sign that says 'Pentre Farm'. At least it's the right place. Who knows, it could *still* be a terrifying murder road, but what choice do they have? He moves the rock to the side and opens the gate fully so Christopher can drive straight through.

He's about to get back in the van when Christopher shouts frantically through his open door, 'No, you have to close it behind us!'

'Why?'

'The Countryside Code?'

Dear God, this country. 'What the hell are you talking about?'

'Just do it!'

Nash slams the van door again, just for good measure. He weighs up the risk of breaking some kind of quaint British law against how fun this argument with Christopher could be, and decides to shut the gate behind them. After all, it is a weather emergency and letting errant creatures wander off in it would probably make this whole situation about twenty times worse.

'Thank you,' Christopher says, as Nash gets back in.

'You owe me for my frostbitten fingers. That must come under short-term lets insurance, right?'

Christopher harrumphs at him, which is enough of a normal Christopher response for Nash to feel relieved that they're back on semi-familiar bickering ground.

The tiny dirt track opens up to a farmyard containing a small farmhouse, completely blacked out through lack of power, and a few farm buildings.

Nash points at one of the furthest away buildings in the yard, from which emanates a soft golden glow. 'He must be in there.'

'In the barn?' Christopher pulls on a woolly hat that covers his ears, which have gone a different kind of pink to the more familiar embarrassed scarlet. 'That seems strange that he wouldn't be in the house?'

'Well, but the power's out, isn't it? Who knows what he's up to.'

Nash reluctantly gets back out of the van, which wasn't *warm* but was still a darn sight warmer than out in the cold.

He can hear sheep softly bleating coming from the direction of the barn, and the rich, earthy scent of hay fills the air. Hopefully any and all livestock are safely secured and comfortable.

The door to the barn is closed, so Christopher raps on the wood with the back of his knuckles. 'Hello?'

There's no answer, and Christopher is hanging back, clearly unsure whether to knock again. It's far too cold to hang around, and this could be an emergency, so after a few seconds of courtesy, Nash cautiously opens the door, just in case there are animals inside looking to escape.

But instead of animals, he's met with a tirade of what he can only presume is Welsh from an ancient, tiny man sitting cross-legged in a pile of straw next to a Border collie. He's wrapped in several layers of coats, but he looks absolutely frozen, the poor guy. Well, he's not frozen solid at least, because he's very animatedly yelling at them.

'Hi! Sorry! We're here to help!' Nash's shouts are drowned out by the continued flow of yells from the tiny cold man.

Christopher follows him in and shuts the door behind them. 'How did you upset him so quickly?'

'I didn't do anything,' Nash growls in return. Turning his Hollywood charm back on, he approaches the tiny farmer, who must be Dai Jones, with palms face forward in an *I come in peace* gesture. 'Hello,' he says slowly and clearly. 'I'm Nash. We're here to help.'

'Bloody hell,' says the farmer in English, peering up at Nash's face with intense scrutiny. 'You're that fella off the telly, isn't it?'

To say that this was not what he was expecting, especially given the man was up until a few moments ago yelling profanities at him in Welsh, would be a major understatement. His fanbase are usually married heterosexual women with a kid or two for a start, and then of course there's the slew of young queers on the internet. Apparently, he has quite a dedicated TikTok fandom, in fact, but he's pretty sure this elderly farmer is not part of that crowd. Then again, you never know these days.

'Nash Nadeau?' Dai prompts.

'That's me,' he says.

'Well, good job you're here. Nessa here needs some help.'

Nessa, who must be the black-and-white Border collie, breathes heavily.

'I think you've mistaken him for someone else,' suggests Christopher, kneeling down in the hay.

'I have not,' says Dai archly, as though Christopher is not paying attention properly. 'He's always saving animals, isn't he? An American vet, but I'm sure you know your way around a farm dog.'

'Canadian,' corrects Christopher.

'Well, technically I usually am playing an American one,' Nash says.

It's not just in the *Christmas at the Clinic* series where Nash plays a veterinarian, now. He's played a vet in several TV guest spots too, and a handful of other Christmas films as a background character. It's almost become a trope, a kind of meta-joke that nods to the audience – *oh look, he's a veterinarian again, everyone*. It's one of those Officially Sanctioned romance movie jobs. After all, who doesn't love a sensitive man who rescues animals?

'I'm really sorry, sir, but I'm not really a qualified veterinarian. I just play one a lot. I'm just an actor.'

'Oh,' Dai says. 'I thought it was like *The Yorkshire Vet* or something, but American. I did wonder why you were always doing things at Christmas, and the sexual chemistry . . .'

He trails off and looks down at his black-and-white collie, whose head is nestled in his lap. Despite how sad she looks, she's a very beautiful animal. Her fur is long and curls softly, and the pads of her paws and her nose are delightfully pink.

'What's wrong with her?' Christopher shuffles closer to the collie. She raises her head with tremendous effort just to shoot Christopher a side-eye, which makes Nash like her even more.

'Giving birth, isn't she?' Dai gently strokes down the centre of her snout. 'I found her in here last night, and I knew something was up, so didn't really want to move her until she was ready. But then the power went out, so we stayed in here because there's the little heater. And then she went into labour, but it's been going on so long. I'm worried something is wrong.'

Shit.

Right now, seeing the exhaustion on Nessa the dog's face, Nash really, *really* wishes he was a veterinarian. Before the first *Christmas at the Clinic* film, he'd convinced a local veterinary clinic to let him come and shadow for a week. They had told him how to properly hold dogs, and he got to see some truly gross but fascinating things that made him realise that, if he'd had the grades and not been a teen actor, he might have actually *wanted* to be a vet. But he'd never watched an animal actually giving birth. He knows as much about assisting a dog giving birth as he would about a human. And that's next to nothing. It's all theory and television – clean towels, fresh hot water, and hope. But he's pretty sure that's not enough here, especially when she's been in labour this long. Is this a normal amount of time?

'Is there a clinic we could call? Did you already try someone?' Christopher asks.

'The phone lines are down, and I hate using those mobile things. I am forever leaving it somewhere. When all the lights went off, I went into the house to look for it, but hell knows where it is. It's probably not even charged anyway.' Dai looks very old and vulnerable all of a sudden. And he's been sitting here all night. No wonder even his sworn enemy sent a concerned email.

Christopher pulls his phone out of his coat and looks down at the screen. 'No signal. You?'

Nash does the same and shakes his head. 'None.'

'We could drive you and Nessa to the vet? Do you know where it is?'

'The guy I use is in Abergwyn, few towns along. He's the best for the sheep. And normally he'd drive up here anyroad,' says Dai.

'Do you know if there's one in Pen-y-Môr?' Nash asks.

Christopher shakes his head. 'I think they closed just after I moved here. And Abergwyn is pretty far in this weather. I'm worried about us getting stuck on the way.'

They share a worried look as Nessa whines. There's only one thing for it. They're going to have to bring up Thelma.

'What about any of the other farmers nearby? Is there anyone who knows much about . . . delivery?' Nash asks.

Dai shuffles in his coat, glancing from Nessa to the floor, to the ceiling. Well, that seems to be a 'Yes, but I'd rather die.'

'You don't have to speak to whoever it is,' offers Christopher, trying valiantly to not give the game away. 'But if you want to get help for Nessa, I think that could be the best we can do right now, especially in this weather. That is, if you know someone.'

Very smooth.

Dai stares up at the little slit window, as if hoping the weather might have shifted dramatically since this conversation started. But it hasn't. The window is frosted over.

With a heavy sigh, he asks Nash one last time, 'Are you *sure* you're not a vet, lad?'

Gently, Nash reaches out and takes Dai's ice-cold, frail hand. 'I promise you that, if I was, I would tell you. We can go get someone who can help Nessa. That might be the best way we can help you.'

The tension seeps out of Dai. 'Fine. Yes, there is one girl. She did her training before giving it up to farm, but she's always been a dab hand with the animals, even if she is, you know, the devil incarnate.'

'Is that Ms Thelma?' offers Christopher.

'Ought to be careful saying her name in a storm like this. You never know what you'll summon.'

Jesus Christ, thinks Nash. Shaz and Tamara weren't kidding.

'We'll go and get her, and she can come and help,' Christopher says, getting to his feet.

But he's interrupted by a sad bleat from the farmer. 'She won't want to help me!' There's a heavy pause, before he sighs. 'We haven't spoken in *fifty years*. Do you have any idea how long that is, boy?'

'I think she might want to help Nessa though,' Nash insists, and as if on cue, Nessa gives a heavy breath out. They need to get moving. He may not be a real veterinarian, but he knows what an animal in pain looks like. 'If she likes animals, she wouldn't want to leave Nessa out here without helping her.'

A little resigned, Dai nods along. 'She always did love puppies,' he muses, and Nash swears that the old man's eyes mist over. Is he lost in his memories right now, replaying happy moments when they were teenagers and in love, before things got twisted and angry and slightly cryptic?

It's all decided when Nessa whines again. It's a plaintive little sound. Dai cradles her head in his hands, softly stroking his thumb over her cheeks. The tip of her tail weakly wags with happiness that he is here with her.

Fucking hell, if he can't help this dog, something in Nash might actually break. 'Come on, Christopher,' he says, getting to his feet.

Christopher looks torn. 'Can we get you anything before—'

'Please go,' Dai says quietly. 'Please be quick.'

'We will be back before you know it.' Nash promises this, hoping that it's true. They sprint back to the van, and this time Nash opens the gate without a complaint.

In hopeful, worried silence, they drive through the snow to Thelma's farm.

Chapter Twenty

Christopher

Even though Thelma's farm is pretty close as the crow flies, the drive takes them up and down the mountainsides, skirting the edges of the valley in a big loop. Snow continues to fall, but thankfully less forcefully, so Christopher can mostly see where he's going. It's as if the skies heard there was a pregnant dog in trouble and gave everyone a temporary reprieve.

Still, the flakes are so thick and huge they look like falling dollops of ice cream.

Beside him, Nash grips the map so tightly that the paper warps. With his finger, he traces the route there and back, over and over, as though hoping to shorten it. They're both worried about Nessa, but it's weirding Christopher out that Nash is so quiet. Not a single joke, or snip. It's more unnerving than the general atmosphere of mild peril.

'Nearly there,' Christopher says, to reassure them both.

'I hope she can help,' Nash murmurs. 'I hope she *wants* to help.'

'I think the email was enough of a sign of that, but . . . yeah.'

Sending an anonymous tip that someone needed help was a very different prospect to sitting in that tiny little shed helping your mortal enemy's pregnant dog.

Thanks to the soft orange glow of the lights, Thelma's farm is visible from quite a way away. It's still only mid-morning so it's not dark but there's a strange, murky quality to the weak light that struggles to get through all the snowfall. It's as though the sun decided it might have a long lie-in, as it's Christmas Eve. Every now and then there's a gust of snow that rolls over them like a bank of fog.

The drive feels like an eternity. Thelma's farm is apparently called Bryn-Heulog – a name that neither of them are sure they pronounce right – but Christopher cannot contain the glee when he spots a sign for it up ahead. When they turn off the main road, the gate is thankfully already propped open as though she was expecting guests. Christopher drives straight down the long drive, past barns of sheep and cows that call after them like drunken patrons at a bar.

They park up right outside her farmhouse, and just as they turn off the engine, the front door flings open.

Standing in the glow from inside is, presumably, Thelma. Her hands-on-hips stance is deeply no-nonsense. Short curly hair springs out from underneath a knitted hat, and she somehow looks formidable in an apron and bright red wellies. She is also possibly the shortest woman Christopher has ever met, but her whole somewhat menacing vibe is enough to make him want to stay in the safety of his vehicle.

'Hello!' calls Christopher cheerily, clambering out of the van. 'Are you Ms Thelma . . . ?' He racks his brain for her surname, trying not to say Agogo.

'Powell, I'll have you know.'

'Yes, Ms Powell.' Christopher has no idea if this is even right, and Thelma offers him nothing else. 'We're from the community response team from Pen-y-Môr, for the snow.'

He has no idea if they actually have an official name, but Thelma seems like a woman who *wants* an official name. She waits silently for more, one eyebrow raised.

'Tamara Yang sent us to do some check-ins on the farmers as we heard that a few people were out of power. We've just come from Pentre Farm.'

She nods, taking this in. 'You didn't bring him here, did you?' She peers into the dark of the van.

'No, Dai—'

'Don't speak that man's name here,' she snaps, and Christopher is fairly sure she spits onto the ground as if to cleanse the name from the air. How did two people who were once in love get like this? Were their feelings warped over time? Or were they always like this? What makes playful barbs become thorns?

They might be truly the strangest pair of people he has ever met.

'No ma'am, he wouldn't leave the farm, but we've come to you because we need your help. I'm Nash Nadeau,' Nash says, turning on his full actor charm, dazzling smile. 'And this is Christopher Calloway. Could we take a few moments of your time?'

She gives them a little upwards chin nod, and ushers them into the ludicrously warm kitchen. Christopher is fairly sure he had some icicles growing on him up to now. He thinks back to Dai, shivering in the shed with Nessa.

'What's the situation then?' She leans back against the counter, her arms still folded. 'Is he too tight to pay the bills? He'd peel an orange in his pocket, that one.'

Christopher decides to take the lead. 'His sheepdog, Nessa, is in labour. We're all a bit concerned that there's something going wrong, and we thought that, as you were near, you might be able to help. He won't leave her and we don't think she's safe to travel to the vet, so we're hoping you might have some ideas.'

She raises an eyebrow at this and sucks her teeth. 'Does he know you came here?'

'He does.'

'Hmm.'

'But we didn't tell him that you originally sent us the tip that something was up,' adds Nash.

She sniffs, as though to dismiss this suggestion that she was the one who reached out to them. Well, Christopher thinks, they can go along with her curious fiction if she'll agree to help.

After an excruciatingly long silence, she finally says, 'You were right to come to me. I'll go.'

Relief pours through Christopher as she grabs a thick coat from the back of the door. She doesn't take off the apron, but fills a reusable shopping bag with towels from under the sink. She hands this to him as she passes, disappearing further into her house.

'Thank fuck for that,' whispers Nash. 'I was worried we were going to deliver a litter of puppies ourselves.'

'Well, that might be a possibility. I think we should be there to make sure they don't kill each other.'

'Can we somehow take this heat back with us. My nipples were going to fall off in there.'

'How curiously specific.'

Christopher's doubly relieved, though. Things were so strange this morning, with Nash acting as if nothing happened at all. Something happened! Something huge! And they just didn't talk about it? Nash just got up and made coffee and toast, which was nice of him, but was that it? Is Christopher supposed to just move on and forget about it? It makes him feel as if they are living in two parallel universes and he doesn't know how to reach out to Nash's.

That whole situation is way too complicated, to the point that dealing with these two cantankerous farmers who might try and kill each other in the world's coldest barn feels like a much better prospect than going back to that tiny flat with Nash in tow. He doesn't have time to think about how he feels about it all, in part because he feels so many different ways at once.

He's grateful when Thelma returns in a blur of activity, so he and Nash are no longer alone with nothing to talk about. She hands Nash a bag this time.

'All right lads. Let's mynd,' she says, ushering them out the door.

Nash holds the passenger side door open for her, but Thelma stomps off into the yard. 'Do you not want to come in the van?' he calls after her.

'I've got my own transport.' She points to a tractor parked alongside the house. The exact tractor that Tamara was despairing that she drives. 'I'll go through the field tracks and meet you there.'

Not ones to argue with a tiny terrifying woman, Christopher and Nash get back into the van. As Christopher backs them slowly out of the farmyard, they see her tiny yet stocky frame perched inside an enormous tractor lurching out of the gloom and chugging out into the field behind them.

'Bloody hell,' laughs Christopher.

'You'd better drive fast or she's going to beat us there and we might be walking into a murder scene.'

'I probably should have packed yellow police tape in my prepper bag.'

It annoys him that this gets a laugh from Nash, even though he was trying to be funny, because *urgh* it just feels strange to slip back into normality after last night. He's probably being weird, and he knows that speaking to the gang would absolutely help, but what's he supposed to do? Text them like, *hey, just to let you know we had sex and I'm behaving not at all normally about it*? Something to worry about when they are somewhere with signal, and when he isn't driving quite quickly through the snow back to Pentre Farm.

Thelma's tractor is already parked up when they arrive in Dai's farmyard, but she's still in the driver's seat, staring straight ahead. How long has she been here? How long must it have been since she was last here? They were childhood friends who inherited their family farms, so presumably she must have spent a lot of time here many, many years ago. Perhaps it's like visiting a memory, or even a graveyard? And any good memories they have must be shadowed by the worst moments of their shared past. There must be so much history, not just here but between them. Even though she wants to help Dai, it sounds as if they've not been alone together for the whole time they haven't spoken. They've been in rooms with other people, and still not spoken.

And now they're going to have to communicate, *really* communicate, for the first time in fifty years, in order to help Nessa.

What must that feel like, to see someone you loved so intensely after so long? After so much time and space and pain? It was pretty strange the first time he saw Laurel post break-up – the party where he met Haf was probably only the second or third time after that, and certainly was the first time he'd seen her with Mark, an odious man who is now thankfully her ex. It was strained, every time. They still loved each other, but time and space had bloomed distance between them.

Like Dai and Thelma, he and Laurel had been childhood friends, then teenage sweethearts. They had grown up together, and tried to grow into new people alongside each other. Luckily, they have developed a supportive friendship that has allowed both of them to become the people they were trying to be. But all that took a lot of honest, and often awkward, conversations. Plus one very drunken snog at her parents' Christmas party. But he can't imagine what that rekindling would be like after a whole life, after marriages and children and the loss of those spouses too, when you also hadn't spoken for that entire time? How do you grow through that? How do you find each other again?

He almost doesn't want to intrude on her quiet thinking, but needs must. They have a dog to help.

Christopher gives Nash a nod, and they clamber out of the van. Hearing them, Thelma comes to life and hops down from the tractor in a swift, surprisingly spritely move. Perhaps she's been thinking about it too, a wholesome, tentative reunion precipitated by some light meddling on his and Nash's part.

But that hope is instantly quashed when Thelma slams open the barn door and strides in. So much for tentative.

'Iesu grist! A witch appears at my door,' Dai cries.

'Move over, you old bastard,' she hisses, kneeling down in the straw next to Nessa, whose panting has got faster since they were last here.

'Oh Nessa,' whispers Nash, as he and Christopher join them on the floor.

'The boys said she's in labour, aye? How long?' Thelma's words are to the point and delivered like a whack to the head.

'Since the early hours. She was a bit off in the evening. The panting started while these boys were gone.' He nervously looks at Christopher and Nash, and checks the watch on his wrist. 'Could be close to twelve hours now.'

Thelma *hmms* to herself, running her hands gently along Nessa's abdomen.

'Is that a normal amount of time?' asks Christopher.

'A tad long,' she replies, her eyes focused on the dog. 'I've got you, girl.'

Nessa seems to understand, relaxing ever so slightly under Thelma's experienced touch.

'Is she going to be all right?' Dai asks quietly. And then, as if that was too much vulnerability, he adds, 'Thelma Edwards, if you kill my dog, I'll—'

'You'll what? Not speak to me for another fifty years?'

'Lord, I've seen what you've done for others—'

'Could we possibly help the dog without arguing?' suggests Christopher, which prompts a chorus of 'No' from Dai, Thelma and, for some reason, Nash. 'Why are you encouraging them?'

'Sorry, I got caught up in it all,' he says sheepishly.

'Also,' Thelma says, with a flick of her hair. 'It's been Powell for near forty years, God rest my Eric's soul. Thelma Edwards was someone else.'

That hits even Christopher like a punch to the chest.

'You,' Thelma says to Nash, taking charge. 'We need hot water. Dai, do you have owt?'

He doesn't look up from the dog. 'Go round to the sheep barn and you'll see an instant hot water tank on the wall. Should be some buckets too.'

Nash gets to his feet but hesitates.

'What are you waiting for? A pat on the head?'

'The keys? Is the barn unlocked?'

This prompts a chorus of laughing from both farmers.

'It's unlocked,' reassures Dai. 'Who the hell is going to break into it in this weather?'

'Good point,' Nash says, disappearing out of the door.

Thelma continues her inspection in silence, while Christopher and Dai share occasional worried glances. At least they're not arguing anymore, but bearing witness to their uncomfortable silence is almost as bad.

Inspection seemingly finished, Thelma nods. 'We'll get the pups out all right, and have you nursing in no time, girl. You've done really well so far.'

Together, Christopher and Dai deflate with relief. She's going to be okay.

Dai, however, might not survive the night. The look that Thelma gives him could turn milk. 'She's a bit old for a litter. You should know better.'

'It was an accident,' huffs Dai. 'Bloody dog appeared over the fields when we were out getting the sheep in, some hiker's pet. I told them to put it on leash so it wouldn't scare the sheep, but . . .'

'It clearly had something else on its mind,' finishes Nash, opening the door with his hip. 'She's okay?'

Christopher gives him a nod, and the huge grin that breaks across Nash's face brings a smile to his own. That's not a look he's seen Nash make before. A kind of childlike glee he wouldn't have thought typical for such a snarky little man.

Nash sets down a washing-up bowl of scalding hot water on the floor between them all, and without batting an eye, Nessa washes her hands in it with some hand cleaner from her bag. Christopher wishes he was even ten per cent as *hardcore* as this tiny terrifying woman.

'The panting means it's puppy time. How many?'

'Eight, according to the vet,' Dai says.

With raised eyebrows, she hands towels to each of the men. 'When the puppies come, clean them up. Rub them warm. It's cold and she's been at it a while, so chances are they'll need our help breathing air for the first time. Us helping takes the pressure off Nessa. Right?'

'Right,' they chorus, towels at the ready.

'You'll be used to this, of course,' Dai says to Nash.

'If the American is such a pro, why am I here?' Thelma snaps indignantly.

'I just play a veterinarian on TV.'

Thelma returns this proclamation with a withering look. 'That does *not* count.'

It doesn't take long for the first puppy to finally arrive, squealing and wriggling, and the room feels lighter for its arrival. One down, thinks Christopher. Seven to go.

Thelma explains that, due to Nessa's age and exhaustion, she's going to cut the umbilical cords for her, and that together they are all going to help remove the sacs from the puppies. That way, Nessa can concentrate on birthing the puppies and then getting them feeding. 'It's unusual', she stresses, 'but unusual circumstances mean cautious medicine.'

Despite, in her opinion, his lack of proper training, Thelma plops this first one in Nash's hands. He breaks open the sac and cleans up the puppy's eyes and nose with such tenderness. The puppy is quiet, so Nash checks inside its mouth for any blockages and the puppy whines indignantly.

'See now, you're a whizz, lad,' says Dai.

Christopher agrees that Nash is definitely a natural, but doesn't say it out loud. He's not sure why.

Soon there's a wriggling puppy in Christopher's hands. He takes a huge breath as he wipes the sac from her face and gives an *awoo* of joy as she starts to wriggle in his grasp.

Nash reluctantly gives his puppy back to Nessa, tucking the little dog in against her side where it immediately begins to nuzzle for her nipples. Poor girl, this is going to be a long night. Once he's satisfied that the second puppy is okay, Christopher plops her down next to the first puppy, just as puppy three is handed over to Dai.

After such a long wait, they're now coming way faster than Christopher expected.

Dai rubs the third puppy a little too vigorously for Christopher's sensibilities, but the pup seems not to mind. A fourth appears, taken up by Thelma, and she does the same kind of vigorous rubbing. Is that something they learned together, whelping puppies as children? Reunited by Nessa, the two puppies chorus in squeals for milk and life.

Another puppy is passed over to Nash. Five down, counts Christopher.

'Not long to go now, girl. You're doing brilliantly,' whispers Thelma.

Poor Nessa looks exhausted, but she keeps going and puppies keep coming. If Christopher had a wobbly sense of time from running his own bakery, it truly has nothing on this.

'She is such a good girl,' says Dai.

Their eyes meet, just for a second, and Christopher swears he can see that old love between them, or even just an echo of it. Love doesn't go away. It can't. It's like energy – all it can do is be transformed into other things. For them, perhaps hate, but haven't the great romance writers spent their careers telling everyone that the line between love and hate is very thin?

Christopher is snapped out of his sentimental musings when the puppy in Nash's hands lets out a roaring burp, and then promptly poops all over the towel.

'He's good at this, isn't he?' Dai insists, as he takes another puppy from Thelma's hands. 'Can't have been all movie magic, surely. Didn't you deliver puppies in that one with the lawyer and the Kardashian girl?'

'It was kittens,' chorus Nash and Christopher. The cringe that rips through Christopher's body could rival the puppy's burp, and the heat that emanates from his cheeks could warm the entire room. That's not even one of the top Nash Nadeau films that most romance fans would have seen; that's a deep cut from his IMDb. The kind of film that now just attracts people wanting to complete their 'weird celebrity cameo' lists on Letterboxd.

Still clutching puppy number five but wrapping it in a clean towel, Nash bursts into peals of satisfied laughter. 'I knew it! I *knew* it. You're *such* an Eve.'

'Who is Eve?' Dai asks, confused by the chaos he's unwittingly unleashed while warming up puppy number six, who is completely bone white, like a tiny ghost.

'*All About Eve*? Low-key movie about superfans turned maybe evil,' Nash laughs. 'And don't worry, Christopher. I'm just impressed that you know the plot intricacies of one of my least successful films.'

'Channel 5 runs all the Hallmark movies,' Dai explains. 'I'm a sucker for a good Christmas movie, but I'll take what I can get the other ten months of the year. Gethin got me onto this.'

Nash sighs. 'I never knew I'd have a fan group amongst Welsh farmers. Marketing are missing a trick.'

'Which Kardashian?' Thelma asks.

'Khloé.'

She makes a noise that Christopher reads as *fine, but not my favourite one*, just as puppy number seven arrives screeching its little head off. Thelma cleans it off and sets it right against Nessa with its siblings, along with Nash's now-poopless puppy. Dai still clutches his all-white puppy in his hands and Christopher is almost certain he hears Dai tell the puppy that she is now named Khloé. Perhaps they'll all be named after Nash's co-stars at this rate.

'So all this time you've been, what, a superfan?' Nash needles, this time looking directly at Christopher.

'I didn't want to be weird!'

'But that's your natural state. This makes the last twenty-four hours even wilder, Calloway.'

'What happened in the last twenty-four hours?' Dai asks, and Thelma shrugs, eyebrows raised.

'Never mind,' huffs Christopher, holding out his hands for the last puppy, who seems to be slowly making an appearance, much to Nessa's relief. Oh God, is this that bad? Worry bubbles through his body. 'You knew I'd seen your movies,' he says, trying to keep the whine out of his voice.

'I just had you pegged as being a casual embarrassed viewer hiding his Netflix history, not a connoisseur of the romance genre.'

'Well. They're good movies,' says Dai, coming to both of their defences.

Is Nash angry with him? Did he cross a barrier by not being upfront about exactly how much of Nash's cinematography he's seen (a lot) before they slept together? Is that the sort of thing you're supposed to disclose to an artist, because that seems like the worst possible option and biggest turn-off. Oh no, did he not tell him *because* part of him knew it was a turn-off?

This is the worst possible outcome, really.

'Can we just move past this?' Christopher asks, trying to ignore how much it sounds like begging.

'Not a chance.' Nash doesn't sound angry as much as amused. Though, Christopher still isn't sure where the line is. Where does fun joking end and being angry at each other in the snow begin?

'I was hoping we could be grown-ups about it.'

'Oh, you have no idea how much *worse* I am going to be now,' Nash laughs, arranging all the puppies alongside Nessa's tummy.

'Quiet a moment,' barks Thelma, lifting the final puppy to her chest.

The three men crowd closer, as Thelma strokes the puppy's soft head.

'My hands are too stiff,' she says handing the puppy to Christopher. The puppy is cool in his hands, a little too cool. Oh god. Does he have a puppy in trouble in his hands? A literal life in his hands?

'You're the baker, right? Good at kneading? She needs rubbing, firmly and quickly.'

Transferable skills, he hopes. Without another word from anyone, Christopher rubs at the puppy's back, mirroring Thelma's suggested movements.

Well, that's one way to find something more important to worry about than accidentally seducing someone on false premises slash being an embarrassing superfan. Sure, this situation with Nash is mortifying, but he might be responsible for this tiny creature taking its first ever breath. Or . . . not, as it currently seems.

Nessa raises her great, exhausted head and looks squarely in his direction.

'I won't let her go,' he whispers.

The room is a held breath as he rubs and rubs, and then at the last minute does a second check of her mouth. In one sweep, his fingers pull away a thick plug of mucus-y something.

And to his delight, she takes a breath.

A deep, very alive breath.

'Oh, thank Christ.' He clutches the puppy against him, but not too hard, worried he might disrupt its breathing again.

Still in his hands, Thelma looks the puppy over. 'She's fine, the colour is coming to her.'

'You scared the living daylights out of me, little miss,' Christopher whispers.

As if in answer, the puppy yips and then farts.

'I love her,' laughs Nash. Finally, he has lost the smug-gleeful look, and instead there's a softness. A smile, not a smirk. A look that Christopher could fall into if he wanted to. A look he wants to touch.

'Good work, lad,' says Thelma, patting him on the back.

Dai nods enthusiastically, but is unable to speak, his face streaming with tears. He gives Christopher a wobbly thumbs up instead.

'Are you going to keep them all?' asks Nash.

'Oh no, I'm too old for that. I might keep one, just for her.'

That'll be Khloé then, Christopher imagines.

Dai smothers his face in Nessa's. She gently licks the tip of his nose where tears have beaded. 'You're such a good girl, aren't you, my Ness? Look at all your lovely babies.'

Christopher hadn't realised until now, but he's still clutching the last puppy to his chest. She's tucked her head against his Paddington Bear scarf, and her tiny pink nose is flushing with life. A yearning rumbles in his chest, but then, perhaps it's quite a silly idea. After all, collies need a lot of time and energy and entertainment. More so than his parents' dogs Stella and Luna, even, and they're a pair of nightmares when they're not asleep. This puppy in his hands is at least half collie, and depending on what the hiker's dog was, she's going to probably have that high energetic need. But then, maybe that could be a good thing for him? After all, he was thinking about bringing someone on to help out at the bakery, to take over some of the responsibilities. Perhaps a commitment like this puppy is a step in that direction? There's no way he can have both.

And if this whole bakery dream falls apart . . . well, he'd still have her.

Plus, he has been lonely without animal companionship. He couldn't have a dog in London – he was in the office too often, which was strictly anti-dog. But here, he could. Here, in this new life he is shaping for himself.

When he looks up, Dai is grinning at him. 'She's yours if you want her. I wouldn't dream of taking her, if you want her.'

'She should meet her mum first,' Christopher says, replacing her back with her siblings, mentally memorising her pattern, the pinkness of her nose, the little black patches on her forelegs. 'But . . . yes. Please.'

Dai nods, and the deal is done, he supposes. Wow. In two months, he'll have a puppy. That feels like a good commitment towards keeping going, to finding joy in his life. A small, brand-new bit of meaning.

'So, what's the plan?' says Thelma with a clap of her hands.

'Well, I can't move her inside where there's no heat. I'll have to wait it out until the power comes on.'

'You can't stay in here forever.'

'It's fine! There's a heater.'

Christopher thinks back to how cold Dai looked when they first turned up, and questions the efficacy of it. The room is warm now with all these warm bodies, but that'll go soon.

'Oh? And what are you going to do, eh? Piss in that corner, wash in the other?'

'Well, where else am I supposed to go?'

Thelma fixes him with a stare. 'Dai, don't be a twmffat.'

A heavy pause follows as they size each other up.

'Thelma, really. I can't.'

'Why?'

'It's an imposition.'

'Not if I've offered.'

'It is.'

'Because it's *me*?' she asks with an arched brow.

'Of course because it's you!' Dai says this with so much hurt that Christopher feels as if he should grab Nash and leave the two of them to their private moment. It's been an emotional day, and everything spills out of Dai in a torrent of tears. 'I didn't mean to stand you up all those years ago. I wasn't supposed to be gone for so long.'

'Then why did you?' Thelma says, her short tone softened. 'I was waiting there for you. You never came back. I felt like such a fool.'

'Maybe . . .' he begins, glancing from Thelma to the nest of dogs next to him. 'Maybe we can talk about it, finally. If you'd be willing to hear me out?'

'I might.'

'But how are we going to get the dogs to yours?'

'We can help,' offers Christopher. 'There's space in the back of the van, and a little fold-down seat. We can pack all your bits up and the dogs and take you over to Thelma's.'

Dai ponders this for a moment, a nervous look on his face.

'I'll drive really slow,' Christopher insists.

'Oh, he will. You can be sure of that,' Nash says.

'All right then,' agrees Dai. He looks to Thelma and repeats a little softer this time, 'All right then.'

A shared flush spreads on Dai and Thelma's cheeks as they gather up the things ready to move the nine dogs over to her farm. For them all, it's perhaps the start of something new. A new beginning, among a whole litter of new beginnings.

Chapter Twenty-One

Christopher

It doesn't take them long to drive over to Thelma's farm. As before, she goes ahead on her tractor, heading straight over the fields like a woman on a mission.

Dai instructs Christopher to bring some blankets from the basket in the living room for the dogs, so he nips into the cold house to get them. It's icy in the house, and he's so glad they're not leaving them here. Despite Dai's insistence that there's no need, Christopher locks up behind him, while Nash helps Dai clamber up into the front passenger seat. Even from over by the front door, Christopher can hear his joints creaking with the cold.

Nash then deposits the puppies into the back of the van, safely ensconced in a cardboard box. Determined not to let them out of her sight, Nessa plods slowly behind him to the van, though the poor dog looks ready for a long sleep.

'Hang on, girl, I'll get you too.'

In one great scoop of his arms, he lifts her gently in, settling her next to the puppies, and settles himself on one of the fold-out seats, the box of puppies and Nessa at his feet.

'Is everyone all strapped in safe?' asks Christopher from the driver's seat, which is met with a chorus of *yep*, *aye* and various squeals from the puppies.

He can't help it; he peers back to check on the puppies.

'They're fine,' Nash says. 'Get driving before we all freeze in here.'

'The lad's right. I don't want to lose any important bits,' murmurs Dai, wiggling further into his coat.

'Okay, off we go,' says Christopher.

And it is a very, very slow drive. The glow of Thelma's farm stretches across the valley even further than before now that they're well into the afternoon. It's like a beacon, calling them all home.

When they arrive at Thelma's, she flings open the back of the van and carries Nessa inside before anyone can even unclip their seatbelts.

'She's one hell of a woman,' sighs Dai, following her inside with a new spring in his step.

'Well, someone's getting lucky tonight,' whispers Nash as he gently lifts the box of puppies out of the van.

Christopher follows them all inside with the bags and sets them down in the kitchen. 'Do you want me to put these anywhere for you?'

Given the lack of response, it's very clear that Thelma and Dai only have eyes for each other.

He finds Nash in the living room, settling the box of puppies on the rug next to Nessa. The box is low enough that she can poke her head in while lying down, and she takes out one puppy at a time to inspect them. Christopher bends down to give puppy number eight, still the tiniest of them all, a little stroke on her pink nose.

'I think we should go. We might be intruding,' he whispers.

Nash growls in some kind of agreement. They drag themselves away from the box of puppies and walk back to the kitchen.

Thelma and Dai have not moved. Between them on the table, Nash places a small square of card, which Christopher hopes is Nash's phone number rather than how to contact him via his agent. 'Call us if you need anything.'

'Aye, thanks lads,' says Dai, not taking his eyes from Thelma.

It's a dismissal, but one that Christopher is glad for. As the door shuts behind them, Christopher could swear he hears, 'Well, I've never had a film star's number before.'

They hop back into the front of the van. 'What a day.' Nash leans back in the passenger seat, arms folded and eyes closed.

'Huh,' Christopher says, looking at the steering wheel.

'What?' Nash asks, sleepily opening one eye.

'I left the keys in the ignition.'

'So?'

'I've never done that before,' he says, pulling out of the farmyard and back onto the winding roads.

'It's been a long day,' Nash shrugs.

'No, it's not that.'

He doesn't know how to find the words for what he's feeling. He'd never have done that in London, and not even in Oxlea, really. But here, he's starting to feel different. The lack of nerves, and perhaps his guard coming down. Perhaps these missions are changing him on a structural level. Maybe now he can really feel that he might be somewhere safe, somewhere that's starting to actually feel like home. And, more importantly, that he's starting to have an impact here. Will people remember him after all this? He hopes so.

'Never mind,' he says instead, brushing past it all. 'Shall we get back to the community centre?'

As they drive up and out of the valley, and over the hill past Dai's farm, Christopher's phone lights up with a text. Before he can ask Nash to get it, Nash has already picked up the phone, unlocking it with Christopher's pin.

'Bloody hell, how did you know that?'

'It's not like you shield it from me. What, worried I'm going to snoop at your selfies? In fact, I should definitely do that…'

Christopher swats at Nash, who leans back cackling.

'Don't you dare.'

'Oh, I do dare, but I'll save that for a time when you're not going to swerve us into a mountain.'

'Who is it from?'

'Priti. Can we swing by Myffy's to pick her up, driver?'

'Your wish is my command,' he says, turning off the main road towards Myffy's village.

'You shouldn't promise things like that,' murmurs Nash in a way that sends goosebumps right up Christopher's spine. 'I've told her we're on our way. She sent the message a few hours ago. Hopefully she won't mind that we were delivering puppies.'

'And when we get home tonight . . . well, it's Christmas Eve, so I should really make my gingerbread house.'

'A tradition of yours?'

'Something like that.' His chest aches a little to think of it. He never really thought he'd miss all the traditions of Christmas – baking in the kitchen while the dogs sniffed at his feet, going to Laurel's family's annual ball and dressing up, Esther's insistence on new Christmas pyjamas, and Otto's on-tap bubbly. And last year was special for a few reasons, not least because it was the first year he and Kit started to come back together after years of awkward barely knowing each other. To make up for it, she's been there by his side the whole past year, helping get this ambition off the ground since he first voiced it.

'And I should call my family,' he says out loud without really meaning to.

Nash gives him a little nod of approval, and something in Christopher's chest flutters at the thought of them being back in his flat, alone. Somehow, after all that's happened today, things have turned a little from *dear god I don't want to be home alone with this man* to *maybe it would be nice to be home alone with this man*. It would be a mistake, perhaps, to sleep with him again, but perhaps he is overthinking. Presuming. Worrying for no reason.

They pop in to say hello to Myffy, whose mind it seems is also on sex. 'Do you want to borrow this one? It's a real bodice-ripper,' she says, brandishing a book at him that has two men dressed in some historical floaty shirts pressed up against each other. Well, perhaps it's obvious to some people.

'Another time,' Nash says. 'But I'll make a note of the title, just for you.'

'You won't regret it.'

There's still nothing from Mohan, and not much else they can do for Myffy today. Priti squeezes her goodbye, and Christopher almost wants to do the same.

They bid her farewell for now and pile back into the bakery truck. Priti sniffs at the air as she gets in. 'No offence, but have you had a dog in here?'

'More like nine,' Christopher says. 'Sorry about the smell.'

'Oh, it's all right. Just a little . . . rustic,' she laughs a little awkwardly, picking a black-and-white hair off her coat. 'At least it's warm!'

They drive along quietly, all tired from the day's activities.

In the overhead mirror, Christopher watches Nash in the back seat, his brows deeply furrowed. 'If you think that hard, you'll get a wrinkle,' Christopher teases, startling Nash from his thoughts.

'Eyes on the road, Calloway,' he growls.

'What's on your mind?' Priti asks Nash, much more delicately than Christopher managed.

'I know it's still snowing here, but is it the same everywhere still?'

'From what I saw on the news earlier, things are better further south. But the trains are still not running,' Priti replies.

'Right. And Myffy said Mohan can drive,' Nash murmurs, as though he's thinking out loud. 'I was wondering if we should try and find a car or something for them so he can get back home? A kind of Christmas present.'

'Oh, bless you, but we already looked and there's nothing,' Priti responds, with a resigned tone. 'Even with the premium prices, which I think Mohan would have found the money for if he could.' She shakes her head. 'It's hard enough to be away from your partner at the holidays, but even more so when they're your carer too.'

'But you think if we could get him a car, he might want to try and drive up?' Nash asks.

'Yeah, he was keen on trying, even if I don't love the idea of him getting stuck somewhere en route.'

'There must be someone we know in London with a car they're not using right now,' murmurs Nash, peering intensely at his phone. 'Londoners don't even drive, right?'

He's right. After all, Christopher had his car just sitting at home when he was in London. There must be someone Christopher knows that Mohan can borrow a car from? This is the sort of thing his dad would be good for; through all his weird business contacts, he probably knows someone with at least three parked up in a garage somewhere.

But is that too much to ask? After all, he doesn't want his own parents taking unnecessary risks, but maybe they could help . . .

'Let's ask my parents,' he says, explaining his train of reasoning. 'There are no promises, but my mother does love to force people into doing what she wants. If anyone can find a car for Mohan in the South of England right now, it's Esther Calloway.'

They pull into the car park at the village hall and Priti hops out, just as Christopher takes out his phone.

'I'll go inside too,' says Nash, half a question, half a statement, but Christopher nods. The last thing he needs is his mother distracted by Nash and their whole situation. That woman has a preternatural sense for knowing someone else is at the other end of a phone call; she'd make a tremendous spy.

His mother answers just as Nash shuts the van door.

'What's that noise, Christopher? Why are you in a van? Are you labouring?'

'What is *labouring*?'

'Being a handyman, Christopher. It's very obvious.'

'Well, no, I'm not. It's the van that came with the bakery. One of the other people in the town managed to fix it up for me.'

Not entirely a lie, but it still yields a suspicious *Hmm*.

'And how did you know I'm in a van?'

'I can just tell these things.' Sometimes it terrifies him how omniscient she is. 'Has that man left yet?'

'Which man?'

'Don't be coy. It doesn't suit you.'

'We found him alternate lodgings,' Christopher says quickly. 'Anyway, Mother, I'm ringing because I need some help and I thought, with your vast network of contacts, you might be able to assist me.' Esther loves a bit of flattery, and he must admit, he's a bit of a Mummy's-boy suck-up, but it always gets the job done.

Christopher takes his time explaining Myffy and Mohan's situation, and that he's trying to source a car that Mohan could drive home.

'Well now, you have been a busy bee,' Esther says, and Christopher is almost positive he can detect a glimmer of pride in her voice.

'Just trying to help everyone out.'

'The insurance would be expensive to take out right now,' he hears his father say in the background. 'Unless the chap has multi-vehicle coverage.'

'Yes, well that's something we'll deal with if we can find him a car to drive. I didn't want to get their hopes up until we could find a car.'

'It's not every day a man asks another man to entrust his vehicles into someone else's hands,' Otto says with all the seriousness of a prophet.

'I know, but it's important. If it was Kit—'

He doesn't manage to finish the sentence because his mother answers. 'I'll make some calls, Christopher, but there's no guarantee. Give me an hour.'

And with that, she hangs up, clearly already beginning her mission to find a car.

Christopher rushes into the town hall, out of the freezing cold of the van, finally thankful for the permanent installation of the hot drinks table, even if both the tea and the coffee are little more than overheated metallic-tasting water. After grabbing a cup of what he thinks might be Earl Grey tea but frankly could be anything, he joins everyone at the Mission Control table. He doesn't see Nash, and tries to act as if this is fine and good and he's probably just in the bathroom, rather than walking back to LA.

'I heard you're after a car for Mohan. You called your mam?' Shaz asks, handing him a hot cup of tea she had already made for him in a mug that says World's Best Grandma.

Unfailingly polite, Christopher takes it, then just stands there holding two blisteringly hot mugs at once. 'Yes, she's on it.'

'It's a Christmas miracle.'

Shaz settles into a folding chair and pats the one next to her for him to sit down, too. It's rather difficult to sit down while holding and not spilling two mugs, but he manages it. Maybe he should ask Nash for some tips about strengthening his core.

'Have you been here all day?' Christopher asks.

'I've been coordinating, slash, on Ursula duty.'

'What does that entail?'

'Making sure she's not pissing off Tammy.'

Without looking up from her laptop, Tamara gives a thumbs up straight into the air.

'See, I'm doing a great job. Plus, I've been walking prescriptions over to people's houses, and I picked up all the dog poop from Mrs Llewellyn's back garden. And I even went home to look after the kids for all of five minutes.'

'You're a saint.'

'You bet I am. And the best part is, I think me being so community-minded might have inadvertently given me some bonus brownie points with Kathy.'

'How's Gar's foot?'

Shaz pulls a face. 'Absolutely grim. I made the mistake of looking and it looks like a pear someone kicked down the stairs. Not broken, but still. Yuck. Priti is going to score us some crutches from her stash.'

'Stash makes it sound so sordid, Shaz,' Priti sighs as she passes them.

'And a little spicy.'

'So, what's our next daring mission?' Nash says as he returns, leaning his hand on the back of Shaz's chair. Christopher offers him one of his two mugs, and luckily Nash takes one. 'Is it dinner and an early night? Please say it is?'

Despite the joke, Christopher wants to ask where he was, and if he is okay. He had looked so tired when they had got into the van, and it's been such a long day . . . but he bites his lip because there's no way he can ask without arousing Shaz's suspicions, and he's pretty sure what Nash said about his seizures was need-to-know information. Instead, he says, 'Any more pensioners need us to facilitate coitus?'

At least this gets a laugh out of Nash.

'Oh my god, are you serious? Look at you love bugs,' cackles Shaz. She turns to yell at Priti across the hall. 'Here, Priti, you'd better go make sure they've not broken a hip tomorrow.'

Priti closes her eyes just for a second and walks over to them. 'I hope you left them some condoms.'

'Do I want to know?' asks Tamara nervously, who has finally looked up from her laptop at the sound of this.

'Probably not,' answers Shaz.

'Sorry. Nurse-mode,' says Priti. 'I can't help it. You wouldn't believe how little the older members of society know about safe sex.'

The last time Christopher felt this uncomfortable about someone saying the word *sex* in his presence was probably when he was about fifteen and in the throes of puberty. But today, with someone he has had sex with sitting just behind him, just acknowledging the act as a possibility between two humans makes him feel naked, in the bad way.

Can Shaz tell? How the hell is he going to tell her? It probably can't be until Nash has left and they can all move on from this.

After he's left . . .

Christopher shakes his head, as if to dislodge the thought, and stands up to speak to Tamara properly. And to get a little more distance between him and Nash. 'Need anything else from us today?' He hopes that she's going to say no, so that Nash can get some rest.

'Well, it's going to be a huge ask,' Tamara says bluntly. 'Thanks to all the volunteers, I think we've managed to speak to pretty much everyone in Pen-y-Môr who is still here. There are quite a few people isolated and without family members here for Christmas . . . so I was thinking we should have everyone here for a big meal?' The only thing is that I don't know where to start. . .'

'I'll host it,' says Christopher before he can think too much about it.

'Really?' Tamara's face lights up. 'It's a lot to ask of you.'

'It makes the most sense. I've got tables and chairs set up, and a much bigger kitchen than in here.'

'True, the oven in the wee kitchen can barely warm a sausage roll,' says Shaz in a way that suggests this has been a major issue they've been trying to solve today.

'With some volunteers in the morning to help me cook and set up, we could make a few courses. It might be rustic, but it'll be something, and no one will have to be alone.' He can feel the flicker of excitement in his stomach. Christopher loves cooking for people, and he never did follow up with Shaz about Christmas at hers what with all the general chaos around them. This way, he gets to be useful and make people happy.

'We'd definitely have to raid all the supermarkets and corner shops,' adds Nash.

'Perhaps I can call in some favours . . .' murmurs Tamara. 'The only other issue is getting everyone up here.'

'If someone else can organise getting people to the bakery, we can focus on cooking,' says Christopher. 'We could lend the van?'

'The van can fit two passengers in the front, one or two in the back, and nine small to very small dogs, but it's hardly comfy and not exactly accessible if anyone has any mobility issues,' says Nash.

'Point taken. Does anyone have anything bigger than a five-seater?'

'Me,' answers Ursula, striding across the village hall in matching furry snow boots and gilet. She looks like the villainous ex-girlfriend from one of Nash's movies. It's kind of a serve. 'I've got a people-carrier for the kids, and we can borrow the minibus from the care home, as they will be doing everything in-house tomorrow. And Mervyn has a black cab he was planning to do up, but it still has all the fittings. Together, we can pick everyone up and bring them over. That's if you actually want to listen to any of my suggestions, *Tamara*.'

The last bit is delivered quite haughtily.

'That's really generous of you,' Christopher says when no one else responds.

Ursula looks about ready to kick off as Tamara, Shaz and Priti are so clearly in the unwilling acceptance stage, so Nash steps in and turns on the golden-boy charm. 'We would really appreciate your help, ma'am,' he says with a smile.

It is truly amazing how quickly Nash can disarm someone, Christopher thinks, especially when he spends most of his time winding *him* up. Perhaps it's all part of the media training – how to speak to journalists and how to calm a storm before it rises.

Except, this time, it doesn't seem to work.

'Please don't "ma'am" me,' she sneers in such a way that Christopher is pretty sure he sees Nash shrink.

Just at that moment, Christopher's phone starts to ring. 'Oh crikey,' he says, wiggling with his two cups. To his horror, Nash slips his hand into Christopher's back pocket, answers the phone and holds it against Christopher's ear for him.

'Christopher, it's your mother.'

'Hi, Mother.'

'I secured a car for your friend to borrow.'

'It's barely been ten minutes, how—'

'I'm just that impressive. Now, I'll send through all the details in a moment so that you can pass them on to your friend. It's one of those 4 x 4s so it should get him through the worst weather. When the snow has cleared, your father and I will drive up to see you, and one of us will drive the car back to London so he doesn't have to worry about that.'

'That's incredibly kind of you.'

'We do what we can for each other, especially in times of crisis.'

'You're right. We've been doing the same here. We were just discussing hosting Christmas Day at the bakery for anyone who is home alone.'

'I'm very proud of you. I always knew you were community-minded like me. Now, let's not get too mushy on the phone. I'll send you the details so we can get your chap on the road sooner rather than later.'

That was alarmingly close to a direct compliment. It feels . . . nice. 'Thank you, Mother.'

'You're welcome.'

'Wait. Before you go, do you have any advice for me?'

There's a distinct pause. 'You're asking *me* for advice? Do I have that right?'

'Well. Yes. Being with people, managing them. Working together for something. I've watched you do that with everyone in Oxlea my whole life and I hadn't appreciated it before.'

Another pause. 'You've never asked me for advice before.'

Generally, that's because you give it before I can ask for it, he thinks, but makes sure not to say. 'I'm asking now.'

'Well,' she begins slowly. 'Firstly, if people offer their help, you have to trust them. Delegate. I can imagine you and I share the same flaw of wanting to oversee everything—'

'Somewhat.'

'It's our cross to bear, and it's important to work against it, otherwise you end up doing everything.'

'And that's bad, yes?'

'Yes. Secondly, you catch more flies with honey than water.'

He's not quite sure he wants to catch any flies but resists teasing her when she's helping. 'How so?'

'Even if someone is royally ticking you off, find a way to work with them, even if it's just telling them what they want to hear. Fundamentally, Christopher, people want to be useful and respected, or at least have the impression that they are either. Give them that and you're on your way to a successful collaboration.'

'Thank you, Mother.'

'You're welcome, Christopher.'

He nods to Nash to withdraw the phone as his mother hangs up.

'Surely there was an easier way of doing that?' Tamara says incredulously.

'She found a car?' Nash asks, ignoring her.

'Yes, she's sending the details now. Can someone take these cups off me?'

Shaz and Nash leap to help, and Nash returns Christopher his phone in an awkward shuffling of hands.

'We'd better get hold of Mohan quickly so he can decide if he wants to set off today or tomorrow,' Christopher says.

'He says he's going to leave right away,' Priti answers for him, her phone to her ear.

Even from here, Christopher can hear the delighted tones from Mohan.

Esther sends over an incredibly detailed set of instructions for where to pick up the car from a garage in London which requires a handful of codes to get into. It's only as Christopher forwards the email that he recognises the Chelsea address – it's where Laurel's ex, Mark Ratliff-Zouch, lives. Well, nice to see he has one single generous bone in his body. Christopher also insists that Mohan drives via the Cotswolds and up the border, a slightly more circuitous route, but one that means if the weather gets bad again, Mohan can hole up at his parents' place. They all agree not to tell Myffy until he's properly on his way, just in case something goes wrong.

There's nothing like a plan coming together.

Christopher decides the next thing they all have to do is to try and solve this Ursula situation. She wants to help but . . . what's this barrier between them all?

He thinks back to Christmases in the Calloway house. Well, not just Christmases. Basically, the whole of his childhood was spent watching his mother wrangle a town's worth of people into doing exactly what she wanted and needed. What was it she said to him? Tell people what they want to hear. It sounded like terrible managerial advice for running a business, but he's now realising that perhaps that's not what Esther meant.

What does a woman like Ursula want? Respect, almost certainly, which she likely doesn't think she's getting at the moment, especially after her disastrous vote and the way Shaz's whole job seems to be running interference.

Perhaps she just wants to be listened to. Christopher decides to channel his mother, and hopes that his big blue eyes make up for the gap. 'Ursula, why don't you and I get out of here for a moment, and get some fresh air? I really haven't introduced myself properly, and I really would like to ensure we're well acquainted. Perhaps you can come over and tour the bakery with me, get a feel for how things could work tomorrow?'

He worries for a second that Esther's words delivered via his mouth might read considerably differently.

But to his great surprise, Ursula ever so slightly blushes. 'That sounds delightful,' she says, taking his arm in hers.

As she steers him out of the village hall, he catches the bemused, amused and horrified faces of Tamara, Nash and Shaz in turn, and flashes them a hopeful smile.

★ ★ ★

The sun is low in the sky and Christopher is grateful to get the last of the daylight, even if it does mean stepping out into the cold with his friend's mortal enemy.

'Shall we go to the bakery?' he asks.

She gives him a quiet little nod, some of the bluster gone out of her, and he leads her across the least icy bits of the road.

For once, he's thankful that he clearly left the heating on in the bakery as it's relatively warm when they arrive. Ursula steps in like a nervous animal, as though ambush awaits. It's clear she hasn't been here before, which is a small sting that Christopher tries to ignore. But it's not as if he's gone out of his way to speak to her either.

'Ursula, I do think you have the power to really help us all out here and make this disaster of a Christmas better for some of the lonelier people, but perhaps we have not been completely fair to you. I would like to make up for that,' Christopher says.

He fires up the coffee machine, thankful that it doesn't take too long to heat up once it's on. 'Coffee?'

'A cappuccino, please,' she asks quietly. It's really rather strange. Now that she's not around Tamara and Shaz and Priti, or the rest of the town for that matter, she seems to have shrunk a little.

'Do you think this would be enough space to host every-one?' he asks as the water in the coffee machine starts to heat up, releasing the hot-metal-and-steam smell into the air.

'If we move all the tables around,' she says, snapping into action, counting them up. 'We could do two long tables, and that would seat about twenty, maybe thirty people. Perhaps a few short ones.'

'I have a table upstairs we can bring down and a couple of chairs. And we can serve right onto the counter buffet-style, which will save us some space.'

The grinding of the beans fills the silence as Ursula tallies up the logistics and seems to make some notes on her phone.

With two cappuccinos freshly made, Christopher encourages her to sit with him at a table together.

'Thank you,' she says. 'This was . . . kind of you.'

'You're welcome. I did mean what I said – we don't really know each other yet, and I want to know everyone here.'

'You're new here, right? You seem determined to stay.'

'I am. And I want to actually be a part of the community.'

She snorts a delightfully piggy snort. 'Oh, don't ask for what you might regret,' she says, but not in a cruel way. It's a little sad. 'I don't mean to be such a stickler all the time. I suppose it's who I've always been. Who my mother was. Who I had to be with my ex-husband, or perhaps who he made me be.'

Ursula sighs and Christopher could swear he heard his own heart break a little. 'And I know being that version of me just makes Tamara and me fight, and means everyone hates me. But I don't really know how else to be.'

How long has she been moulding herself into someone she doesn't even recognise?

Christopher reaches across the table and takes her hand. 'I think there's always time for us to reinvent ourselves. I'm trying it right now.'

'How's that going?'

He pulls a grimace, and she snorts once again. 'It's hard, but I'm trying to find out who I am, I suppose. And, like you say, *how* I want to be, which I think is halfway to who.'

'That sounds nice. I think I've been here too long. No one will think I'm being genuine,' Ursula replies.

'When is there a better time to turn over a new leaf than Christmas?'

It's quite possible that he really has watched too many holiday movies in the last few months, as he's almost certain that's one of Nash's lines from *Mushing Home for Christmas*. It's one of Christopher's favourites, even if it is a very thinly veiled *Balto*-rip-off-turned-romcom, where Nash played a musher called Forrest Tenzing opposite an Anna Kendrick-type. No wonder he's so good at being around snow, though it's quite possible it was all fake for the movie. Hopefully they don't still make that stuff out of asbestos, like the snow in *It's a Wonderful Life*.

In the end, they sit and talk for half an hour over their coffees. Christopher shares his recent adventures in baking, while Ursula opens up about how tricky it is to co-parent with her ex-husband. In the end, he finds he likes her – there's some elements of Esther's bristliness that he recognises. He's used to brusque people bossing him about, after all.

The thing he needs to remember is that someone might have an attitude he can't quite place, but it's so often because strangers are unknowable. It's only when you can see where someone is coming from that you might be able to understand their slightly cranky exterior.

Sure, that absolutely doesn't excuse someone being a total dickhead, but that was how it had seemed to be with Nash too, wasn't it? Christopher had thought him rude and cocksure and demanding, when really he was stuck in a new country, alone, with seemingly no one knowing where he was, with a tricky disability to manage alone. No wonder they sparked off.

And they still have so much to talk about, he and Nash.

As the last of the light fades outside, Ursula says, 'I'm going to do it, you know. Try and start afresh. I always was going to.' Her confidence appears to wobble and she falters slightly as she adds, 'If you think they'd like that?'

'I think everyone would like that.'

He's not one hundred per cent sure of that, but hell, if the village took *him* in, an outsider, maybe they can stretch to find space for Ursula to be a different kind of person than the one they've always known.

* * *

They walk back to the village hall together, and everyone seems ready to embrace Ursula's help . . . Perhaps that was all it took, someone else to disrupt old habits, for them to work together? Or maybe, a quiet part of him says, maybe it was you. Maybe all it took was Christopher putting himself out there and bringing someone else into the fold. It feels good, he must admit.

Thanks to all the visits they'd made over the last few days, they already have a list of people who are going to need a hot dinner on Christmas Day.

'Ursula, do you want to join us ringing everyone?' Shaz asks, all the former snark dropped now. 'We were going to ask Nash to ring, but we thought everyone would just say yes to him no matter whether they need it or not.'

'Yes,' Ursula nods happily. 'Please. I want to help.'

It takes a couple of hours to ring round everyone, and together with Ursula, they work out the best routes to pick people up, so that everyone can be at the bakery for mid-afternoon the following day for an early dinner – late enough to give them time to cook, and early enough that the older members of the community wouldn't be asleep before it was served.

When Ursula nips to the bathroom, Shaz nudges Christopher. 'How did you get her to agree?'

'I just listened to her,' he says truthfully. 'I think she wants to turn over a new leaf.'

Shaz raises an eyebrow. 'Might take the whole tree.'

'I know it's not my place when you all have history, but perhaps it could be a kind of Christmas miracle.'

'You've been watching too many of his films,' she says, thumbing in Nash's direction. Christopher shushes her, and he swears he sees a tiny grin in the corner of Nash's mouth.

'All we need now is the food,' says Nash, who this whole time has been scribbling down ideas on a piece of paper, whole menus of dishes, what ingredients are essential and what could be substituted.

Christopher has no idea where he's pulled all this from, but it aches his heart a little, in a good way. Despite Christopher's accusations of him not being serious the other night, Nash has kept showing up. All this time. He fits in here, Christopher thinks, but quickly banishes the thought. It's not as if Nash is going to be here much longer. Would he even want that?

He can't get lost in daydreams and wishes right now. He needs to focus on the real challenge: cooking for God knows how many people tomorrow with hardly any ingredients.

An ominous rumble sounds, growing louder and louder, and for a second Christopher worries that the real danger is some kind of avalanche. But to his relief, it's just the sound of an enormous tractor pulling up outside the village hall, one giant wheel visible through the window.

And in strides a tiny farmer, carrying what Christopher is pretty sure is at least half an animal, followed by another tiny farmer, carrying bags and bags of potatoes.

'We heard some rumours of a Christmas dinner,' Dai says.

'And we thought you might need something to cook!' Thelma finishes.

The pair of them look like post-Christmas Future Ebenezer Scrooges.

Nash grins, and rushes to take the food from them both. 'Now *that* is a Christmas miracle,' he confirms. 'And I should know.'

Chapter Twenty-Two

Christopher

With the food from Thelma and Dai, and a quick run to the supermarket and corner shops, they have *just* enough food to feed everyone tomorrow. Hopefully, Christopher thinks, everyone will just be glad of a hot meal and company, and not mind what ends up on the table.

For starters, there'll be a cream of vegetable soup using all the sadder bits of veg they rescued from the supermarket. And through a stroke of luck there was only UHT non-dairy cream in stock, so if any vegans show up it'll work for them, too. Christopher will bake some sourdough loaves to go with the soup. Easy – he'll just have to be up nice and early to get going on that.

They've got what is essentially almost *all* of one of Thelma's lamb's legs to roast, which should be more than enough meat for everyone. Dai threw in a couple of hams, too, which Nash wants to cook first so there's time for them to cool ahead of slicing. For the vegetarians, they'll make a kind of Wellington-cum-nut-roast, which Nash insists he has done before. And then there are all the various veggies scrounged from the supermarkets and whatever anyone had going spare, and more potatoes than Christopher has ever seen in his life.

As for dessert, Christopher remembers he has some of the Christmas puds left in the cupboard, ready to age for next year, but they'll be good to eat now.

As evening really draws in, Nash carries all the food home from the community centre, making several trips, while Christopher unloads the supermarket shopping from the van. He's just about to unpack the bags, too, when Nash stops him.

'Don't you have a gingerbread house to make?'

'It's not essential.'

Nash gives him a look he can't quite place. 'I can handle this. Go make your silly little biscuit building. It's important to do your traditions, right?'

Something catches in his throat, and Christopher wants to speak, but he's so tired that all he can really do is nod. He tries not to watch as the shopping piles up, and Nash meticulously organises it, packing things away in the bakery kitchen as though he has been doing so for years.

It's bordering on night by the time Christopher is finally able to start on the dough for his gingerbread house. If he was being sensible, he would go to bed early, and put this off another day – or until after Christmas. After all, he has to cook a whole Christmas dinner for, best estimate, about twenty-five adults tomorrow. And that's after a long day of puppy birthing and healing old resentments between former friends, and dealing with annoyingly helpful yet still egotistical and handsome film stars he'd only just slept with. It's been . . . a day.

But because nothing about this is a normal Christmas, baking gingerbread is at least a tradition he can ground himself in.

Funny how much Nash could sense he needed it, really.

Over the last few years, he'd done a real showstopper, mostly because his mother always wanted to give one away for the Christmas fête she organised. If he had time, he'd always make one for himself, too. The thing about making a house out of biscuit is that so much can go wrong, but that's bizarrely what Christopher likes about it. Every step has to be meticulous – the structural integrity of the biscuit, the design of the house, the decorations placed outside, which must not overbalance the building itself. Really, it's a little like the bakery window displays he likes doing: the balance of bright and edible, the eye-catching and the stable.

Given the general lack of supplies, he'll have to think on his feet more about decoration, but he falls back on his usual recipe for gingerbread. It's a dough not dissimilar from a *pepparkakor*, but not as thin, so probably more akin to a *speculoos*. He's tried a few other variations in the past – including golden syrup instead of treacle – but this one feels right. It feels like home.

He feels a little embarrassed when he takes down his notebook of recipes from the supplies shelf, self-consciously flicking through to the right page, slightly spattered with icing sugar and spices. It's silly but this book feels like the sum of all his hopes and dreams, in some ways. He started filling it out when he was at pâtisserie school, determined that writing things out by hand would help techniques stick in his brain. And now, whenever that dark overwhelm appears, threatening that this dream isn't going to last because *how could it*, he comes to this book and flicks through the pages, filled with hopes and knowledge and promises to himself.

A stillness settles over him as he measures out all the spices – cinnamon, of course, ground cardamom too, and a kick of ginger. Thelma had also brought a couple of boxes of eggs fresh from her farm, so they go into the mix, yolks so golden-orange they might be red. The lid of the black treacle comes away in a deliciously gooey pop, and the dark syrup folding into all the dry ingredients feels like a kind of alchemy.

As Christopher works the dough, he can't help but watch Nash from across the kitchen, settled in a contemplative quiet as he makes the plan for tomorrow with all the timings. He's thorough, and generous with his time and thoughts.

Christopher doesn't mind the number-juggling part, but he's really quite glad that Nash has taken the thinking out of tomorrow for him. Naturally, he'll double check – he's still

Christopher after all – but still. As he'll be the one leading the cooking, he's glad he'll have Nash's plan to work from.

Perhaps all this planning has the same effect on Nash as working the dough has on Christopher? Nash certainly liked it when they were cooking for everyone a few days – and what feels like a lifetime – ago. He wonders, just for a moment, how this side of Nash shows up in his life in LA, away from Christopher. Being a working actor sounds as if there's a lot of showing up when someone tells you to, so where does he find the time to take charge and plan something? Or even cook?

There's so much he doesn't know about this man.

What he does know are things like his remarkable handiness, the easy ability to charm people, and how he sounds when . . .

Spices and sugar crowd the air and Christopher feels for a moment as if he can't breathe. He shakes his head, and flips the dough round, clapping flour into his hands. He has to move. If he stays too still, the thoughts rush in.

'Are you okay?' Nash asks, his concentration replaced with concern.

'Yes. Fine.'

His phone hums with a text, and he's grateful for the distraction.

Shaz: Tell Nash I sourced the pastry. Also, be proud, I'm helping Ursula wrangle the guests for tomorrow. Personal growth, a Christmas miracle x

'Err, Shaz says she sourced the pastry?' he says to Nash with confusion.

'Oh great. Tell her thanks.'

'You know this *is* a bakery. We can just make it from scratch ourselves.'

'For vegans? This seems to be a very butter-central kind of bakery.'

'Oh,' he says, suitably chastened. 'That's a good point.'

'Plus, who can be fucked to make pastry?'

'Me? I'm quite literally a baker.'

'Oh, don't worry, none of us have forgotten that,' Nash says with a smile.

Christopher huffs but can't keep the grin from his lips. 'Fine, I take your point, I probably don't have what we need to hand.'

'Nah, but luckily the vegans insist that pre-made is in fact usually vegan, so I set Shaz a mission to steal as much as she could from people's freezers.'

'Excellent thinking.'

'I'm really not just a pretty face, Calloway.'

His mouth goes dry thinking about kissing that pretty face just last night.

'Are you almost done?' Nash asks, when Christopher doesn't respond.

'Yeah, I think so. I just need to let it rest for a while.' He wraps it in a rather finicky bit of clingfilm and places it in the fridge, in a space Nash had left for it. Gingerbread always rolls out better when it's chilled, he finds. Plus, he gets a more reliable size of biscuit if the butter isn't starting out half-melted.

He turns to find Nash, who is fiddling with a bit of clingfilm he'd ripped off. 'Is this Britain's excuse for plastic wrap?'

'Yeah, it's not very good, is it?'

'Well, it's a point in your favour of not being a murderer, because you'd never be able to wrap me up in this stuff. The whole premise of *Dexter* would have fallen apart.'

'Always glad to hear you're still coming round to the idea that I'm not going to murder you.'

'It's a work in progress.'

Christopher peers over at the paper Nash was working on, only to see it is actually many, many pages full of timings, diagrams and instructions. It's meticulous. 'Have you worked out the plan of action?' A slightly redundant question considering the depth of what he's looking at.

Nash guides Christopher through the timings and his ideas. 'I think so. And I've got the recipes to hand for us so, if you're too busy and you need me to cook anything, I can just follow that. We're going to have to do more individual dishes rather than batch-cook a couple of big things, as we don't really have *enough* of any group of ingredients to do that, but I think it's doable. There'll be food.'

'Speaking of food, I think it might be beans on toast for dinner.'

Nash winces. 'I knew I'd be participating in a British culinary exchange, but does it have to be that?'

They stomp up the stairs together to investigate what's left in Christopher's rather bare cupboards.

'Aha!' cries Nash, on his hands and knees with his head deep in a cupboard. He wriggles out with a packet of instant risotto. 'I can work with this.'

'I didn't even know that was in there.'

Nash flips the packet over. 'Well, that date is close enough to being this year that I'll take the risk.'

Christopher watches as Nash navigates the kitchen, setting a pan filled with cold water on the stove. He tears the packet open, and tips the powdered cheese, rice and dehydrated vegetables into the water.

'Let's not get food poisoning right before Christmas,' Christopher says, peering into the pan.

'We'll nuke it. It'll be fine.'

'While . . . erm. While we wait for that, I was wondering . . . if we could perhaps discuss what happened last night?' Christopher stares resolutely at the wall as he speaks.

Nash glances at him. 'About us having sex, you mean?'

'Well. Yes.' The heat of his cheeks burns.

'What do you want to talk about?'

That's a good question, really. It just feels as if he's surrounded by unknowns here. He tries to find the words for the feelings that swarm him, but the words flee his tongue. There's not been enough time to really process any of this, and that's half the problem.

Nash must see him drowning, so softly offers, 'Do you want to not do it again? Because that's fine.'

'No,' Christopher blurts, surprising himself, but finding it is actually true. The little grin on Nash's face is intoxicating. 'I'm just worried it's a bad idea.'

Nash tilts his head, like a dog listening for command. 'Talk me through the bad.'

'It just complicates things.'

It hangs in the air for a little while, and Christopher is half waiting for Nash to ask him if he's catching feelings so that he can furiously refute it, but Nash doesn't. Perhaps that can of worms is best left unopened. Like the beans.

'That's true,' Nash says slowly. 'So why don't we set down some boundaries?'

'Like what?'

'Well, other than the very obvious points of consent in the moment, we can stop doing this if it becomes not fun for anyone for whatever reason.'

Christopher nods along.

This does all sound reasonable, and he absolutely *does* want to sleep with Nash again. But there's a pang in his chest that won't shift. Perhaps it's just the knowing that this can only be finite. After all, he has got the chance to spend the next few nights with the man of his literal dreams, while also knowing that that same man will be leaving the country when the snow lifts. That's got to be doing a number on his overtired brain. 'Yes. Right. That makes sense. But also . . . we didn't talk about what *you* want and don't want.'

'Christopher,' Nash says, a little too softly. A little too tenderly. He looks up at Christopher, and God, he could sink into Nash's green eyes.

* * *

Nash

Nash wondered when this would come up, but then, Christopher really seemed to know what he was doing when they first fucked, and had taken directions well enough to keep him focussed on what Nash liked.

After all, it's been no secret that Nash is trans, as Christopher obviously knew who he was from the off. That role on *Parental Units* had landed in Nash's lap specifically *because* they were looking for a trans teenager to play his character, Luke, and because they'd seen his various *x many weeks on T* videos on the early days of YouTube. His transness has been on public record for so long that sometimes Nash forgets he still has to come out with some people.

Still, he'd purposefully left out his testosterone gel on the bedside table, just in case everything wasn't obvious enough.

He stirs the ancient packet risotto, which is just about starting to smell like real risotto he might want to eat.

'Am I the first trans guy you've slept with?' he asks, and Christopher nods. 'But you've slept with men and women, right?'

'Not loads of either, but yes. You're not the first trans person I've slept with.'

'Well, everyone has their own preferences,' he says, trying to keep this as matter-of-fact as possible. 'Your mouth on my cock was pretty good. Penetration is a maybe, we can talk about that if you want to do it, else we can just use hands and mouths. I also like to top if you are into that, but I don't have a strap with me.'

This conversation is always awkward, but the way Christopher is trying to be so serious and stay present in the moment, rather than turning into a gigantic beet like he normally does, is kind of endearing. 'I don't have one either,' he says, which Nash takes to mean a strap.

'Oh well, that'll be someone else's first with you. Is there stuff you don't like?'

Christopher blinks a few times, as though this might be the first time someone has asked him. Fuck, he hopes it's not. 'Err, not that I can think of. I'll just say, in the moment.'

'Are you sure, Calloway? You're not really a *say it in the moment* kind of man.'

He smiles, a little embarrassed. 'I will endeavour to be.'

The watery risotto starts to bubble, and Nash turns the heat down, beginning the laborious constant stirring you have to do even with the packet stuff.

'And,' Christopher continues, 'just tell me if I'm not doing anything right or saying the wrong thing.'

'I will.'

The thing is, as uncomfortable as Christopher looks, Nash would quite like to kiss him after this. Too many cis guys don't take a moment to ask basic questions about his body and his wants, which is one of many reasons why he doesn't seek them out anymore. But against all the odds, Christopher keeps standing out.

And it's not that alone that makes Nash want Christopher more, but it does make him respect him more. Perhaps even *trust* him more. There's a lot of trusting he's had to do in the last few days, so why not let them have fun, too?

Nash is just about to reach up and grab Christopher's collar, push him up against the kitchen door, when his phone starts to buzz. At first he thinks it's the timer going off, but in fact it's Kurt.

Time to face the music and forget about making out with the hot English man for a bit. There's nothing like his impending work crisis to numb his desire.

'I need to take this,' Nash says, staring at his phone. 'Can you deal with the risotto?'

'Yes, just stir, right?' Christopher responds.

'Until it looks like risotto, yeah.'

Nash dips out of the kitchen and pulls the bedroom door closed. 'Hey Kurt. Not sitting on my doorstep today, are you?'

'Not today, unfortunately for your doorstep. Happy Christmas Eve.'

'And to you. Are you driving home?'

Kurt grew up in the Bay Area, where his entire family still lives, even his many siblings – Nash tried to memorise all their names at first, but they just keep sprouting up, like hydra heads. In the end he just resolved to pretend he knows who anyone is whenever he needs to.

'Yeah, man. The car's loaded with gifts and I am ready to hug my Bubbe. Auntie Catalina is cooking this year, so you know it'll be a good one.'

'So, you're making me your last work call of the season?'

'God, no offence, but I hope so. Look, I know they pushed back negotiations, which is a good thing for both of us. But I also know they'll be back in the office and ready to talk on the 29th, which means you and I need to be on the same page by the 28th, right?'

'Right.'

That's an even bigger relief. This weather has to let up soon. He'll be back in LA way before the 29th. His mind whirs over the logistics, and he half wishes he could click off the call to check the forecast for the next few days.

'Is there anything else you want to say?' Kurt nudges him.

'Not right now,' Nash says, a little too shortly. His mind is still thinking about flights.

He can hear a kind of frustrated groan from Kurt's end. 'Dude, I know you think you're very subtle and clever, but I always know when something is up. You go all squirrelly and quiet—'

'I do not.'

'You *do*. I wouldn't be a good agent if I didn't notice when you were quietly pissed or worrying about something, as looking after you is a major part of my job. We've been working together for what, fifteen years now? You're like a little brother to me, and anything you want to tell me, well, we can work with it. But you gotta tell me what it is before we go back to the table, *capiche*? I'm not asking you to tell me now, so you've got the next few days to make a bullet-point list, a mind map, anything. But you do need to do *something*.'

'Okay, Kurt. I'll try.'

'Good. I hope whatever that situation you were dealing with has resolved itself?'

'Err. Yeah.'

'Are they cute, at least?'

Nash can't help but laugh. 'Am I that obvious?'

'Probably not, but I know you. You're a romantic who hates to admit they are, and you love a fixer-upper, so I put two and two together.'

Well. He's not entirely wrong.

'Go have fun. Happy holidays.' Kurt says, after a pause.

'Merry Christmas, Kurt. Have a good one.'

When he gets back to the kitchen, Christopher has plated up the risotto and topped it with some fresh parsley leaves picked off a plant, and some grated Parmesan. His back is still to Nash, so he takes a moment to just watch. There's something so domesticated about all this that it's doing something strange to his insides. He's been wanting this, quietly, for so long. Someone to make dinner with. Someone to make dinner *for*.

The thing about being a workaholic is that you can always put those relationship wants on the back burner by pretending that you're 'just too busy for it right now'. He can tell himself that, maybe one day, when the film industry or wherever he ends up next inevitably gets a little fed up with him, it'll be different. He'll have more time for his people then, right?

But what has that got him? Sure, it's not changed things with his parents because they've always been somewhat arm's length, but pleasant, about it. It does mean he sees his friends only in between shoots, when usually someone will chastise him for not texting back, or there'll have been a huge piece of news that he's missed in the interim – admittedly because of the not-texting-back issue – that he has to roll with on the spot. It makes him an outsider in his own life.

If he's honest, that's not enough.

That's only part of why he wants a career change, but it's a big part of it. What could his life and relationships be like if he was more present? If he had time for people. If he wasn't afraid of committing to someone . . .

That's a whole other problem in itself, though. What he and Christopher have is probably the most emotionally intimate thing that wasn't built on a pre-existing friendship that he's had with someone in, well, years.

But this is just blowing off steam, right? That's clearly what they're both doing here. It's not as if they *like* each other in that way. It's fine. They'll have a nice time together, unite Christopher's community for Christmas, and then he'll go home. That's all this is.

He's not ready to examine why exactly that makes his stomach ache a little, but it's probably just hunger.

Finally, as he turns to place the plates on the tiny kitchen table, Christopher notices him. And smiles. It's a soft, small smile that feels reserved just for him. The kind Christopher is trying to keep for himself.

God, he's getting too sentimental this Christmas.

'Thanks for this. My agent just wanted to wish me happy holidays.'

They both squeeze in round the kitchen table and eat in exhausted but companionable silence.

'Are you going to assemble the gingerbread house tonight?'

Christopher glances up at the clock on the wall that Nash is pretty sure has never worked. 'What time is it?'

'About nine.'

He groans. 'Apparently not.'

'There's still time. You guys have Christmas for longer, right? The whole Boxing Day thing?'

'Yeah. I guess you're right.'

'Plus,' he says, pushing his empty plate away. 'I was thinking we could do something a little more fun this evening.'

'What's more fun than assembling a gingerbread house?' Christopher snorts, and then looks up, clocking Nash's hungry look. 'Oh.'

They lose all their clothes on the way to bed, kissing as they go. Their desire for each other is less furious tonight, probably because they're so tired, and under Christopher's gentle touch, Nash comes quickly, as though Christopher's been doing just that to him for years. Nash takes his time with Christopher, stroking him gently with his hands so that they can keep kissing. Nash thinks that he could never get tired of kissing Christopher.

It's only in the quiet when his lips are bruised from kissing that he feels some small part of himself come undone. Is this . . . relaxing? It's not something he's felt for a long time.

Christopher rolls over and fixes him with those big baby blues. 'If you want to talk about work things, I'm happy to be an ear. Especially now, you know, we're not pretending I don't know who you are any more.'

Nash snorts a laugh. 'Now that *you* are no longer pretending, you mean.'

'Well. Yes.'

'I'm not sure you'll want to hear it, Superfan. You've no idea what you're asking.'

'Tell me.'

'No, it's . . . long and complicated and probably really dull.'

'Nash, of all the things I could call you, dull is hardly one of them.'

'The situation is dull.'

'Okay, but it matters to you?'

Nash lets Christopher's words hang in the air. After all, what is the risk of talking this through with him? It's not as if he's connected to the industry, and from Nash's limited snooping, Christopher's social media seems to be confined to taking photos of things he's baked. He's hardly *DeuxMoi*.

'So, the acting thing. I might be . . . done.'

He can tell Christopher is trying to squash all his shock. What Nash is pretty sure was a gasp quickly turns to a yawn.

'Done? With acting?' Christopher asks, trying to look casual. 'But what about the last *Christmas at the Clinic* film?'

'See, this is why I didn't want to talk about it with you. You sound like I just told you Santa isn't real.'

'He *isn't*!?' Christopher smirks, and Nash rolls his eyes.

'Very funny.'

'I can be, on occasion. But I'll restrain myself.' Christopher is doing that earnest look now that makes Nash want to tell him everything. It's . . . disarming. He must never let Christopher know how powerful it is.

'It's just . . . it's a weird thing living your dream when it's just not your dream any more. Getting scouted for *Parental Units* was unimaginably cool when I was just this dorky little kid making my transition progress videos on YouTube. Like, yeah I'd always been a bit of a theatre kid.'

'No. You, a diva? A drama queen? I'm *shocked*.'

'Yes, very funny, I've never heard that one before.'

Christopher squeezes his arm. 'Sorry. Keep going.'

'Anyway, I loved that, although going through puberty on television and being a teenager in the public eye are two experiences I, on the whole, would not recommend to anyone.'

'And then the Christmas films happened?'

'Eventually. It took a while but, yeah, I kind of fell into that. It was Barbie who kicked my career off. I kind of rode her coat tails for a while.'

'You were known already,' Christopher disagrees.

'Yeah, but it's not the same. She was Instagram famous in 2014. Do you remember what that . . .' He trails off. 'No, I imagine you won't.'

'Harsh.'

Nash furrows his brows, because he has looked up Christopher's Instagram account, and scrolled quite far back, past the baking content of last year to a whole load of nothing beyond a few fake-coupley photos with Haf. 'Accurate?'

'Yes. Fine. But you like acting, don't you?'

Nash leans back and sighs. 'I do. I did. I do? It's complicated.'

'Well, you've done a million festive romcoms by now. I swear the only person who has you beat on sheer seasonal output is Lacey Chabert.'

'She's a powerhouse. And yeah, I love romcoms, genuinely. I think there's so much power to them, a universality. That's why people gravitate to them, over and over. Plus, I've had a pretty steady career being one of the hot guys they like to wheel out from the stable every year.' Christopher chuckles at this, so Nash adds, 'Just to be unclear, there is unfortunately not a literal stable of hot guys.'

'The greatest disappointment of my life. So . . . it's not your dream anymore, is that it?'

'That's what I'm trying to work out. The deal that's on the table isn't just for the next Christmas Vet . . . I mean *Christmas at the Clinic* film. It's more than that. They want *me*, and if I don't sign, there're a lot of people's jobs on the line.'

'Like Barbie's?'

He doesn't answer, and Christopher takes a sharp breath in. It's horrible to have to explain to him the way the industry rapidly dumps women once they've passed a particular age and area of stardom – those Instagram followers seem less and less relevant to the execs now that she's over thirty, and that fucking sucks.

'And you don't want to sign this big deal?' Christopher continues.

'I don't know really.'

'Right, but what is the thing you *do* want to do, that you're not saying?'

Urgh. Stupid smart tall man for spotting the gaps in what Nash is saying. 'It's embarrassing.'

'Tell me.' He says it so softly that Nash finds he does want to tell him.

'I think . . . I want to write?'

'Why is that embarrassing?'

'Being a writer is fundamentally embarrassing. All your feelings on the page thinly veiled for entertainment?' He fake-shivers. 'I think I'd like to direct, too, maybe? I got to help out a little on a few episodes of *Parental Units* but I was still a bit too young and inexperienced for them to trust me with the reins on such a big show. The thing is, I've been on screen for nearly two decades and I just think I've had enough of being a public person.'

'You're hardly doing interviews every day.'

'It's not that so much . . . like, *yes* I've slowed down on doing those but part of that is because people are significantly less interested in me than say the latest Marvel ingenue. It's more the *being perceived* part. Like physically? I don't think it's all dysphoria, and I don't think it's none, either. The only time I wear a packer is when I'm filming.' He pauses to catch his breath, because this is spilling out faster than he expected. It's weird; he's held this all in for so long. 'I think the general having to worry about my appearance so much when it's filming season is the problem. Too much policing what I'm doing with or to my body. I don't think it's very good for me overall. The exercise keeps my brain from boiling over, but is it only doing that because I'm constantly having to think about being on? Would I be constructing home gyms in your bakery if I wasn't thinking about acting? It's an ouroboros.'

'A what?'

'That snake thing that eats its own tail and goes in circles. You're posh, aren't you? I'd have thought you'd know what that is.' Christopher makes an indignant noise but doesn't move away. In fact, his hand is still placed on Nash's arm, a quiet reassurance.

'Have you started writing?' Christopher asks, doing that goddamn earnest face again that makes Nash want to tell him things.

'Yes,' he quietly admits for the first time. 'I've got a couple of script treatments. Like a proposal or synopsis of a few films or shows I'd like to work on. It's all pretty amateur stuff, but I think they're good ideas. I still want to work on rom-coms, but not as the leading man. I want someone else to act out the stories I tell, and I want to make space for other actors coming up the ranks.'

His mouth feels dry. Talking about his writing makes him realise how different it is from acting. When he acts, it's all about embodying someone else. He's not really Nash when he acts; the disappearing is the point of it. But when he writes, it's *all* him. He *has* to be himself, and that is both thrilling and terrifying in equal measures.

'Basically, I want to try something new, and I worry that if I sign that deal, I'm locked into this life that doesn't fit for so much longer.'

'What does your agent say?'

He shuffles. 'I haven't spoken to Kurt about it. The execs pushed the deadline until after Christmas, which saved me from having a conversation about it.'

'Wait a moment, is that why you're here? To avoid all this?'

Nash can feel his cheeks redden, and he's grateful that the lights are off.

'Nash. That was a very silly idea,' Christopher softly admonishes.

'Perhaps, but if I hadn't come, I wouldn't have been roped into this Christmas-movie-come-to-life, would I?'

There's so much else he could say here, words that sit on the tip of his tongue but that he refuses to acknowledge. If he hadn't come, they wouldn't have met, and while Nash is still trying to work out what that means for him, he knows it isn't nothing. And that scares him a little.

'Speaking as someone who is truly terrible at talking about things,' Christopher says slowly, 'I think you should probably talk to Kurt about it.'

'I know,' he says, his voice quieter than he expected. 'I've spent the last, like, decade and a half of my life always pushing forward, looking for the next thing and hustling for more work. It feels against my nature to stop and say, actually this isn't it, especially when so many people's employment is linked to this deal.'

'Like Kurt's?'

'Well, yeah, he does get some money from my work.'

'Well, I'm sure he'd rather that money came from something you *wanted* to do, rather than something you were doing just for him. Don't you think? Doesn't he get a say in it?'

Nash narrows his eyes. 'You know, it's quite annoying when you're so unusually perceptive.'

'Am I not usually?'

Nash makes a teasing *hmmm* noise, and Christopher tickles him. He *actually* tickles him, and he can't help but laugh. All the pent-up anxiety flowing out of him as he tries to escape the gangliest man alive. 'Please, no more!'

'Only if you're going to talk to Kurt about it.'

'Sure, but after Christmas. I have some boundaries.'

Christopher lets him go, and Nash feels the cool air rush in where Christopher's touch leaves him. Christopher yawns and stretches his body out in a way that reminds Nash of the puppies.

'We should get some sleep. We've got another full-on day tomorrow.'

Christopher starts launching into sleepy scheduling for the next day, and Nash shushes him with a hand over his lips.

'Shush. I'm already starting to regret it,' Nash says.

'What are you going to do? Hide? Shaz is like a bloodhound. She'll find you.'

'Nah, I was thinking something more sophisticated like turning the truck into a teleportation machine. I've probably got enough time if I get started now.'

'You could just make it your Christmas Wish.'

'My what?'

'Oh. It's a Calloway tradition. Kit and I would always make a wish at midnight on Christmas Eve, like on a star in the sky or the one on the tree if it was too cloudy to see any.'

'Is it like a birthday wish? One of those you-can't-tell-people-or-it-won't-come-true situations?'

'Yeah, I suppose so.'

'I can't believe you didn't come up with any new wish rules. That's very unimaginative.'

'Oh sorry,' Christopher scoffs. 'I'll use that teleportation truck to go back and tell five-year-old us that we need to do a second draft.'

'Don't be ridiculous, Calloway, you're talking about a time travel machine. That's something completely different.'

'Now look who is being a nerd.'

What a funny man he is. Who would have ever guessed that such a buttoned-up man would hold onto his childhood traditions quite so tightly. But then, Christopher definitely has some kind of whimsical, childlike side, what with the Paddington Bear, the gingerbread houses, and his general love of bickering.

In a swift move, Nash stands up on the bed, opening the curtains for the skylight above it. The sky above is deep navy peppered with silver, and a bright shining moon fills the bedroom with soft light.

'Well, come on then. It's wish time.'

He pulls Christopher up to stand next to him, and of course he has to crouch a bit because the ceiling is too low.

'I'm not going to say it out loud,' he says, a little indignantly.

'This was your idea.'

'Yeah, and my rules. You don't share the wish.'

'Fine.'

Nash cracks open the window a little, as though they might need a direct line to the sky to make it work. It's cold but the air is so fresh that he could gulp it down. They stand together in silence, watching the stars, and Nash wishes he could remember any constellations. Is the sky here even the same as the one in LA, or above his childhood home?

He's not sure what to wish for, if he's honest, and perhaps it's a cop-out, but he wishes for happiness and for clarity, whatever those two things mean.

Chapter Twenty-Three

Christopher

Christopher wakes early to get started on the busy day of cooking with an unmitigated glee. It's Christmas. And, even if it's not the Christmas he had in mind, he gets to spend it with his friends, feeding a lot of people who might have nowhere else to go. That feels right.

On one hand, it feels normal waking up before sunrise, but it's the waking up in Nash's arms part that feels strange and a little too comforting.

He decides to wake himself up with a hot shower, but before that, he opens the Spanks Squad chat, where he sees a few post-midnight messages he missed while he was asleep.

Kit: merry christmas dickheads x
Haf: HAPPY CRIMMUS
Haf: Is christmassssss
Haf: MERRY CRISIS
Laurel: Are you all right darling?
Kit: Haf discovered limoncello tonight. She'll be fine.
Ambrose: merry chrysler!
Haf: see AMBROSE gets it
Haf: ily all
Laurel: Merry Christmas darling. Take a paracetamol before bed x
Haf: where is christopher
Haf: why has he not wished us christmas yet

Ambrose: hopefully he's celebrating in his own special way
Haf: making gingerbread???

This is followed by several lines of cry emojis from Haf.

Ambrose: if that's what we're calling it now
Ambrose: oi oiiiiiii
Kit: ????
Haf: wait are you doing an innuendo

Oh god. Trust Ambrose to have borderline psychic powers. Luckily no one has said anything for a good four hours, so it's probably safe for him to drop a greeting and leave.

Christopher: Morning! Merry Christmas everyone. Love you all.
Ambrose: did you shag him
Ambrose: did you?????
Christopher: Why are you awake? It's 6am.
Ambrose: thats a yes then
Ambrose: lads lads lads lads
Ambrose: and the answer is that i'm always perceiving you x
Christopher: Horrifying.
Christopher: I have to go make Christmas dinner for about twenty-five people.
Christopher: Speak to you all later. Have a nice day.
Ambrose: WAIT WHAT ABOUT THE SHAGGIN

As he's finishing in the shower, Nash jumps in too, passing him with a quick peck on the cheek. It happens so fast that Christopher isn't even sure it was real.

By the time they make it downstairs to the bakery, it's getting worryingly close to seven.

'It feels late to be starting the loaves,' Christopher says, partly to himself. If they hadn't been fooling around last night, maybe he could have got them done. Or woken up earlier. A thick wad of guilt pools in his stomach. What if he fucks this up?

'Do you have to get up really early?' Nash says, already busying himself with chopping vegetables for the starter soup.

'Yes. Usually four to get the dough proving.'

'Gross. I hate it when I have a call-time that early, because it always happens on the days after I finish late.' Nash yawns. 'So, you're just here all day then?'

'It's not just me. Tegan serves the customers.'

Nash gives him a look. 'So it's just you.'

'I'm not sure what you're implying.'

'Oh nothing,' Nash says airily. 'Just that you're a bit of a control freak.'

Before Christopher can reply and insist that actually he's not a control freak, he just really likes things to be done in his own specific way, there's a knock on the window in the café.

He walks through the bakery kitchen to find Tegan herself at the door, dressed head to toe in black. The giant hat on her head is fluffy and has cat ears sticking out the top of it, but boy does it look warm. The men are barely awake, and yet somehow Tegan has had the wherewithal to draw on the sharpest eyeliner he's ever seen, presumably before caffeine. Oh, to be young again.

'Morning,' he says, which turns into a question as she walks past him, stomping the snow off her enormous platform boots. 'We're not open today you know?'

This is met with a blank stare.

'And it's Christmas?'

She rolls her eyes, and hands him a carrier bag. Inside are a couple of rolls of frozen pastry. 'For the vegans,' she says, by way of explanation.

Older people might find Tegan's special brand of communication offensive or rude, but Christopher just accepts that she's working on a different wavelength to him. She does a really good job with the customers so what does it matter if she's a bit blunt with him on a one-to-one basis? Nash would definitely agree with Tegan that he's a bit annoying, so he can hardly hold it against her.

Either way, this mostly non-verbal conversation seems to be the best he's going to get for now, as she goes behind the counter and hangs her things up in their usual places.

'Morning,' Nash says, as he wanders in to start up the coffee machine, and he sees a flash of recognition cross Tegan's face.

'Hiya,' she says, giving him a Tegan's top-customer-service-level smile. 'I'm Tegan.'

'Nash. Nice to meet you.'

'Look at you trying to run an industrial coffee machine,' Christopher smiles to Nash as he passes.

'I'll have you know I was a great little barista in my teens in between TV jobs, Calloway. When did *you* start working in customer service? Yesterday?'

This garners a smile from Tegan, and Christopher admittedly feels a little jealous as well as awkward. Of course he'd never worked in a café before. His first job when he was a teenager was doing data input for his dad. All his professional kitchen experience was from the internships he did as part of his course. 'I mean, yes, it was last year.'

'Getting down with the plebs, aren't you?' laughs Nash.

'I don't think . . . *plebs*,' he says, struggling to get the word out, 'is a fixed category, and I think, Nash Nadeau, that as a man easily visible on all streaming services internationally, you might have transcended that class category.'

'God, you lot really are obsessed with class, aren't you?'

There are several tea towels within reach, and Christopher has a great desire to whip one into a rope and flick Nash with it.

'Tegan, do you want a drink?' Nash asks the empty space where Tegan was previously standing.

They find her on the café side, picking up one chair at a time and moving it carefully to the edge of the room.

'What is she doing?' whispers Nash.

'I'm not sure,' Christopher whispers back. Then, more loudly, he calls over to her, 'Tegan, what are you doing?'

This garners a loud groan. 'I've been sent to help, haven't I? I'm going to clean the floor and then I'll set up the tables. No point moving stuff around first if the floor is covered in muddy footprints.'

'It's not—' protests Christopher, but he sees that it is. All the stomping through from him and Nash over the past few days has left a spatter of muddy marks all over the centre of the café. 'Oh, it really is. And that would be a great help, Tegan. Thank you.'

She raises her eyebrows in a face that definitely means *well yes obviously*. 'The floor will need to dry and stuff, and setting everything up won't take me that long, so if you need some help in the kitchen, just say.'

Normally, when she offers the help, Christopher bats it away. But he thinks of what his mother was saying about trust and delegation. Tegan has quite literally turned up on Christmas morning to help them out. There couldn't really be a greater show of dedication.

'Well, we were just about to start the loaves. I know you usually miss that part. Would you like to learn how to first?'

'You're not going to make me start coming here at four to make them, are you?' she asks warily.

'No, I won't,' Christopher reassures her.

A beaming smile spreads across her face. 'In that case, yes please!'

Armed with fresh coffees, Christopher sets out a number of proving baskets, and flour on the central kitchen work surface. It'll be so much quicker with two hands, even if one is learning on the go.

'Can we have some music on?' Tegan asks.

'I'll be DJ,' says Nash, pulling out his phone. He starts up a playlist of Christmas songs, which opens with an upbeat song about being nice from a Christmas movie, a deeply ironic choice from Nash Nadeau, a man who Christopher would never describe as *nice*. Charming, perhaps. Handsome, yes. But nice? Nice is too small a word.

'Do you want to try, Nash?'

'Sure. Three hands are quicker than two.'

Strange, he thinks, that they thought the same thing. Perhaps they've been spending too much time together.

His yeast starter has been a trusty tool of his for over a decade. The original tiny jar came from one of his Baking Soc friends at university, who had got it from a witchy aunt known for her rustic bakes and myriad of possibly illegally grown plants. The sourdough recipe is one he's been using since he was a teenager, which he tweaked while at pâtisserie school when he learned all the ways he wasn't making the best loaves he could. Now they pretty much always turn out perfect. Sourdough isn't particularly fancy, in truth, but people love fresh bread. Cakes and treats are shinier and easier to sell, especially on miserable days, but what makes a meal is a still-warm slice of softly pillowy bread with a thick crust, slathered in melting salty butter. That's what people need today. Some comfort, some nourishment.

He guides Nash and Tegan through mixing up the dough, and how to knead it consistently to develop the gluten, which will be important later, after it's proved and filled with microbubbles that need to be incorporated back into the dough. The more kneading, the tighter the crumb will be in the final loaf.

Naturally, Nash is very good at this part. Christopher tries very hard not to look at his toned arms working the dough, and it looks as if Tegan is doing the same.

The dough in his hands has been somewhat mangled in the last few moments of arm ogling, and he pats it back into a more acceptable blob shape. He's always worried about overworking it, going past the point of activating the gluten into mashing it all up into a tired mess. It's possible he's arriving at the point where one turns into the other.

Still, there's magic to the whole process that Christopher is glad he's not lost, even after making his hobby his job. It's truly a wonder to take all these individual ingredients and, in combining them, create joy and full tummies.

Despite the distraction, Tegan does a really good job following his instructions, and even asks questions when she's unsure. Why hasn't he asked her for help before? He always thought that working with other people would destroy the sense of calm, but with Nash and Tegan, he can still tap into that feeling, even when they're all singing along to a song that features Mariah Carey alongside a few other singers . . . which he's pretty sure is *also* from a Christmas movie.

'Hang on, is this playlist made exclusively of songs from Christmas films?' he asks with a laugh.

Nash shrugs awkwardly, clearly embarrassed to have been caught out in something so obviously self-referential. 'They're all bops!' he cries, kneading the dough a little harder.

'Don't take it out on the bread,' scolds Tegan.

Nash pretends to look chastened. 'Yes, chef. Sorry, chef.'

'Damn right,' she laughs. 'This is actually kind of fun.'

'Thank you for coming to help,' Christopher says. 'It was really thoughtful of you.'

'Means I get to be away from my little siblings. I have done *way* too much babysitting this week. There's only so much *Bluey* I can watch.'

'Don't go slandering *Bluey*'s name in front of me,' says Nash, flipping the dough round. 'Bingo is an angel.'

'Yeah, but I've seen all of it. Three times at least. And they just want to keep watching the sad ones, because they're little demons.' She sighs with the kind of world weariness that you can only associate with being a teenager. No one could pay him to be a teenager again. 'Plus, Grandma is driving my mum nuts, which makes the whole thing much worse.'

'How's your mum doing?' Christopher says, remembering suddenly that Tegan had mentioned her mum had been under the weather.

'Better,' she says, and he decides not to pry into what she might have been recovering from.

Tegan is flagging as she kneads, but she keeps going, eventually patting the dough into round loaves. She's a little powerhouse of fury and eyeliner. He makes a note to have a proper conversation with her about what she would like to learn – after all, that's the point of her being here, isn't it? She should get to learn how to do any part of the business she's interested in so it'll be on her CV for wherever she goes next.

Eventually, they have ten proving baskets with dough quietly rising, and a timer set to check back on them in a few hours.

'What's next on your plan?' Christopher asks Nash.

'We're going to slow-roast the lamb legs. The oven upstairs is little but if we use that, then we can leave them in low and slow for the next few hours.'

'Good plan.'

'Also, Dai and Thelma gave us these hams but I'm not sure I've ever cooked one. Usually, it's just like a thin steak of ham that tastes of despair. The internet says to boil it in water, which for some reason sounds disgusting to me.'

'Boil it in Coke,' says Tegan sagely. 'That's what Nigella does. I've seen it on TikTok. I'll ask Danny from the shop to bring some up now.'

'That sounds somehow worse, so I'm going to leave you to it,' Nash says, hoisting the lamb legs under his arms, and a bagful of herbs in the other.

It doesn't take Christopher long to find the recipe online, so he takes over the hams, scoring the skin and studding them with cloves plus a coating of brown sugar and some ancient mustard powder he finds upstairs, squeezing around Nash's intense lamb preparation.

If Christopher was sceptical that an Angeleno would know how to handle two whole legs of lamb, he shouldn't have been. In Christopher's trusty and huge casserole dishes, he makes a trivet of the saddest-looking supermarket vegetables for the lamb to sit on. The lamb legs have been rubbed and studded with garlic and rosemary and salt.

'Worked in a lot of kitchens too?' he asks, peering over as Nash breaks up the sprigs of herbs.

'Not in real life. I played a chef in—'

'*What Christmas Means to Leigh,*' Christopher finishes and, realising he said it out loud, the heat creeps up his face.

To his relief, Nash just cackles. 'All right, *Ingrid Goes West.* You don't need to recite my IMDb back to me.'

'I just think it's quite a good one,' he huffs, walking down the stairs.

'That's the one with Khloé Kardashian in it isn't it?' Tegan calls, presumably so they can both hear.

'It is,' Nash calls back down, clearly amused by his little burgeoning fan base. 'I didn't realise I was so popular in this corner of North Wales.'

'With him and my stepmum, sure. Maybe the dinner will turn into a meet and greet.'

Christopher realises he really doesn't know much about Tegan's family, other than that she has tyrant little siblings. Perhaps her father is remarried? It seems kind of a weird thing to ask her about, though, as her employer.

In record time, Danny from the shop arrives with two carrier bags straining under the weight of many large bottles of Coke. Christopher instructs him to pour it right into the big saucepan on the stove, which houses the hams and some onion halves, but this is met with a very confused look.

'I'll show you,' says Tegan, dragging him over to the hob. Christopher feels a swell of pride at everyone working hard in his little kitchen.

Once the hams are on the go, Tegan takes a few pictures of the food prepping, before going back through the café to let Danny out and to finish cleaning.

Soon the lamb is roasting, loaves are proving, hams are cooking, and Christopher gets a start on making a mountain of chopped and prepped potatoes and vegetables ready to be roasted, boiled, even sautéed, depending on what pans they have left. Nash also returns and gets started on his mysterious vegetarian Wellington, and, seeing quite how much puff pastry he needs, Christopher is glad that they opted for *raiding freezers* rather than it being yet another thing they had to make themselves.

Christopher's little greenhouse of herbs has been stripped bare, but now they have a glut of mint sauce for the lamb, and the start of both a vegetarian gravy and a meaty one made with some stock cubes from his cupboard upstairs.

The hours roll by quickly as they tick off each step on Nash's list, taking things in and out of ovens, and wrapping hot things up in foil to keep warm for serving time.

He didn't see her arrive, but eventually Shaz walks into the kitchen and surveys the large amount of food already laid out ready. 'It's a Christmas miracle!'

'Christ, are people arriving already?' Christopher asks nervously.

'Relax, we rounded up everyone nice and early, and they're at the village hall being topped up on hot drinks. Tamara even managed to get some proper salt for the road so everyone could get across without going arse over tit. And have you seen what my girl has done out here?'

They follow her out to the café side and Christopher gasps. The tables have been aligned into a couple of long ones, covered with various tablecloths that do not match but that are all along the same holiday colour palette of red, green and gold. Each setting has cutlery and something to drink out of – along with café supplies, Christopher recognises some of his glasses from upstairs, plus some of the ancient plastic juice cups from the village hall. He's not quite sure where she got all the salt and pepper sets, but they're dotted along the table, along with jars of horseradish, redcurrant jelly and mustard.

Also on the tables are small centrepieces of piled-up Christmas decorations that must have been stolen from someone's tree, balanced on a few of the fake present boxes from the window.

The counter is clean and clear ready for the buffet, with a huge stack of plates at one end, and large serving spoons ready.

Finally, instrumental Christmas music softly plays from a speaker in the corner.

It's everything they could have dreamed of.

'Wow, this looks amazing in here,' says Nash.

'Tegan, this is . . . this is just magical,' Christopher says, his voice quiet with awe. 'Thank you so much.'

She smiles down at her shoes. 'Danny from the shop helped too.'

'Everyone who is coming today brought a bag of useful bits with them, and we've used everything we can,' Shaz explains.

'I took photos of everything so I think I can match it all up at the end too.'

'Great thinking,' Nash smiles, yielding another beam from Tegan.

'How long do you have left on the great Christmas master plan?' Shaz asks.

Christopher does some quick maths. 'Maybe ready to dish up in an hour if we have a couple of hands to help with serving?'

Nash snorts. 'You can probably divide that time estimate by how long his legs are. Takes you half the time to whip round as the rest of us.'

'I'd be quicker if I didn't have imps like you underfoot,' he sniffs.

Shaz stares at them in disbelief. 'What are you on about? There's like two inches of height difference between you both. Maximum.'

'It has to be more than that,' Nash murmurs.

'Nope,' agrees Tegan from across the room where she holds up a hand presumably to match up their heads. 'Basically, the same height as each other.'

'Well. Now I feel a bit ridiculous,' murmurs Christopher.

'Why don't we move this along?' Nash says, clearly just as embarrassed.

'On it. Bee R Bee,' she says, sounding out the acronym and heading back over the road.

There's luckily not much left to do, but it's all the awkward bits that all seem to need twenty minutes or so. The loaves are done, and after taste testing to make sure they're good, Tegan ladles the gravies into an array of borrowed boats. They all work fast and efficiently, and Christopher can hardly believe how much they've got done in the last six hours of near constant cooking.

Just as they're almost done, Shaz and Ursula nip back over to help tidy up, so they are ready to help plate up dinners for people. Tamara, Mervyn, Priti and Carl slowly help people over the road in small groups, while Danny from the shop takes coats and bags up into the flat for safe keeping and so that no one trips over them. All the while, Tegan and Nash serve drinks to the waiting guests, while Christopher manages the final touches.

Soon, the bakery is packed out with people waiting patiently in their seats for dinner. To Christopher's delight, Myffy arrives on her mobility scooter accompanied by a man with hair almost as curly as hers and a bright smile, despite the deep bags under his eyes. Mohan. He made it; what a relief.

He recognises a few of the other guests: Cecil, who lent them a thermos. Mengsan and Nancy, who almost made black ice. Joan, who loves her garden birds. Dai and Thelma, who are now never out of each other's reach. Hot Drinks Lady, who he finally remembers is called Enid. All of the people he has met and helped, or was helped by, over the past few days, and yet there are still as many again he hasn't met before.

These are all people who are his community now. People who he gets to celebrate his first Christmas in Wales with. This is all he ever hoped for.

'All good to go?' Shaz asks, stunning him out of his thoughts enough for him to hear, but not enough to halt the inevitable oncoming spiral of worry.

And part of Christopher wants to say, well, no, because what if they hate it? What if this was his one chance to ingratiate himself in his new community and he blows it?

But just as the worries threaten to engulf him, he locks eyes with Nash through the door into the café; a smile is returned with a thumbs up, and every fear falls away.

He can do this. He *has* done this. All that's left is to let people eat, before it all gets cold.

'Yes. Let's serve up.'

They bring out the food to rapturous applause, and a few *oi oi*s from Shaz and Myffy, who has an impressive yell on her. Christopher slices up big wedges of sourdough, slicked with bright yellow butter, as Tegan ladles out thick creamy soup into mismatched bowls. It all disappears so quickly that, for a moment, he wonders if he even served it at all.

When it's ready for the main course, Christopher tackles plating up vegetables and sides, while Nash carves up the lamb, seeing as he's the one who cooked it. The meat is so tender it practically falls off the bone.

'It's the good stuff, I told you,' Thelma announces to everyone proudly, and Christopher can't help but smile when he notices her and Dai holding hands. Well then, another Christmas miracle in what is starting to feel like a sea of them.

Priti, Tamara and Shaz take orders so no one has to stand, and they bring full plate after full plate to empty tummies, while Danny and Tegan top up glasses and pass around sauces and seasonings.

It's all a blur, but soon everyone has a plate of food, a raised glass and a cheer on their lips, crying Merry Christmas and iechyd da in turn as glasses clink together.

Mervyn is, it turns out, a dab hand at making cocktails, and although Christopher has no idea where all the spirits have come from, he doesn't overthink for once, because everyone seems happy and merry.

In the doorway to the kitchen, Christopher and Nash stand together, aprons covered in gravy and oil and seasonings, holding a glass of mulled wine each, handed to them by Ursula.

'I can't believe we did it,' Christopher whispers.

They clink their glasses together and, as they sip, their eyes meet.

'We make a great team, Calloway,' says Nash with a soft smile. He slips an arm around Christopher's waist, and they share what is really just a tiny squeeze of a moment, but which feels like an eternity to Christopher, his heart flipping back and forth with joy.

But it's not *just* because of this moment with Nash. It's also due to the community he has built right here in his bakery. He doesn't know how long his business will last, but it feels as if he's finally put down roots. He's made something, and fed people, and created a moment that everyone will remember.

What more could he ask for?

Myffy taps a glass with her knife. 'A toast for the very best Christmas elves our little town could ask for!'

'To Nash and Christopher!'

They're surrounded by a chorus of 'To Nash and Christopher'.

'And everyone else too,' Christopher says, feeling the blush rise over him in protest.

'Just let them celebrate you,' Shaz says, patting his arm as she passes.

And so, he decides to just accept it. It's a funny thing really, he spent all this time worrying about fitting in and finding a community, and now, as he's just about starting to find and feel that, accepting it feels like a whole extra step.

He can't quite believe that this town, this whole town, saw something in him.

He's just about to make himself up a plate when he notices something very strange out of the windows at the front.

A van he doesn't recognise pulls up and parks in the village hall car park.

Strange, he thinks.

Hunger overrides curiosity, and his stomach growls loudly. While standing at the counter, he remembers he hasn't checked his phone since this morning and, keen to avoid using it actually *at* the table, he decides to check it now. As he turns it over, he realises he has over a hundred unread messages in WhatsApp.

Perhaps a glitch?

But no, he can see there are over 200 notifications in Spanks Squad. Yes, Ambrose and Haf can be really chatty, but that seems like a lot even for them. The last visible message shows Haf saying, 'Crap he must have turned his phone off.'

When he actually opens the group chat, WhatsApp is so overwhelmed that it automatically navigates to her last message, above which are messages from Kit, Haf, Laurel and Ambrose repeatedly typing his name over and over. They must be having some kind of joke, but unease pools in his stomach. Why were they trying to get his attention? Had something happened?

Instead of scrolling all the way up to find out what they've been talking about, he writes a new message at the bottom.

Christopher: hello?

Haf: GUYS HE'S HERE

Kit: where the fuck have you been??

Christopher: What's going on?

Laurel: We don't want to scare you darling but there's been some kind of leak.

Christopher: a leak?

Laurel: To the press.

Ambrose: the whole world knows Nash is in your bakery

Laurel: He's gone viral, darling.

Chapter Twenty-Four

Christopher

'What the?' Christopher murmurs, trying to make sense of what his friends are saying.

'What's wrong?' asks Nash.

Rather than explain in front of the others, he takes Nash by the hand and leads him into the bakery kitchen.

'Something weird is going on, and I don't think it's a prank.'

In the group chat, Haf replies to a message sent earlier that's just a Twitter link.

Haf: Open this
Christopher: I don't have Twitter.
Ambrose: it doesn't matter just open it!!!!!!

It's a tweet that says 'spotted on TikTok: Nash Nadeau in Wales??'

It has hundreds of retweets and quote tweets, and so many thousands of likes that there's only a 'K' after the first three numbers. Attached to the tweets are grainy screenshots from a video, zoomed in as far as possible, showing Nash in the kitchen.

A cold shiver runs down his back.

'Oh fuck,' groans Nash, peering at the screen.

Laurel: I think I found the source. Do you happen to know this teenager?

At the same time, a screenshot and a TikTok link arrive in the chat from Laurel and Ambrose respectively. And while Christopher might not understand TikTok, he does absolutely recognise the heavily eyelinered teenager smiling and grimacing at the camera, dancing around a café, *his café*, showing off all the things they have been cooking for Christmas dinner and the beautiful table settings she spent all morning on.

It's Tegan.

And when he plays the video just for a flash in the background you can clearly see Nash and Christopher working in the kitchen. It's not the best-lit shot, but it's very clearly him.

Ambrose: there's a whole hashtag where they're cross-referencing Nash in the background with side profiles from his films, it's wild

Ambrose: his fans were sharing it with each other

Haf: And somehow that got out of fan circles onto like everyone's Twitter

Laurel: It's all over Instagram too. They think you're re-enacting one of your films or doing it for PR. The press has gotten hold of it too, and keep talking about a deal?

'Oh FUCK.' Nash turns a spectacular shade of green for someone with a seemingly permanent California tan, and starts pacing back and forth in the kitchen.

Christopher: Christ this is bad. Thank you for warning us.

Ambrose: idk how we can help with this one im sorry

Haf: Do you have a Santa costume lying around? Perfect disguise right now?

Kit: Or, you could just hide him upstairs?

Laurel: That's terribly dull darling. What about the possibility for hijinks?

'What do we do?' he asks Nash.

'I have no idea. But I'm fucked if this gets back to my team, which it probably will, even though it's Christmas Day. And I've heard that the British paparazzi can be vicious.'

There is no script for how to proceed here, and Christopher is floundering. He needs to help Nash, but how?

'Do you think any press will even be able to get here? The roads are still pretty bad, right?' Nash splutters.

His gut twists. *That van.* What if the van that pulled up outside is the press?

How are they going to even explain this? Though the press obviously know Nash is trans, they otherwise seem to think he's a somewhat reclusive straight man. What if this outs him? What will that do to his career options? He's spiralling, and they need help. They need Shaz.

'Shaz,' he calls, trying to keep his voice calm but deeply aware he's doing that *we need your help because a crisis is unfolding* voice.

'What's up?' She walks into the kitchen bringing a stack of dirty plates with her. 'Is a crisis unfolding? You're doing your stressed voice.'

He hands her the phone.

'Oh shite.'

'Indeed. I think they're here too.'

'Fuck,' mutters Nash, his hands running through his hair.

'Tegan!' Shaz barely raises her voice, but her tone is sharp.

It surprises him a bit that Tegan comes running so quickly, but when she does, her face is frantic. 'I've just looked at my phone! I'm so sorry, I didn't realise what was happening and I had notifications turned off and my account is private so someone *stole* the video from there and leaked it and—'

Nash sets his hands gently on her shoulders. 'Tegan, it's not your fault. It was probably going to get out eventually that I was here. Someone was going to spot me, and if it wasn't on TikTok it would have been on someone's Facebook photos or something. It's not like I laid down the law on privacy.'

'I'm really sorry,' she whispers, deep sobs punctuating her words.

'Discussions on internet safety coming for you later. Right now, we possibly have a situation to be dealing with,' Nash reassures her.

They poke their heads out through the kitchen door, only to see that the van isn't just one van anymore. It's a gaggle of photographers and reporters, and several more vans.

'Christ, do they have nothing better to do? It's literally Christmas Day!' Christopher hisses.

'Like what? Report on the weather? Give over, this is the most exciting thing in celebrity news that's happened round here since Will and Kate left Anglesey.'

In one horrifying singular motion that feels right out of a horror movie, the mob turns towards the café.

'Hide the American!' Shaz yells, and Tegan yanks him as far back into the kitchen as possible without knocking anything over.

Christopher can just hear his muffled cries of, 'I'm *Canadian*,' before Nash disappears entirely from sight.

Making himself as tall and broad as possible, the latter rather difficult for him, Christopher takes up the full doorway to the kitchen like a guard, just as the front door bursts open. The reporters and photographers attempt to shuffle inside, clearly not expecting it to be quite so full in here. A photographer looks around the café with lens raised to eye just in case they can grab a candid photo.

The guests go deadly silent, eyes focussed on the intruders.

'Can we help you?' asks Tamara, standing up from her seat and assuming her usual role of Being In Charge, hands on her hips.

One particularly smarmy-looking chap saunters forward with a grin like the cat who got the cream. 'We have it on good authority that actor Nash Nadeau is here . . . assisting the community, apparently. We would really like to just get a few words with him about what he's doing here.'

'You are interrupting a private event, and we are not speaking to the press at this time. Please vacate the premises immediately.'

'And who are you to speak? His PR?'

'Tamara Yang, I'm the local councillor. I'm in charge.' This yields a cheer of *yeahs* from the townies. 'So now, you all must leave.'

'And will you shut that bloody door?' cries Dai. 'Letting all the heat out, you are.'

'He is here, though, isn't he?' presses another photographer.

'No, he's not,' says Priti, getting to her feet.

'Why would an actor be here in our quaint little village?' sniffs Cecil.

'We don't even know who you mean!' yells Myffy extremely unconvincingly, but Christopher's heart aches for the effort anyway.

The journalist looks not remotely amused by the solidarity on display. 'Funny you'd say that, because I'm pretty sure this is the same establishment as seen in this TikTok here.' The photographer next to him holds up their phone where Tegan's TikTok is playing. 'So, unless he's already left, which I sincerely doubt, I'm sure he's here.'

'Regularly watch videos of teenagers, do you?' Christopher snarls from the doorway into the kitchen, and one of the photographers chuckles before remembering they are essentially all here from the same tip-off.

'We know he's here,' yells someone from the mob.

'Teegs,' whispers Shaz. 'Record this, will you? In case they kick off.'

Still keeping out of sight, with shaking hands, Tegan points her phone camera to film through the doorway by Christopher's knees.

'We *also* heard that he's been delaying signing his next contract,' someone from the mob shouts from the doorway. 'I'm sure his production team would be very happy to know that he's hiding out all the way over here. Especially with Barbie Glynn's contract on the line, too.'

Christopher gasps. There must have been a leak. It's all out there now. Poor Nash.

'Is that some kind of threat?' Christopher asks, his hands curling into fists at his side.

'Please leave, or I'll be forced to call the police,' says Tamara.

'For what? For entering a public place?'

'I repeat, this is a *private* party,' Tamara emphasises, 'and you are currently trespassing,' she growls, with all the fury of a warrior. Though, God bless her, not a single one moves.

Christopher can hear some faint whispering coming from the kitchen behind him, and wills Nash to stay where he is.

'We're just after an interview, my guy,' the reporter calls to Christopher again. He tries to walk around the tables, presumably to get through Christopher to the kitchen behind, but people keep pushing their chairs out, or standing up to block him.

'I'm not your *guy*,' growls Christopher.

'You seem to care a lot about this. Why else would he be here, in the middle of nowhere? Perhaps then you're Nash Nadeau's guy? Care to comment on *that*?'

There it is, laced in just enough plausible deniability for them to say they're not being completely homophobic and trying to out Nash. And just as the boiling hot rage is about to spill out of Christopher's body, the room explodes with shared furious protest.

Shaz abandons her place in the kitchen with Nash and Tegan and instead storms right up to the reporter and stabs a finger into his chest. 'Oi. Dickheads. I have no idea what you think you've seen but have you ever heard of a deep fake? One, why would a film star be here in the middle of winter? Two, how would he have even got here? And three, this is private property and FOUR—' she roars, just as the reporter tries to interrupt her. 'We are doing a community initiative to feed the members of our community who are without a Christmas dinner and maybe youse would all like to fuck right off back to your own sad little dinners so we can get the fuck on with it, yes? Yes?'

Shaz is radiant, glowing and wholly terrifying – Christopher sends a thanks to the gods that he has never faced her wrath.

One of the photographers clearly decides this is more hassle than he can be bothered with and turns tail out of the front door. But too many remain, including the smarmy guy who has managed, in all the chaos, to make his way round to the counter. He's merely steps away from where Nash is hiding, and if Nash moves to go upstairs, they'll all spot him. He's trapped. '*I* don't have to move.'

'Oh yeah?' Shaz takes the tea towel slung over her shoulder and starts whipping it round in her hands, winding it up into a twisted rope.

'I think it's time you left,' growls a deep voice that belongs to someone who looks the spitting image of Tegan. *Her mum?* Christopher wonders. He is not quite sure when she arrived, and for some reason, she is wearing a medical boot on one foot. 'You don't get to come here and intimidate everyone.'

This is a slightly ironic thing to say because she is one of the tallest, broadest women he's ever seen and she could *absolutely* kick the shit out of basically anyone, boot or no boot.

'Oh, what are you going to do? Kick me with your boot?' stammers the journalist, losing a bit of his bravado.

'I'll do something much worse with it, which you definitely won't enjoy. And now, look, all your little photographer friends have left,' the tall woman snarls.

She's right. They're all hurrying outside, the door barred behind them by Mervyn and Ursula.

'It's just you, me, and my wife with that towel. You want to risk it?'

The man takes one look at the towel and Shaz, then back to the tall woman, and bolts.

The bakery is filled with triumphant cheers as the reporters and photographers dive back into the van and drive away. Christopher locks the front door behind them, just to be safe.

Nash emerges from the kitchen, and everyone cheers again. 'Thank you, everyone. You really didn't need to do that.'

Thelma pats him on the arm. 'You helped us, lad. It's only right that we help you.'

'Shaz, did you know you're absolutely terrifying?' Nash laughs with relief.

'You know, that's the loveliest thing you've ever said to me? You can stay.'

Now that the moment of terror is over, Christopher's brain finally catches up with him. And he realises that the tall woman has her arm around Shaz's shoulders. Wife? Did the woman say *wife*? As if to confirm his suspicions, she bends down to give Shaz a kiss.

'My wife is the scariest woman in the world. I'm going to have a bite to eat if that's all right.' Shaz sends the tall woman off to take a seat at the table with a pat on the bum.

'Hang on a minute,' Christopher says to Shaz. 'You're . . . together?!'

'What, Gar?' she asks, thumbing in the direction of the tall woman, now happily eating her dinner.

'*She's* Gar??'

'Who else did you think Gar was? That's Gabrielle! Gar for short.' The look Shaz is giving him lies somewhere between baffled and extremely amused.

'I . . . I don't know,' he murmurs and then realises the embarrassing truth of it all. 'I thought you were married to a Gary.'

'You thought my wife's name was Gary?' Shaz snorts with laughter.

'Well, no . . .'

'Hang on,' says Shaz. 'Did you not notice that Tegan is my step-daughter?'

'You talk to everyone so . . .' Christopher stumbles to find a word, 'so *Shazly* that I didn't think you were actually related. I thought that was just a You Thing.'

She bursts into raucous laughter. 'Oh dear, I am either a shite step-parent or really good at bossing everyone around if that's the case.'

'And I'm . . . I'm really sorry, I presumed the straight default. That was weird of me.'

At this, she softens a little, her laughs subsiding if not diminishing completely. 'Christopher, you big lug. Why do you think I was so insistent on coming in every day and getting people to come? Why do you think Gar and I were so keen for Tegan to come and work for you?'

Dizzy with the revelations, Christopher doesn't answer, because how do you answer when all your preconceptions are so obviously wrong in the first place?

'Because I wanted to support a new queer business, you big wally. One of my friends, Kim, is obsessed with bakestagram or whatever you call it. She sent me your announcement about opening here, and I clocked your subtle little blackberry and raspberry layer cake on International Bisexual Visibility Day, so I wanted to come out and make you feel part of the community. Hell, it's not like we're overrun with gays here, but I thought it might be nice to know one seeing as you were coming up from London. And luckily, I liked you, so I stuck around.'

'Oh,' he says, a warm ache forming in his chest. Before he can say anything, tears prick at the corner of his eyes.

'Come here, you big fanny.' Shaz wraps her arms around his middle and he bends down a little to tuck his head against hers.

'No one's ever said that before,' he murmurs into her hair.

'What? *Come here, you big fanny*?'

He snorts with laughter. 'Not that, thankfully.'

'I don't know. Could be a good come-on. I'm sure you'd oblige it if Nash asked.'

Oh no. 'Is it that obvious then?'

'Oh, you bet, you're giving me all the gory details tomorrow. While you two were back here cooking, half the gossip in the village hall was about whether we reckoned you'd snogged yet. Thelma wanted to start a betting pool.'

He laughs and takes a moment to find the words to say what his heart is yelling. 'This is a little hard to explain,' he begins. 'So, you know my sister is gay.'

'I know, Gar and I met her when you guys were up here in the summer. She and Gar couldn't stop talking about shelving, the fucking weirdos. I think they swapped emails and everything. They're like mutual close friends on Instagram now.'

'Wait, hang on. So everyone knew but me?'

'Apparently. Not that it was a secret. You just apparently can't put two and two together. Or just two lesbians I guess.'

'Well, I feel very silly.'

'Anyway, we were having a *moment*, let's not get sidetracked,' she urges. 'What were you trying to say?'

'So yes, Kit is gay and a few of my friends are queer or trans, and I'm still really kind of finding my feet with everything . . . with being bisexual. It's . . . it's not *new* news. But it's new that I'm *embracing* it, and have been doing so since Laurel and I broke up.'

'I guess you didn't so much have to think about the options when you were not looking?' she offers.

'Something like that. I mean, I knew. And Laurel knew to some extent. The first new person I told last year was Haf, and since then I've been trying to feel comfortable in it. And with, like, *the community* in general, I was never brave enough to join any societies at university or anything. What I'm saying is . . . it means a lot to me that you saw me that way, before I was even brave enough to say it.'

'Oh God, now I'm gone,' laughs Shaz through a sea of instant snotty tears. She grabs him back into a huge cuddle, all laughter and love and joy.

As they break apart, he spies Nash sitting with the townies, regaling them with stories. All these brilliant people together. He couldn't be luckier.

'Christopher,' Shaz interrupts his moment suddenly. 'I don't want to alarm you, but there appears to be a cat eating your ham.'

Chapter Twenty-Five

Christopher

'What on earth am I going to do with him?' The cat sits in Christopher's lap enjoying a chin tickle and the last bits of ham.

The cat, which seemed to have an alarmingly strong preference for pork-based products, had clearly decided that actually it didn't mind if Christopher picked it up, provided there remained steady access to said food. They would have had to throw away all the bits the cat had been chomping on otherwise, just for safety's sake, and so it seemed a waste to not let it eat, even if Christopher was pretty sure Coca-Cola-baked ham isn't on a cat's dietary plan. The poor creature still looked as skinny as the last few times he'd seen it.

After a possibly worrying amount of salt for one small cat, it had attached its claws into his woollen jumper as if to say *congratulations you are in charge of me now.*

No one had recognised the cat, and after Shaz's scroll through the various Facebook group posts for missing pets, everyone resolved that it probably was a stray that had survived kittenhood, especially due to its nose for meat.

And so, it made sense for him to just bring the cat upstairs with them.

'I don't think you have much of a choice.' Nash touches the cat's little pink nose with the tip of his finger. As if on cue, sensing the most perfect moment to really seal the deal and ensure a home for life, the cat begins to purr.

'What do you mean?'

'Have you not heard of the old *cats pick their owner*s thing? Or the universal cat distribution system?'

'The what?'

'You know, how some people just find a cat somewhere and then that cat won't belong to anyone and so they then own a cat.'

'Is this an LA thing?'

'It's an *everywhere* thing! Plus, I think he's pretty set on living here.'

The cat chirrups in agreement.

'I have to check it's . . . they're not microchipped first.'

That's the responsible thing to do, after all. Though if this cat does belong to someone, how did they end up in this malnourished state? Christopher dreads to think about it.

Once all the guests had been picked up by various transport methods, everyone remaining had insisted Christopher and Nash go upstairs with the cat for an early night. There was still cleaning and tidying to do, even after everything had been loaded into the industrial dishwasher. But still, they'd been sent away.

Tegan's photo documentation of whose dishes and plates and condiments belonged to who turned out to be really handy, and a plan was drawn up to drop them round to everyone tomorrow.

At first he'd felt a little strange leaving people in his kitchen alone, but he's so bone-tired that he doesn't have anything left in him to protest.

Plus, it's quite nice being up here on the sofa with Nash and the cat.

'It's kind of incredible that in the last two days you've gone from zero animals to two, like you're Doctor Doolittle or something,' Nash says.

'He just spoke to animals. I don't think he amassed them. And can't I just be me?' The cat stands, stretches and promptly curls itself into a neat little croissant on Christopher's lap.

'No.'

'Fine. Anyway, why are you so sure it's a he?"

Nash shrugs. 'The unseasonal desire for sausage?'

'Stop,' hisses Christopher. 'I'm too tired for your mischief.'

'I doubt that. You love it.'

Christopher could swear there's a hitch in the air. That word spoken out loud, even in jest, feels so awkward, like it's ripe for misconstruing. Either way, Nash decides to steam-roller past it.

'We should call him Karma.'

'Because he stole my sausages and now I've imprisoned him?'

'No, because of the song lyric, you know?' He points at the cat curled up in Christopher's lap, purring like a steam train.

'Did . . . did you just make a Taylor Swift reference at me, Nash Nadeau?'

'Don't look so surprised. I'm a man of taste. I saw the Eras tour. Plus, you're the one who recognised it.'

'Fair point. And yes, I quite like a few of her songs. Just as long as you don't start singing—'

'Darlin' aye fancy yewwww,' Nash sings in his very loud faux cockney accent. After delivering his performance, he leans back and laughs loudly, extremely pleased with himself. It's terribly annoying, but Christopher can't help but smile.

'There it is.'

'Well, you are a London Boy.'

'Not any more. And arguably, it was only temporary. I'm an Oxlea boy, if you want to be technical.'

Nash waves this away like it's far too much detail. 'Close enough.'

'It really isn't.'

'Has no one sung that to you before, really?'

'Surprisingly no. Thank you for bringing about that experience for me.' He feels heat in his cheeks. Every word feels heavy, laden with some deeper meaning, now that they're just sitting here alone again after another busy day. Perhaps he's just overthinking things, but obviously Nash picks up on it too because he raises his eyebrows and laughs awkwardly.

'Stop it,' groans Christopher. God this infuriating man.

'You're the one who is being all weird. Look, you'll upset the cat.'

Naturally, the cat looks completely unbothered, and has started softly snoring in his lap.

'Fine, if not Karma, which personally I think is a fun little suggestion, what are you going to call him?'

'I was thinking something classic. Perhaps something like Felix.'

'When I used to make my videos, I had, like, three British trans friends called Felix.'

'I'm not sure what to do with that information, Nash.'

Nash clearly doesn't know either, because he just repeats Christopher's words back in a sleepy bad English accent, before yawning loudly.

'Do you need to eat?' They had come upstairs with a plate of leftovers each, but they had put them in the fridge wrapped in clingfilm for later. After cooking all day, Christopher is not sure he's even that hungry right now, but he knows Nash hasn't eaten anything for a while. Is it weird that he noticed that? He hopes not.

'You could call him Paddington?' Nash says as the cat's ears stand up straight and he hops over to Nash's lap instead.

'Why?'

'A little lost creature that you rescued . . .'

'He's not even a bear.'

'So? You love Paddington.'

'I do but I like names that make sense too. He's not even *brown*.'

'He doesn't even have a suitcase, Nash,' Nash says in a now rather uncanny version of Christopher's voice.

'Hang on, you can actually do my accent?'

'Yeah, of course I can. I just prefer doing the bad one that annoys you.'

'Well, what if I started going on about . . . I don't know . . . moose. Moose and Tim Hortons. And lumberjacks. Or smoothies and wellness cults.' It turns out that his frame of references for both LA and the entirety of Canada are a little thin on the ground.

On Christopher's lap, the cat is sat right up, head tilted looking over to Nash, who, for some reason, doesn't spar back. Perhaps he crossed a line somewhere?

'Nash?'

Something is clearly not quite right. And not just because Nash isn't making fun of him.

His face has this kind of minutely slack quality to it that Christopher has never seen before. He looks distant. As if he's left for just a moment.

'Nash?'

No response. Only a few blinks. Christopher pulls out his phone and sets a timer. The cat looks up at Christopher as if to say *is this what he normally does* and he gives the cat a little pet on the head for realising what was going on far before he did.

'I'm here,' he whispers, as Nash's brain quietly misfires in its own private way, his systems rebooting. It's strange to see him gone, though of course he is still *there* physically.

Nash is such a big presence in this tiny flat, and his life. His personality and self seem to take up all the space, in a way that Christopher finds he has grown remarkably used to.

He shuffles along the couch so he's sitting alongside Nash, and slings his arm around the top of the couch, just in case he needs to catch him. He doesn't want to touch him while he's out – they didn't talk about whether that was something he wanted or not.

He's propped up safely and Christopher is pretty sure that he said he didn't convulse, but still, there's nothing he

can hurt himself on. Just to be safe, Christopher pushes the
coffee table away with a foot.

Hopefully he knows, in some quiet part of his brain, that
Christopher is here. That he isn't alone. The cat gently pads
its paws on Nash's thighs and wiggles its whiskers, clearly
thinking the same thing.

'I'm here, Nash,' he says softly. 'We're here. It's okay. You
can come back when you're ready.'

★ ★ ★

Nash

It all tastes like metal.

That's usually a big warning sign that something is wrong,
and sometimes it happens early enough that he can tell
someone, but today everything comes rushing at him like
a truck. First metal, then smoke in his nose, followed by the
slow slide away as speech and movement stop being things
his brain can do.

It's like a blink of nothingness that he falls into.

And then, very slowly, things start to come back. It's a
strange feeling to know he's been gone, while also not knowing how long he was seizing. Has he been out for seconds or
minutes?

The fog clears, and his brain latches onto Christopher
sitting beside him. His huge eyes are startlingly blue in the
low light.

The cat is still on Christopher's lap, its paws padding gently on Nash's leg.

He goes to speak but the connection isn't there yet. The
muscles don't know what he's trying to tell them to do, that
he's trying to speak. The words in his head are staccato
attempts at sentences that die off quickly.

This part always feels like an age to him. Not surprisingly, really, that he had a seizure given all the change and stress of the last few days. All the rushing around and probably not sleeping enough. The big emotions and decisions. It's like a checklist of all his triggers. His neurologist would probably call it a melting pot of micro stresses or something. The exact kind of jumble of messes he tries to avoid just to keep his brain going.

And yet, Christopher sits here, watching like a guard on duty. An ache swirls through his stomach as the anxiety of what happens next manages to brew up, even though his brain is still coming back online.

The pink of Christopher's bottom lip is curled under his front teeth ever so slightly, and Nash thinks, once again, about touching it. About kissing it again.

His body is still disobeying him, even if he wanted to. Not that coming out of a seizure is exactly the time when he wants to instigate a make-out session.

'Nash?' Christopher calls, probably not for the first time. His voice is a soft, guiding light. Nash wants to follow it. He wants to wake up.

He tries to say hi, but he knows the sound that comes out isn't quite right – his tongue and lips and brain have not yet linked back up, which feels especially rude when Christopher is literally kneeling before him *looking like that*.

The cat hops off his lap, and curls down between the two of them, seemingly satisfied that he's awake enough now.

'Hey. Are you back?'

Nash nods. His body shakes slightly with the adrenalin and misfiring, everything a little disconnected. To his embarrassment, a few tears run down his cheek.

'Can I touch you?' Christopher asks, which makes the tears run faster.

Without another word, Christopher wraps a quilted blanket from the back of the couch around him. Then he takes Nash's face in his hands, gently wiping away the tears with his thumbs.

'It's okay, you're safe.'

Fucking hell. This is not what Nash needs right now. He does not need Christopher to whip out his goddamn humanity and kindness just when Nash is at his most vulnerable. This sort of behaviour could make you fall in love with a man.

'Shall I get you a drink and a snack now? In fact, I'll just get it now, so then you have it if you want it. You don't have to have them now. I'll just be a few moments.'

Nash's smile is almost certainly wobbly and uneven, and he manages the smallest tilt of his head in a nod through the heavy thickness that still settles in his brain.

As Christopher leaves, Nash runs through his senses. He rubs his hand on the soft cushion of the couch – though this is interrupted by the cat who insists he is a much better thing to touch, pushing his little head right into the soft pad of Nash's palm. The cat smells like *warm*, a scent he can't narrow down but knows isn't one conjured by his own brain at least. Plus, he can still smell the lingering flavours of Christmas dinner on his clothes and hair.

In his lap drops a Snickers.

'I know you said it didn't *have* to be a Snickers, but when you mentioned it I thought I'd make sure we had some in. I hope that it fits the bill and – sorry I'm rambling.'

Nash's heart catches on the *we* of that sentence. How is it possible that this man can be so thoughtful and kind while also still being an enormous dork? Or is it Nash he's reducing to dork status?

Christopher drags the coffee table closer and sets down a glass of water and a steaming cup of tea on it. He's still muttering about the Snickers. 'To be honest, I'm not even sure if they're the same here as in the States or Canada, but hopefully it's the kind of thing you need right now. Lots of energy.'

He sits down on the couch on the other side of the cat, which seems to have taken up permanent occupation of the middle cushion.

'If you'd rather—'

Nash stills Christopher's babbling with a hand on his arm. 'This is perfect,' he says, each word heavy on his tongue and leaving a residual ache in his brain.

'Do you want some quiet? Or I can help you to bed?'

Nash shakes his head very slowly and then regrets it when his brain swirls like it's in a pot of stew. 'Stay. Let's watch something.' He tucks his legs up underneath him, sprawling a little into the middle cushion, but the cat accepts the intrusion and curls up into his side.

'You should drink some water,' Christopher urges.

His hands shake slightly but a couple of slow sips later, he feels a bit more himself. 'Thanks.'

Christopher gets up and refills the glass from the tap. He hovers, clearly looking for something else to do.

'Christopher, come sit down. I'm fine.'

He means to say this in his usual snarky way. *Sit down, you giant oaf, and stop stomping around me, you're frightening the horses.*

But no, instead it comes out as a soft plea. And possibly one of the first times Nash has called him Christopher instead of Calloway. It makes him feel even more vulnerable.

It works, either way, and Christopher sits down on the couch, narrowly avoiding both Nash's toes and the cat.

Clearly, Christopher has been so shaken up by this whole incident that he doesn't clock what he's doing until he's logged back into Netflix and navigated to the main page, which shows his Watch Again list. It's essentially just everything they show that Nash stars in. To add insult to injury, a teaser trailer starts playing at the top of the screen and of course it's for the *Christmas at the Clinic* series.

On screen, Nash wears reindeer ears and veterinary scrubs, but let's be real, he *did* look very handsome when filming this scene.

Nash cackles to himself as he unwraps his Snickers, and Christopher finally seems to realise what he's done.

'Oh God. Well. This is rather embarrassing.'

'I *knew* you knew who I was. This is too good.'

Christopher flushes and rolls his eyes, trying to style it off as though he's not deeply embarrassed. 'This is totally normal. They're just good films!'

Nash laughs, almost choking on a peanut.

'I might have downplayed how *aware* I was of your work when we first met. I'll admit that.' He looks sheepish.

'Christopher, if your Netflix is any indication, I am pretty sure you are singlehandedly supporting my whole career. I'd say thank you for all the residuals if I got residuals.'

'I've just seen a few!'

'A few?' Nash laughs, reaching for the remote. 'Scroll back up. Go on, search my name! I just want to see how many you've liked.'

'Get off,' Christopher laughs, playfully slapping his hands away. 'I'm not going to go easy on you just because you're feeling poorly.'

'If I were not quite so mentally incapacitated right now, I'd make some kind of innuendo there,' Nash says. 'You'll have to imagine it yourself, but be assured it was funny and just a little flirty.'

'Just a little?'

'Just a little.'

'Fine. I might have seen . . . all of them.'

'Of course you have. I'm excellent. Now come on, Kathy Bates, pick something.'

'What?'

'*Misery*? Going to keep me in the basement for your own entertainment?'

'The point of *Misery* is that she chains him up so he can keep writing. How would you make more films if you were trapped in a basement, which to be clear, I do not have. That would be useless if I wanted to watch more of your movies.'

'Could be a sexy dungeon basement?' At this Christopher flushes, which makes Nash cackle again.

'You are very irritating,' he huffs, resuming his scrolling.

'I can't believe I'm running out of obsessed-fan references. What have I used so far?' he says, counting off his fingers. '*All About Eve. Misery. Ingrid Goes West.* Ooh, does the second act of *Gone Girl* count?'

'For someone so nervous they're about to get kidnapped you are very aware of related media. And you missed *Perfect Blue.*'

Nash leans back to peer at Christopher's *trying-to-be-casual* face. 'What's that?'

'A psychological horror anime about fandom and celebrity through the lens of a pop idol.'

'Hahaha, you absolute nerd,' Nash says, kicking Christopher in the thigh.

'It's not nerdy to watch foreign films. Wasn't one of the ones you mentioned before a German film?'

'Yeah, but anime? And not even Studio Ghibli anime. Come on, Christopher, you're making it too easy for me even in my post-ictal state. Give me a challenge.'

'I liked you better when you were quiet,' he says, which produces the biggest laugh from Nash.

'A total lie, but that's more like it. I knew he was in there still.'

'Who?' Christopher frowns in a way that scrunches his nose up.

'Bitchy Christopher. Bitchstopher.'

'Do not call me that. I do not need more nicknames.'

'Fascinating. I'll be sure to pick up that train of thought at some point, if I don't forget it. Anyway, tis the season and all that, put on a Christmas movie if you'd like,' he says, scratching the cat behind its ears.

'Is that not too close to work for you?'

'Only if you insist on putting on one with me in it, which I rather you didn't.'

Christopher hesitates. 'Are you going to judge me?'

'Based on what you pick?'

Christopher nods, remote poised in mid-air.

Slipping a hand out from the blanket, he pats Christopher on the arm and says, 'Probably.'

He chuckles. 'You're the worst.'

After a few loud objections, they settle on *Single All the Way* for the Jennifer Coolidge of it all. Definitely. No other reason.

Nash feels the heavy lure of sleep flood his bones. He shuffles in his seat, and blinks in and out of a nap.

Much later, he wakes during the 'third act argument' – always his favourite bit – to find he is curled up against Christopher. He breathes in the smell of ginger and cinnamon which seems to have impregnated itself in Christopher's skin.

'Do you need anything?' Christopher whispers, not taking his eyes off the screen.

And Nash could answer him. He could say all the things that he's thinking, tell Christopher all the needs in his heart. All the things he wants right now.

Like, to pull Christopher's arm around him, and curl up more deeply against him.

To kiss him again, with less fury, but no less desire.

Or how terrifying it is that Christopher has been so gentle with him tonight, when that's all he's ever wanted from someone.

But he's too afraid to voice any of it. So he keeps his eyes closed, pretending to be asleep.

After a moment, Christopher's attention drifts back to the film, and without a word, he wraps his arm around Nash.

Chapter Twenty-Six

Christopher

Rather than wake him with breakfast, Christopher lets Nash sleep in. Even after his nap on the couch, Nash still looked bushed last night, and so Christopher had led him to bed, helped him undress down to his underwear and tucked him in. It was a tender moment. So different from the night before, when they had spilled out of their clothes, tearing fabric from each other's skins.

This was different. This was careful. Gentle.

When he woke, Nash was curled up in a little ball against him, completely dead to the world; his long eyelashes fluttering against his cheek as he dreamed. Christopher had been worried that moving would wake him, but Nash didn't even move when the sun rose and bright light poured in through the window.

Outside, there's a fresh dusting of snow but the gloomy clouds are long gone. It's sunny and bright, his favourite kind of weather.

It's practically lunch by the time Christopher decides to start the day proper.

It's probably safe to leave Nash sleeping, but he doesn't want to just disappear so he writes a little note and leaves it by his bed. Ideally, he'd text him but, one, he's worried that might wake him, and two, he doesn't even have Nash's number. A kind of wild lapse in admin given the last few days.

Hopefully, he'll be okay. The cat is curled up at the bottom of the bed, and gives him a look as if to say *I've got this*.

So, he gets dressed and makes himself a tea, picking at the plate of leftovers from last night while the teabag stews. Boxing Day is always such a strange day if there's nothing planned, a quick slide into the blur of Betwixtmas. Last year's was a little chaotic, so he's ready for a quiet day at least.

Downstairs, the bakery is so clean and tidy that he could have sworn he dreamed yesterday. The only sign that Christmas Day happened at all is yet more leftovers in plastic containers in the fridge. He'll have to find a way to redistribute those today, if he can.

And that's when he remembers that he never baked the gingerbread. He'd been so insistent on making it on Christmas Eve when they were both so tired, and yet he didn't bake it at all. Is this perhaps his first ever Christmas without doing a gingerbread house before the actual big day? Well, nothing about this Christmas is particularly normal, he supposes.

With nothing better to do, he takes the clingfilm-wrapped gingerbread dough from the fridge and slowly starts rolling it out, ready to cut it into shapes. There's more than enough for a small house, and he can also make a bunch of reindeer to give to everyone who helped yesterday. Plus, they'll make a nice treat for Nash.

While he's rolling the dough out, his phone buzzes. It's Kit checking in again, after the panic of the reporters yesterday, and so he makes the decision to just video-call rather than get his phone all sticky.

Her sleepy face appears on screen, hair still sleep-mussed. 'Morning. Are you baking?'

'The gingerbread.'

He hears a chorus of groans. 'Noooo, I'm so sad I didn't get to eat it,' whines Haf. 'Also why are you up and dressed? It's Boxing Day. Go back to bed, you weirdo.'

'Unless . . .' says Kit raising her eyebrows.

'Yes he's in there still and no it's not what you think.'

'I highly doubt that.'

'Plus it's lunchtime. But, actually,' he says, setting down the reindeer-shaped cutter. 'Erm, he wasn't very well. I don't want to go into specifics because I don't know if it's public but it's—'

'A disability thing,' Kit says, but it isn't a prompt for more information. She just gets it.

'I just want to make sure I was looking after him okay.'

'Did you follow what he said to do?'

'Yeah.'

'Then you're okay. Just keep doing that. And maybe, you know, dial down on the you.'

'The me?' he startles a little. He can't help it.

'You know. The worrying thing,' Kit drawls.

'Oh,' he says, blushing. He starts measuring out the sides of the house, slicing fine tracing grooves into the dough while he makes sure he's doing it right.

She softens. 'I don't mean you're being annoying. I just know you'll be worried about how to help him, but this is normal for him, right?'

'It seems so, yes.'

'Okay, so he might feel a bit weird about it because it's the first time you've seen whatever it is happen.'

'And because you two have some kind of sexy emotional entanglement going on,' giggles Haf.

'Exactly what I mean, though. Like I was pretty embarrassed the first time Haf knocked my hip out while—'

'Please for the love of God do not finish that sentence.'

The two women dissolve into mischievous giggles. The hazards of your best friend dating your sister is that sometimes they forget that you absolutely do not want to hear a lot of this stuff.

'But I take your point. I'll dial it down. It must not be nice being unwell when you're not at home, though.'

'No, that's true. Do you have anything planned for today?'

'No. Everyone told us we had to take a day off after cooking yesterday. But maybe, I was thinking, I might take him down the road to the beach. It's finally stopped snowing from the looks of things. We can practically drive onto the front with the van so if he's too tired to walk we can just sit and watch the waves, or toddle about a bit.'

When he looks back at the phone, both Haf and Kit are squished into the screen beaming at him.

'What?'

'You're just cute,' Haf says.

'I'm just trying to be . . . hospitable.'

'Mmhmm,' murmurs Kit, completely unconvinced. 'Let us know how you get on with that.'

They talk for a bit longer about their weird individual Christmases, and he moves the camera so they can see him working away, laying the sides and roof of the house, and then each reindeer down on the baking trays. With the sudden free time, Kit and Haf had watched the entire *Lord of the Rings* trilogy back to back, only moving to make more food or top up the wine.

'Not gonna lie, it was much easier than last Christmas with everyone,' admits Haf.

'To be fair, last year, you and Lovestruck over here were pretending to be together while you were trying not to snog me, so the stakes were a little higher,' laughs Kit dryly.

'Yeah, but this time I got to pick all the best treats and I only cried once.'

'You cried multiple times during the movies?'

'Why did you cry the other time?' Christopher asks.

'Oh, you know, the cutlery was just too loud.' Kit pats her gently on the head.

Christopher nods sagely. Sometimes it is too loud, and sometimes Haf says things that are all too familiar to him. Ever since she got her autism diagnosis this year, he's been quietly wondering some more things about himself, but his possible . . . likely . . . neurodivergence is not something he's entirely ready to look at head-on.

'How many times did you cry, Christopher?' asks Kit, dragging him from his thoughts.

'Not once.'

'Wow. That's impressive. But maybe you should have a little cry? You know, a nice little festive one. As a treat.'

'I think we have very different ideas about what *treats* are, darling,' Kit says.

They sign off with a chorus of *love yous*, determined to get a walk in around the York walls if it wasn't too icy, or at the very least get some kind of chocolatey delicious thing to eat. They'll have their time together when the snow is gone, he hopes. Though Lord knows when. He'd have to keep the bakery shut for longer, and he doesn't know if he can afford to do that, especially when he's due to reopen in a few days anyway.

'Morning.' Nash is wrapped up in Christopher's dressing gown. His golden hair sticks up in a truly impressive variety of angles, and there are deep dark furrows under his eyes.

'Hi,' Christopher says breathlessly, trying not to beam at the sight of him. 'How are you feeling?'

Nash blows out his lips and shrugs. 'Mid. Not bad but I don't feel as sparkly as I might normally do.'

'You're sparkly in the mornings?'

'I might be.' Nash sniffs the air in a move that reminds Christopher of the cat. 'What are you making?'

'Gingerbread, finally.'

'How long until I get to eat some?'

On cue, the timer goes off, and Christopher removes several baking sheets of wide shapes and crisp-looking reindeer from the oven, setting them on the wire racks to cool.

'You have to wait for them to cool or it'll be all squishy and gross.'

'I hate the interminably slow passage of time,' Nash groans. He bends down to closely inspect the reindeer. 'These are cute.'

'They're Shaz's favourites. I thought perhaps I'd drop a few round to people to say thank you for their help yesterday.'

'That's a nice idea and you should do it, but know that I am also objecting to it on the grounds that it means I don't get to eat them all.'

'Noted. Do you need some breakfast? I'll whip up something for us.'

'I was just going to have some toast. And then I'll take a few of those cookies.'

'Biscuits.'

'Whatever.'

They make their way back upstairs, Nash taking each step with slow consideration. Christopher regrets going ahead, wanting to hang back to help push him up. He holds out a hand, and Nash takes it, so he leads him up the last few.

'Do you have Boxing Day in America?'

'A free day off for no reason? Of course not. Canada does, though. I figure it's generally pretty similar to what you guys get up to here.'

'Usually nothing?'

'Sounds about right. Over on Newfoundland they have a whole mumming thing. Like a parade mixed with a play where everyone has to take part, or like they go knock on doors and ask for admission. Sounds fucking dreadful.'

'Oh, they have that here. Well, not here, but in South Wales they do that but with a horse's skull on a stick throughout midwinter.'

Nash spins around to stare at him, an incredulous look on his face. 'I'm sorry, but the casual way you just dropped that bomb on me might be the thing that takes me out today.'

Christopher stops a step down, so their faces are level. He could just reach forward and kiss him. There's so little space between them. 'Well, before the very fascinating culture of Wales takes you out, why don't we go on a very small adventure?'

Nash

They bundle up in as many layers as possible before getting into the van. Christopher insists Nash adds at least another jumper layer even when he thinks he's wearing enough, which they bicker about for a few minutes until Nash relents, the arms of his coat nearly bursting at the seams from so many layers.

To be fair, he always struggles with regulating his temperature after a seizure because his nervous system is so whacked. In LA, this isn't so much a problem because he can just turn the air up or down. In snow, it's a little more complicated.

Christopher drives them through the now slushy snow right onto the promenade, and Nash is briefly worried he's going to drive right onto the sand and cause an incident, but he turns the ignition off when the truck faces out to the grey sea.

Christopher turns to look at Nash. 'We can just sit in here, in the van, if you'd like?'

'Nah, let's get some air.'

It's ice cold, the wind whipping at the exposed skin on their faces. Despite the sun, it's much colder today, way below zero, so the cold is dry for once. The tide is going out (naturally, Christopher claims to have checked the tide tables like a good Boy Scout). The sea rolls back in coils of grey and white, revealing dark sand and glistening pebbles that whoosh along together in harmony.

'It's kind of beautiful here, isn't it?' Nash sighs. 'Weirdly fucking beautiful.'

'Did you grow up near the sea in Canada?'

'No, I'm from inland Ontario, but near the Great Lakes. LA is the closest geographically I've ever lived to the sea, but, like, it's still a long drive to get there. It's amazing to just be here in minutes.'

'I'm really lucky to live here,' Christopher admits. 'For however long I get to.'

'Thinking of leaving?' Nash asks.

'Oh, no. It's just . . . you know the statistics. So many businesses fail in their first year. The previous occupants ran a little café, and that struggled for a long time.'

'Sure, but you're dedicated. It's your dream.'

'Chasing the dream is half the fight,' he says with a sad smile. 'You still have to live it, make it work. Turn it from a dream into a reality and keep it that way. That's pretty hard in and of itself. Plus, making your hobby the thing you do for a living means you no longer have a hobby not tied to your personal finances.'

'You've thought about it a lot.'

'I've had a lot of time alone to think.'

'It's brave, though. Even if it is just a dream for now, you still did it. That's not a failure. You tried something new that mattered to you. Most people don't even bother doing that.'

As if making his point for him, he feels his phone vibrate in his pocket. It's not a phone call from Kurt, but it *is* a calendar invite for them to have a talk tomorrow.

Fuck's sake, it must be barely six in the morning over there. Can he not just have a moment to enjoy the view? Not just the sea, but Christopher, too.

Nash has barely been awake long enough to process everything that happened last night. First off, having a seizure in front of someone, which is just a whole other level of vulnerability that most people will never experience. But secondly, how gentle Christopher was with him. How he's continued to be that way this morning. If Nash is honest, part of him was half expecting the other shoe to drop, for Christopher to realise what an imposition it was . . . he is.

But he hasn't.

He's a little afraid of the things that he's feeling and trying not to notice. He thinks about trying to tell Christopher what it all meant to him, but the words stick in his throat.

And that's when a perfect snowflake lands right on the tip of Nash's nose.

Above them falls a fresh flurry.

'It's snowing,' Christopher whispers with such boyish glee that it grips Nash's heart.

'Snow on the beach. I thought that was impossible.'

'*Magic*. It must be magic.'

* * *

Christopher

Snowflakes gather like icing sugar all along the brim of Nash's hat, peppering the fringe of hair sticking out at the front. They lock eyes and Christopher feels the weight of what's growing between them. Can either of them deny it anymore? It feels increasingly difficult to say it's 'just blowing off steam' after the last couple of days.

'Nash,' he says, his voice low and soft.

'Christopher,' Nash echoes in the same tone.

'Can I kiss you?'

'You've been doing that for the last couple of days.'

'Yes, but I wanted to ask you again. Just to be sure.'

Their kiss is the only warmth in the world right now. It's soft and tender, as if they're just finding each other for the first time. He doesn't want it to end.

Christopher wraps his arms around Nash, deepening the kiss. Even through all the layers they're wearing, he's sure that Nash can feel his heart beating, furiously joyful.

He knows this is dangerous, to kiss a man who is destined to leave. But hang sensibility. He wants this. He wants *Nash*.

He wants Nash Nadeau, who tastes like the sweet warmth of home . . . and a little of gingerbread, which means he's getting a telling-off later. His kiss, this kiss, is more than he could ever have imagined. So much for movie magic; he has the real magic of a kiss in the snow.

An improbable, impossible kiss.

But it's all real. It's all theirs.

And it's all he's ever wanted.

When they break apart, Nash's cheeks are pink. 'I was wondering when you were going to do that again.'

'I didn't know if you wanted me to.'

'Of course I wanted you to.' And he grabs Christopher by the coat lapels and pulls him into another kiss. It's like being dragged into Nash's orbit. He never ever wants to leave.

They walk on a bit, hand in hand, and Christopher dares to dream of another day at the beach. What would it be like in spring, or summer, when they could brave the chill and swim in the sea? He wants to walk along the beach with Nash in all seasons, in all weathers. It's dangerous to think about, but he's realising he really wants more days like this. More time together.

Nash's phone buzzes and he takes it out, dismissing whatever it is, probably a call from his agent. Part of Christopher wants to tell him to answer it, to speak what he wants out loud, but that's letting the real world in. Can't they just stay in this wintry fantasy a little longer? This is their time to be selfish and together, and so he pulls Nash into another deep kiss as the salty sea laps the shore.

How impossible it is to be here, kissing the man of his dreams, under a sugar-coating of snow? This Christmas was never going to turn out like he expected but what are the chances of *this*? It makes it all feel that bit more magical, as if they were meant to find each other in the storm.

The wind whips up into a gale, and they break apart from kissing with shrieks.

'You'll have to carry me back to the van. I'm too frail and tired,' Nash says, burying himself against Christopher.

'You know I'd love to be able to lift you, but I'm afraid that's definitely not going to happen.'

'That sucks,' Nash pouts. 'I've always wanted to be carried. You're letting the side down.'

'Well, maybe you should carry *me*. You're much stronger than I am.'

'Have you seen how long your limbs are, Calloway? I'm not sure I can lift high enough to get your giant tree-trunk legs off the ground. I swear you're part ent.'

'Is this our thing?' Christopher laughs, wrapping his arm around Nash's shoulders and guiding them forward through the snow and sand back to the van.

'What?'

'Bickering and getting annoyed with each other and then kissing?'

'I think so,' Nash says with a sharp flash of a grin.

Our thing feels like a tacit admission of something. Or a wish.

He doesn't know how long this will last between them.

'Maybe . . . we should go home and bicker some more then.'

'I'd like that. Also, I'd like to eat, for the first time, some of that gingerbread you made.'

'Nice try.'

'I didn't eat any! It was the cat.'

'I'd know that taste anywhere.'

'Oh, all right then,' Nash says, giving up the pretence almost immediately. 'But you better let me have some more.'

Even though the drive is short, Nash falls asleep in the van. Christopher feels awful prodding him awake when he's so exhausted, but he manages to coax him upstairs and tucks him into bed. His bed. Their bed.

This is the kind of thing he can imagine doing forever. And it's kind of horrifying to realise, but maybe he wants to do this forever. He could be the man Nash can come home to, the one to look after him when things get too much.

Is he really thinking about this?

The gingerbread is cool so he decides to distract his mind with decorating, but the thought doesn't shift. What-ifs run through his mind, one after the other, and the thing is, he'll only get an answer if he talks to Nash about it. That was his advice for Nash thinking about his future career and what he wanted, wasn't it? To actually address it? Perhaps he should take that same advice too.

But for now, he'll let him sleep.

Chapter Twenty-Seven

Nash

Nash doesn't manage to sleep for long before Kurt calls again. Groggy-headed, he accepts that the conversation needs to happen, and answers the phone.

'Hey Kurt.'

'Hey bro. Sorry to get back on things so early, but I was just thinking of picking up some breakfast and swinging over to your place so we can talk business. What do you fancy?'

Oh no. He sits up, the blankets pooling around him.

'Kurt. I'm not there.'

'Oh. Can you be back this afternoon? I can bring dinner?'

'No, Kurt. I'm . . . I'm in Britain.' The other end is silent for so long that he briefly worries the connection died. 'Hello?'

'Sorry, I got coffee all down me, because I was taking a moment to consider why my favourite client left the continent and didn't tell me about it.'

'Urgh, don't be mad.' He regrets the whine to his voice.

'Dude, why are you in England?'

'Wales actually.'

'What?'

'I'm in Wales, not England. It's a whole thing.'

'Okay, sure, Wales. But why?'

This is it. He needs to tell him. 'I got scared and ran away.'

'From what?'

'The deal on the table.'

He can't hear it, but he knows Kurt is currently cursing him under his breath for not talking to him directly and for being a *fucking idiot*. This is the side of Kurt he never sees, but very occasionally hears if he takes a phone call in his presence. Exasperated-with-clients, getting-the-deals Business Kurt.

'You're going to have to explain this one for me, buddy.'

'I know. I've been cowardly, but the reason I've been delaying is that I'm feeling a bit burnt out from acting, Kurt. And I really want to try something new, like writing or directing. I've got ideas I don't know what to do with yet, and I'm worried that getting tied into this deal is not going to give me any space to grow as an artist.'

The last part feels embarrassing to admit, but there we go. He's said it now. Radical vulnerability is the mode of the day.

Kurt breathes out slowly, a soft fuzzing sound through the speakers. 'Well,' he begins slowly, 'they're interested in you as a brand. I'm sure that if we took this back to the negotiations to see what investment they'd be interested in making in you branching out, we might be able to find a middle ground.'

What? Is it really that simple?

'Are you serious?'

'Yeah, like they really want this franchise to keep going, and these kind of development partnerships are not unusual – look at Amazon with Donald Glover and Phoebe Waller-Bridge.'

'Yes but they're Donald Glover and Phoebe Waller-Bridge. I'm just Nash.'

'*Just* Nash? My dude, did you cross the Atlantic and forget who you are? You're Nash *fucking* Nadeau. You're King of the Seasonal Screen. These guys are *desperate* to nail you down so you won't go off and make films with their competitors, who, for the record, have also been sniffing around recently. You're a hot commodity and a rising star, and the reason I've been harassing you is because they're desperate to get you signed up.'

'Oh.'

'Oh?'

'Well, now I feel really stupid for not talking to you.'

'And running away to Wales.'

'And running away to Wales and getting stuck here because of a snowstorm that knocked out all the international travel for like an entire country.'

'Oh no, for real? What have you been doing there anyway?'

'Accidentally cohabiting with a baker.'

'Is that slang for something dirty?' Nash can practically hear the accompanying eyebrow waggle through the phone line.

'It's not.'

'Pity. Well, be nice to this mystery baker. I know what you're like.'

'Look, the stunt guy recovered and anyway it was just a misunderstanding—'

'Yeah, yeah.'

'I can be nice.'

At this, Kurt suppresses a loud snort. 'Yeah, maybe when you're playing the vet and having a temporary personality transplant.'

'Aren't I paying you to be nice to me?'

'I only get paid when you sign the contracts, my dude,' Kurt says gently, in a way that makes Nash feel incredibly guilty for all this mess, especially when it apparently seems to have been entirely unnecessary. 'Hang a moment, will you?'

He does as he's told, cursing himself for not speaking to Kurt in the first place. How did he take this so casually? And while complimenting Nash and his work? God, this is maddening. He really should have just spoken to Kurt from the first moment he started having doubts.

But then, if he'd been brave from the off, he'd never have met Christopher. Maybe he needed that in order to be brave.

'Okay, I'm back. So especially with this on the table, I need you back in LA as they're going to want to talk. I know ideally you'd get to stay in Wales for now and we do this all over Zoom, but you're the asset and we need to pony you in front of them a little, if that sounds all right? I'll set up a meeting. From what I can see, international flights are back on, we can book you onto a lunchtime flight tomorrow from Manchester from the looks of things. I'll arrange for Tessa to send you a car – I'm going to assume she knows where you are?'

'Yes,' he says quietly.

Tomorrow? Is it over already? He'd stopped checking if flights and trains were operational a few days ago, when some small part of him had accepted that this is where he was going to be. Where he *wanted* to be.

'OK, I'll send you an itinerary.' Kurt is in full business mode, springing into action as always, and Nash is struggling to keep up. 'If you could write up some notes so that we've got something to talk through before we meet the bigwigs, that would help me no end, and then we can present you as a rounder package, OK?'

His mouth is dry. This is happening. So much is happening at once that all he can do is bleat out, 'OK.'

'Are you sure?'

No. Yes. Absolutely not.

'Sorry, I had a seizure yesterday so I'm a little foggy, that's all. I'm fine,' he says, the lie souring on his tongue.

'Are you safe?'

'Yes, the baker . . . Christopher looked after me.'

There's a pause on the line, just for a moment. 'Good, I'm glad. And look, don't get all caught up in your head about everything. This is *exciting*! I'm excited for you and for us to enter a new era of Nadeau. The cards are all in your hands, bro. I'll pick you up from the airport in like thirty-six hours. Sleep well!' Kurt hangs up.

Fuck.

He drops the phone in his lap. Why does he feel so numb? He did the thing, finally! That's what this whole fucking mess has been about – speaking his truth, asking for what he wants. And yes, deep down it feels good that he is apparently on track to maybe make his dreams come true . . . but tomorrow?

Tomorrow.

He must have slept for longer than he thought because it's nearing four, which means he has barely any time left with Christopher before . . . the inevitable.

Nash scrambles out of the bed and walks carefully down the stairs. When he reaches the bakery kitchen, Christopher doesn't look up, too absorbed in decorating a tiny but perfect gingerbread house. Something catches in Nash's throat as he watches him pipe frosting, delicately bringing a world to life.

That's how it feels. For the first time in a long time, Nash feels animated. Alive.

This man, this strange, awkward, but impossibly kind tall man has worked his way into Nash's brain and heart and now he has to say goodbye? It's some kind of special cruelty that he has to leave the only person he's had any kind of romantic connection with who didn't act as if the way his brain misfires is a problem. The last person he loved told him outright that it was a burden to love him, and that it was too much to expect someone to look after him *and* love him at the same time.

And he's believed that was a universal truth for so long that he closed off that part of himself, too scared to show his own vulnerabilities to someone who could love him lest that person throw it back in his face.

Alongside that sharp pain is the waning of friendships, people who have loved and cared for him in vulnerable moments. Yes, perhaps due to a lack of tending by him, but also other things like geography and changing personalities. But his personal life has quietly felt like a place of loss, fast and slow, of people still living but moving forward and away from him for so long now. It makes him feel ever more stuck.

He'd become an island. And he's just realising that he'd been starting to consider a change. A bridge to land of sorts.

What he's frankly terrified of is that Christopher might be someone who could choose to love him not in spite of his differences and difficulties, but *alongside* them. They might spark and bite and snap, but he sees Nash as a whole person, and hasn't backed away.

He knows, deep down, that he would stay, or ask Christopher to follow, if one of them was brave enough to ask and the other to agree, but then he would never want Christopher to accept. So that would be two people's dreams-in-progress destroyed, and for what? A glimmer of lust? Foolish hope? Or, instead, something that could grow to be so much more if they just tended it?

God, he's going to miss him. He misses him already, and they're just across the room from each other, Nash on the stairs and Christopher gently spotting the edge of a ginger-bread roof with red and white. He could watch him forever.

And when he looks up, there's just this huge, unafraid smile on Christopher's lips that Nash wants to kiss and kiss and kiss.

The truth of the matter, which he doesn't want to look at too closely, is that Nash is going to have to break two hearts to leave.

But not tonight.

He wants one last night when they can just be Christopher and Nash, whatever that means. Another night where he can pretend it's not almost over.

Chapter Twenty-Eight

Christopher

Christopher wakes in an empty bed.

They had been up late, far later than he'd expected Nash to want to be after his Christmas Day seizures, but he had insisted that he hadn't been tired, some kind of sleep cycle thing. So, they'd watched movies and kissed and eaten yet more leftovers, and when Christopher had shown Nash the gingerbread house, he'd taken photos and even told him how good it was. Kind of a perfect evening really, especially because they got to eat the gingerbread house, something he hasn't been able to do in decades, what with his mother always offering them up to Christmas fêtes over the years rather than letting him enjoy them.

He stretches out, his hand finding the cool of the sheets where Nash usually is. Hopefully he's not constructing another gym somewhere.

Karma/Felix/Paddington is curled up around his feet, and grunts in protest at being disturbed, presumably for the second time this morning.

'Do you want some breakfast, cat?' Their eyes prick up slightly, and he takes that for a yes.

While Nash was sleeping yesterday, Christopher had managed to drop off some supplies at the community centre, only to be presented with several pouches of wet cat food from Tamara, whose own cat had shuffled off this mortal coil several months ago. That saved him yet another trip to a shop, though realistically he's going to have to go today. God knows what food is even left, and even if the cat is an obligate carnivore, he's not sure how long he and Nash can live off leftover lamb alone.

He finds Nash in the kitchen making coffee, dressed fully, with his hair properly done for the first time in a few days. Perhaps he's feeling a bit more himself today. The cat, who looks particularly tiny next to Nash's broadness, weaves around his ankles.

'Morning,' Christopher says, leaning against the door frame.

It's a curious look that passes over Nash's face. He looks happy to see Christopher, he's pretty sure, but there's something else there in the eyes.

'What? Do I really look that terrible?' Christopher laughs.

'You look lovely,' Nash says softly, kissing him on the cheek, which sets Christopher's alarms running even louder.

Something tells him not to look at the stairs, to stay focussed on Nash and this cat they've taken in. But he does turn, and there, he sees a suitcase. Nash's suitcase.

His heart is beating so loudly that it thunders in his ears in desperate pleas.

'What's going on?'

Nash closes his eyes. 'I have to go.'

'Go? Now?'

'Yes. There's a car coming for me, and I'm flying home to LA in a few hours.'

Christopher's mouth is dry and he's begging himself to wake up because this has to be a dream. It cannot be right that Nash is leaving right now?

'Don't be silly,' he says, shaking his head. 'The airports must still be closed. And the roads too?'

Nash holds up his hands, as if placating a wild animal. 'It's cleared enough that I can go. Flights are running again too.'

'Oh.'

'We always knew I had to go back,' Nash says, carefully not looking at him. 'Kurt booked everything for me. I have to go.'

'You spoke to him? When?' Christopher asks.

'Yesterday. I spoke to him yesterday.'

Christopher doesn't know where to look or what to say because speaking to Kurt was exactly what Christopher himself *told* Nash to do, but he's drowning. He thought they had more time.

'Can't you go another day? Later?' God he feels foolish, desperate to say this.

'I can't. It has to be now.'

'Please. Please, don't go.'

The distance between them feels enormous and he wants to cross it, he really does. But he watches something shutter across Nash's face, as if everything that they were is gone in an instant. 'It's over, Christopher.'

It's over.

His words echo in Christopher's body, a ricochet of hurt. 'You spoke to him yesterday?' he repeats.

'Yes.'

'So you've known for definite that you were going to leave today?'

'Only since last night.'

'Oh, well that's fine then, isn't it?' Christopher spits, his hurt turning bitter and sharp. 'And you didn't tell me?'

'I didn't want to hurt you.'

'So, what? You were just going to pack your things and disappear in the night instead? How very fucking chivalrous of you.'

'I was always going to say goodbye.' It's barely a whisper, and Christopher can't quite believe it, either.

'Well, go on. Goodbye.'

'It doesn't have to be this way, Christopher.'

'What way?'

'Angrily. Bitterly. Can't we say goodbye as friends?'

Christopher can't grasp all the things he's feeling, but that word feels absolutely terrible on Nash's lips. He feels hot tears pricking in his eyes and, for Christ's sake, he will not cry in front of this man, not when he seems so unmoved himself, so willing to just disappear without a word. Without a *conversation*, because clearly he's decided that's it.

There is no future for Christopher and Nash, not as far as Nash seems to see it.

The space between them is a gulf.

The only sound is Nash's phone vibrating on the counter.

'You should get that,' Christopher says, his voice flat.

It's only now that Nash looks at him, as he answers the phone, and Christopher doesn't hear what he says, because he's just looking at him, pleading with him to change his mind, to stay a little longer.

'That's my car,' Nash whispers. 'They're here already.'

'Stay. Don't go.'

'I have to.'

The cat loudly miaows in protest, and Nash bends down to stroke them between the ears.

Christopher steps aside to let Nash past, but can barely follow him towards the door. If he hangs back, maybe it'll prolong this goodbye? There must be something he can do to slow Nash down.

But it just means that he watches Nash pick up his case from the top of the stairs, while he grips the back of the couch, knuckles white with desperation.

'Don't hate me, Christopher.'

And with that, Nash Nadeau is gone from his life, forever.

Chapter Twenty-Nine

Christopher

Christopher doesn't get out of bed for two days.

At the end of the second day, Shaz breaks into the flat and finds him and the cat curled up in their misery pit. She joins them, holding him while he cries through this terrible heartbreak.

He knew Nash would leave. He knew they could only be temporary.

The trouble was that he had dared to imagine that it could be a fairy tale ending, where somehow they'd find a way to exist together. Either way, he deserved a proper goodbye, an ending that resolved some of their feelings and gave him somewhere to put all this hurt.

On the bedside table, he finds one of Nash's cards, the very same kind he gave to Myffy. His number. Nash might see it as an olive branch, but it's one that Christopher is not ready to take. He throws it into the rubbish.

On the third day, he finally notices the snow has gone. Completely, utterly gone. The whole world has gone back to normal while he's been crying in the dark. He takes Nash's card out of the bin and goes back to bed with the cat.

On the fourth day, he finds Tegan downstairs in the bakery and he does start to wonder whether, between Tegan and Shaz, there is some kind of familial ability to break into places they're not supposed to be.

'Life goes on,' she announces with the kind of deep solemnity only teenagers can manage. Apparently, things with her and Danny from the shop had not been going well either.

But she was right. It was time to get back to work, and even if he didn't feel able to open to the public just yet, he decided instead to throw himself into work as a distraction. He could get his orders to the suppliers, plan for the next couple of months, and, finally, teach Tegan how to bake some things. She wanted to know this stuff, and if he was going to be a good boss, and a good member of this community, growing her skills and talent had to be part of that, right? He had to keep giving back; things couldn't just go back to the way they were before the snow. Before Nash.

* * *

The fifth day, New Year's Eve, starts with Shaz informing him that he is taking the afternoon off.

'I'm busy,' he mumbles, not looking up from the open spreadsheet on his laptop. He'd never normally work at the bakery counter like this but Tegan wanted another afternoon practising her breadmaking with his supervision, so he sits perched on a counter stool, hunched over his computer, trying to avoid the occasional plume of flour or splodge of dough.

'It's a national holiday, Christopher.' At this point, he assumes Shaz must have cut herself a key, by the ease with which she keeps appearing without anyone having to let her in.

'Not for lots of businesses. Pubs do a roaring trade, I hear.'

'Yes, and you're a *bakery*. What are you going to do? Offer buns at midnight? Hardly the same.'

'You say that, but you'd be into it.'

'I would. But also look at Teegs, she's desperate for some time off.'

He raises his head finally. 'Are you, Tegan?'

She has finished kneading the loaves, which sit in their baskets proving on the counter, but she hesitates before answering. 'No. I mean, yes. I mean! This has been really nice today and thank you for teaching me all the new things, but I'd like to go to the . . . thing later.'

Shaz shoots her a wide-eyed look, and groans exasperatedly. 'Tegan!'

'Thing?' Christopher asks. 'What thing?'

'Well, he was going to find out anyway. That's why you're here to bully him into closing the shop up, isn't it?' Tegan huffs, arms folded.

'I do not *bully*,' she hisses.

Christopher is not entirely sure that's true.

'It's just a light cajoling.' She fixes him with a soft look that he'd almost call maternal if she wouldn't absolutely hate that.

'Fine. I'll stop working so you can tell me whatever this thing is.' He shuts the laptop and looks up to find Tegan already pulling her coat on.

'See you later!' she yells.

'Bye then,' Christopher says to the back of Tegan's head as she flies out of the door. 'So,' he turns to Shaz. '*The Thing*? Hopefully not the film, it's not really snowy enough for that to be thematic anymore.'

'You're rambling.'

'Yeah, because you're being all mysterious and unnerving.' She sits down next to him. 'The thing tonight is a party Tammy has organised as a thank you to everyone who helped out.'

'Oh. That's so nice. Do you need some help?'

'Please, no. We wanted to surprise you as you'd done such a big job with Christmas Day and knew you'd try to get involved.'

'Oh. All right then. So why do I need the afternoon off if it's tonight?'

'Because I arranged an extra surprise. For you, specifically.'

'A surprise? Do I like surprises?'

'I think you'll like this one.'

There's a strange grumbling sound from the café. Did the cat somehow get downstairs? They seem happy enough upstairs and obviously he can't have the cat wandering round the bakery, but perhaps he didn't lock them in?

Except the sound seems bigger than the cat could make. There's a knocking of crockery and a hiss and . . . he's pretty sure he heard someone say *fuck*.

'Guys, you missed the cue to jump out,' Shaz shouts.

'Oh. Shit!' Up jumps Haf, *his Haf*, wearing the world's puffiest winter coat. Her hair is enormous, but it's really her. She's here in the bakery, and so is Kit, who she helps up, all the while muttering a series of foul curse words. From the other side of the counter appear Ambrose and Laurel in a much more dignified fashion. There's something so disjointed about it all that he can't quite believe it's really happening.

'Surprise!' cries Shaz.

He can't believe it. They're here?! His friend-family and also actual family are *here*.

Christopher rushes through the bakery to the counter and soon he's wrapped in all their arms. 'You came? You came all the way here?'

'Shaz told us to,' Haf says. 'We've been *scheming*.'

'And we wanted to,' adds Kit.

'Because we were worried about you,' says Ambrose, which is so out of character for them that everyone in the hug steps back to look at them askance. 'We *were*!'

'Yes, darling, but the way this works usually is that you say something rather rude and then I follow it up with something wholesome,' Laurel explains, threading her arm through their elbow crook. They both look so elegant, dressed in contrasting tailored coats – Laurel in an ecru woollen wrap coat, Ambrose in a belted bright red coat with oversized lapels and a matching belt. God, he'd missed them all.

Ambrose sniffs. 'I was trying something new.'

'Horrifying,' Christopher says, and they all burst into giggles.

'But yeah, Shaz is the mastermind,' Haf says.

'Haf's parents made it onto their cruise so we're staying at theirs instead of squeezing in upstairs with you,' Kit explains.

'Unless you want us to.' Haf waggles her eyebrows. 'We can all get snuggly.'

'I think he's had enough only-one-bed this year,' says Ambrose, and everyone but Christopher shushes, hushes and even hisses at them. 'What?'

'Ixnay on the Ash-Nay,' growls Haf.

'What??' Ambrose repeats, looking around at the others. 'So what, we're going to just avoid talking about it?'

'Yes because *his feelings are hurt* and we're trying to be sensitive about it,' she urges.

Kit groans, her face in her hands. 'I think that ship has sailed.'

His heart aches with how much he loves his friends. 'Guys, it's fine. We can talk about it.' He's not ready to say his name out loud just yet.

Shaz takes his arm in hers. 'Are you sure? I only just got you out of your sadness pit.'

'I prefer misery pit. But yes. It happened. He left. It sucks and I'm sad and no I haven't heard anything from him and, yes, I . . . technically have his number but I'm not going to be the first one to reach out either. That's pretty much it. Now, let's have a nice time together, shall we?'

There's a pause as the others seem to digest this list of non-news, and he gets it. It is a weird end-of-a-situation to walk into while trying to be happy and excited and united. And he knows that's why they've come – they want to cheer him up. But there's nothing they can do except be here, which they are.

'Can we see the cat?' blurts Haf.

'Have you been waiting to ask that this whole time?'

'God yes. We just, you know, had to do all the polite, normal-people bits first.'

They all file upstairs and find the cat curled up on the bed. On Nash's side. Since he left, the cat has taken up residence there. Christopher wonders if the cat feels the lack of him too.

'Oh, you're so cute,' babbles Haf, tickling the cat under the chin. 'Aren't you the sweetest little creature?'

'What's their name?' Kit asks.

'Karma/Felix/Paddington.'

'Bit of a mouthful isn't it, darling?' Laurel sniffs.

Shaz fills the kettle and flicks it on. 'Did you hear about his escapades with the puppies? He's going to be a daddy twice over in two months' time.'

'Christ, please do not call me Daddy. Why do I always have to end up with a horrible nickname?'

Naturally, this leads to everyone calling him Daddy at every opportunity for the next few hours. They all squeeze into the living room, balancing cups of tea and gingerbread reindeer on armrests and tables and laps, as the cat weaves itself around them all. It feels so easy being together that time slips away, moving a little too fast if anything. The flat doesn't feel quite so empty with all the people he loves packed in tightly.

Well. Almost all of them.

'Right, I'm going to go get my glad rags on. See youse all in a bit?' says Shaz, and before she can get away from him, Christopher wraps her up in a huge hug.

'Thank you, for everything,' he whispers.

Once she's gone, Laurel insists that they spend the next couple of hours getting ready and dancing and being silly. He finally remembers all the treats he'd made to bring to Christmas, still packed in his suitcase, and so hands them out to everyone, while Kit strictly controls the party playlist. It's so nice, and just as he's about to pick out something to wear, Ambrose holds out a wrapped parcel to him.

'What's this?'

'Something I made.'

'You *made*?'

'Yes, don't be weird about it. Just open it.'

The shirt is beautiful. It's a simple dark navy linen, but it's edged with floral Liberty fabric, and when he turns up the cuffs, as he always does, there's a flash of golden thread woven through the flowers. It fits him perfectly.

'I can't believe you made this,' he gasps.

'I'm naturally talented.'

It all feels complete when Haf pulls out a pot of gold glitter gel and swipes a couple of lines across his cheekbones, like golden blusher. He feels more himself – no, more *than* himself because of their love and belief in him.

Everyone is dressed up to the nines. Kit wears a slinky structured black dress that just screams *I'm an architect* but in a way that works for her so completely, which clashes with Haf's pink sequin mini dress and cowboy boots. Any party is a reason for Laurel to wear silk, and she slinks along in a champagne gown. And tucked into high-waisted wide-leg trousers, Ambrose wears a shirt in the same floral Liberty fabric that trims his own shirt, making them a matching pair.

They walk over to the community centre at seven to find it packed full of faces that are now so familiar to him. There are still people to meet, and a herd of small children that he doesn't yet know, who are frantically stuffing Party Rings into their faces. But he doesn't feel like the stranger walking in any more.

In fact, he ends up doing the rounds, introducing his friends and family to his new friends and family.

It turns out that Ursula was tasked with decorating and she's done an incredible job. No longer is there sad taped-up tinsel – instead there are well-placed fairy lights, and even a disco ball hanging from the ceiling over what seems to be a dance floor. There's a huge Christmas tree, which Christopher's not entirely convinced wasn't actually Ursula's, decorated in black and gold and glowing with soft light. There are also paper chains being made by some children in the corner, who throw them up onto the walls with abandon once they're created.

'Look, Christopher, there's mistletoe!' shrieks Haf, pointing back towards the doorway. She lunges at him and he just about ducks out of the way in time. 'Come on, for old times' sake.'

'Get off,' he laughs, pushing her away as she comes in for a second attempt. 'Christ, there've been more than enough mistletoe kisses for one lifetime.'

'Don't say that. You never know what will come next,' Laurel says sweetly. He's pretty sure their drunken kiss last year also started out as a mistletoe kiss, but there's not much he remembers from that part of the evening.

A few children start doing sock slides across the floor and for just a moment, Christopher thinks about joining them. Maybe later. He's always enjoyed a good sock slide.

The tables have been dragged together for a huge buffet of picky food from the supermarket, and a whole table of various alcoholic and non-alcoholic drinks, which for some reason is not manned by Enid, but Thelma.

'Can I interest you in some sloe gin?' Thelma asks, waving a bottle of murky thick liquid.

'Oh yes,' cries Laurel, holding out a fresh glass.

'Are you sure?' Christopher murmurs. 'It looks *lethal*.'

'When in Rome, Toph.' She takes a sip and her eyes go wild. 'Cheese and rice, that could power a car.'

'I'll take one,' adds Ambrose immediately, and Thelma fills up glasses for them and Haf too.

'Now I regret agreeing to be the designated driver,' says Kit sulkily. As Ambrose's glass is filled up, she takes a sniff. 'Fucking hell, actually, I take that back. You're all allowed only one. There'll be no vomiting in my car, thank you very much.'

'Oops,' says Haf, her glass conspicuously empty.

'Dear God.'

He leaves them to fight over Thelma's rocket fuel, and finds Shaz and Gar by the tree, arms round each other's waists. They look so right together that he can't even imagine not realising they were each other's person.

'Happy New Year,' he says.

'Blwyddyn Newydd dda,' says Gar, but not in a correcting way. He gives repeating it a good go, which seems to satisfy them both just enough to suggest it was vaguely correct.

'I can't believe everyone did this,' he whispers.

'Of course they did,' Shaz says. 'Everyone loves you.'

'Especially this one,' says Gar, squeezing Shaz tightly. 'It was her idea.'

'Give off, it wasn't.'

'It was,' Gar insists to Christopher.

Before Shaz can resist, he wraps his arms around her. 'You nightmare,' he says. 'If you admit it, think of all the gratitude cake you'll get from me.'

'Oh all right, it was me then.'

'Ha! Too easy,' says Gar.

'There's one thing I was thinking, though,' Christopher says. 'Have you thought about doing this the rest of the year?'

'What, celebrating New Year's Eve? It's a rogue choice but—'

'No, you dingbat. Organising. Getting involved. You've done so much the last week, smashed it, *and* you loved it.'

She pauses. 'You really think I did a good job?'

'Yes,' he urges.

'I had been thinking it was time to go back to work,' she said, with a glance up at Gar, who looks down at her with glowing pride. 'Maybe I can speak to Tammy. Get into local politics and terrify everyone.'

Gar nods. 'You are very good at that part, bab.'

'Thanks,' she says. 'It kind of . . . knocked my confidence when I lost the school job. It's nice to be reminded I'm good at something.'

The sound of someone knocking on a microphone cuts through the party, and everyone turns to see Tamara standing in the middle of the room. 'Good evening everyone. Thank you all for coming. I think Pen-y-Môr has been through a real trial over the last couple of weeks, and you all rose to the challenge. So, this is our thanks to all of you for your hard work and community spirit. Have fun, be merry, and Blwyddyn Newydd dda.'

She raises a glass of bubbly, and everyone does the same, chorusing variations on 'Blwyddyn Newydd dda' and 'Happy New Year'. The music is turned up fully, and Ursula drags Tamara onto an impromptu dance floor with Joan, Cecil and Mervyn.

There's a bittersweetness to all this that he doesn't want to notice, but can't help but feel. The lack of *him*. He would be flirting with Myffy or dancing with Ursula and Tamara or he'd have picked up a tray and would be serving everyone snacks and drinks. All the time flashing that Hollywood smile of his.

It's not the first time Nash has crossed his mind in the last few days, but on this occasion, Christopher allows himself, just for a little while, to dream.

★ ★ ★

Quiet dreaming ends up not being the vibe of the night. Everyone of drinking age gets into Thelma's rocket fuel, and soon the party is quite lairy. Having nursed a beer for the last hour, Christopher is feeling rather out of step with everyone else.

Especially so when Tamara appears in front of him with the microphone, which appears to be on, and slurs, 'Christopher, you should give a speech.'

'A . . . speech?' he murmurs, but the microphone picks it up, blaring his words out over the speakers.

This, naturally, causes everyone in the room to start chanting the word 'speech' like a horrifying chorus.

Now he regrets not drinking any of Thelma's gin. *Courage, man*, he tells himself. *Just tell the people what they want to hear.*

And perhaps even what he wants to say to them.

'Ahem. Hi, everyone,' he says, which is met with a couple of whoos from the crowd. 'I just wanted to say, I'm so glad to be part of this community. Thank you for taking me in and giving me a home here. I hope that I get to stay here a long time with you all.'

His mind casts back to Christmas Day, the last time he was with all of these people. Celebrating then, too, yes, but also working together to protect Nash.

He takes a breath.

'And, while he's not here right now, I'm sure Nash would want me to thank you all for the way you took him in too. I've never seen a group of people so determined to fight the press. So, thank you.'

They're all looking at him with big, sad eyes. It's not pity, though, or at least it doesn't feel like it. It's more a shared grief. They're taking his burden and splitting it out between them. But then, they got to know Nash along with him. Maybe not on the same level. After all, they tended to see Hollywood Nash. Christopher saw that version, the pissed-off version, and the quieter, vulnerable version of Nash that he hides away.

'I . . . I miss him too. It feels wrong in a way, celebrating everything without him here with us. But maybe one day, Nash will come back for us to thank him properly.'

And the man he's been waiting for this whole time walks through the front door.

Chapter Thirty

Christopher

Nash is here?

At first, Christopher worries that he's imagined Nash being here. That all his hopes and dreams of the last few days have manifested in seeing him everywhere. But no, all the townies see him too, and they go wild, raised glasses being happily waved.

Their eyes meet across the room, but neither man moves, as though they're both unsure this is really happening.

Why is he here? Wasn't leaving the first time hard enough?

The Spanks Squad sidle up to him.

'Is that him?' Haf hisses.

'Yes,' Christopher whispers, at the same time as Ambrose says it very loudly.

'Well, ding dong, darling,' says Laurel, who it appears has definitely had a bit *too* much of Thelma's home-brew spirits.

Ambrose gently takes the glass from her hands. 'I'll take that, thanks.'

Kit places a hand on his back. 'Go talk to him.'

'I . . . I can't.'

His heart hammers in his chest, because *why?* Why is he here? And how dare he come back when he hasn't spoken to Christopher since he left?

That's when it hits Christopher finally. Nash isn't just *here*. He came *back*.

Christopher has to find out why.

The world falls away as he crosses the room towards Nash, who hovers in the doorway. He's never seen Nash like this, afraid to enter a room or take up space. Normally, that's Christopher's problem if anything.

It feels as if the air is sucked out of the room as they get closer.

Gone is the leather jacket or the too-thin fancy sports jacket. Nash stands in a caramel peacoat that reaches his knees, a red scarf at his neck. He looks smart, possibly even purposefully dressed up.

'Erm. Hello,' Christopher begins.

'Hi.'

'Right.'

He's not sure what to do or say. Nash waves to someone over Christopher's shoulder, and when Christopher turns to look, all of the party attendees suddenly turn away, knocking into each other and spilling wine and causing a ruckus.

'Christ.'

They both laugh, and there's this tiny moment where Christopher thinks, *There it is, there we are.* It feels traitorous because he can't get his hopes up.

Not again.

'Happy New Year,' Nash says.

For some reason, the casualness of this spikes his chest. 'It's not midnight yet,' Christopher grumbles.

'Fine, Happy *About-To-Be-A* New Year. Better?'

'Yes. How did you know we'd all be here?'

'The Facebook group for community organising in Pen-y-Môr is both regularly updated and not even remotely secure.'

'And . . . how did you get here?' For some reason he can't stop asking about logistics because his mind is still reeling.

'The same way I left. Sadly, I didn't get chance to get the teleportation truck working.'

'Probably for the best.' *God, get on with it,* Christopher's head and heart scream. It's too easy to slip into this casual back-and-forth, as though they were old friends at a party, not briefly lovers who separated on a fight. 'Why are you here?'

'Is that not obvious?' Nash asks, his voice low. 'I'm here for you.'

His heart flutters with hope, but it's such a vague word.

'What do you mean here *for* me?'

'Exactly what I said. I'm here for you.'

'Nash, you lied to me about leaving, then you left, and you asked me not to hate you, and that's all you have to say to me? I've not heard from you since you went.'

Nash blinks hard. 'I left you my number.'

'Yes. You left, and you left it, and you left *me*.' He hates how much the hurt bleeds out in those words, but it's true, and he needs to say everything just in case Nash gets up and leaves again.

'I know. I know and it fucking sucked how I did it. I'm owning that, and I'm not denying it. I'm sorry I hurt you, Christopher. I really am. But I had to go back and sort some things out, and I was too afraid to leave the door open to me ever coming back. I was worried you wouldn't want me back either.'

Nash steps forward towards Christopher, and all the air disappears. God, he's so beautiful.

'So why are you?' he manages to gasp. 'Why do you even . . . want *me*?'

Nash reaches out and takes Christopher's hands in his. They're still a little cold from being outside, and Christopher wants to wrap them up, blow warm air into them. A few days ago, he would have, but then just a few more before that, and they wouldn't even have been holding hands.

This month might have been the strangest one of his whole life.

'Christopher, no one has ever known me like you. When I'm with you, I can be the person I am. I don't have to put on the front all the time, and no one has ever gotten through that exterior before when I didn't want them to. But you? You barged in. You cared for me. You made me see you. No one else has got that close and wanted to stay.'

'Is that the only reason you like me?' Christopher says, a little too bitterly, but by God he needs to hear something about him. 'Because of how I make you feel?'

'No! Fuck, I'm going to suck as a writer if I can't say this right.'

Christopher's heart jumps. 'So, you're going to do it? Quit acting?'

There's a series of small heartbroken gasps behind him that he can only assume are coming from Shaz and Dai.

'Yeah, erm, Kurt convinced the execs to change the deal to be more of an all-rounded development deal. Less emphasis on me on camera, unless I decide to write something for myself, you know? Obviously I have to do the last *Christmas at the Clinic* film for that to happen—'

'HALLE-FUCKING-LOO—' yells Shaz. They turn to look and she goes pale. 'Jesus, sorry, I didn't mean to yell. Or eavesdrop. CARRY ON.'

'The point is,' Nash continues, as Christopher realises their hands are still entwined. 'This deal gives me not just what I want career-wise, but more flexibility about where I can be when I work.'

Christopher's mouth goes dry. Does he dare to hope? 'And where did you have in mind?'

'Well, I'd like to be here. With you. There's stuff we'd have to sort out, and I'd have to fly back to LA to shoot, obviously, and be there for meetings when I stop acting, but there's no reason why I can't be here the rest of the time. If you'll have me?'

This can't be real, surely? Christopher doesn't know how to feel, but it's *huge* and bubbles up, and somehow, he finds himself saying, 'You think you can just show up and ask to move here and tell me you love me and that's it? Everything between us is then just fine?'

Nash laughs quietly. 'Well, actually, I hadn't got to that part yet. But yes, I do love you.'

His breath catches. 'You do?'

'Yes, you absolute clod. I love you. I think you're completely ridiculous, but also beautiful and kind and so creatively talented and brave for chasing your dreams and annoyingly quite funny at times, especially when you're being petty. When I left, the first thing I regretted was that I'd spent so much time arguing with you that I hadn't told you any of the things I liked about you. And that's exactly what happened just now, too. I think the world of you, and I want you to *be* my world.'

'That's a lot to ask of one person,' Christopher whispers, still taking all this in.

'OK, well how about we be each other's world? We build a world. Us, and the puppy and Karma—'

'Paddington.'

'To be discussed.'

'They're my cat.'

'Our cat. The point is, I want to spend the rest of our lives telling you all the good things, in between the bickering.'

The life that he dared to wish for on Christmas Eve is coming true, somehow. It's impossible magic. Together, under the stars and crouched on their bed, he had wished for a world where their life together kept going. It can't be this simple, can it?

The whole room is silent, hanging on his next words.

He looks to Haf and Kit, cuddled up together. It was simple for them, wasn't it, in the end? They knew they were each other's person. Is that how it is? Does he just need to be brave enough to say yes to this man, this incredible man, who has flown halfway across the world just to tell him that he loves him? This man, who wants to love him.

'Nash, I'm not sure I can bear you leaving again.'

'If you'll have me, Christopher, I'll never leave like that again.'

'Then, stay. Stay with us. With me.'

'I will.'

'Just kiss him already!' shrieks Ambrose, causing all the other townies and his friends to cheer in agreement.

'Christopher, look up!' cries Haf, when everyone falls silent.

And there, above them, in the doorway, is a sprig of mistletoe.

That ridiculous custom that started everything, that shook up his entire life, and brought him to places he could never have imagined, is right above him now, at what feels like another turning point in his life.

This time, it feels like the most obvious choice. The right choice not made out of silliness or fear or loneliness, but out of hope for a future together. Christopher looks at Nash, at the man he loves who is begging to stay, and he kisses him. There are cheers and the sound of glasses clinking and the music being turned up, but all that is drowned out by their kiss.

It's more than just a kiss. It's a promise, and his wish come true.

'I love you too,' he says, when they break apart, still clutching onto each other. 'I'm terrified of what all this means and there's so much to sort out, but I want to try. For us.'

'Even though I'm half quitting acting?'

'Yeah, but I don't need you on my screen if I have you in my heart.'

'Christopher, that might be the dorkiest thing you've ever said.' Nash sweeps him into another kiss, and while this one doesn't come with cheers – presumably everyone else has moved on with their lives and evenings – it still feels like the start of something. 'Also, are you wearing glitter?'

'Yeah . . . and now you are too. Sorry about that.'

'No sorries needed. It suits you, C-3PO.'

'Oh good, more nicknames.' He rests his forehead on Nash's, and tries for the life of him to catch his breath.

'Ahem. Are you going to introduce us?' says Ambrose.

Kit elbows her way forward. 'Excuse me, I'm his sister. I'm arguably the most important.'

'I'm his fake ex, though,' says Haf.

'And I'm his real ex,' swoons Laurel, who has somehow got another glass of Thelma's terrifyingly strong liquor.

Nash looks at him and smiles. 'And I'm his boyfriend, I think?'

'Yes, you are.'

'Cool. I'm Nash Nadeau. The boyfriend.'

They all shake hands and gush excitedly, and this is the moment where Christopher finally sees it. His future, his past, all the people he loves together, celebrating another turning of the year.

Author's Note

Hello readers, it's me, the author. I hope you've enjoyed reading Christopher and Nash's sparky little romance. This book is, in part, a love letter to the trans boys and trans mascs in my life, and the people who love us fiercely. Honestly, I wrote it for myself, too.

I want to remind readers that the words trans people use for their bodies are individual. Nash's are based on his preferences.

I made the decision to gloss over most of the transphobia that Nash will undoubtedly have faced in his career because my aim with these books is to create an uncomplicated space of joy for my marginalised readers. However, while I've chosen not to focus on transphobia in this story, we cannot turn our eyes from its very real repercussions in our world. When I was drafting this story of queer community, the Club Q shooting happened on Trans Day of Remembrance, and then the murder of Brianna Ghey. I cannot separate the story from the context in which it was created.

If this is your first time reading a book with a trans main character, please do not stop here. Keep reading, listening and learning. Please show up, protest, use your vote. As Mother Jones said, mourn the dead and fight like hell for the living.

In love and solidarity, Hux. x

Acknowledgements

This book has been a long time coming. Ever since I finished the first draft of *Make You Mine This Christmas*, I knew Christopher's story was not over. I'm really glad I got the chance to go back and tell it. Writing a book is an act of collaboration and, five books in, I know I have a lot of people to thank, including some people who supported *Make You Mine This Christmas* from the off.

Thank you as always to Abi Fellows, my incredible agent, who guides me so gently and with such love (and jellycats!). Five years together, and here's to many more. Thank you to the teams at The Good Literary Agency and DHH Literary Agency for all their support too.

Special thanks go to my former editor, and now author extraordinaire in her own right, Bea Fitzgerald. These two books would not exist without her, and I'm so glad I've got to watch her own success alongside my own. She's my favourite person to be unseasonably loud with at fancy award shows. We did it! Look at us!

Thank you to Amy Batley and Lucy Stewart for your hard work on the structural and line edits, and for bringing this book into the world! Thank you to the team at Hodder Fiction for everything else, especially to Charlea Charlton in marketing, Kallie Townsend for the publicity, Juliette Winter for her hard work in production, and to all the sales reps who work to get this book out in the world.

Thank you to Becky Glibbery and and Zahraa Al-Hussaini for the gorgeous cover designs, to Joanna Kerr and Kerry Hyndman for both their wonderful illustrations, for all editions of this book, and to Natalie Chen and Debs Lim for the matching paperback cover of *MYMTC*.

Huge thanks to the team at Illumicrate and Afterlight for supporting my stories. You are a dream team to work with.

I also want to thank Monika Buchmeier and the team at HarperCollins DE for bringing my stories over to Germany. Your original email lives on my phone for when I need reminding of why these stories matter. Thanks to Leni Kauffman for the illustrations!

Thank you to all the lovely authors who gave lovely quotes for *MYMTC* after I sprang on you that I'd written a Christmas romance, and to everyone else in publishing who has supported me or said nice things about the book!

Special thanks go to: Cameron Haberberg for the guidance and encouragement for Nash; Adam Jenkins for teaching me about weights, including how to construct them in a bakery; the Honks for helping me think of movie references to replace the twelve instances I mentioned *Swimfan*.

Thank you to my friends in general for keeping me sane through a three-book-year. The Murder Cat Biker Gang, Peps and alt have been cheering me on so hard. Thank you to Alice and Lauren for always feeding me when I need it. Thank you to all the friends who collectively lost their brains over Taylor Swift with me this year, especially Nell who started it all for me. Thank you to all the dogs, cats and babies I have hung out with.

Thank you as always to my family for being so supportive of The Family Author™, especially my sister Julie who remains my biggest champion. Continued apologies to Nerys the dog that more books keep being delivered, when it should be exclusively treats for her.

He always gets the last thanks because he's there at the beginning, the end and the afters. Tim, thank you for loving me, all the versions of me that have been and are to come.

If you loved *Under the Mistletoe with You*,
why not try Lizzie Huxley-Jones's,
first festive romcom...

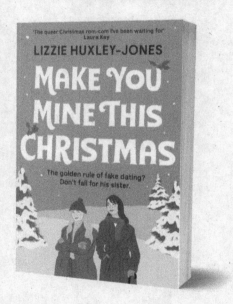

The golden rule of fake dating?
Don't fall for his sister.

Available to buy now!